Rogue

Luke Phillips

First published in the United Kingdom in 2023
by Black Beast Publishing

Print Book ISBN: 978-0-9562987-7-5
e-book ISBN: 978-0-9562987-8-2

For my Dad.

Thanks for letting me watch 70s bigfoot movies when I was far too young, and for sharing my interest before you became a sceptic.

ACKNOWLEDGMENTS

As I put the finishing touches to my fourth novel, I am reflecting on how lucky I am. I am incredibly fortunate that my books are popular enough to make continuing to write viable and worthwhile for me. I think I'd do it anyway, even if it wasn't, because I'm a story teller at heart.

Rogue is a book I have always wanted to write. I have been fascinated by bigfoot stories since I was young, when, like many, I watched *The Legend of Boggy Creek* one rainy Sunday afternoon, and was scared out of my wits yet intrigued at the same time. This book is dedicated to my Dad, for letting me watch it.

But it's also dedicated to all of my readers that have helped me get this far. You've had to wait whilst I changed careers, fought mental health battles, and found enough money to do a half decent job of packaging a book. So, this one's for you – all of you. Your messages and support have really kept me going.

It has long been a dream of mine that *my* bigfoot book featured a cover by the incredible Sam Shearon. Sam has been incredibly patient over the course of years, from my first mentioning of it to the stunning cover you see on the book. Thanks for making it even more memorable for me.

And to my friends and family, who have stood by me through COVID, getting back on my feet, and beyond, thank you for being there. I hope you all enjoy Rogue immensely.

FACT OR FICTION?

Like my books before, I have tried to centre Rogue in reality. Some of you may be rolling your eyes at the thought of this – but there are thousands of eye-witness encounters reported every year. Native American tribes and indigenous peoples across Canada have long feared and revered these creatures, separating them firmly from those they consider 'spirit' animals.

Furthermore, giant unknown ape-like creatures are a global phenomenon, with legends and aural histories found on every continent except Antarctica.

Many of the cases mentioned in the book – such as the history of Portlock, are a matter of historical record. I have even had my own unnerving, but ultimately unexplained encounter in the woods of California.

Rogue is of course fiction, but just like the big cats of my previous books, they, bigfoot, and the truth, may just well be out there.

CHAPTER ONE

BIGFOOT AND THE HENDRICKSENS

John Henriksen glanced in the rear-view mirror. His teenage daughter, Maggie, was staring out the window with the same look of frustrated boredom she had worn since they'd left the house nine hours ago. The expensive headphones covering her ears prevented intrusion from the deep and otherwise penetrating snores coming from her younger brother, Josh, slumped in the seat next to her. John let out a sigh as he looked across to Melinda, his wife. She was fixing him with a stare that warned her own tolerance of the journey was dangerously close to collapsing.

"Maybe we're a little too early in the season," he offered, apologetically.

"You think?" Melinda replied, a little short but as good naturedly as she could manage.

"If the next one is shut too, we'll just stop at a motel in the next town. We don't have to camp."

"And you'll cover the extra $60 a day we'll have to budget for?" she scolded.

He half-smiled at her, thinking it would be a small price to pay compared to the nagging and told-you-so attitude he'd have to put up with otherwise. And the thought of a warm, comfortable double bed certainly had more allure than the camping cots stowed away in the trunk. So far, they'd been to four camping grounds, only to find thick chains across the entrances of each.

He fixed his eyes on the road, guiding what had been his father's 1987 Ford County Squire station wagon, through the sweeping curves of the scenic forest setting of north Washington state. Towering pines, sequoia, and oak, rose in steep banks on either side, the road climbing the mountain in natural undulations and tight corners. The car leaned and wallowed in these, showing its age with tremors along the chassis and groans from the suspension.

"Even the car's had enough," Melinda said, rolling her eyes.

As they rounded the next bend, John spotted the damaged sign out of the corner of his eye. He couldn't make out the first part, but the word "campsite" was still readable. He had to stamp on the brakes to avoid shooting past, but he wasn't too worried, having not seen a car in the rear-view mirror for hours. Melinda and Maggie glared at him, but weren't ready to escalate into all-out argument yet. He stared out of the window at the track that led into the darkness beneath the trees. It was heavily overgrown, but something in the pit of his stomach was telling him it was worth exploring. He turned the wheel and pushed the car over the grass verge. The suspension bucked and protested along the deeply rutted trail, but after a slight rise it was all downhill, and he coasted the car down to the campground.

The first spring flowers had already begun to push themselves through the knotted mass of overgrown grass. Red columbine, bearberry, and great camas dotted the meadow. Surrounding it were clumps of fireweed, and beyond them were the trees. By the close clumping of the trunks, John guessed it had once all been Forest Service land. He turned off the engine and looked back at Melinda, who didn't seem quite so enamoured.

"You're not serious, are you?" she exclaimed.

"What's wrong. It look's great," he replied, offended.

"It looks deserted," she snapped back. "What about toilets?"

"We've got tissue and wipes. Back to nature baby," he replied, smiling smugly.

"I thought it was only bears who shit in the woods," she said shrewdly.

John checked his phone. It had one bar of signal, and he tapped on the GPS app he'd installed. It took a while to load, but eventually the screen became populated with green and white squares, and a yellow roadway that led to the north. The area known as Paradise, on the southern slopes of Mount Rainier, was a little over three miles away.

"How about a compromise," he suggested.

"I'm listening," Melinda shrugged.

"We camp here, but we head to Paradise for dinner, at the inn. Means we don't have to do anything but set up the tents. And if it's not working out, we move on tomorrow. But for now, we get out of the car, get the tents up before dark, and don't have to cook."

"Sold," Maggie interjected from behind.

Melinda rolled her eyes, but couldn't quite hide her smile.

John woke up Josh, who was more taken with the campsite they had to themselves. John watched as the twelve-year-old boy busied himself with getting the tents from the trunk and putting them up. There were two modern dome tents for his parents and his sister, and his own backpacking bivouac and cover, which offered slightly more basic shelter. As soon as he'd finished one of the dome tents, he offered it to his sister, who hadn't budged from the car. She grabbed her bag and flung it into the empty space beyond the door flap. Josh grinned as he bolted back to the car for one of the camp beds. He passed it to Maggie as he sped past, ready to get going on his parents' tent.

John stopped him, placing a hand on his shoulder.

"You set yourself up, me and mom will do ours."

"Mine won't take a minute though," Josh offered.

"Gives you more time to explore," John offered.

"It certainly looks and smells like uncharted territory," Maggie called from inside her tent.

Josh had his tent set up within a few minutes, with just a roll mat and his sleeping bag pushed inside. A clear strip of plastic, which would be by his head when inside, would give him a brilliant view of the stars and any wildlife that wandered into the camp. He'd seen deer, turkey, and even a black bear once. There was just enough space in the entrance for his backpack to sit upright. He left it there and returned to the car to grab his hiking boots.

He headed straight for the far tree line. It was cool and dark between their branches, and he knew he wouldn't have to go too much higher before he would find snow clinging to the frozen ground. He did his coat up and stood for a moment. He noticed a Lewis's woodpecker, flicking its tail and watching him from a bough high above. In the close grouping of the trees, it and everything else was in silhouette, but its size gave it away.

There was no real path to guide him, so Josh decided to make his own. He intended to circle the campsite in a wide arc, not straying too far, but getting a good idea of the surroundings at least. Straight through the maze of trunks, about a hundred feet ahead of him, he could see a large, wide stump. Beyond that, the trees seemed to close in, and he couldn't see much further. He decided to head towards the stump and use it as a marker to turn south, back towards the far border of camp.

He picked his way through the towering trunks, occasionally having to pull branches out of his way, or duck to avoid thicker protruding limbs. He had gone about thirty feet when something made him stop. The dripping melt water, the call of crows, even the sound of his boots digging into the dirt and slime, had filled his ears until that moment. But it had all been replaced with unnerving silence. He'd been keeping his gaze trained on the ground as he picked his path, but now, he looked up sharply on alert. Nothing. He squinted in the low light at the stump. For a second there, he thought he'd seen something, a glint of reflected light. Only now did he realise how big it was. At least six feet high, and nearly four feet across. It piqued his interest, making him wonder what species of tree it could be.

He looked down as he lifted his foot over a low, torn branch that lay across the ground. Immediately, there was a sharp, savage sounding grunt from up ahead. Josh froze again, this time in fear. His eyes slowly rose, once more seeking out the stump. Nothing had changed, but the remnants of an icy breath of water vapour clung to the air in front of it. Josh shuddered as he realised his own laboured breathing was creating similar clouds of mist.

Just then, he heard his mom calling in the distance. He turned instinctively to look. The movement he caught in the corner of his eye stopped him, and his head snapped back to the stump one more time. It wasn't there anymore. That was as much as he could take, and he broke into a run, crashing back through the trees in a straight line towards the safety of the camp. As he burst back out into the sunlight, a rock the size of a softball flew past his head and smacked into the side of his hammock. He came to a stop, and stood trembling for a moment, unsure if he should turn around. When he did, the ominous feeling he'd felt among the trees had vanished. Bird song had returned, and the sounds of his family laughing and going about camp business filled his ears. He went to join them.

~

Despite being quiet, and back from his exploration of the forest a little earlier than expected, John put Josh's edginess down to being tired from the journey. He checked on him with an occasional glance in the rear-view mirror, as they headed to dinner at the Paradise Inn. The boy stared out of the window, his brow wrinkled, and his eyes darting to the trees with a nervous energy and intensity that seemed unusual. John decided to try and talk to him when they were back, after a good meal. After all, the quickest route to the heart was through the stomach.

By the time they had piled into the Paradise Inn's dining room, good spirits overtook them all and Josh's disposition became solely focused on the long, generously plated buffet table. John and Melinda also ordered some extra entrees from the menu, as a reward for the long journey and the possible cold night ahead. John felt much more reassured that things were going well, and they would soon be settled at the campsite. Despite its relatively rustic amenities, they'd all cope – even Maggie. They'd soon get into the spirit of things. By the time dessert came around, he had completely forgotten about trying to talk to Josh. He tipped the waiter extra for an unopened bottle of red wine to be subtly delivered to the table, which he slipped into his jacket for later. Melinda would appreciate seeing in the holiday with style, and with the kids in their own tents for the first time, who knew what else she might be in the mood for. It had been a while. No reason, other than busy, tired lives he thought. That's what vacations were for.

They were still laughing and rough-housing as they made their way back to the car. The night had crept up on them, and John checked his watch. It was a little after nine. They'd been out longer than he thought, but that was okay. He was glad they'd set the tents up and had nothing left to do but climb into their cots when they got back. He'd start a fire though, just to be sure and safe. The Washington woods at night harboured more than just trees after all. And he liked the firelight too. The warmth, the glow. It felt good to sit around a fire and take it all in.

John went slow on the road back, wary of deer that might dash across as he passed. He always wondered why they did that, wait to the last moment. They always waited until you were right on top of them, testing your reflexes and heart condition at the same time. In the dark, it was even more difficult to spot the entrance to the campsite. As before, he had to stamp on the brakes to avoid shooting past. He pulled the car around and onto the track. He was more confident this time, and the car bucked and strained even more than the first time. The kids laughed it off as Melinda rolled her eyes, smiling contentedly. As John applied the brakes sharply a second time, bringing them to an abrupt halt, the smiles and laughter vanished.

"What the hell...?" John stammered, peering over the steering wheel through the windshield.

Melinda followed his gaze. She felt the piercing looks of the children behind her. It was as if a tornado had been through the meadow. Maggie's tent, to the far right, had been torn in half, revealing a mash of poles and mangled nylon. The contents of her bag were strewn around the meadow. It was the same for the others too. One of the camping cots, impossible to tell who's, had been bent and crumpled into a ball like papier-mâché, then deposited into the boughs of an oak some twenty feet up. Josh's tent had been reduced to shreds. The split and ruined frame poked out of the ground where the rest of it had been hammered into the earth. But it was John and Melinda's tent that drew their attention. Four long slashes had been clawed along the side that faced them. They sat in silence for what seemed minutes, then John opened the door and stepped out of the car.

It hadn't rained, but a dank smell hit his nostrils. A putrid mix of musk and urine. The headlights were the only source of light, and offered two thin corridors of illumination, stretching from the car to the trees at the back of the meadow. John took a few steps forward, each one revealing more of their possessions, ransacked, destroyed and distributed across the open ground. A cooler hung from a tree. Beer cans that had been ripped apart littered the floor below. A trail of Cheetos led into the grass and abruptly stopped. Blue polystyrene trays were all that remained of their meat stash. Hamburgers, steaks, sausage, and bacon had all been stripped from their packages, presumably devoured. John guessed a bear had found the campsite, and taken advantage of their absence. He was surprised it had managed to get the coolers and storage containers open, which were meant to be tamper-proof.

As he took another step forward, onto the torn remains of a sleeping bag, he flinched at the sound of a heavy impact somewhere in front of him. Whatever had made the noise was beyond the reach of the headlights, but he still peered into the gloom. For a brief moment, he thought he saw a dark shape take form. It was like a void in the shadows, blacker than the night surrounding it. Then it was gone. He turned as he heard Melinda approaching from behind.

"What do you think happened?" she asked.

"It... it must have been a bear," John replied, turning back to the scene of destruction.

"I want to get out of here," Maggie whined, leaning over the open car door, gripping its frame intensely.

Melinda's frightened and alert eyes told John she felt the same way.

"Why don't you guys get back in the car. I'll see if there's anything worth salvaging," he suggested.

"Something just doesn't feel right," Melinda said, her eyes scanning the darkness as she began to back up.

John looked towards the car, intending to call Josh over to help him. But the boy was still as a statute, sat in the car with his seat belt fastened. He had twisted his head around to look through the window towards the nearest grouping of trees. Something there held his attention. John slowly turned his head in the same direction. He could see nothing. The haze from the headlights dulled his vision, and made the shadows blur into swirling shapes that disappeared into the vortex. He was about to look away again when a low, guttural grunt emanated from the trees. The sound hit him in the chest like a punch. As he flinched instinctively at the noise, he felt his stomach spasm in readiness to dispel his dinner.

Melinda was looking at him in terror, her head snapping back and forth between John and the darkness.

"Get in the car," John ordered.

She was about to protest, when a rock appeared out of the gloom. About the size of a cantaloupe, Melinda had just enough time to duck back into the car before it would have smashed into her head. Then, John saw there definitely was something there in the gloom. It crossed the track behind the car in a single, fleeting rush of movement. Now, there was nothing between it and John. It had purposefully moved around the car to get past the obstruction. John only had to contemplate its possible intentions for a moment before he was running full tilt towards the open driver's door.

He grabbed at the keys in his panic to get the engine started, stamping on the gas, and throwing it into reverse as it roared into life. The elderly Windsor V8 screamed at the abuse, as he yanked the steering wheel round. The car pirouetted through a slush of mud and debris, scattering it across the trail in an untidy arc. John shifted into drive and felt the back-end shudder as the rear tires fought for grip. For a second, they were immobile, before the big car catapulted forwards, bouncing precariously along the track. Just before he swerved back onto the asphalt of the main road, the rear window shattered as a spruce limb jettisoned into the car's interior. Neither Maggie's nor Melinda's screams were enough to make him stop, or even look back.

CHAPTER TWO

CODE 10-20-67

Park Ranger Roger Gimlin guided the beaten-up Park Services truck along the short patch of trail that led to the ranger's station. It was Sunday, and it was way too early in the season to expect anything like a busy day. So, the old station-wagon containing a family, waiting for him as he drew up, was something of a surprise.

He took his time gathering his stuff, pretending not to look in their direction. Four pairs of eyes were fixed on him, watching his every move. He swept everything on the passenger seat into his rucksack and got out. As he walked towards the ranger station and fumbled for the keys in his pocket, he met the gaze of the man sat in the driver's seat. Long wisps of greying hair sprang from his balding scalp, out of place and unkempt. Pale blue eyes met his in awkward, almost apologetic desperation. Whoever they were, they looked pleased to see him. He wondered how long they'd been there.

"Guess you folks had best come on inside," he said, as good-naturedly as he could manage.

He already knew the story he was probably going to get. Most likely city folk. Hadn't put their food away. A black bear had wandered into camp, and they had run from it, terrified. It was only as he passed by the rear of the car that he noticed the smashed back window. Just what I need he thought, a habitualised bear that's doing the rounds and breaking into cars.

He opened-up the front door and went through to the main counter and desk. He switched the lights and heating on. As he began to loosen the blind slats, the family of four shuffled in. They found it hard to meet his gaze, looking down at their feet or nervously back out of the window towards the car. Roger walked back to behind the counter and closed the partition. For some reason, he knew people felt more comfortable when things felt more official. The snap of the wooden catch seemed to spark something in the man who had sat in the driver's seat. Roger guessed he was husband and father to the group.

"We thought we should report something that happened to us last night," the man murmured. "While we were camping."

"Uh-huh," Roger replied. "And what might that be, sir?"

"We… well, we were attacked."

"Attacked?" Roger paused for a second. "Were you able to identify the animal or persons concerned?"

He picked up a yellow form from one of the boxes. He asked the man for his name and particulars, slowing him down and helping him regain some control in the process. He stood in silence as he looked back over the report.

"And all of you back this up, this is how it happened?" Roger asked.

Each member of the family nodded in turn.

"I know how it sounds," said the man, who had identified himself as John Henriksen for the report.

"Sir, my job is just to take the report," Roger explained. "I can see you folks are pretty shaken up, and I don't doubt you had a horrible experience. I can see that all clear enough." He was trying to be reassuring, but knew he wasn't quite pulling it off. "A bear recently out of hibernation stumbles across a campsite, goes mad trying to get at your food. It's happened before."

Something seemed to harden in the man, and in his young son standing behind him.

"Bears don't throw rocks," the boy objected.

"And that thing, when it crossed the road. It stepped," John stammered. "I remember now, the movement was like something walking on two legs. And it got into our food stash."

"Again sir, I'm not questioning you. But bears can rear-up on their hind legs, and there's not much that'll stop one determined to get at food. They're able climbers, and once they know something's worth their while, that's kind of it. Probably somebody fed it once, and it now knows what's inside those containers."

"And do they have a habit of throwing branches through windows like a god-damn spear?" the woman demanded, despairingly.

"No ma'am, but you might want to consider that two things happened to you, not just one. Those big tree limbs come off all the time. A sudden gust of wind, and wham, it's raining branches. Just bad timing to happen straight after the bear," Roger explained, as patiently as he could. He could see they weren't convinced.

"I'll make sure someone looks into it, and I have your name and address. I'll get your stuff back to you," Roger offered. "In the meantime, I think you folks could do with a decent breakfast and some help with your car. Let me make a few phone calls."

He took the report with him to the more private office out back and closed the door. First he called a mechanic he knew out in Longmire, a couple of miles down the road. He wouldn't be able to replace the glass, but he'd be able to patch up the hole and get them on their way. He then called Alice Mahoney, who ran a diner in Ashford, a little further more down the road. He knew she would look after them, and it would handily get them out of his jurisdiction too. After he put the phone down, he opened the drawer of the desk he was sitting at and took out the procedure manual. It took him a little while to find the right page, towards the back. There was little to draw attention to the phone number, other than the words that preceded it. Code 10-20-67, report immediately. He lifted the phone receiver and dialled. It went straight to voicemail, as he knew it would. He repeated the details of the report, citing location, the file number, and an approximate grid reference – then he hung up.

The bell over the front door to the reception area chimed, and Roger was pulled away from his thoughts. He stuffed the report in the drawer and walked out of the office. The Henriksen family had taken a seat together, on a bench, left of the counter. Standing in front of it were a new group of people, hikers by the looks of them.

"I'll be right with you folks," Roger nodded towards the Henriksen family.

The hikers were just checking in, and they didn't take up too much of his time. He got them sorted and saw them on their way.

"If you folks follow me, I'm going to set you up with a mechanic to look at the car," Roger beamed. "Then we'll get some food into you. Things'll seem a whole lot better, you'll see."

~

Agent Cordell Jones listened to the recorded message a second time, glancing at the map on the wall of his dark office. A patch of yellow dots marked an area just east of Paradise and Mount Rainier. He absentmindedly scratched at the scar underneath the fabric of the plaid shirt on his right arm, as he filled in the rest of his own paperwork. He assigned it a new case number and hesitated before filling in the final box on the form. Looking at the little nest of dots again, he took a new, singular red dot and placed it north of the yellow ones. He went back to the form and wrote POSSIBLE INCURSION. RECOMMEND INVESTIGATE AND IF CONFIRMED, TERMINATION.

CHAPTER THREE

TERROR ON THE TRAIL

Jake Sutton was enjoying the challenge of an early Spring hike in Washington. His senses seemed sharpened by the frost, as the scent of spruce and pine permeated his being, invigorating him and encouraging him to increase his pace. But he had volunteered to bring up the rear of the group, being one of the more able hikers. To the east lay the winding paths of the Pacific Crest Trail, which he would join again in a couple of days. Today though, something a little gentler beckoned and he was happy to take his time and enjoy the beautiful scenery. The group of hikers he'd joined were in their 50s and 60s, and he was glad of their company, as well as being able to help them out. They had found even the easier trails a little challenging, and he'd suggested an alternative, thanks to a little research and map-reading.

He'd use the more relaxed pace to rest a little he'd decided, and he could part company with them once they got to the next major trail camp. One of the things he loved most about the PCT was the community. He knew that there would almost certainly be someone willing to take up his temporary mantel of unofficial tour guide, and no matter the time of year or the weather, you were never completely alone for too long. Company was usually there if you wanted or needed it.

Mercifully, the path was in good condition, and the little party seemed to be enjoying themselves. Occasionally, one of them would look back and flash him an appreciative smile, or give a solemn nod of thanks. The little bit of space he afforded them was his own choosing. It gave him an opportunity to watch for any wildlife they inadvertently disturbed, usually flushing it his way. And it also gave him the opportunity to get lost in his thoughts, which was another thing about the PCT he loved. Quality time. He realised they'd gotten a little ahead of him again, and he pressed on.

~

The others could sense the alpha was restless. They had returned to their grass nests at dawn as usual, but Adotey had been unable to settle. His beta and son, Cona, noticed and joined him, scanning the trees on alert. Katshar, Adotey's mate, called nervously, urging them to return to the nests. Fala, the daughter, growled sullenly. With a single commanding grunt from Adotey, they joined Cona at his side instantly. They were a close family group, and they slept, hunted, and defended their territory together. As Adotey's rumbling growl grew in his throat, Cona caught the trace of the scent his father had locked onto. There was an intruder on their patch. They moved off into the trees in a silent, sweeping formation.

~

Jake was really beginning to enjoy himself. The pace was so leisurely that he considered it restful, and the forest was brimming with sounds and scents that enlivened him. He always found himself wondering what might just be out there, hidden from sight and creeping through the foliage. He remembered a wonderful encounter on a trail in Oregon, where a mountain lion had trotted past him, snarling at his presence before slipping back into the trees. It had taken him a while to shake off the feeling he was being stalked, but now, he was glad of the experience. Another close call had come as a momma skunk and its babies had nonchalantly walked up to him and his mountain bike, investigating at their leisure. That had been in Idaho, and the only stink he'd gone home with was his own, as his girlfriend and mother had been very keen to point out. They'd even joked the skunks could have accepted him as one of their own. He reminded himself to put in a call to them once he was back somewhere with cell reception.

~

Adotey was moving quickly, trying to pin down which direction the intruder's scent came from. It was old but hung tantalising in the air. He could tell it was a male, and the musky, penetrating odour hinted that it had moved into the territory purposefully. Adotey stopped and turned his body to allow him to look back at Fala. He made a soft cooing noise by pursing his lips to show his concern and affection. Both Cona and Katshar closed ranks around her immediately, and she thumped her brother in agitation. But now, something else drew their attention. A series of sounds off in the distance alarmed them further. They dropped to all fours and made their way towards them.

Adotey stopped at the foot of a large, broad-headed oak tree. He took hold of the lowest branch, some ten feet high, and effortlessly pulled himself into the boughs. The others selected their own trees and did the same. From a height of about thirty feet, they were granted a view of the noise makers. The large group of humans were slowly making their way along a forest path. Adotey knew it didn't lead deep into the trees, and it eventually turned back towards the strange, hard surface they used to travel on at great speed in even stranger contraptions. He'd broken into a few of those to forage for food, but generally, he avoided people.

He swung down from his vantage point. Cona and Fala, being young, were more fascinated with the humans, and had to be encouraged to give up their entertainment with a well-aimed pebble. They followed their parents along a game-trail that paralleled the path the people were on, but at a higher elevation. The four of them stayed low, with the humans in distant earshot. Adotey was increasingly becoming more agitated, and Cona realised why, as the musky scent intensified. The male they were tracking was close.

Katshar let out a long, intense breath. Adotey and Cona took immediate interest and doubled back towards her. In a small depression, where some melt water had collected, there was a muddy impression. It was a print, left with deliberate care. It was immediately obvious that the maker of the impression was even bigger than Adotey. The intruder was being brazen and blatant. In their language, Adotey was a name that meant 'great tree', and it was one he lived up to. His size and power had kept them safe for a long time. This male was the first they'd encountered that seemed like true competition. Adotey pushed his shoulder against his son's. Together, it didn't matter how big the interloper was. They pushed on.

~

Jake had caught up with the others again and was already dropping back. As the group reached a bend, he let them go ahead and venture out of sight. He took off his backpack and opened it to fetch his canteen. He took a long, wholesome drink of water. As he put it back, he was suddenly aware of the unnerving silence that seemed to have fallen on the little section of forest they were passing through. He looked around. The trail was bordered on both sides by dark-coloured rock formations, forming a natural corridor.

A slope ascended to his right, with large boulders and rows of tobacco-barked trees marking the natural contours. Directly ahead of him, where the path turned a corner, there was an opening in the wall of rock. Grass tussocks had formed around a large, dead stump of a tree that sat in in the centre of the opening. It was the only place the sun could truly penetrate all the way down to the ground, and the rays of light showed steam and dust gently lifting from the hair-like bark of the stump. As Jake sat and stared at it, he smiled, thinking of what it reminded him of. If he didn't know better, he'd say that a monstrous creature was crouched in the opening, grimacing at him. He could see how somebody not used to the woods might panic, or report what they were seeing as genuine. In this light, the stump really did look creepy. He closed up the backpack and lifted it onto his shoulders.

It was as he was passing the stump that he thought he heard a strange, wheezing grunt. He stopped and turned to look at it again. It made him shudder. Now a mere six feet from it, it looked even worse. The notched recesses of the bark looked just like thick, matted clumps of hair. In its shape, he imagined an immense, hulking form squatting down with its hands on the ground in front of it. Even this close, it was hard to tell the difference. He reassured himself that the size was wrong, as the stump stood at least seven feet high, and nothing crouched like that would be so tall. As he looked up towards where he imagined the face would be, the stump turned its head.

Whatever was looking back at him was the ugliest creature Jake had ever seen. The golf-ball sized eyes, the colour of burnt amber, seemed too far apart, and were housed under a thick, protruding brow ridge. The ears were very small in contrast – flat, pointed, and to the side of the head, below where the eyes sat on the face, but in line with the raised flaps of its flattened nose. He got the feeling that hearing wasn't nearly as important to this animal as sight and smell. As Jake began to back away in shock, a flash of the creature's canines set within a powerful, square jaw, spurred him into flight.

A thick, burly, six-foot long arm reached out and plucked him from the floor with ease. Jake yelled and bucked as he was lifted higher, his legs dangling helplessly in mid-air. The creature pulled him in closer, as if to examine him. Now facing it, Jake kicked out and screamed louder. Leisurely, the thing opened its mouth and sank its teeth into Jake's shoulder. As it did so, Jake felt the breath driven from his chest as it crushed him within its grip. He heard something in his abdomen pop, and a crack from his ribs. There was no air to fuel the cry of pain he wanted to release. As if the struggling annoyed it, the creature dangled him at arms-length by his hair and looked him over. Jake kicked again, his foot slamming into the thing's stomach. It was like hitting rock, but the ape-like beast reacted all the same. It used its free arm to hold Jake at his injured shoulder, while its other hand began to pull at his head. Jake screamed in panic as he realised what it was doing, but it was too late.

The sound of his skin beginning to tear came at the same time as the burning, searing pain. His neck broke a second later, separating from the spine. There was a pop, a rip, and then his head was separated from his body. The sasquatch lifted Jake's flesh-wrapped skull high above it and drank the cascading blood that drained into its welcoming throat.

It was then that it heard the noise behind it. It spun on its heels, looking up to the top of the wall of rock where it had set its ambush. It saw Adotey and Cona looking down, their teeth bared in savage smiles. It sneered in disgust, ripping an arm from the body of its prey and throwing it in their direction. Cona braced to jump and charge, but Adotey slapped a restrictive hand across his chest. Sounds were erupting from back up the trail. The people were returning. As father and son looked back down, the interloper had vanished, along with the mangled human corpse.

As they returned to the trees, Adotey let the back of his finger run along an ancient scar on his shoulder, hidden by his hair and over time. He now knew who the intruder was and how much of a threat he was. His own father had called him Shartale – Dark Claw.

CHAPTER FOUR

ALIAS SMITH AND JONES

Nina Lee took a deep breath, glancing at her cup of coffee that had gone stone cold. She waited for the sobs to reside at the other end of the line. She stared back over the missing persons form. Jake Sutton, nineteen years of age, last heard from three days ago as he hiked south, away from the Pacific Crest Trail and along the eastern border of Mount Rainier National Park. He had abandoned a group of elderly hikers he'd been with, and hadn't picked up the supply pack waiting for him at the forestry post he'd been scheduled to stop at yesterday. It had now been 24 hours, so he could officially be listed as a missing person. His hysterical mother sounded like she had been counting down the seconds before picking up the phone.

People went missing all the time up here. Some even wanted to. That's what the families sometimes failed to grasp. After finishing the phone call and completing the report, she filed it and printed out the missing person poster for the board. Whilst there, she took down the outdated ones, the oldest, to make space.

Nina had been with the Forest Service for just over five years, joining straight from the University of Washington at Tacoma. Despite majoring in Wildlife Ecology and Management with a minor in Forestry to boot, her aspirations of working with wildlife had quickly been grounded. It was mainly campers, timber firms, and water treatment that took up her days. She walked through to the morning briefing. The call had held her up, and she was the last to enter.

"Now that we're all here," barked the agent at the front of the room.

The unidentified agent wore darkened glasses and looked like Chuck Norris's meaner, truck-driving brother. Nina ignored his stare and took a seat. The guy had already waltzed in like he was the President, not even bothering to tell the lowly rangers which agency he and his suit-clad partner were from. Whoever they were, they seemed to make the chief and the other supervisors nervous. They didn't seem like the Forest Service's Law Enforcement and Investigations Unit types. Although his partner could easily pass for FBI, bad Chuck most certainly couldn't. With long red hair, a hunting jacket, and a dark camouflage tee underneath, he looked more like one of the bikers that might occupy any of the local sheriff drunk tanks. He dressed like a hillbilly and spoke like an asshole, that's all Nina knew.

"Anyway," stammered Marty Johnson, her boss, as he stood up. "North of the Resolute Campsite is currently out of bounds, and will remain so while these men are in the area."

"I'm still not clear on that," another ranger spoke up. "Who are these guys and how come they have that kind of authority?"

Travers was young, but spoke his mind. Nina knew everyone else was thinking the same.

"Fuck you, that's who I am, son," growled the Chuck Norris wannabe.

Nina glowered in her seat silently. She really didn't like this guy.

"This grizzly is nothing like you've dealt with," said the agent in the suit, changing tact. "We're here to help and sort it out. We're operating a curfew and closing most of the trails for the time being. You'll also be paired up for the remainder of your patrols until we clear the area, just to be on the safe side."

"Excuse me," Nina interjected. "But most of us are hunters, from native backgrounds. We also deal with aggressive bears and other wildlife all the time. Why the extra precautions?"

"He's a killer," snapped the Chuck wannabe. "And the reason he's a killer is because some little sweetheart like you in the Forestry Service took a pot-shot at him. We're clearing up your mess."

"And the fact that none of us here have seen neither hair nor hide of this supposed grizzly?" Nina challenged.

"Trust me darlin', that speaks volumes," bad Chuck chimed smugly.

Nina sat back, bristling at the man's rudeness. She was Crow Nation on her mother's side and Skokomish on her father's, and had probably known more about tracking and handling wildlife by the time she'd turned five than this guy would ever know. She was certain his attitude stank as much as he did, and looked at Marty for back up. She couldn't believe he was standing for this. Marty failed to notice, as he was too busy staring at his feet. The meeting appeared to be over.

As the rest of the Forest Service Rangers got up and began to make their way back to their desks, Nina hung back. She noticed she wasn't the only one. Scott Travers was too. Concerned his youth and brashness would get the best of him, she was determined to get to Marty and the two agents before him. She walked over, hurriedly.

"The others may be prepared to put up with this anonymous juris-my-dick-tion crap, but I won't. I want to know who you guys are, I want to see your shields, and I want to see written authority. Until then, you, especially you," she declared, pointing at the rude redhead, "can check your egos in the parking lot, whilst I run your plates."

Marty fixed her with a look of panic that did little to dissuade her. She couldn't believe that a few seconds ago, she had been worried about Travers being too blunt.

The agent in the suit stood up, a half smile on his face.

"Okay, settle down, I get it. My partner here can be a little forthright. My name is Special Agent Gregory Smith. This is Agent Cordell Jones," he explained, nodding towards Chuck.

"Agents Smith and Jones… I'm seriously meant to believe that?" Nina exclaimed.

"Believe what you like, it's the truth. And it's all you're getting," Jones growled in her direction, stepping forward.

"What department are you with?" Nina asked, ignoring him. "You guys aren't LEI, that's for sure."

The Forest Service's Law Enforcement and Investigation special agents were rare visitors to the remoter parks, and only ever investigated criminal cases against property, visitors, or employees, for the most part.

"We're… from a branch within the Bureau for Land Management," Smith replied.

"That's even harder to believe," said Travers, who had walked up behind Nina as they were talking. She realised he was making it clear she had back up, but was keeping a respectful distance. He wasn't stepping in, but he was prepared to. She appreciated the gesture.

"The Bureau for Land Management are investigating an errant grizzly?" Nina continued.

"Imagine if you can, there may be shit you don't know," Jones grinned.

"What I can imagine," shrugged Nina, "is that's a two-way street."

Marty met her gaze. He seemed more in control now, but his glance still warned her to back off.

"Maybe they can be of help," Marty suggested to the

agents. "You've got a lot of ground to cover, a lot of people to talk to. Maybe it's a case of many hands make light work."

Smith gave a nod signifying his approval to Jones, who didn't seem quite as taken with the idea. Then, smiling smugly, he reached behind him and grabbed a large pile of manila files from the table.

"Well, seeing how good you are at running your mouth n'all, maybe you can carry out some interviews," he sneered. "It'll keep you out of our hair, and we won't have to waste our time with a bunch of drunk natives."

Nina glowered at the man. She was on the brink of losing control of her temper. She imagined darting forwards and slamming her elbow into his face, breaking his nose. It would be easy, and satisfying. But she guessed Marty was nervous for a reason. She clenched her fists, only a little shake in her arms hinting at her pent-up fury. She snatched the files from him.

"Happy to be of help," she replied, turning her back.

"One more thing," Marty said, calling her back. "The patrolling in pairs thing is mandatory. Take Travers with you."

"What?" Nina exclaimed. "Marty, there isn't a thing in these woods I haven't come across on my own before. I can handle it. Plus, up on the res, I can't vouch for his safety, especially among them drunk natives," she scowled, staring at Jones.

"My partner was out of line before," Smith offered, "but you're close to being the same way. It's our way, or no way. If you want to be involved, this is it."

Nina looked at Travers. He shrugged. He was trying to look nonchalant, but he clearly wanted in. She sighed. It seemed like a hopeless fight anyway. And Travers wasn't a terrible choice of partner. Despite his youth, he was tall, well built, and could handle himself. He was a little impetuous and thoughtless, but nothing she couldn't keep in check. And he knew not to push his luck with her, which was a major plus. As soon as her demeanour softened, his bright blue eyes sparkled mischievously. She often told him he'd only been recruited because his brown hair matched the uniform, but compared to everyone else, she knew they could at least work together.

"Come on you big lug," she sighed.

Travers followed her out of the room back to her desk. As she flipped through the files, she saw some familiar names. Some she dismissed, shuffling them to the bottom of the pile. Others she took an interest in and brought them to the top.

"Well, it might not be a dull day after all," Nina quipped, looking up at Travers. "We'll head up to the reservation like they want us to, but we'll do some sightseeing on the way."

"Where to?" Travers asked.

"Well, there's Lucas Christian," Nina replied, raising an eyebrow.

"The writer?"

"The very one. Bought a huge piece of land out in the forest and built a luxury house out there. Rumour is that it's less writing retreat, more fortress. I don't know about you, but I'd like a look around that place."

Travers nodded, impressed.

"Then there's Patwyn Dalton, owner of Dalton logging. He's been complaining about guys from the res moving stuff around his camp, damaging equipment and such like. And he just happens to have been the guy who sold the land to Lucas Christian."

"Think that's just a coincidence?" Travers asked.

"I think it'd be interesting to see how they're linked to each other, that's for sure."

"Isn't it like you said, guys from the res causing trouble,

with chunks of the forest being sold off?"

Nina sighed. "No, I don't think so. But I think you're right about one thing. I think it's about territory. Let's go find out."

CHAPTER FIVE

MEMORIES

It had been three days since Shartale had killed and eaten the human. The metallic, fatty taste of the blood was electrifying, and he had sucked it from the torn head with relish before he had retreated with the rest of his meal. The others had been hesitant to follow him, cautious about the other humans returning. He knew they were right to be concerned.

He had eaten on the move, tearing the legs from the torso and carrying them with him. He had scattered the half-eaten remains through nearly a mile of dense forest. The coyotes that often followed him would make short work of what was left. If not them, there were others in the forest who would: wolves, racoons, and a multitude of opportunists waiting to take advantage.

He had been keeping to the outskirts of the family's territory, only eating what he could find or happened upon. They were sticking together, as he knew they would. It made them easy to track, and even easier to avoid. They would instinctively protect the young female, and he was counting on them to do just that. But it did restrict his hunting to a few narrow corridors of forest, most of which took him closer to the humans and their habitations.

Shartale remembered the first time he had taken closer interest in the strange, hairless animals. It had been many summers, but he could remember the warm breeze and the strange scent it carried. He also remembered the rhythmic, melodic sounds drawing nearer. Curiosity had lulled him closer, and from the low boughs of a pine, he watched the young female approach. She was picking wild flowers, and scampering from tree to tree with her head down. As she did so, soothing sounds emanated from her mouth, in a pitch that thrilled and incited him. Even then, he had been three times her size. As she had passed beneath the tree he was in, he had learnt everything he had needed to. The light touch of sweat on her skin. The brisk, bright heartbeat in her chest. Her pungent scent. This was flesh and blood. This was meat. This was prey.

He had dropped from the branch then, smashing into the ground behind her and dropping to all fours. He still towered over her, his shadow blocking out the sun and causing her to turn around in surprise. He had tested her then, driving his arms down with purpose, sending a tremor into the earth where they both stood. He curled back his lips, revealing his fangs. Soon the prey would run. But she didn't. Quick as a flash, she had scooped a rock and flung it directly into his eye. He had stumbled backwards, more in shock and surprise than in pain. Except for others of his kind, he had never encountered anything that would stand its ground against him. He couldn't comprehend something so small attacking him and showing no fear. When he had come back to his senses, she was already running at a blistering pace, back towards the habitations and the safety they offered. With a roar, he had thundered after her, quickly closing the distance. Each of his steps were equal to ten of hers, and he made enormous gains on her with each bound. He dropped to all fours again, where he was even faster. She had already made it to the edge of the trees and was now streaking across a meadow. He would be on her in moments.

Then, just as he was about to pass into the long grass, he had pulled back and skidded to a halt. There had been the sound of impact on the trunk of a redwood, and a long, smooth stick sat quivering at the point it had struck. The gash in the bark was exactly where his head would have been had he not stopped. He could smell the oil on the metal at the tip of the stick, and he looked up, further out into the meadow. The little female was running towards an adult human male, which stood facing him. In one hand he held another stick, and in his other, a bent piece of wood with a thin, tight material attached to it, joining the two curved ends. As Shartale watched, the man threw both to the ground, only to reach behind him and reveal a weapon he was more familiar with. A thick piece of wood with a sharp, curved, metal plate attached to it.

Shartale had lost his advantage. He roared once, then bowled back into the trees, crashing through the thick foliage recklessly and venting his anger and humiliation, until he remembered the sounds would give his position away as much as his movement. He had slowed and quietened his pace, listening out for any signs of pursuit. None had come, but he had learnt his lesson. The hairless ones operated in family groups too, and although smaller, they used tools to protect themselves in ways he was unable to comprehend.

Since then, he had stalked and hunted humans many times, observing their ways and responses. He learnt that if he was discovered, he would be hunted. He also knew that unlike his own kind, different families and groups would band together in large packs. They would search for the ones he took, and their methods of protecting themselves had grown more sophisticated. Then, just as now, his actions had to be carefully planned. Killing and eating a human had the same consequences as being seen, or foraging for food near their habitations. The risk had to be worth the reward, and the meagre offerings he found in what they discarded weren't. Only if he could take a human was it worthwhile.

He smashed a rotten log with a crushing blow from his foot, splintering it. He pulled the shards apart, reaching into the cracks and recesses in search of grubs. He found some, hooking out three and squelching them between his teeth. He contemplated the family and what he knew of their territory. The humans would be coming.

He remembered running, his chest heaving, passing through a clearing where three of his kind had stood, surprised by his sudden appearance. He hadn't stopped, fearful of his pursuers. They'd attacked upwind and silently, just as he would, and they were close. As he passed back between the trees, he heard them. Ricochets of sound, bursts of explosions, and whoops and roars from the three he had left behind in the clearing. The humans had found them in his place. He had hidden, listening for hours as things descended from the sky, and the men walked through the trees. They were noisy now, relaxed. It was clear they were no longer searching. And he had learnt something new. The humans would settle for any quarry like him, if he could lead them to it, as they could not tell the difference.

He would leave the territory tonight, and head for the habitations further out in the forest's perimeter. If the humans came, he would be able to hunt in relative safety whilst the family were forced to run or defend themselves. The males would be protective of the females, and more likely to become casualties. If an attack did come, he would still have to intervene to avoid the men also taking the females, but he was willing to risk losing the older one, and the humans wouldn't expect to be flanked. He gulped down the grubs and stood up. His path and plan were now clear.

CHAPTER SIX

WOOKIE PATROL

There was a southerly breeze that brought hints of the warmth back home to Second-Lieutenant Wade Garric, as he looked out at the darkening Washington state sky. Over 2,000 miles away in New Orleans, the sky would be painted molten shades of pink, gold, and scarlet red. Here though, less than 150 miles from the Canadian border, the sunset was cloaked in mauves, indigo and swirling black, all too ready to descend. He waited at the gate, knowing he was a few minutes early. A foot patrol crossed the yard, the two soldiers moving quickly, purposefully, and silently.

A side door in the gate tower he was standing next to opened, and a figure emerged, the silhouette lit from behind by the ghostly glow of the halogen wall lamp in the stairwell. The man was stocky and well built, and was wearing an army cap. As he stepped towards Wade, he recognised the man as Major Clarke. Clarke was a professional soldier with significant notches from America's recent military history on his belt, and years of experience under it. He was known for being tough but fair, and Wade felt a slight swell of relief as the Major stopped beside him.

"All ready for tonight?" Clarke asked.

"Yes sir," Wade snapped in reply, knowing it wasn't really a question.

"Hope you enjoyed your dinner, as you're gonna be seeing it again real soon when that smell hits you," came a cackle from behind.

Wade didn't need to turn around to know Master-Sergeant Amos Dugas had joined them. The two had been friends since they'd first arrived at Fort Skookum, both being New Orleans born and raised. Despite his loud and unsubtle demeanour, he was glad the skinny blonde Cajun would be on the patrol with him. He was still bothered by Clarke's presence though. No regular patrol he'd ever been on required a senior officer to tag along. He wondered how true the rumours were, what he might see out there. He tried not to think about it.

Garric turned as he heard the rumbling engine of the approaching vehicle. The Humvee drew up alongside them and stopped. Clarke climbed into the front passenger seat, nodding to the driver as he did so.

"The Second-Lieutenant will take it from here, son," the Major commanded.

The Private behind the wheel nodded, even seemed relieved, as he climbed out and left the door open. As Wade got behind the wheel, he stowed the M4 rifle to his side. This also aroused his suspicions further. As the driver, he would be the last to get to his gun. So, if an initiation or prank of some kind was being planned, the guy with perhaps the only gun clipped with live ammunition wouldn't accidentally maim or kill anyone.

"Keep that handy," Amos chided him. "I guarantee you'll need it."

"Up top, Dugas," Clarke ordered, his impatience showing.

Wade smiled as Amos snapped to and threw open the hatch, giving him access to the Humvee's Browning M2 50-

caliber machine gun. He swivelled it left and right on its mount to check its movement wasn't restricted. He thumped the roof to signal all was good.

"Sir, if you don't mind me asking, what exactly are we going to be encountering that requires a 50-cal machine gun?" Wade asked.

"Maybe nothing," Clarke replied. But I have an OP coming up that might require a few good men, and I've had my eye on you two for a while. Let's just say this is an opportunity for me to see how you cope when things get hairy. As you may have gauged, this isn't Dugas's first Wookie patrol. But when I said I was looking for someone else, he mentioned you. Don't let me or your friend down, son."

"No, sir," Wade replied.

He'd heard the others talk about the so-called Wookie patrols. The word Skookum, after which the fort was named, was a Chinook word that meant 'evil god of the forest'. He knew what to expect. They'd go out, complete their rounds, then at some point, they'd be attacked by a group of Marines in gillie suits, a type of camouflage material that had the appearance of long strands of matted hair. It made anyone wearing it very difficult to see in the undergrowth, and at night, there was almost no chance of detecting them. Wade would go through the motions of being surprised when it happened, at least at first. He knew the drill.

As he pressed down on the gas and passed under the large gate between the two guard towers at the front of the fort, he looked left and right. Then, he looked over at the fence that hugged the boundary. 10,000 volts of electricity ran through it, constantly. Twenty clicks out, another fence, intersected by just the front and rear gates, encompassed the entire fort and surrounding forest. It too was electrified and patrolled under guard. He'd never thought about it before, but tonight, the setup bothered him. He'd never come across anything like it on any base he'd been stationed at previously. As a special forces training facility, it wasn't unusual for there to be a slightly less orthodox layout. But he still couldn't help wondering. What are they trying to keep out? He thought.

Clarke indicated for him to turn left, and he found himself driving through a gully bordered by the fort on one side, and the forest on the other. The bushes and underbrush began to intensify, and Wade eased off the gas a little. Clarke's eyes were fixed on the treeline, and he seemed to be acutely listening to the night's sounds. A little further on, the gulley swept right, away from the fort. The lights of the buildings and the hum of the fence faded quickly, disappearing altogether within a few seconds.

"I think we've got company sir," Dugas yelled down into the Humvee's interior.

Wade stifled the grin that wanted to spread across his face. They still weren't too far from the fort, but were out of sight. This was the perfect place to launch the ambush. He was resolved to play along, even if he did feel slightly disappointed they weren't going to wait until they were further round to stage the performance.

Clarke banged the dashboard, and Wade instantly brought the vehicle to a stop.

"Whatever you do son, don't turn the engine off. You just sit here idling, understood?"

Wade nodded.

"Three bogies, approximately eighty yards to the east," Dugas whispered.

It was then that Wade heard Dugas pull back the slide of the 50.cal, and he caught the gleam of the brass, chain-linked cartridges in the magazine. The bullets were real. This time, he couldn't quite repress the chill he felt. If this was a set-up, they were trying real hard to convince him otherwise. Nobody was inclined to take chances with that kind of fire-power. His eyes snapped to the treeline.

For nearly a minute, there was nothing but the sound of boughs and branches creaking gently in the wind. Then, from within the darkness, the booming hoot of a great horned owl pierced the night. Wade was just beginning to feel the edge of the adrenalin wearing off, when a deliberate, decisive crack emanated from nearby. As he peered into the black, he thought he saw movement, a blurred shadow moving between the trees. A second later, a good-sized branch smacked into the side of the Humvee, and dropped to the floor. Wade heard Amos swing the Browning in the same direction.

Wade didn't know why, but he felt a certain urge to check the rear-view mirror. He glanced up, and froze. Glimpsing past Amos's legs, out in the gloom, he saw two amber dots low to the ground, and appearing to edge closer. He recognised them instantly as eye-shine.

"Sir, directly behind us, about thirty yards out. Potential tango," Wade reported, not taking his eyes off the mirror.

"Sneaky sons o'bitches ain't they," declared Amos, swivelling the gun around.

With the windows cracked open, there was no escaping the sudden, seeping stink that crept into the cabin. It was as if a skunk, rolled in dog faeces, had died in the back seat, and been left to rot there for a few days. It took all his self-control to force down the vomit that wanted to fly from his throat as it filled his nostrils.

"Jesus H. Christ, that's one unhappy monkey," Amos declared under his breath, wiping at his streaming eyes.

"Throw a flashbang Corporal, let him know we've seen him," Clarke ordered.

Amos picked a canister up from the seat below and pulled the pin, tossing it gently behind the Humvee. Wade instinctively covered his eyes as he saw the others do the same. Above the sound of his thumping heartbeat, he distinctly heard the thuds of heavy steps coming towards the vehicle. Then he heard the fizz, pop, and crack of the flashbang, and the dazzling blaze of light projected onto his closed eyelids. Something behind the truck was screaming in rage and pain, moving away at high speed. Something else on Clarke's side was roaring, but also moving away. The noise seemed to penetrate every fibre of his being, resonating in his chest. At one point, it was so loud he almost couldn't hear anything at all. As the glare from the flashbang faded, he opened his eyes wide in terror, unsure of what he would see. In the rear-view mirror, all he could see was Amos's grin. And to the front, the reach of the headlights showed only the trees.

"They don't like bright light," Clarke explained. "You may want to remember that."

"They sir?" Wade asked.

"I'm not rightly qualified to tell you exactly what they are," Clarke replied. "But tonight, and on the op, they are your enemy. Let's move on."

As Wade shifted the Humvee into gear and pressed down on the gas, he heard something large thrashing its way through the scrub on his right. Through the open window to his left, something there too, was mirroring their movement. It agitated him. There was little cover there, he would expect to be able to see it. He kept glancing out into the shadows as he drove, trying to get a fix on what he was listening to.

"Maybe time to roll up the windows, bud," Amos suggested.

"Not a chance, I want to hear them coming," Wade replied. "Plus, I'm not sure how much good a pane of glass will do against the thing that threw that tree branch. That pitch must have been from over a hundred feet, and if it hadn't hit the truck, it would've been out of the ball park."

"Maybe when we catch up, you can try signing them up to the Mariners," Amos laughed.

"They certainly need all the help they can get this season," Clarke replied.

Wade wasn't much of a baseball fan, but the Seattle Mariners were pretty much the only Major League team in Washington state, and they got game tickets every now and again. It was more about hot dogs, beer, and buddies for him though.

Wade felt, rather than heard, the impact of something hitting the ground, again somewhere to his left. He came off the gas, letting the Humvee roll along as he reached for the M4. Clarke was watching him out of the corner of his eye, but said nothing. The thing, whatever it was, was too close. He didn't have time to say anything or warn the others. He slammed on the brakes, whipped up the rifle and thrust it through the open window. He closed his eyes, registering the slight crumple of grass underfoot a few feet away, almost parallel to him. He eased the barrel an inch to the right, slipped the safety, and fired.

There was a sucking sound, like an inhalation of breath taken in surprise. Then a low, guttural, curdle of a growl started somewhere in the darkness. It built in resonance and pitch. The sound exploded into a series of shrieks, whoops and utterances that when heard together, almost had the same rhythm and pace of language. For a moment, he felt like he was being scolded. As he heard Amos swing the big Browning round, Wade caught the flash of something white, as a shadow loped off into the darkness. He realised it was a set of long, yellowish fangs, being bared in his direction. It slowly registered with him that they were eight feet off the ground.

"Well, look at you, shooting down range on your first Wookie-patrol," Amos declared, grinning.

"Tell me straight sir, I didn't just shoot a Marine in a gillie suit, did I?" Wade asked, disturbed and confused by what had just happened.

"No son, you didn't."

"So, what did I shoot then, and shouldn't we be going after it?"

"As to what it was, you'll find out soon enough," Clarke replied, meeting his gaze. "And in terms of going after it, no point. Even at that range, that rifle's basically as effective as a pea shooter."

Clarke shrugged, ending the conversation, but he looked Wade up and down for a moment, as if sizing him up.

"Welcome to the Skookum squad," he finally said.

"Report to the briefing at 07 hundred. But in the meantime, get us the hell out of Dodge."

Wade felt a chill as they drove back to the safety of the main fort. He looked once again at the perimeter wall and electric fencing. That's when he realised, they were designed to keep something in, not out.

CHAPTER SEVEN

INVASIVE SPECIES

Nina was about to grab the keys to her truck when the phone on her desk rang. She stared at it, tempted to let it ring. But duty called, literally. She sighed, slumping down into the chair, and lifting the receiver.

"Ranger Nina Lee, Forest Service," she answered.

"Bout time you picked up, I've been trying to get through all morning", came the deep, gruff voice she recognised. "I've got problems on my land, and I need you to god-damn do something about it,"

"Mr. Dalton. I was actually on my way out, to see you amongst others, believe it or not," she replied.

"Really, how convenient. Guess I must be one of them clairvoyants. I'll be here for the next hour, then I'm taking things further. They're not getting away with this kind of harassment."

"They?"

"Your friends, down on the reservation. I mean it Miss. Lee, next time they come on my land, they'll pay for it."

"First, it's Ms, and second, I doubt anyone on the reservation is harassing you. As far as I know, they were very happy to make the sale. But we'll be along shortly. I hope all your permits are up to date before you start throwing around accusations at other people Mr. Dalton. After all, I'm sure you're not doing anything that would antagonise or upset anyone."

The line went dead, and she put the receiver back. Travers was standing across from the desk, smiling knowingly.

"Charm school candidate huh?" he queried.

"Let's just say he suffers from what I call Custer syndrome," Nina quipped. "Symptoms include being an asshole, and consistently underestimating dem Indians."

"I think we already met one of them back there," Travers replied, pointing back to the meeting room with his thumb.

"Well, it's highly contagious, widespread, and there's no known cure," Nina sighed, less humorously.

She picked up her keys again, and nodded her head towards the door.

"You ready to go?"

Travers nodded back, checking his radio and holster. Forest Service Rangers experienced the highest number of assaults in all of law enforcement, and Washington state was no exception. Whether hiking, hunting, or even in their homes, most people they encountered were likely to have access to a weapon of some kind, even if it was just bear mace. People didn't see Park and Forest Service agents as they did police officers, or even the sheriff department, whom the rangers had jurisdiction over. For some reason, they either thought they had more leeway, or were less likely to be charged with something. They often reacted badly when they found out that wasn't the case. That's why shoulder-holsters and weapon carrying had become part of the uniform in recent years. Travers had a government-issue Sig Sauer P226 pistol, whereas Nina favoured the punch of a 357. Magnum in the classic frame of a Colt King Cobra revolver, her personal gun, and a gift from her father. With a

4″ barrel and wood grips, it had an old west feel she liked. It was also accurate and as reliable as hell.

As they walked out of the office, Travers was surprised to see Nina turn left, walking away from the back lot where the trucks, emblazoned with official Forestry Service decals, were parked up. Instead, she was heading to the side lot, where the staff parked their personal vehicles.

"Why not use a works truck?" Travers asked.

"The guys on the res will see it as me pushing authority. If we go in mine, they know I'm there for a one-to-one. It's a little more respectful," she answered, whisking a set of keys from her pocket.

She walked up to a black GMC Syclone. It had clearly been modified, with raised suspension and a serious set of off-road tyres sitting on large, heavy-set wheels. But it still maintained its low-slung, purposeful stance. Travers smiled in surprise as she opened the driver's door and beckoned for him to get in the other side. On the interior, other than a new looking stereo system, the truck was as GMC had intended, bare, basic and alluding to its performance focus.

"I always liked these," Travers said.

"I found it abandoned alongside a Chevy Baja, - both kind of useless in Wyoming, where I lived at the time. So, they'd sat unloved and unwanted on the lot. I couldn't leave them there," Nina replied. "I traded a wrangler for them both, and this was their love child."

"Did you do the mods?"

"Kind of, I had help," Nina replied, pulling out onto the road. "Those factory slicks weren't exactly built for Washington state forest roads and trails. Now it can go fast, and anywhere."

"Best of both worlds," Travers grinned.

"That was the idea," Nina laughed.

The drive out to Dalton's camp took about half an hour. It was a large, ugly scar that cut into the forest. Trees had been felled, and the earthy, rock-strewn ground looked barren in contrast to the lush greenery of the surrounding woodland. Dalton was using it as a base from where he would cut new logging roads into the forest, but for now, it was just his cabin and some equipment. As they pulled up, the camp's bombsite-like appearance was further underpinned by the excavators with smashed in windows, bent and twisted panels, and worst, one that had been turned completely on its side.

"No wonder he's pissed," Travers stated.

"Nobody on the res did this," Nina exclaimed.

As soon as they brought the truck to a stop, the front door of the cabin opened, and Dalton stepped out onto the veranda. He was tall, and stocky, with piercing blue eyes and thick brown hair. He looked a little overweight, but his entire demeanour suggested he knew how to take care of himself. He made straight for the truck as Nina and Travers climbed out.

"Well, you're a woman of your word Ms. Lee, I'll give you that," Dalton acknowledged. He looked tense, and his eyes had the sluggish, strained nervousness that came with tiredness. He was covering it well, but the man clearly hadn't had a good night's sleep in some time.

"As, it appears, are you Mr. Dalton," Nina replied. "This would take some serious doing. I think it's well beyond the remit of anyone on the reservation though. You'd need some serious equipment to do the damage here."

"I figure you're on the money there," Dalton agreed. She could see the reluctance in admitting it on his face, and the worry that followed it by doing so.

"Any rivals in the area, maybe someone who you beat to the land sale?" Travers offered.

"Not that I know of. Guess that is something you can ask them," Dalton replied.

Nina began to look around the site. She made her way over to a large, tracked, yellow bulldozer. The vent panels that covered the engine, sitting behind the cabin, had been pummelled and dented over every inch of their surfaces. A side window had been smashed, and the door ripped from its hinges. As she looked behind, Dalton nodded towards where the misshaped, ruined frame of the door was hanging in a tree, its glassless window panel hooked over a branch nearly twice her height above them. She walked around the bulldozer, and saw on the other side that the track had been ripped off, making the earth-mover slump over.

"That thing must weigh ten tonnes," Dalton exclaimed. "Same as the one over there," he indicated towards the machine they had seen turned on its side.

"Were you here when it happened?" Travers asked.

"No, I was out with one of my crews. It was Jerry, one of my work-chiefs who found the camp like this yesterday morning. I'd only been gone a couple of hours. Whatever happened here, it happened quick."

Nina walked back and forth, scanning the ground. She was no longer paying any attention to Dalton, and ignored Travers completely as she moved past him. Other than the trackways of the equipment in the camp, there was no sign of similar machinery having been used to do the damage.

She knew it would have taken many determined men, armed with sledgehammers and maybe even fire-fighting equipment to do the damage inflicted on the excavators and earth-movers, and she couldn't imagine how many it would take to turn one over.

"I'll head up to the reservation, Mr. Dalton – I'm as interested as you are if anyone might be trying to harass you off your land. But don't go picking any fights, that's our job," Nina nodded.

"Fair enough," Dalton agreed, the frustration showing. "But you figure why I'm upset, right?"

Nina nodded. "This is a big deal, and would throw anyone off their game. This wasn't done lightly. This is serious, and it's just become my top priority. What made you think it was people from the res if I might ask?"

"I'll show you," Dalton replied, beckoning them to follow.

They walked around to the rear of the cabin, which overlooked a grass meadow bordered by treeline on three sides. Dalton led them out a little way beyond the deck and took a knee beside something. As Nina and Travers reached it, she saw it was a short, broken-off stick pushed into the ground. Dalton pointed to another a little further along, and then another back further out where they'd come from.

"What are they?" Travers asked.

Dalton stood up and turned around, taking a step towards the cabin. He raised one hand and waved it casually. Immediately, a series of lights fitted to the rear of the wrap-around veranda illuminated in a soft glow, even in the middle of the day.

"These mark the reach of each individual light, all the

way round," Dalton explained. "Clever, simple, practical," he shrugged.

"Guess that's a compliment," Nina quipped.

"All I'm saying is, I think we can rule out racoons," Dalton replied.

"This is pretty serious," Nina said, changing tack. "Have you thought about cameras and security?"

"Got some on order. There are guns in the cabin if I need 'em."

"We'll be in touch," Nina nodded acceptingly. "It's now an official investigation. Given there's property damage, you'll likely be contacted by an LEI agent once I write up my initial reports, but for now, I'm on it."

A short while later, Nina and Travers were back in the truck, heading north to the Packwood Reservation. Covering over 2,000 square miles, it was home to nearly 30,000 Native Americans spread across ten different communities. Klikitat, Palus, Wallawalla, Wanapam, Wenatchi, Wishram, and Yakam peoples made up the Confederated Tribes and Bands of the Yakama Nation who had been assigned to it. It was also where Nina's father lived. He was from the northern Skokomish nation but had met her mother whilst working as a ranch hand in Wyoming. When they had separated, he had stayed, and Nina and her mother had gone back to Wyoming. Following the death of her mother, Nina had recently returned. It still didn't feel like home. In his youth, Nina's father had been a fierce and well-respected leader, but in his old age, drink and depression had taken some of that respect and authority from him. He was still affectionately referred to as "General Lee", in good-natured irony by those close to him, perhaps due to his first name being Robert like the respected Confederate General known for his shrewd tactics during the Civil War. To Nina, he was dad, and to everyone else, he was simply "Bob".

Nina steered the truck through the township of Grey Swan, nodding through the windshield at some of the residents she recognised. Her father's cabin was the other side of a set of crossroads, facing a patch of evergreen forest. Beyond that, Mount Rainier crested the skyline. Not only was the 4,392-metre-high peak Washington state's tallest mountain, it was also considered one of the most dangerous active volcanoes in the world. Although it's last period of activity had been between 1820 and 1854, it's official status of "dormant" was questioned, when in 2016, permanent seismic monitoring stations were deployed throughout the region. Mount Rainier threatened the lives of nearly 80,000 people living within its vicinity if it erupted. Its native name was "Tahoma", meaning "the Mother of waters", and it was an apt one. If it were to erupt, its enormous glacial deposits could be turned into vast lahars - mudflows that might engulf the entire Puyallup River valley. Or, due to its sheer size, ash from an eruption could penetrate Vancouver, San Francisco, Canada and huge tracts of the North-West. Everyone who lived in Packwood lived in the shadow of potential death and destruction. It seemed to dull life there, like a serpent coiled around a heart, ready to squeeze.

Nina pulled the truck up outside her father's cabin. The teal-coloured, slatted boards hugged white-painted windows that were well kept. Like most of the houses in the township, a simple raised deck, covered by a slanted wooden roof, graced the front. On it, Nina's father sat in a wooden rocker, watching them as they got out.

"You're home early," he stated, an amused expression on his face. Although talking to Nina, Bob Lee's gaze was fixed on Travers. "Who's the Belagana?"

"Dad, this is Scott Travers, my partner," Nina replied, rolling her eyes. "Scott, this is Robert, my father." She never called him Bob.

"Pleased to meet you sir – Belagana?" Travers queried.

"It's a Navajo word for white folk," the old Native American smiled. "Would you prefer pale face? You can call me Bob," he winked.

Scott and Nina made their way up onto the deck. A menacing growl and the sound of claws on wood made Travers freeze in his tracks. A black-coloured blur barrelled across the decking from around the corner of the house and flew at him. To the young ranger's credit, he stood his ground but found himself eye to eye with an enormous wolf, standing on its hind legs and with its front paws draped over his shoulders. It growled again and turned its head slightly towards Nina.

"Jesus," Scott muttered under his breath, his right arm bent across the chest of the animal and keeping it at bay.

"Friend," Nina said, laughing.

The wolf whined slightly, then sprang excitedly at Nina. Scott noticed the animal didn't bark or wag its tail like a dog. He watched as Nina returned the greeting, rubbing the side of her head against that of the canine. She looked up, a huge and genuine smile on her face. It wasn't something Scott could remember seeing all too often.

"Travers, meet Achak," Nina offered. "The name means spirit in Algonquin and is a traditional name for the wolf."

"Really? And is he a…" Scott trailed off.

"Well, for a spirit, he sure can make food disappear," Bob laughed. "But yep, almost at least. There ain't much dog in him, if at all."

Scott went to stroke the animal but noticed Nina's cautionary shake of the head. "He doesn't like that. He'll tolerate it, but that's not how to make friends with him. Come here," she offered.

Scott walked over, a little hesitantly.

"Take his head in both hands and rest yours on his. Don't close your eyes," she suggested.

Scott only held back for a moment, then committed. He was surprised to find the wolf compliant, and it relaxed immediately after he did as instructed. Scott stood back a little, admiring Achak. His amber eyes gleamed, and his tongue lolled out of his mouth as he took a few steps to the edge of the veranda and surveyed the track back up to the crossroads. Close up, Scott could see the wolf had flecks of grey throughout his black coat. But he couldn't have been that old, probably four or five years at the most, and clearly in his prime.

"Dad, do you know anything that might be going on up at Dalton's place?" Nina asked.

"Like what?" Bob shrugged.

"He's had a bunch of equipment busted up pretty bad," Nina explained. "Would have taken several men, and some tools to do it."

"Land was sold fair and square. He got a good price and so did we. We have no quarrel with Patwyn Dalton," Bob replied, frowning.

"Nobody's accusing you of anything," Scott assured. "We just wondered if there might be other buyers out there with a case of sour grapes, something like that."

"I like him," Bob nodded towards Travers, as he turned back to Nina. "He's more polite than you."

Scott grinned at Nina as she rolled her eyes.

"Give him a chance to get to know you," she shot back. "But like he says, can you think of anyone?"

"Dalton was the only one interested in that land," Bob sighed. "And I warned him about making tracks in certain places or clearing certain areas, that it would disturb the wildlife. I'll go down and talk to him, see what he's done. If he listens to me, he'll be fine."

Nina fixed him with an unamused stare.

"With the greatest of respect sir, I don't think wildlife would have been responsible for what we saw, not unless an entire family of pissed-off grizzlies decided to go apeshit," Travers said, shaking his head.

"All depends on what kind of wildlife we're talking about, don't it," Bob smiled. "Apeshit might be more apt than you think."

Travers noticed Nina stiffen slightly as she shot her father a warning glance.

"There's something in those woods that can crush up those diggers like paper," Bob warned, with no trace of the smile.

"I don't mean any disrespect sir, I'm sure you know what you're talking about," Scott replied.

"See, more polite," Bob nodded at Scott.

"Well, if there's nothing else you can add to the investigation other than phantoms in the woods, we have another stop to make," Nina sighed.

Bob nodded acceptingly.

Scott walked up to Bob and offered his hand. The old man took it and returned the shake with a surprisingly firm grip of his own. Scott could see the fierce intelligence in his eyes, and that Bob was quite lucid. It surprised him. He made his way back to the truck, where Nina was waiting for him.

They made their way out of the township of Packwood and headed north towards an area known as Cougar Valley. It was about five miles, via a road usually closed in winter, but it was just about accessible now, being early spring. It was pretty much untouched wilderness, although a number of trailheads began in the area. It was also where a multi-millionaire author named Lucas Christian had decided to build an incredible house after buying up acres of land. He had donated heavily to several wildlife charities and Native American communities, gaining him considerable support as he moved into the area. But Nina knew the purchase of the land from Dalton prevented it from being logged – which may have upset his competitors. The publicity surrounding Lucas Christian's move to the state had been focused on a return to nature. It was a retreat where he could write and head off on a hike, whenever he wanted. It was rumoured there wasn't another house like it in all of Washington state.

The entrance to the property was marked by a stone archway, housing an electronic gate that opened onto a long gravel drive. No other fencing or barriers could be seen, and neither could the house from the road. Nina pulled up to the com and pressed the button. After almost a minute, she was about to press the com again when a voice answered – a male voice, with an English accent.

"Hello, can I help you?" it asked.

"Good afternoon, is this Mr. Lucas Christian?" Nina replied.

"Answering a question with a question," the voice laughed. "It is. I'm guessing you're law enforcement. If my ex-wife..."

"We're rangers with the Forest Service," Nina explained. "We're closing off some sections of the area following reports of an aggressive bear. Some of those trails and sections come very close to your land Mr. Christian, and we wanted to talk to you about the situation. Word has it you're a very keen wildlife watcher."

"One of the reasons I moved here," came the reply. "Please, come up to the house."

There was a loud buzzing sound, then the imposing double wooden gates swung inward. Nina put the truck into drive and pushed down on the gas. The track was a slight incline, with a bank of thickly entwined Douglas fir and ponderosa fir trees to the left. It was the same to the right, but as they sat on a downward facing slope, Nina and Scott could see over the treetops and out across an area known as Goose Prairie – a patch of open scrub to the south. It lived up to its name too, as the grassland would attract huge flocks of migrating snow geese, and the rarer emperor geese. They did as good a job as buffalo as natural grazers.

As they rounded a long and sweeping bend, the track opened up and the house came into view. It was substantial – a perfect architectural blend of stone and hardwood. Completely modern in style, almost every aspect featured floor-to-ceiling windows. It somehow looked like a lodge, despite being the size of a mansion and spread over at least three floors. Nina noticed the design was very angular, like a bunch of boxes had been placed on top of one another. Only one section had an A-frame style roof, on the top floor. It looked like it formed the centre of the house, from front to back, with wings dispersing outward from it. These blocks had more gently sloping roofs, she noticed.

Nina parked the truck at what she assumed was the front door and got out. Scott followed suit and walked up the steps with her.

"How much d'ya reckon?" Travers asked.

"A lot," Nina said, her eyes trying to take the property in again. "It's amazing to think he had this built almost without anyone knowing."

There was the sound of several locks unbolting, and the big door made from western red cedar swung open. A man with short, neat grey hair and spectacles that partially hid steely blue eyes, stood in the doorway, smiling at them. He was relatively well-built yet lean, and Nina placed him in his late forties. Two enormous black and tan dogs with long but well-groomed hair stepped up, flanking him on either side. Nina recognised them as Tibetan mastiffs.

"Don't mind the boys, they're well trained," Lucas laughed. He looked down at the dogs, and they instantly turned on their heels and padded off back down the corridor beyond. "Come on in," he beckoned to them both.

Nina and Scott followed the author down a wide, wood-panelled corridor. The walls were adorned with framed posters of the horror movies that had been made from his books, and large pieces of original artwork. Everything was in good taste and suited the property perfectly – no doubt the work of an especially good and talented interior designer. It had been rumoured that a famous British firm had been responsible for the look of the property both inside and out.

Lucas led them into a huge open room at the back of the property, where the dogs lay on an enormous rug, facing a window that ran the length of the room from floor to ceiling. Nina stepped close to take in the view. Washington state wilderness stared back at her in all its glory. Huge red-barked, evergreen firs and pines sat either side of a crystal-clear stream that gave way to a waterfall and pool. The forest thinned out as it approached the house, almost creating a natural path. Huge slabs of rock had been perfectly placed to serve as viewing platforms, or perhaps to entice wildlife for photographic opportunities. She got the sense that even this lush and natural-looking scene had been planned and designed. That's when she noticed the thickness of the window itself.

"That's some safety glass you've got there Mr. Christian," Nina stated, looking round.

"You have a good eye, Ranger…?"

"Lee, Nina Lee," she replied, realising she hadn't formally introduced herself or Scott, as they had been taken in awe of the house.

"Well, Ranger Lee, that glass is tougher than steel, and it's three-inches thick. It could take a hit from a 50-calibre round and barely crack. It was developed by the University of California, at the Berkeley and California Institute of Technology. What you're looking at is basically metallic glass."

"Worried about something?" Scott asked.

"More… preparing," Lucas answered. "The walls and doors have titanium linings too. There are motion sensors throughout the woods, as well as perfectly-hidden infrared cameras. There might not be any fences, but the security has been designed so I see anything coming from a long way off."

"And why's that?" Nina asked.

"You probably know that I write monster stories," Lucas shrugged. "And as you said, I'm here for the wildlife. What if I were to tell you that there's a monster in those woods, and I'm going to catch it?"

CHAPTER EIGHT

SEEKING SASQUATCH

Agent Cordell Jones smiled at his partner, Special Agent Smith, as the big-rig truck swung into view. The "Prowler" was a mobile-command-unit and would help distance them a little from the local sheriff department, state police, and even the rangers. There would be no need to operate out of borrowed offices now, and it came fully equipped for even the most arduous of missions.

"Greg, my boy," Cordell grinned, "there's no part of this job I don't like."

"Really," Smith mocked, "because it didn't seem you liked co-operating with the rangers much. We need them, and you'd do well remember that."

"We're not the ones keeping the truth from them," Cordell growled. "I figure there's a reason for that. As it is, they're clueless, and therefore in our way."

Gregory Smith sighed, his utterance lost as the truck pulled up and its air brakes let out a blast beside them. A second vehicle trailed behind – a brash, over-styled, modified, six-wheeled, white Jeep Gladiator with blacked-out windows. It pulled up a little way back along the road. The bureau lackey driving the Prowler climbed out of the cab and handed a clipboard to Smith, who duly signed the paperwork and handed it back. The agent, who was young, well built, and probably a Langley reject, nodded and climbed back into the cab obediently.

"They shouldn't be following the truck," Cordell muttered, nodding towards the six-wheeled Jeep. "Have the Forest Service relinquished that campsite yet? It's not like we can all book into the same motel."

"I'm sure it's being taken care of," Smith answered, with a non-committal shrug.

Cordell shook his head as they both climbed the steps into the back of the unit. The Prowler was a mobile fortress on the outside and a cutting-edge communications centre inside. There were no windows in the rear section, and the door they entered through was solid titanium with locks to match. To their right, as they entered, banks of expensive and covert-looking hard drives blinked green and amber operating lights at them from behind glass doors. On the wall opposite the entrance, a huge flat screen was angled slightly down towards them. Three smaller screens, in a column, bordered its right-hand side. All could be used together or separately as required. Secure, military-grade satellite, GPS, telephone and internet connections serviced every piece of hardware and the two workstations that sat at a 90-degree angle to the screens. Beyond them, separated by another steel locked door was a significant armoury, complete with body armour and tactical gear. There was even a bunk, in case they needed to work shifts. The only thing the truck didn't have was a bathroom, hence the need for a base camp. With the Prowler, along with its all-wheel drive and bullet-proof all-terrain tyres, they could run operations from anywhere. As the truck got underway, both Cordell and Smith braced and got their sea legs back. It had been a while since they'd been onboard. They knew they were headed to the requisitioned camping ground, where their task force and backup would also be stationed.

"First thing's first," Smith commanded, nodding towards the radio unit, "let's get the circus out from under our feet and get them to run interference. They're all set up and ready to go."

Cordell grinned again and picked up the radio.

"Why Gregory, don't speak ill of the PR department," he chuckled, "otherwise, people might think there's something other than fluffy forest giants with bad teeth out there. Let's let them get the show on the road."

A few minutes later, at the next junction, the Jeep pulled off from their tail and headed north.

~

Scott eyed Nina cautiously as they drove back towards the Ranger Station. Her anger was evident.

"So... what that author guy was saying is basically what your dad was saying, right?"

Nina glowered at him.

"An elderly Native American who believes in superstition, and a writer of horror novels who is probably planning to cash in on the hype and nonsense surrounding the bear story. All we've found out is there are at least two people in the community more than willing to waste our time."

Scott went to reply, but the radio mounted on the dashboard suddenly bleeped.

"Unit 8, pick up please, over."

Nina snatched up the radio.

"Unit 8, receiving, over."

"How close to Bumping Lake are you folks?"

"About six clicks I'd say," Nina replied. "But I'm not in

the mood to round up wayward hikers. Give the feds something to do."

"Nothing so mundane, 8," the dispatcher reported, some amusement in her voice. "We have a TV crew who need permits signed. You're closest."

Nina rolled her eyes. "Fine dispatch, we're heading there now. Are they at the camping ground picnic area?".

It was the only place Nina could think that had anything even nearly resembling a parking area. And it gave rather scenic views of the water against the backdrop of Mount Rainier in the distance.

"That's a ten-four unit 8, over and out."

Like everything else at this time of year, even if there hadn't been a fed-enforced lockdown in place, Bumping Lake campground was closed for the season. Nearly three miles long, Bumping Lake was a significant stretch of water, although only half a mile at its widest point. The campground offered a boat ramp for summer guests, but it was still pretty remote. You kind of had to know it was there. Compared to some of the other local lakes, it got pretty deep – well over a hundred feet in places. It wasn't a bad place to fish either. Brook, cutthroat, and bull trout could be found in the glacial water – although there was a current restriction on bull trout. It was one of the maddening things about her job. Every year, the forest service co-ordinated with Washington Game & Fish to release rainbow trout into the lake. But the rainbow trout outgrew and out competed the native bull trout, which was now disappearing fast from the state's waterways. But they would keep doing it to keep the fishing folk happy. Politics, conservation, and common sense rarely made good bedfellows, especially when there was a profit to be made. Fishing permits and game licenses brought in a lot of money, and no agency was in a rush to bite the hand that fed it.

But it wasn't anxious fishing enthusiasts looking for a trophy trout they were heading to meet. Nina scolded herself for not asking more questions about the TV crew, but she'd felt bad about the flippant remark about rounding up hikers. If that had been required, she knew that was her job, and not something she'd be able to pass off. And she wouldn't even want to. It bugged her that her mouth was often smarter than she was – or at least faster. She made a mental note to make it up to Bonnie, the dispatcher, later, as she pulled into the Bumping Lake campground.

"Oh no, not them," she growled, stomping on the brakes.

Crowded around the hood of a big, metallic white, six-wheeled Jeep that Travers instantly recognised, were four people also familiar. He grinned.

"That truck is the Wendigo and that's the crew from Seeking Sasquatch," he said, taking in a quick breath as his eyes widened.

Nina felt his glance as he checked to see if she too was experiencing the same, giddy reality he was. She wasn't. She wasn't even listening to him. Instead, she was fantasising about the supposed rogue grizzly obediently rounding the corner and suddenly setting upon the four people now looking in their direction. Her nostrils flared as she near pulled the handle from its socket and kicked open the door.

"You know you're glaring, right," Travers asked her, quietly, joining her.

When she didn't respond, Travers shrugged and set off towards the four people – the hosts of TV's 'Seeking

Sasquatch'. Nina knew it well enough. It was a hugely popular show. Over the course of the last eight years, they had travelled up, down, and across the country to "investigate" the existence of the mythical creature known as bigfoot. In almost every native culture, the entity was known by several names, and often treated as very real. She neither dismissed it nor believed. She often felt intrigued by what people reported and said they had seen. But when it came to the show, she did dismiss it. It was pure, nonsensical entertainment at best. Whilst they did interview witnesses and collected reports, their investigation techniques ranged from walking through the woods with marching bands to leaving out peanut butter – which was always taken. They called it gifting, which was maybe how the racoons and chipmunks saw it too, Nina guessed. What remained clear was that in eight years, the animal they sought had never been seen by them – at least not on camera. They all claimed to have had several encounters when the cameras were conveniently switched off.

The team were led by a woman named Katie Cash, who right now, seemed to be in the middle of a serious phone call. Nina estimated her to be in her late forties. She was tall, with an athletic build, and long, silvery blonde hair. Her eyes were more grey than blue, and her skin came with an authentic tan tone that only California seemed to be able to produce. Before the show had started, she had written several books on bigfoot and the paranormal. Bodhi Prince was an Australian adventurer and survivalist who looked every bit the part. He had claimed to have encountered yowies – the Australian version of bigfoot, many times. His dark brown hair was almost as long as Katie's, but tied back in a ponytail. He was compact rather than short, and Nina could tell plenty of muscle made up most of the bulk beneath his jungle shirt and khakis. In contrast to Katie, his eyes were sparkling blue, and he sent a wink and a mischievous grin the team leader's way as she came off the phone. Nina wondered if there was something there. That certainly hadn't been on the show. Next, was the team's resident scientist. Dr. Mary Beth Benoit was an African American, proud of both her Cajun roots in Louisiana and her renowned, global reputation as a primatologist. She had joined Jane Goodall in agreeing that people must be seeing something when it came to bigfoot, and her journey from sceptic to authenticator had been well documented on the show. Her short, dark hair escaped in tufts from the John Hopkins Blue Jays cap she was wearing, and her shrewd brown eyes were the only ones currently evaluating Nina and Travers for now. The other member of the team, a self-declared paranormal investigator, Joe Beazley, was crouched, rummaging through the contents of his serious looking backpack. His hair was a wayward mop of light brown strands slicked back for ease. He was wiry, but not out of shape. On the show, he came across as nervous and geek-like, endorsed by his darting green eyes that hid behind thin glasses with octagonal lenses.

"Come on," Scott beckoned, "it's not like we get to do this sort of thing every day. Make the most of it."

"That's what I like about you, Travers," Nina sighed with a smile, her shoulders relaxing as she did. "You haven't lost your optimism yet."

They walked towards the TV crew, side by side. But before they got to them, a large, brown Chevy Tahoe SUV pulled into the parking lot behind their own truck. Katie Cash instantly looked up and waved. Nina glanced, and noticed a man and a woman climb out of the rear of the Chevy. They driver, another man, stayed put. Nina thought there was something about him – she'd seen enough ex-military swaggers to know the type. As the man and woman opened the trunk of the SUV, Nina noticed the cameras and equipment cases in the back.

"Camera crew," Travers said in realisation.

"Aw, has it spoiled the magic?" Nina teased.

Travers laughed and shook his head. They continued over to the cast of Seeking Sasquatch. Introductions were brief, formal, but not unfriendly. The crew joined them and passed over the paperwork.

"This is Tilly Miller and Jason Berman," Katie explained, "Tilly is our producer, and Jason is our cameraman."

Nina nodded without looking up. She headed towards a nearby picnic bench and sat down. Katie Cash watched her go and glanced at Travers.

"Non-believer," he explained, kindly.

"How about you?" Katie asked, tilting her head to the side. She moved a little closer and studied Travers with an unblinking gaze.

Travers thought about his response carefully.

"I've seen the show," he shrugged. He looked up, noticing that Nina was heading back to them.

"There's a problem," Nina explained, passing the permit request back. "I can't give you permission to stay at the Resolute campsite overnight. Even we're not allowed in there at the moment. We have reports of a grizzly, out of hibernation early and in the area."

"I can assure you, we are competent hikers and campers, and we can deal with dangerous wildlife," Katie replied, nodding towards Bodhi Prince.

The adventurer stood up, and took pride in turning his hip towards them. Holstered to it was a black and silver-coloured revolver with a scope attached to it. Nina recognised the gun as a Taurus Raging Hunter. It was a gun she wouldn't be against carrying herself if she could afford it, although she preferred the shorter barrel and the less flashy, all-black version.

"I have a permit – cleared that before we came," Bodhi explained. "Once took down a water buffalo in Argentina with this little beauty. Not much a .460 Magnum round won't stop dead, if you get my drift."

"The crew also have a shotgun in the vehicle, and are never far away," Katie continued to explain. "We've encountered bears and mountain lions, and know what to do. We also always surround our camps with a battery-powered electric fence."

"It's simply beyond my authority," Nina explained. "I'm not trying to be difficult, I just can't do it, and it's for your own safety. Those kinds of fences are good in summer when bears are well fed and happy, but to one determined or desperate, they offer little deterrent."

"That's disappointing, excuse me for a moment," Katie replied.

Nina knew from her tone that she wasn't taking no for an answer, and wasn't surprised to see the cell phone come out again as she walked towards the production crew's Tahoe. She did wonder who she might be calling though.

"Good to see she's as impertinent and pushy in real life

as on the show," Nina scoffed.

"You watch it then?" Dr. Mary Beth Benoit asked, walking around the side of the Chevy, which they were gathered around.

"I've caught bits here and there," Nina replied, a little guarded. "My dad watches it," she added, as if to explain.

Dr. Benoit examined her with a cool, collected gaze. Her eyes were kind, and Nina could see she recognised and understood the hesitation, but pitied it a little too.

"I joined the team holding my sceptic card loud and proud," Dr. Benoit continued.

"And now?" Nina challenged.

"I've heard and seen things I can't explain. I've heard calls that are undoubtedly primate, only I've been in Ohio, or Oregon. Several thousand miles from where any apes are meant to be. And..."

Nina stared at her, waiting for her to finish.

"Guess you really don't watch the show," Dr. Benoit smiled in realisation. "A few years back, something bluff-charged me in the woods of Pennsylvania. We'd finished filming for the day, and we'd headed back to the campground we were staying at."

"Thank god it had cabins," Bodhi chimed in with his signature wink.

"Anyway, I needed the bathroom and headed out," Dr. Benoit continued, rolling her eyes with amusement. "I was about halfway across, when something grunted at me. At first, I thought it was a wild boar, but then, whatever it was thundered out of the scrub. It was huge. I could see an outline, and two glowing gold eyes. Then it veered off, crashing away back into the brush. It was enough to make a believer out of me."

"And for you to take a break from the show," Travers added, sympathetically.

Dr. Benoit nodded.

"We managed to get great tracks from that encounter," Katie Cash chimed in, re-joining them. "It's just a pity that we didn't have our cameras rolling. Somebody wants to talk to you," she said, handing the mobile phone to Nina.

Nina took the handset.

"Ms. Lee?" came the voice of Special Agent Gregory Smith down the line.

Nina was impressed at Cash's ability to find friends in low places, and how quickly she'd been able to do so.

"Let me guess, you want me to okay a TV crew to operate in an area you expressly told me not to go into just this morning," Nina snapped.

"They have impressed upon me that it's of the utmost importance," Smith replied.

At least he doesn't sound smug, Nina thought. On the other hand, she could see from Katie Cash's expression that she most certainly was feeling awfully pleased with herself.

"If they can go in, I can," Nina stated, matter of fact. "If civilians are using the trails, Forest Service personnel should be on hand to respond if necessary. There's a dangerous bear in the area I hear."

"Ms. Lee, I doubt anything I say will stop you from entering the red zone if you need to," Agent Smith replied. "But I'm sure you have better things to do than babysit TV crews looking for something that isn't there."

"Do you mean the bear or something else?" Nina mocked.

The phone went dead. Nina handed it back to Katie Cash, who in turn returned the permit papers.

"Got a pen?" Nina requested.

Tilly Miller, the producer, handed her one with an embarrassed, apologetic smile. Nina signed the permits and tore off the receipts so she could log the numbers. She handed the paperwork back to Katie Cash, who was still smiling triumphantly.

"It's easier if we work together," Cash said, raising her eyebrows in a victorious 'told you so' shrug.

Nina stared at her hard. Her own shrug in reply was more in the spirit of 'whatever' than acceptance.

"Let's get out of here and leave them to chase shadows," Nina said to Travers, wheeling around and marching back to the truck without a look back.

CHAPTER NINE

YOUR BEARS AIN'T BEARS

Agent Cordell Jones stepped out of the big rig mobile-command-centre, nicknamed the 'Prowler' – and took a deep lungful of the forest air. They had travelled some way into the woods, following an old logging road north of the Resolute camping ground. It marked the boundary of what they called the red zone. The area was strictly out of bounds to all civilians and even the Forestry Service and Park Rangers. The area hadn't been logged for years, and even if it were still active, no logging took place until the onset of summer. That was months away.

Special Agent Gregory Smith stepped out of the truck and let out a deep sigh. He'd changed out of his suit into some brand-new outdoor gear, including some heavy-duty boots. All part of the truck's inventory. Cordell snickered.

"I don't know why you insist on suits still," he shrugged.

"Makes me feel superior to you," Smith shrugged. "And you like the fieldwork a lot more than I do," he added, nodding towards the carbine in Cordell's hands.

The M4A1 carbine Cordell had selected was fitted with a Special Operations Peculiar Modification kit – or 'SOPMOD' accessory system. In this case, it enabled both a foregrip and a Trijicon 4x Advanced Combat Optical Gunsight, or 'ACOG' scope to be attached via the rail interface. Smith glanced at his side holster, which held his standard issue Sig Sauer M17 pistol.

"At least tell me you've loaded that thing with something more impactful than a strong breeze," Cordell asked.

"115 grain, solid copper rounds. Armour piercing for all

intents and purposes."

Cordell didn't seem convinced.

"M993 cartridges – actual armour piercing," he responded, tapping the extended magazine plugged into the carbine. "There's a reason they used to be called stone giants, y'know.".

"I'm not convinced the term stone giants referred to these... things," Smith replied, looking agitated.

"Point is, taking them down needs more than a pea shooter."

"We're just the eyes on the ground. If we have to shoot anything, things have got way worse than I ever signed up for," Smith sighed. "Anyhow, let's get going. I know this is the shit you live for."

"Why, Gregory, haven't you heard how getting outdoors is good for your mental health?"

"I see that shit all the time," Smith laughed. "Connect with nature, get lost in the woods... you know what really happens? When you connect with nature, it rips your goddamned arm off. And if you get lost in the woods, you die."

"Not the outdoors type, huh," Cordell laughed. "But you're not wrong. Which is why we do the macho bullshit," Cordell tapped the gun again.

They did a quick equipment check, tested their radios and frequencies, and went over their planned manoeuvres with the agent staying with the Prowler. As they set off into the forest, Cordell was still thinking about what Smith had said. The stone giants. It was a generic name that referred to a number of Native American legends. The Iroquois called them 'Ot Ne Yar Hed', which meant stone giant, or stone coated. The Genoskwa was a broader native legend, also believed to be a type of very aggressive stone giant. The Tuscarora tribes named them 'Ot-Nea-Yar-Heh' – a powerful tribe of hairy men from the wilderness they fought against. They were known for their incredible strength, as well as being violent cannibals. They devoured men, women, and children without mercy. Smith's confusion came from how many native cultures viewed them as another tribe. But Cordell knew what they were. He'd seen it with his own eyes.

He remembered waiting in the river bottoms for the glimpse he'd been promised. He had been upwind and in the forest for days. His scent had mellowed and blended with his environment. And the camouflage blind he'd built was one of the best he'd ever constructed. He'd lain flat against the warm forest floor. Bugs had welcomed his presence and he'd felt their squirm and toil against his skin and clothes. More netting and camo covered his back and legs, and he wore them like a shroud over his darkly painted face. He had only been a few hours from giving up when he'd heard it. Somewhere, high up on the opposite bank of the river, something large made its way down to the river. At first, he could only see a shadow. He had been surprised by how little noise it made. That was the day he realised the creature's signature oversized feet helped it achieve this. Its mass was so enormous that as it placed its feet down, they pushed into the ground. When a human foot hit normal ground, it was usually a case of a stoppable force meeting an immoveable object. Not so with these things. The earth gave way to them, extinguishing the sound of impact. But he had still felt it coming.

It had paused at the bottom of the riverbank, where the slope gave way to a sandy, clay-packed shore of a shallow pool. The creature was alert and slowly turned to look both ways up and down the river. It raised its head, and he presumed it was scenting the air. From what his father had told him, and what he had learnt since, the fact that the animal walked upright, in a bipedal fashion, was no surprise to him. But its size was. It had been hard for him to imagine what eight feet looked like. At the time, he'd thought of Randy Breuer, an NBA star of the Milwaukee Bucks. He was seven feet and three inches tall. Breuer towered over most people on the court, and to this day, was still one of the NBA's tallest players of all time. The thing in front of him would have been literally head and shoulders over Breuer. In fact, it wouldn't be hard to imagine the thing picking its teeth with the wiry basketball player.

Cordell remembered how, from his hide, he couldn't see its face, so he'd had to imagine where its eyes were. It wasn't looking in his direction. Some of its physique was obscured from him, but he had seen how its arms were longer in proportion to its legs. It had been extremely thick and broad and had a conical crest to its head, but smaller than he'd envisioned. A tuft of hair at its crest reminded him of the husk of a coconut shell. Seemingly satisfied it was alone, the animal had dropped to all fours and approached the water's edge. Even this it did in a way Cordell had found strange. It didn't move like a gorilla would – walking on the knuckles of its hands and with its legs bent awkwardly in a typical 'ape' waddle. Instead, this creature reached its arms out at a 45-degree angle to its body and commando crawled down to the water, staying flat and low. It had reminded him of a cut scene from a horror movie, featuring a demonic, unnatural sequence known as the spider walk. He couldn't see its lips, but he could hear it taking big sups of water.

It had finished slaking its thirst, but it wasn't done. The animal had lain on its side, close to the water's edge. It scooped wet clay from beneath the wet sand and had applied it all over its body, doing so with a fanatical level of attention. The creature had smoothed the grey-coloured muck over its torso, and along its arms and legs. When it had finished there, it used its impressive reach to coat as much of its back as it could. Finally, it had wiped what was left of the clay across its face, head, and neck. He'd watched as the thing rolled and lumbered to its feet. And he remembered how, suddenly, its whole demeanour had changed. The creature had stuck its face out across the water, lifting its nose and hunching its shoulders. Cordell had imagined static electricity rippling over its hair. It had slowly moved its head from side to side, then stopped as its gaze came to rest in his direction. Cordell had known there was no way the animal could have seen him, yet it had seemed to be staring straight at him.

Then the stink had hit him. Like a wet dog had rolled in a dead skunk. It had been enough to make his eyes water, and he'd winced automatically. Cordell remembered the cold dread he'd felt as the slightest rustle escaped from the camo blanket pulled over his head. The growl, clearly emitted by the creature, had come in instant reply. It had taken one step towards the water, then paused. He'd watched, too scared to breathe, as it looked down over its clay-caked body and limbs. Then, it had grunted and lifted its chin as if in dismissive acknowledgement of Cordell's presence. Cordell remembered how he'd felt; like he'd been pulled over by the cops and let off with a warning.

Later, a Tuscarora elder had told him a creation story. In it, two brothers – one a spirit of good, the other of evil, created creatures. The Eagwehoewe were people, but the Ronnongwetowanca were giants, and their enemies. It seemed obvious which spirit had created which. Whereas Cordell had taken parts of the story with a grain of salt, he had played close attention when the elder described how these "stonish giants" would coat themselves in clay and mud. Once hardened into their long, matted hair, it became almost impossible to kill them with an arrowhead.

Therefore, a favoured method of execution was to trap them in caves and block the entrances with enormous fires. But it came with great risk, and many warriors were lost in such confrontations. The stone giants were real enough.

Even without clay armour, the creatures were not easy to take down. Their outer layer of hair was dense, and often interwoven into clumps. Like the best insulation, it kept them cool in summer and warm in winter. It was often enough on its own to absorb a huge amount of energy, say that of a small to medium calibre bullet. Then there was their skin, which was unusually thick and tight. It didn't stretch too much, but it was pudgy enough to take a significant dent. It reacted like latex – like an expensive Hollywood special effects costume. Underneath the skin there was a blubbery layer of protective fat, which was especially compact around the torso. And the knit of their musculature was as good as natural Kevlar. Even if you did get through all that, their skeletal tissues were as strong as steel. After that, their internal organs were as vulnerable as anything else's. Cordell smiled and raised an eyebrow as he saw Smith check his pistol again.

"Second thoughts?" Cordell asked.

"Maybe," Gregory replied, admittedly.

"To be honest, if we encounter one in a bad mood, the two of us won't make much difference," he shrugged.

Smith's glance was not appreciative. Cordell smiled, heaving his pack on. The trail beckoned, and they had some way to go. He wanted to get a good idea of the territory they were covering. It had been some time since they'd been to Washington. The last few months had taken them to Idaho and Tennessee. It was early for them to have come north. They climbed slowly for five minutes, scanning the ground carefully with each step. They stopped, taking nearly half a minute to scan the forest and listen to the woods. A Douglas' squirrel barked, and a pileated woodpecker scolded back. They carried on. They left the hiking trail almost immediately, following a steep ascent mostly used by elk, judging by the stink. Cordell took point, knowing that Smith had his back and was checking his work. Nothing would be missed. They built random stops into their trek, an attempt to catch anything that might be following them off guard.

Most of the game trails they followed were unrewarding. A few hours later, another steep climb took them back to the hiking trail. Cordell knew that a little beyond that, the Pacific Crest Trail joined it. Cordell's brain kicked into gear, processing missing persons reports he'd read and taken interest in. Hikers, wild campers... not many more than would be considered average for any place of wilderness – especially one where every American apex predator was well represented. Wolves, grizzlies, black bear, and mountain lion all called the place home. But Cordell was pretty sure something else did too. One recent disappearance was bothering him. He'd read the file with interest. Some people came up here to disappear. But this kid had been different. He did everything right – and he'd hiked through before. Several times in fact. Something in Cordell's gut had told him to pay attention, and that same thing was directing him now.

Cordell glanced to his right. For a moment, he thought there was nothing there – until he looked again and noticed how the brush didn't quite seem right. It wasn't an obvious game trail. The path of a single, large animal instead of many smaller ones. Cordell imagined thickset swinging arms, and mitt-sized hands with palms facing backwards attached to them, naturally pushing knee-high scrub back into place as it went. But not all of it. He stepped off the trail, Greg falling in behind him immediately. A few more steps and suddenly, Cordell was following his nose, literally. He knew the coppery scent he was picking up on all too well. Then he heard it.

It was a sound similar to rain hitting moss, but more rhythmic than that. Not loud, but you knew there was life to it. Something was making the sound. Like hundreds of fingers softly tapping a wooden desk. The odour was stronger now and he could pick up the taint of the rotting wet wood surrounding it too. Cordell knew if they'd been on the trail a few days earlier, he might never have picked it up. A few days more, and Stevie Wonder could have led them straight to it. He knelt close to a deadfall pine. A jagged scar of a crack ran along the trunk, and pumpkin-coloured mulch seeped from it. With a deft kick from his steel-capped boots, the bottom half of the log gave way. Smith recoiled, stepping back instinctively as a mob of insects spilled from the log. Cordell recognised them as carrion beetles. They clicked and scurried back into the darkness of the soil and detritus. They formed army lines as they exited the log, abandoning their prize. Cordell watched the last of them emerge from the eye socket of Jake Sutton's skull before it dropped to the forest floor and disappeared.

Both agents retreated to the trail immediately. Smith got on the radio, requesting the assistance and presence of a medical examiner. His next call was to Washington D.C, to secure jurisdiction over what was quickly going to become a joint investigation with the FBI, maybe even the Ranger Service. Everyone would want a piece of the pie, until they could prove it wasn't homicide. The radio code for such a crime was 55-A. Smith had deliberately used the code 55-K to report their discovery of the remains. It meant a dead body had been found, but homicide wasn't suspected. It would keep things quiet until word got out they'd only found the head. But Smith was confident they'd be able to convince most parties it was an animal attack. At that point, the FBI would lose interest and drop it. Technically, they were still on Forest Service turf, and they had the right to investigate the crime. They did most of the grunt work, and as the young ranger they'd spoken to had pointed out, the Bureau of Land Management rarely wanted to help. From the outside, it would look like they were glory hunting. Regardless of how it looked, they couldn't be more wrong.

Cordell had only one call to make. A specialist dog team had been brought in for this purpose, waiting for word back at the camp the bureau had hopefully by now, taken over. For both the medical examiner and the dogs, the biggest issue was logistics – how to get them to the location quickly. Part of the bureau team were tasked with facilitating this. The Prowler's equipment stores would supply most of their needs. By the time the FBI and M.E arrived, the area would be floodlit, with paths marked and the perimeter of the area of investigation secured. Cordell and Smith weren't really interested in the remains. There was no mystery for them here. They knew what had killed Jake Sutton. They just had to find it.

Whilst their bureau colleagues did the grunt work, the M.E and dog team got the full VIP treatment. They were transported to site in an Army UH-60M Black Hawk helicopter. Cordell watched as the dogs were lowered down to the path on a harness, one at a time. They had been trained for this and many other unusual circumstances. The M.E less so. He looked dishevelled and annoyed as Cordell pointed the way for him. Within another half hour, their bureau team arrived – more obedient Langley rejects and rookies, as Cordell saw them. They took up sentry positions and set up the floodlights as instructed. One of them, and Cordell made a mental note to find out who, had the presence of mind to hire a trailer and bring up two four-seat Polaris General all-terrain vehicles, or ATVs. These would act as shuttle transport between the area of investigation and the mobile command centre. That kind of thinking showed potential.

Cordell moved over to what he was really interested in, the dog team. Cordell had worked with the tracker before, a tough old woman named Janine Nelson. She was a civilian, but she was also the best, and that's why Cordell had asked for her by name. A former Army dog handler, she had trained search and rescue dogs for most of her working life and beyond. But that wasn't her specialty anymore. Her dogs were cadaver dogs. They had been taught to seek out death. Decomposing human flesh in particular. It wasn't that they couldn't seek out the living though – just that it wasn't what got them worked up and excited. Their training meant they associated real reward with finding a dead body, or parts of one. Her small pack of four dogs were all majestic tree hounds, her favoured breed. On a previous investigation, she had told Cordell how their nose was just as good as a bloodhound, but they were a little more rugged and suited to working outdoors for long periods.

"Good to see you, Janine," Cordell nodded. "Thanks for coming".

"S'okay," Janine replied. "Unless I had a choice not to?"

"Nope," Cordell smiled.

"Let's get to work," Janine grimaced.

They passed the agents along the path subtly and quietly. Cordell went and spoke with the M.E, who passed him a large, clear, polythene evidence bag. Not only had the M.E worked with dog teams before, but Cordell had already asked him to secure a scent source for them. That meant that a piece of the remains had been removed with instruments and placed in the bag for isolation. This was no small request, as it usually meant surrendering that specific piece of remains. Once the dogs placed their noses in the bag, it would be contaminated. That meant no DNA testing could be carried out. It also meant that the specimen had to be something innocuous or of no interest. They couldn't give the dogs a piece of a body with a tattoo for example, or fingers, toes, or anything with potentially unique identifying features. In this case, the M.E had provided a hair and scalp sample, along with scrapings from the back of the neck.

"Will that be enough?" Cordell asked, offering the bag to Nelson.

She looked at him and sighed, as if tired of being asked the same question by every investigator she worked with.

"Imagine an olfactory system a thousand times more powerful than ours," she explained. "Now imagine years of disciplined training honing that skill. It's more than enough."

"Good," Cordell said. "Guess we'll have no problem finding what we're looking for then."

"If the rest of him is out there, we'll find him," Nelson replied.

She took the bag from him and carefully opened it, rolling back both sides of the zip-lock opening. The dogs eagerly wagged their tails and fought each other to be first. As each dog lowered its nose into the bag, it whirled around and pulled on the leash. They bayed exuberantly, their eyes all set on the brush ahead of them, beyond the trail.

Janine held the two cadaver dogs, her grip on the leashes tight. She trusted the search and rescue dogs to Cordell, who followed in behind. Agent Gregory Smith brought up the rear. More than once, Cordell caught him looking over his shoulder. That had made him raise his eyebrow and acknowledge Smith with a wide grin. Smith in turn had dismissed him with a shake of his head and a wave of the hand.

"Shadows getting to you?" Cordell quipped.

"Just keeping track of where we're coming from... be easy to get turned around in here," Smith explained.

"Uh-huh," Cordell nodded.

They certainly weren't following any official trail. But the dogs seemed to know where they were going. Cordell could feel the strain on his thumb as the hounds pulled and fought to race off. He wrapped the leather around his wrist, shortening the reach of the tethers, but strengthening his control over them. Even then they threatened to pull him over with every step. It took considerable stamina to keep the dogs under his command. He realised that without the leashes, the dogs would soon be miles from them, chasing down the scent in single-minded, blinkered pursuit.

"Harder than it looks, huh?" Janine chortled.

"Let's just say my respect for you, which was more than I give most already, has reached new, dizzying heights," Cordell huffed.

His heart was beating pretty fast and he could feel the sweat on his brow. The incline was subtle, but it was there. They were headed uphill. And they were losing light. It would soon be dark – certainly before they got back. Both he and Gregory had head torches in their packs, but it wasn't not being able to see that worried him. It was what might see them. Predators did their best work at night.

One of the lead dogs held by Janine – a dappled white hound with grey, pendulous ears, came to an immediate stop and let out a long, mournful howl. The gaze of the dog was fixed on a fallen tree, a little way off the game trail and to the left of them. Janine approached carefully, shortening the leash of her dogs accordingly. Cordell added it to the long list of reasons he preferred to work with her – not every dog handler would know to stop their dog nosing its way into potential evidence. He passed the leads of the two dogs he had to Gregory, and walked forward.

What he was looking for didn't take long to find. Stuffed into the recess of the rotting timber was a human arm. What was left of the flesh and sinew at the shoulder had withered, and looked tight and pale without its supply of living blood. But the rips in what was left of the muscle showed it had been torn from the socket with significant force. As Cordell looked closer, he could see the teres major, deltoid, bicep and triceps muscles had all been stripped from the arm, and presumably consumed. He could see where canine teeth had scraped their pointed ends across the bone. The flexor and radialis muscles further down were more or less intact. Cordell pulled out the GPS tracker and the radio. He marked the position and gave the co-ordinates to the ME. But he knew the job wasn't done.

The dogs worked fast, re-finding the trail and heading deeper into the trees. They didn't have to go far. The two legs were found close together and showed similar wounding. Torn from their sockets and missing the significant muscle and fat. The morsels less rewarding, or those too tricky to strip quickly, were left. The predator had eaten on the run. Which annoyed Cordell, as they still hadn't found a single track, despite the dogs easily finding the trail. Continuing, the four hounds bayed eagerly, pulling on their leashes with renewed vigour, as they broke into an avenue of trees on either side of them, looking up at another incline ahead of them.

Then, just as suddenly, they stopped in their tracks and silenced their baying. Janine pulled at her dogs, but they would not budge. Their eyes were wide, revealing the whites. They also didn't look at Janine. Instead, they began to lay flat on the ground and tried to tunnel under each other. Cordell looked down at the dogs he was holding onto, and noticed they were trembling. As universal signs of fear went, it was a pretty good one. He'd never owned dogs, but he knew a scared animal when he saw it. One of the dogs Janine was holding onto let out a whimper and raised its head towards the treeline on the ridge ahead of them.

"They're shitting bricks," Janine shrugged. "They ain't going no further. Something up there's got them real spooked."

Cordell looked around to Gregory, who acknowledged him with a resolved nod.

"It's okay, we'll walk up and take a look," Cordell said. "You can head back."

"I'll wait around," Janine replied, sucking her cheeks in and stiffening a little.

"They don't like dogs, and dogs don't like them, it's as simple as that," Cordell added. "You're not letting anyone down, or being dismissed. Just the end of the road."

"We.... we haven't found..." Janine didn't finish the sentence.

"All of him," Cordell nodded. "But I think we're about to."

"Your bears... they ain't bears, are they."

Cordell looked back at her, blankly.

Janine let a flicker of a smile show before she turned around, taking the dogs from Cordell as she did. Cordell and Gregory waited until she was out of sight before they began the short but sharp ascent towards the ridgeline. They pushed their way up through the maidenhair ferns and the broad leaves of deerfoot shrubs. They were making their own path now, determined to reach the high ground fast. They were about halfway when the stench hit them.

"God, you never get used to it, do you," Gregory muttered.

Cordell shook his head, knowing better than to open his mouth.

"Smells like a dead skunk's asshole," Gregory grimaced,

coughing up spittle and half retching.

Cordell just kept climbing. He knew Gregory did not like the fieldwork aspect of their job. Which was fine, because Cordell didn't like the paperwork. It was just one of the reasons they made such a good team and had lasted this long. Maybe survived was a better word. Not everyone did. He moved quickly, hoping the scent would dissipate as they climbed. After a couple of hundred more feet, it did. Fifty feet beyond that, and they were on the ridgeline.

"We got pretty close," Gregory exclaimed, getting his breath back. "For it to hit us like that."

Cordell shook his head with a knowing smile.

"The wind was in its favour," he explained. "It was probably curious, could hear or smell the dogs. Soon as it saw we had guns, it skunked us and let loose."

"Think it's still around?"

Cordell slowly scanned the ridge and the treeline on either side. The forest was quiet. The wind was now cutting across them, instead of heading straight at them. But nothing was being carried on the breeze. He put down his pack and pulled out what looked like the head of the robot from the movie Short Circuit. In reality, the FLIR Recon B2-FO was a military grade multi-sensor binocular. It delivered crisp thermal imaging on vehicle-sized objects up to five miles away. It could then also handily add target geo-location data and stream it to a compatible weapon's system. But right now, Cordell just needed to see if anything was there, hiding among the trees.

"Can't believe you got them to pay for those," Gregory laughed.

"Might catch one off guard," Cordell shrugged. "Plus, I figure they can only do it for so long."

Nobody really knew why the creatures only sporadically showed up on thermals. They would disappear suddenly, their heat signature evaporating as if into thin air. Or only the tiniest flickers of red, yellow and orange would drift across the screen. To an untrained eye, it would be dismissed as a much smaller animal. One of the lab rats had told Cordell that the creatures' hair was so thick and dense that it acted as thermal camouflage. Another had suggested that the animals were able to thermoregulate. Which meant they could drop their temperature at will to match the environment. If so, it meant they somehow stopped or changed the blood flow around the surface of their skin. Cordell privately figured both the theories were on the money. Their hair was dense, and they could thermoregulate. But if they cooled off for too long, it was dangerous for them, just like any animal. He figured it was kind of like how some Buddhists, not to mention special forces operatives, could lower their heart rates and control their bodies to minimise pain. There was no way to verify his thoughts, but it made sense to him. It was as simple as that.

He scanned slowly from left to right and back again with the fancy thermal viewer. The ambient warmth of the air was enough to make the optics glow lightly orange. He switched to the mono settings, instantly turning the world black, white, and grey. He watched a woodpecker of some kind flit from a nearby tree. As it landed on another, it took up the characteristic, straight-backed stance of its kind, its slicked back head feathers and beak illuminated against the slate grey background of the trees beyond. He paused, focusing quickly on something further out. It was a momentary glimpse, but he was sure he'd seen it. Thick, sausage-like digits wrapped around a tree that blocked the rest of the hand, arm, and body they led to from sight. He found them again, just as they slipped from the trunk and from view. Cordell dropped the thermal imager from his eyes and looked straight into the trees. They were a long way from the trails here, and this was undisturbed forest. The Sitka spruce were untouched and immense.

Cordell was torn. He wanted to charge towards the treeline and let loose a spray of bullets, but he knew the animal – or animals, had the advantage. They could cover five times as much ground as he could. Five times faster too. By the time he got anywhere near the trees, it'd be gone. Or worse, on top of him. He reminded himself this wasn't a hunt, and the weapons were there for defence. But he knew he still had to go and investigate. He knew the rest of Jake Sutton's corpse was up there. If nothing else, they would recover the body, dismembered as it was.

"Got my back," Cordell asked.

"Always," Gregory replied.

Cordell put the thermal imager back in his pack and brought up the M4A1. He flicked the safety off and checked the magazine before shouldering it. Semi-crouched, he made his way forward. The ascent was slow, as he both checked the trail for signs and scanned the nearing trees for movement. Even so, it took less than five minutes before he was standing in their shade. He paused for breath. He planted his back against the nearest fir and closed his eyes. The sounds of the forest told him all he needed to know. It was gone. Somewhere to the west, a young wild turkey gobbler was calling. Songbirds, none of which he knew, sang. Then, almost out of earshot, a Steller's jay sounded out an alarm. There was no way to be sure, but he guessed what might have caused its upset. If the creature was here, he knew the forest would be silent and still. But with his eyes closed, he could pick up other things too. Pine sap came to him on the breeze, perhaps the spoils of the woodpecker he'd seen. Beneath that and the ozone smell of the rainforest though, was something else. At first, it always seemed sickly sweet – but it was a lie. There was sourness there. It reminded him of rotting apples and cider making for some reason. It was like covering the stink of a ruined pork roast with a few drops of cheap perfume. Cordell knew it would only get worse as he got closer, but at least finding the remains was now a simple case of following his nose.

Next came the mothballs and rotten eggs. As a body decomposed, it would release up to thirty different compounds. Almost all were generated by bacteria. When indole was released, it smelt similarly to mothballs. Hydrogen sulphide was more easily identifiable – perhaps just because more people encountered rotten eggs. After a few more steps, the heavy stink of shit hit him. But again, he knew that wasn't quite the case. Skatole was what gave faeces its unique odour, but it was also generated as certain proteins and amino acids were broken down in the gut. In small concentrations, it was actually quite pleasant, not dissimilar to orange blossom. This wasn't the case here, and the foul, garlic-like odour that hit his nostrils confirmed it. He knew he was now within a few feet of what he was looking for, and the guts were split and spilled. He almost stepped in them.

What remained of Jake Sutton's torso was carefully hidden in a structure made of bent over saplings. Covered in a thin layer of lady fern leaves and fleeceflower, the creature had been able to eat its prizes in relative peace. It would have hunkered down, eating its meal like an ancient Greek, sprawled on a chaise lounge and sucking at grapes. Cordell marked the GPS position as Gregory radioed it in. The final piece of the puzzle for now. He peered into the bizarre, morbid shelter. It was strange, as it almost felt like the body had been laid to rest. The limbs and head, as they'd discovered, had all been removed. Ripped from the sockets. The removal of the head seemed messier and more savage than the arms and legs. On one side of the torso, four slits that could have easily been made by steak knives, had torn through the skin and into the flesh. The other side of the torso had been ripped open at chest level, then right down the middle like a zipper. The ribs there had been snapped off. Broken shards of them were scattered around the deathbed – for want of another name. The thing that had dined on Jake Sutton had sucked the marrow from his bones. He knew the rest of the cavity would be empty, with the heart and liver removed. He wouldn't be able to tell until the medical examiner got there, but Cordell guessed that the trapezius muscles and latissimus dorsi would likely be missing from the back. If Jake Sutton had been a cow, those parts of him might be known better as T-Bone, sirloin, or for some of the less favourable pieces – strip steaks and jerky.

~

The creature had been able to return to its kill several times before the humans had tracked it down and reclaimed it, as he knew was their way. He had stayed close until he had caught the scent of the dogs and heard them bay. He had left his own markings on the trail, knowing they would not follow beyond it. Only the strongest or most desperate of wolves dared to, and these were not wolves. They smelled different, acted different. Even full grown, they acted as younglings. But he would not tolerate any canines interloping on his territory. He and his kind felt instinctive hatred towards them. So, he hunted them. The ones that lived with humans were often easy kills and meals.

He retreated quickly and quietly as he watched the men ascend the ridgeline. They laboured heavily and their progress was slow. Despite his instinct to flee, he dropped to the ground instead, spreading his limbs wide. He continued to back up on all fours until he found a tree to his liking and of significant girth. From here, he crouched and watched. He controlled his breathing and heartbeat; both became shallow shadows of their normal rapidity and rhythm. He let his arms fall to the ground, aware his fingers were too far round the tree and potentially in the line of sight of the humans. The bolder of the two had approached at that point, looking in his direction. But his nerve held and he saw the man turn away. Only then did he let out a sharp exhale and reach up to dig the clawed tips of his digits into the bark. He pulled himself upwards and watched the men discover his kill. They showed little despair or emotion. Which confirmed to him that they were not looking for the one he had killed, but him. He would move on and leave no trail. He would go to the dwellings where the prey lived and slept.

CHAPTER TEN

HOME INVASION

Patwyn Dalton opened the door to his cabin and walked out onto the front porch, grasping a can of Mac & Jack's Log Boom Pale Ale. The beer was a simple brew, not too fussy or over complicated – but good. He guessed he liked both the taste and its principles. The brewery was an independent one based in Redwood, and he liked to support local businesses. And hell, his own business could do with all the log booms sent his way. His face fell when he looked out onto what had become his front yard, filled with the damaged equipment and vehicles. He let out a deep sigh and walked around back, following the veranda to the rear porch. There, two rocking chairs greeted him, as did a much-improved view.

A small meadow separated his back porch from the nearby treeline. It was mainly made up of new growth Douglas fir and western hemlock, planted over the last thirty years. The land had been a tree farm for decades. But that time had taken its toll. The high production rate and the densely packed trees reduced the fertility of the soil and the biodiversity of the forest. With only two species dominating the acreage and with little light reaching the ground, the trees grew well enough but little else thrived. Slowly but surely, Dalton logging would remove more and more of the hemlock and firs, opening the land up and replanting a broader mix of native trees in their stead. It would take another few decades, but this place would be a much healthier ecosystem as a result. And in the meantime, he'd profit from the logging. Of course, it never looked good at first. Felling timber was an act of destruction, no two ways about it. But so was a forest fire, and both were transformative and encouraged new growth, if done right.

He fell into the rocker heavily and cracked the beer open. Lifting it to his lips, he took a long sup. He closed his eyes and savoured the flavour. He took a deep inhale, trying to force his body into relaxing. It kind of worked, so he opened his eyes, only to notice he was no longer alone. At the very edge of the treeline, some fifty yards or so into the meadow, a Rocky Mountain mule deer buck had stepped out and begun to graze. Head to the ground, its large ears flicked with tension as it fed. Having harvested what it could from the small patch of ground immediately within reach, it took another step out into the meadow. It lifted its head and scanned its surroundings, the ears continuing to flick as it did so. Dalton knew he was downwind and wouldn't spook the deer if he stayed relatively still and quiet. The deer seemed to relax and returned to foraging. It spent more and more time with its head to the ground, as it worked its way further into the meadow.

Being well beyond the season, fetching his rifle was far from Dalton's mind. Instead, he watched the buck graze. It used its hooves to smash the damp meadow soil to reveal the shoots and buds that hadn't quite made it to the surface yet. From time to time it would raise its head a little and pluck a mouthful of dead, dry meadow grass – no different from the hay a rancher would feed their stock really, he thought. Dalton was just raising the beer to his lips again, slowly, so as not to spook the buck, when the deer's head shot upwards, as if spring loaded. Its rear quarters quivered with nervous energy as it looked around the meadow, almost in panic. With a short bark of alarm, it glanced once at the trees and sprung away in quick, fluid bounds. On the far side of the meadow, it disappeared into the darkness beneath the trees and Dalton heard it utter another cry. The woods fell silent in its echo.

Dalton stood up and walked to the edge of the veranda. He wondered what had spooked the buck. Instinctively his eyes lifted to the trees, where the deer had concentrated its own gaze before fleeing. He was amazed at how quickly the atmosphere had changed in one brief moment. The tranquillity and connection he'd been feeling had evaporated instantly. Mother Nature was always on hand to remind you that the real world wasn't an episode of "Wild Kingdom". Now, everything that had heard the buck, was heeding its warning – something that might kill and eat you is nearby. Suddenly, his thoughts did turn to guns, and the fact that he wasn't even wearing his sidearm. He had taken it off when he'd got home. Feeling uncomfortable, the thought of a grizzly charging out of the treeline or a cougar creeping through the grass towards him, encouraged him to take his beer inside. He turned towards the back door. Then something hit him in the side of the head with enough force to make his vision blur.

Dalton somehow stayed on his feet, but only for a moment. He staggered towards the rocker, then the world began to spin, and he pirouetted down towards the decking. He landed on his side, and it flushed the air from his lungs. Gasping for air, he couldn't focus. But when he blinked, he saw the baseball-sized rock on the decking, a foot away from him, in perfect clarity. As his head spun, he wondered if it was his blood dripping slowly from one of its ragged edges. Time seemed to slow as he noticed what he thought were marks where the stone had been chipped away, creating a series of razor-sharp crests that ebbed and flowed across the surface of the otherwise round-shaped rock. It seemed flint-like and deliberately unsmooth in texture. Dalton rolled onto his back. His vision was still blurred, but he noticed the dark mass as it blocked out the light at the far end of the veranda. A bear, it had to be a bear. His head throbbed, but he tried to force himself up.

"Getouddahere," he slurred, rolling up onto one elbow.

Unable to see anything else clearly, he reached for the rock and picked it up. He was surprised by how heavy it was. He dragged it back towards his body and cradled it into his chest. The bear hadn't moved, but as some of his senses returned, Dalton realised he could hear it breathing. Deep, gurgled rasps as it inhaled, and short, sharp, grunting huffs as it exhaled. It sounded enough like a grizzly alright. But something didn't feel right. Mustering his strength, he rose and hurled the rock with all his might. There was a slight movement. The black mass took a slight step to the side and caught the rock confidently, with a palm the size of a baseball mitt, turned out towards him. Dalton had enough of his vision back to notice the animal's arm leave its side momentarily to accommodate the catch. His mind began to clear quickly. This bear had been standing on its hind legs for way too long. It had occurred to him that a bear might kick a rock up accidentally, or dislodge one on purpose, but it couldn't throw one. As for catching, it wasn't even remotely in the realm of possibility.

"What the...?" Dalton exclaimed.

The black mass leapt forward in a fluid bound and landed on all fours directly over him. Suddenly, his foe was revealed to him in unequivocal clarity. This was no bear. The eyes that met his were human-like, yet completely animalistic. Small, round pupils coloured brownish red, perhaps even maroon, glared at him. They were set too far apart to be a man. Grey, wrinkled skin, flecked with pink, covered the face, from the heavy brow ridge down to the wide, ape-like nose, which protruded a little but not enough to be the snout of a bear. Its ears were small and placed much further back and farther down on the face than any human. As it curled back its plum-coloured lips, Dalton shuddered as the vicious canines of its upper and lower jaw were revealed. Between each set of fangs sat a row of four, large, chisel-like incisors. A crest of grey hair swept backwards across its scalp and down onto its neck, where the hair grew gradually darker. From the shoulders down, it was a uniform jet black. Its upper lip, cheeks, and neck were accented by a long white beard and moustache. When he'd been a kid, a friend at school had an emperor tamarin for a pet, and it kind of reminded him of that. But that monkey had weighed about a pound and had been less than a foot tall. This thing had to bend down to fit under his eight-foot-tall veranda, and it no doubt matched the biggest grizzlies for weight.

The thing growled at Dalton as it drew close. It sniffed at the side of his head. Its snort of breath cooled the blood flowing freely from the wound inflicted by the rock. It sent a shockwave of pain through his body, like he'd been stabbed in the cranium with a blade of ice. The creature screamed as he spasmed, flecks of spittle flying from its mouth and covering his face as it did so. Its arm flew upwards, and Dalton saw the rock cushioned between the clefts of skin of its palm. Dalton's eyes widened in realisation, and he gasped. It was the last breath he consciously took.

The creature brought its arm down in a swift, heavy downswing. The impact caved in the left side of Dalton's face, popping out his eyeball. This seemed to amuse the creature, and it bent its head down and sucked the eye into its mouth. It squeezed the succulent morsel against its cheek and savoured the jelly-like texture. It stuffed two fingers into Dalton's mouth. Claw-like nails tunnelled downwards through unresistant flesh, piercing the skin above the throat. Nonchalantly it tugged, ripped out Dalton's lower jaw. What was left of his life flickered, trying to find neural pathways that no longer connected. His body simply did not remember how to breathe, so it just stopped.

~

The human had offered little resistance. Shartale found them to be weak, easy prey to hunt when alone. He recognised the coverings on the body to be inedible and he peeled the flesh from them with ease. The structure of the dwelling the human lived in offered him seclusion, and he ate in privacy, confident that he wouldn't be disturbed. He had watched from the treeline, on many nights. There were never any visitors, and the human lived alone. For his plan to work, he would not hide the remains once he finished his meal. He needed other humans to be alerted. He needed the others of his kind to be hunted. He would not be able to stash the limbs of his prey or allow it to age and grow more tender. So, he ate. He poked through the fragments of the skull and fished out pink, spongey fragments of brain from inside, which he licked greedily from his fingers. He punched through the chest cavity and removed the heart and liver, feasting on them. Then he stripped what muscle and fat he could from each limb, severing each one in turn and laying them back in place, shredded and torn. Satisfied, but not fully satiated, he bent down and stepped off into the meadow, heading towards the treeline. Beneath the trees, he dropped to all fours and headed deeper into the darkness. As the wind changed, a new scent came to him, and he stopped in his tracks. The smell was herbal, woody, and earthy. But with it also came the scent of his newly favoured prey, and he moved towards it.

CHAPTER ELEVEN

TALL TALES

Dr. Mary Beth Benoit picked her spot carefully. The firepit was full of burning logs and the flames were growing tall, teased by the wind. Three wooden benches, carved from felled trunks, had been arranged in a triangle around the central spectacle of the fire. She sat, letting the fire warm her as she gripped the ceramic cup of cocoa she cradled in her hands. She knew the camera was there, but she ignored it. This was a time-honoured tradition of the show, and viewers couldn't get enough of it. Tonight, two of the team would spend the hours of darkness looking for their elusive quarry. But not before they had heard a tall tale, just to help put them on edge. And everyone's favourite storyteller was the African American from Louisiana. A scientist of course, but thanks to the show and the marketing people, there was always a hint of the old ways of the South too. Most of the time, she didn't play up to it, but every now and then, she gave in to the theatricality. It wasn't like she didn't enjoy it, after all.

She waited patiently as the rest of the team joined her, sitting on the benches across from her and anxious for her to begin. But as always seemed to be the case, Bodhi Prince had to have the first word.

"Before we get our bedtime story," the Australian beamed, "who's braving it out there with me?"

"It's you and me, Bodes," Katie sighed.

Mary Beth shared a knowing glance with Joe Beazley and smiled, rolling her eyes.

Bodhi smashed his fellow male team mate on the shoulder.

"Hit the jackpot, eh," he said with his customary wink.

Joe looked out into the darkness, seemingly deep in thought.

"Oh, I wouldn't be so sure," Mary Beth interjected, seeing her opportunity. "They like the fog. And the mist is coming in tonight."

Katie Cash seemed to tighten her grip on her own coffee mug. But she forced a smile. Mary Beth could never tell if the concern was genuine, or just for the cameras. It didn't matter really, she figured. But she took her role seriously, and she did her research. She looked at her colleagues, assessing their readiness. Joe ran his hand through his long hair and rubbed the back of his neck whilst avoiding eye contact. Bodhi was smiling, almost swaggering, but he was rocking back and forth on his feet too. Mary Beth leaned forward, her elbows on her knees as she held the mug close to her face. Her cold breath was visible in the steam rising from the hot drink.

"There's a forest in Alaska, much like this one," she began. "It sits on a remote, hard to get to peninsula. If you were to visit today, you'd never know that seventy years ago, a small town thrived there, built upon a booming salmon fishing industry."

"You're talking about Portlock, also known as Port Chatham," Joe said, his head snapping in her direction.

Mary Beth nodded, as if in silent reverence.

"In 1785, a Captain Nathaniel Portlock landed in a secluded bay, on the Kenai peninsula of Alaska. Whilst surveying, they found the remnants of an abandoned native village. Nobody could fathom why they would have left such a prime area, full of untouched game, fish, and shellfish. But, as members of his party grew sick and scared, they began to beg their captain to depart. Little did they know, just six years before, Spanish explorers had trodden the same soil as them. But they too had fallen sick. Some even died, and those that lived, lived in fear. Fear of what had driven the original native settlers to leave too. Horrible, morose cries would be heard in the night, edging down the mountains towards them. As with the Spanish before them, Captain Portlock's party begged him to leave, and so they did, only leaving his name to bear on what they saw as cursed ground."

Mary Beth wet her lips with a sip of the cocoa before continuing.

"But our story really begins in 1867. A new community of nomadic Sugpiaq set up a camp in the bay of what was to become Portlock. They were amazed by the abundance and size of the clams and other bounty they found on the shoreline. No doubt, it signalled to them that this was a place they could spend the winter and never be without food. But their joy was short lived. Within a month, they were attacked. What they described as cannibal giants began to raid the village, almost nightly at times. They fought with an animalistic savagery the Sugpiaq have never encountered before, and they named the giants Nantiinaq – or the hairy man. At first, the people fought and were unwilling to give up their new home. But as the months turned into years, the attacks did not stop. Whenever game became scarce, the cannibals came. And they showed no mercy. In the same year, the San Francisco Chronicle reported on the events, stating 'the giants rip people to shreds in the streets every time they need a square meal'. In 1905, the village is abandoned, and the Sugpiaq leave."

"So, that's it?" Bodhi exclaimed, unimpressed.

"Nope," Joe said, shaking his head and almost to himself.

Mary Beth nodded in acknowledgement. "In 1921, a small community of Russian-Alutiiq are attracted to the bay for the same reasons as the Sugpiaq. But this time they have 20th century industry with them. They build a cannery to process the salmon, a post office, and a school. But they very quickly implement strict rules. There is a curfew at night. Armed guards patrol the streets, and especially the school and entrances to the cannery. And nobody, ever, ever goes out in the fog or into the forest. It seems that they know... the forest belongs to Nantinaq, and in the fog, it will stalk the streets of town too."

Joe leaned forward and casually lifted another log from the small pile beneath the fire pit and added it to the flames.

"The rules worked... for a while," Mary Beth continued. "But as the community grew bigger and more successful, perhaps they became overconfident and let their guard down. Whatever happened, in 1931, a man named Andrew Kamluck ventured out into the forest to log some trees. They found him with his head caved in. It was said a piece of equipment, heavy enough to have been hauled there by Kamluck's dogs, had been the murder weapon."

"And the dogs?" Katie asked in a whisper, her shoulders tightening.

"What they could find of them... torn to ribbons," Mary Beth replied. "After that, the rules weren't enough to save Portlock. First, a few gold prospectors disappeared. Then the

Dall sheep and bear hunters. Each time, a little closer to town. Something was moving in on them. They all felt it. Occasionally, a body would wash up in the bay with strange bite and claw marks, or worse, beyond recognition. Twice, on the foggiest of nights, something broke into the cannery. On the second occasion, it caused enough chaos and damage for it to burn to the ground. One day, they found a man that had been missing for months. His body had been swept down the mountain by the Spring rains and into the lagoon. His remains were torn and dismembered in a way no bear was capable of. Official reports list fifteen people as having gone missing during that time, but the Alutiiq say it's far higher. The community describe themselves as being terrorised by the creatures, and in 1950, almost overnight, they finally abandoned the town."

"Jesus, is this for real?" Bodhi exclaimed.

"Every word," Mary Beth nodded. "And it doesn't end there. In 1968, a goat hunter is stalked and chased by a creature making horrendous screams as it followed him through the woods. Then, in 1973, three hunters take shelter in the remnants of the village during a storm. All night, their camp is circled by something that growls at them and utters unintelligible, threatening sounds. Each swears it walked on two feet. Then, in 1989, a native paramedic attends an elderly man who has suffered a heart attack after returning from a walk in the woods. The native is an Alutiiq, and he knows the legends. He asks the old man if he saw it, if it bothered him. The old man nods, looking terror stricken towards the treeline. He dies in the paramedic's arms. And until this day, the Alutiiq know to stay away from the forest, and to never go out in the fog. The point is, for over two hundred years, Portlock has been repeatedly abandoned, and it appears to be because of a murderous clan of bigfoot. Enjoy your investigation tonight folks. I hope the mist clears... for your sake".

Mary Beth let a shudder of cold move through her shoulders as she finished her tale and leaned back.

"Okay, from now on, the only one of us who seems to actually do decent research, isn't allowed to tell stories anymore," Bodhi declared, standing up and walking over to a cooler to fish out a can of beer.

"I'm not sure the monster is what you think it is up there," Joe said, regarding Mary Beth coolly.

"Oh?" she replied.

"Our own government has used ghost stories to scare people off valuable land before, during the Cold War."

"Great, another conspiracy theory from the paranormalist," Bodhi quipped.

"It's no conspiracy theory," Joe objected. "During the Cold War, the Philippines was a trusted U.S ally. But a group of communist rebels had power and sway over the islands, and we began to lose our valuable footing"

"We're getting two stories for the price of one tonight, eh," Bodhi nodded to Katie.

"It was known as the Hukbalahap rebellion, and the C.I.A were called in to quash it," Joe continued, ignoring Bodhi's scepticism. He was more than used to it by now. "And the C.I.A sent one of their best – an expert in psychological warfare named Edward Lansdale. Lansdale learned that in Filipino culture, a monster named the Aswang was greatly feared – a basic, run-of-the-mill vampire for all intents and purposes. Lansdale's solution was simple. His special forces would ambush Hukbalahap patrols, often targeting stragglers or those lingering at the rear. The unfortunate rebel or rebels would then be dispatched, with a special instrument designed to penetrate the throat. The wounds would look like fang marks, and to complete the illusion, the body would be strung up to drain of blood. Then, the body would be placed where it would undoubtedly be found by those looking for the missing men."

"And it worked?" Mary Beth asked, intrigued.

"Absolutely," Joe grinned. The Hukbalahap rebels were so terrified, they abandoned a key post, in an elevated position, practically losing their tactical advantage overnight. So, sorry, when I hear of things that are heard but not seen, and mangled bodies found, I tend to think man before monster," he shrugged. "I have no doubt sasquatch is out there, but I'm not convinced he's a killer."

"So, why would governments or whoever, want to drive people away from nowhere-ville Alaska?" Bodhi exclaimed.

"There's gold in them thar hills," Joe replied, putting on a comical accent of an elderly prospector type.

"Come on darlin'," Bodhi scoffed towards Katie. "Let's go make daisy chains with the forest people."

Mary Beth smiled kindly at Joe but sighed.

"Do you know what my biggest issue with conspiracy theories is?" she said.

Joe shook his head.

"I've worked in government," she replied. "Getting different departments in the same organisation to liaise and work together is hard enough... but suggesting that multiple agencies, bureaus, and other factions can seamlessly coordinate a multi-faceted operation and do it so well it remains a secret over decades?! For me, that takes a much larger leap of faith than an intelligent, unknown primate being out there and just being good at what it does."

Joe nodded.

"I get that," he said. "But you're not naïve, Doc. You know who we're shadowed by, and who we work with off camera."

"Yeah, but it's one, small, dedicated unit... well-funded, naturally, but still... I get the impression it's just them. And they only turned up after..."

"After you were nearly killed by one."

Mary Beth nodded.

"You know you still stiffen every time you tell the bluff charge version of the story, right?" Joe asked.

She nodded again, lowering her head.

"Well, whatta ya know... two different groups working together and keeping a secret," he laughed.

She smiled. Joe got up and walked towards the trucks, and Mary Beth returned her gaze to the fire.

~

West of the Resolute campsite, in a secluded and hard to get to valley, the air was filled with a skunky scent. In truth, it was more like an open sewer. The cannabis plants had clearly gotten the message that Spring was on the way and were beginning to bud. Noah Johnson wore a mask as he patrolled "the fields" – as he and the other guards called them, but it didn't seem to help. Especially as the fields were, in fact, a series of undulating ridges and ditches that snaked their way through the forest for roughly a square mile.

Legally grown cannabis was Washington state's fourth most valuable crop – worth $2.1 billion. But despite how the market was turning and how things were going politically for cannabis, illegally grown weed, like on this farm, was not only more valuable, but better quality, and still very much in demand. Everyone under the age of 21, and anyone who didn't want to pay commercial prices, still turned to the black market. And regardless, growing it on public land was of course, a federal crime. They'd never had a problem this far out in the forest, but still, a small arsenal was made available to the guards. Noah carried a CMMG Banshee, an AR-15 pistol-style, short-barrelled rifle. He liked it because it was finished in white and looked like something off Star Wars. It also handily took the same magazines as the Glock he carried as a sidearm. He fired both regularly enough, out of sheer boredom – though they'd been told to keep target practice to a minimum outside of any hunting seasons. Noah smiled and shook his head as he thought about that – there was no hiding the stink. You could pick it up from a mile away at times.

As he picked his way through the groupings of the plants, the other reasons it would be impossible to keep the place a secret, should anyone get close, was made clear. It was a wreck. Each cannabis plant needed fifteen gallons of water a day. It was why Washington State had always been popular for cannabis farms in the first place. With an average rainfall of 73 inches a year, and an average snowfall of 17 inches per year, there was a lot of water around. But not always enough. So, creeks and streams were dammed and diverted. The soil was pumped with nitrogen, potassium, and phosphorous to give the plants nutrients.

And the whole place was laced with poisons and pesticides. Any living thing that walked into the hemp was unlikely to walk out. The rotting corpses of everything from foxes and bobcats to rodents and birds, were discarded at the borders of the fields.

Noah and the other guards weren't ignorant of the impact the operation had on the local environment. Once, he'd found a dead fisher. It had looked like it was sleeping, curled up with its head beneath its tail. The fur was a deep, chocolate brown and he hadn't been able to resist touching it. He had decided to take it home and skin it, maybe make some gloves with it. But as he had worked with the pelt, a strange yellow rash had spread across his hands and wrists. It didn't take him long to discover the same markings under the marten's fur. A day later, the hair on the dead marten and the ones across the back of his hand, had shrivelled and fallen out. It was a good reminder that with one wrong step, the poisons were enough to kill them too. But the money was hard to turn down and walking out of the forest each week with trash bags full of empty pesticide and poison containers would be both impractical and suspicious. And so, it continued, until they moved base, or they were caught.

He was about two thirds of the way through his patrol when the sound of a branch breaking, off to his left, made him stop. His eyes darted to the trees, and he searched the shadows beyond them. Nothing moved. He'd grown used to the silence. In any other forest, twilight and evening would mean a cacophony of noise as birds went to roost. It was the time deer came out to feed and predators went on the hunt. But not here, not near the fields. They'd pretty much killed everything, he figured. Or the animals knew this place wasn't right. The smell of death, decay, and the plants themselves put them off. And there was always a human presence. That's why the sound disturbed him. It had been loud, and whatever had broken the branch was big. He stood another few moments then shrugged it off. It was probably just a deadfall, he thought. Noah moved on, keen to get back to the central camp and a cup of coffee.

~

Bodhi Prince went to the back of the modified Jeep Gladiator known as the 'Wendigo' and opened the sloped, angular trunk. He pressed a latch on a side panel, and it flipped open, revealing a small stash of weapons. He lifted out a short-barrelled shotgun with a military look – a Fostech Origin 12. He fitted it with a 10-round stick magazine, checked the safety and slung it over his shoulder. The rest of his pack had already been put together by the production team, and he lifted it off the tailgate and placed one strap over his other shoulder. He lifted Katie's pack out of the car and turned, finding her walking over to him. She took the pack from him and nodded an acknowledgement of thanks. They stood in silence as Tilly Miller, their production assistant, helped them with their wearable camera systems and checked everything was working, including their GPS.

"I know the audience love it, but I could live without the stories before we set off into the woods," Katie grimaced.

"It serves as good warning to be prepared," Bodhi replied, tapping the shotgun. "Besides the doc, we've never really been in trouble. Be nice to get the fuckers on camera, just once. Then we can all retire."

Katie nodded. "Where we headed?"

Bodhi took a map from a pocket in the truck's rear and

opened it up. He ran his finger from the campsite along a trail that ran west. It was an 'out and back' trail – one you followed to its end and then retraced your steps. This one seemed to follow a creek to a ridgeline.

"Let's follow the trail in here, then scramble up to the ridgeline," he suggested. We'll get a good enough view from there, and a little privacy," he winked.

"Do you ever think about anything else?!" Katie laughed. "Work first, dessert later, maybe."

They spent a few moments with Jason and Tilly, who filmed them walking off towards the start of the trail, with the remnants of the sunset sending cascades of magenta, coral, and tangerine across the bluffs of the ridgeline to the west.

~

Noah Johnson trudged his way past a small cluster of cannabis plants nestled between the root arms of a large Madrone tree. The open ground was partially covered by camouflage netting. This patch was the last in a series of hollows that led to the ridgeline. A little way ahead, he'd be able to peel off and head towards the centre of the plantation, shoot the breeze with the other guards, and get something hot down his parched throat. The smell really was getting to him now... but it seemed worse and somehow different. He paused and noticed as the last of the light projected his shadow on to the incline that led towards the ridge. Then, his shadow seemed to grow – becoming colossal and changing form, and the stink was now bad enough to make him gag. As he watched, he could only think it wasn't his own shadow, but that of something far larger approaching from behind. He spun, the gun raised and his finger half-pressed on the trigger already. There was nothing there. Off to his right, a cannabis plant swayed back and forth, as if something had just brushed past it. From beyond the trees, a crack sounded as another large branch break sounded out. Noah took off towards the camp kitchen, doing all he could to stop himself sprinting the whole way.

"It's just nerves," Jackson Adams, one of the other guards acknowledged, after Noah told him he had the creeps. Jackson was a little friendlier than the others he'd met, and they shared cigarettes and coffee when time allowed.

"I ain't saying you're wrong," Jackson continued. "Couple of times I've felt like I was being watched. But expecting the feds to descend at any given moment kind of makes you jumpy, you know. Probably ain't nothing."

"Something just don't feel right," Noah said, shaking his head.

"Well, at least it ain't gonna be cold, dark, and misty soon... oh shit, yes, it is," Jackson replied, grinning.

Standing water, generators, and heat lamps where needed, created a rainforest-like micro-climate. As soon as the sun dipped below the horizon, the hollows would become shrouded in water vapour. Washington was already the foggiest state in the union, with an average of 165 days of mist each year. Such nights made patrolling more difficult – torches in the fog going back and forth would look like a beacon to the authorities, so they made their rounds in the dark by memory. It was routine now. Noah took another sip of his coffee. The tents that made up the kitchen and mess were camouflaged on the outside, and thermo insulated on the inside. It kept their heat signature small, if not completely concealed. The guards slept in shifts, using temporary basic shelters and bivouacs. It had been part of the original appeal for Noah, having a bit of a Survivorman vibe. But right now, he'd be happy with the shittiest of motel rooms, if it meant not staying here.

Just as Jackson had predicted, the mist rolled in as soon as it got dark and cold enough. Noah watched it roll down into the hollows from the ridgeline – as if it was being billowed like dry ice. He moved slowly and cautiously, keeping as quiet as possible. His eyes searched the mist and his hearing sought out the slightest of sounds. He knew it was ironic that earlier in his shift, it was noise that had unsettled him. Now though, it was the comforting silence that he knew so well that he found eerie.

CRACK.

Despite his senses being heightened and on maximum alert, the sound still surprised him. It came from behind, and he whirled around, raising the gun. The mist swirled around something moving away from him. He heard the faint squelch of mud. Footsteps maybe? He knew better than to give his position away, so he moved in silence in the same direction. He began to recognise the landscape as he moved over the ground. Twenty feet further, and he came across where he and Jackson slept in shifts. The dugouts kind of resembled the spider holes used in WW2 and Vietnam. Just deep enough to hold a man and his weapon, with a weatherproof, camouflaged lid made from boards and foliage.

As Noah neared, he saw the one nearest to him had been damaged somehow. The trapdoor top had been broken in the middle, as if something heavy had fallen on it. He realised this was what he must have heard. He edged closer, peering into the hole. The military-style bivouac inside, khaki green in colour, was in shreds. The insulating stuffing was falling out of four long slits that's ran across its top. It sent a chill down his spine. Had someone been in it, the slashes would have run across their face or throat, depending how they positioned themselves. It seemed deliberate. Noah looked around and decided he could chance a quick look at his watch. He lit up the dial with a momentary flash of his torch. It had just gone 9pm. Under normal circumstances, he realised he would indeed have been taking an hour's break – but he had been too jumpy and lost track of time. He fumbled with the flashlight, putting it away quickly and bringing up the gun again. It was as though something had known he should have been there. He remembered Jackson's comment about being watched. It was tracking their movements, waiting for the perfect time to strike. It had been his good fortune and the attacker's bad luck he hadn't been there.

The thought was all it took for Noah to wheel around, headed in a straight line for the far side of the camp. He knew his course would take him through the fields, instead of around them, and he'd undoubtedly be damaging some of the crop. But he didn't care. Right now, he didn't want to be alone, and he wanted to know where Jackson was. This was his best guess. He had gone no more than forty yards when he froze. Off to his right, near where he guessed the nearest treeline was, something had snorted. The noise reminded him of a time he had cut across a field, only to be greeted by a very pissed-off and bad-tempered bull. Whatever this was, Noah had the impression it was every bit as big and as aggressively focused on him. Noah pointed the gun in the direction the sound had come from.

A new sound, something akin to the yikker of a coyote, came from behind him, but this time a little closer. He spun on his heels, the adrenaline surging through his body now sending a tell-tale shake into his hands. Ten seconds later, what sounded like a great horned owl called out to his left – but the volume and bass were wrong, unless the owl weighed around 800lbs. Noah tried to keep control of his nerves, slowly revolving on the spot to try and get a bead on whatever it was out there in mist. Then, from behind again, came an ungodly sound, half growl, half demonic laugh. He broke into a run.

"Noa..."

Noah turned out of instinct and blind-fired, pulling the trigger as he reeled back in fright. He hadn't been expecting something to sound off so close to him. The yell that came next was from the ground, not far from his feet.

"You fuck, you shot me," he heard Jackson spit.

"Holy shit, I'm sorry..." Noah stammered.

He peered down and saw Jackson was sat about a yard away, holding his thigh and rocking back and forth. Noah had never felt quite so terrible as he did right then. He offered Jackson his hand and helped him onto his feet.

"I think you just grazed me, but you're still an asshole," Jackson grumbled.

Noah supported him as he helped Jackson limp in the direction of the main camp, where at least there was a first aid kit.

"Did you hear it?" Noah asked.

Jackson nodded.

"Why I was coming over to you. Thank fuck you got me

in the leg."

"I'm swapping it out for a shotgun as soon as we're back to camp," Noah replied. "What are you carrying?"

Jackson held up the Ruger PC Charger, another AR-pistol style gun that fired 9mm ammunition. Noah wondered if he felt as stupid as he did now, realising that it probably offered them little protection against anything big or fast. And whoever, or whatever was out there, seemed to be both. The guns looked great, and it had been a good enough distraction to play soldier and wile away the boredom. But from now on, if they got through this, he'd be carrying something that gave him a little more confidence. He couldn't believe the thought of not surviving had crossed his mind. It had gotten very real, very fast.

As if reading his mind, Jackson held up his hand, indicating he wanted to stop. Noah obliged. He watched Jackson, who seemed to be scanning ahead. Somewhere out in the darkness, something growled a low and guttural warning.

~

"Was that gunfire?" Katie asked, stopping so fast that Bodhi nearly walked into her.

"Sure as hell sounded like it," Bodhi replied.

"Nobody else is meant to be out here," Katie said, as if demanding an explanation.

"I wanna get up into those trees on the ridgeline and take a looksie – you game?" he asked. "I completely understand if you'd rather get out of Dodge."

"We take a look, but no chances, okay?" she replied.

He nodded and started scrambling up the bank where the trail had ended. If the map was accurate – and it usually was, he knew it would be a good vantage point. If it wasn't for the good old Washington fog, he'd be able to get a good lay of the land. But he had just the thing in his pack to help with that. He helped Katie up behind him, and he found a good-sized Western hemlock tree for them to put their backs against. He tried to get a view of the valley and hollows that lay beyond, but all he could make out were the dark treetops that peeked above the mist. He opened the pack and pulled out a large, black leather case. Inside was one of his favourite toys. The FLIR Recon B2-FO thermal imager was military-grade kit. It not only provided crisp, thermal-clear, pin-sharp, detailed imagery with a range of up to ten kilometres, but it also had live-streaming and wireless capabilities. Whatever might be hidden in the fog below them would soon be revealed, at least he hoped. He switched it on and booted through the start-up menus before raising it to his eyes.

The landscape burst into colour before him, etched in vivid purples and magenta. He was surprised by how much heat seemed to be seeping out of the forest. But the biocular did its job, and he soon made out the clumps of cannabis plants. The nearest, some thirty yards from them glowed a faint orange. In real time, he was able to watch them cool and more closely match the surrounding purple of the forest. He slowly and carefully scanned forwards and across, methodically mapping the area in his head and looking for the guards. This wasn't his first rodeo, and he knew how operations like this worked. The gunshot made sense now – probably a bored local letting off some steam. But he wasn't inclined to get any closer. He'd just see where they were and make sure he and Katie could leave without being noticed. A good way off and to the left, he saw two bright orange blobs. He adjusted the zoom and focus, and what he was looking for appeared in the view finder in sharp definition.

The two human forms glowed like fire embers against the violet and magenta hues of the background. The detail was excellent, and he even noticed the wound on one of the guards – the blood seeping down his leg the same colour as a lava flow. The other guard had his arm around his waist, and both were standing still, with their weapons raised. The barrel of the gun held by the unwounded guard was almost gold yellow. Bodhi smiled. Silly bastard shot his mate, he scoffed. The intensity of the colours was a little dayglo for him, so he took his eyes away from the viewfinder and switched to the monocolour mode. He could have done this with a press of the button, but he took the opportunity to hold his finger up to his lips and let Katie know to stay quiet. He recommenced his surveillance.

The built-in range finder signalled the guards were 871 metres from them, and 9.77 metres below them. In between was the maze of cannabis plants, and a series of rises and dips. Some of these dips were irrigation channels, and he could see the water vapour rising from them. He saw this as good news, as it meant that he and Katie could not be reached easily. But only if the guards were alone. He decided to keep scanning ahead to make sure. Slowly, he moved the biocular back and forth, slowly scanning. Then he froze. He might not have seen it if he'd not been paying attention to the ground and the plants so much, but there it was. The mass was almost the same colour as the background, indicating it was very well thermally insulated, but it still gave off a little more heat than its surroundings.

He took a sharp intake of breath as he realised what he was looking at. The creature was on all fours, its arms and legs spread wide, so its body was close to the ground. But its rear was raised slightly in the air, and its face appeared to be bent in the direction of the two guards. Bodhi used the rangefinder to gauge how close the creature was to the guards. 47 feet, it determined.

Once, as part of the show, the doc had conducted a series of experiments at an ape sanctuary down in Florida. They had shown that chimpanzees could leap over 30 feet. The gorillas had made it to 26 feet. Both species struggled to jump more than three feet straight up though. The exact size of the creature he was looking at was hard to gauge, but without doubt, it was extraordinarily large. The other thing that surprised him was how broad it seemed to be – easily equivalent to two good sized men. He had no doubt that this thing had physical abilities that easily surpassed all the great apes. The two guards were well within reach of it, at least he guessed so.

He realised Tilly and Jason would be seeing what he was. He quickly reached down to his waist and turned off the radio clipped to his belt, indicating that Katie should do the same. She did, but he could see the apprehension on her face. He tried to reassure her it was okay, but he couldn't risk any noise being made – especially by an excited producer shouting down the radio at them. He put the thermal camera back up to his eyes. It took him longer to find the creature this time. It had moved – sideways, but its focus was clearly still on the guards. Bodhi watched its muscles glow slightly as they tensed. Then it launched itself at the two men.

~

There was no noise. One moment, Noah was holding Jackson up, his arm underneath his friend's, then he was gone, and Noah was on his back, gasping for breath. He had been thrown several feet. He'd landed in a clump of cannabis plants, and it took a few moments for him to untangle himself. Then, through the fog, came Jackson's screaming. High-pitched, uncontrolled, terrorised wailing. Something grunted in reply. There was a resounding crack, and the sound of something splattering, like rainfall on soft sand. The screaming stopped and Noah shuddered. He pulled himself up into a crouching position and raised his gun, pointing it in the direction the sounds had come from. A hyena-like, cackling garble of excited, rasping shrieks erupted out of the mist. It sounded like a language, and it sounded like he was being mocked and insulted. Their tormenter was enjoying itself.

He'd heard the stories of course. You couldn't be from Washington State and not have heard of bigfoot. The films he'd watched as a kid had depicted the creature as some kind of friendly forest giant. But he'd seen documentaries about the missing loggers and hikers. About the clusters of disappearances in the national parks and the hunters that vanished without a trace. They'd caught his interest, but he'd never given it much thought or credit. He'd grown up in the woods and seen all manner of wildlife – but never anything that could be considered so out of the ordinary. But there had been whispers. Every now and then, he'd see some of the other guards in a bar in town or coming off shift. Like him, for the past few weeks, they'd been jumpy. They felt watched, threatened even. It hadn't been paranoia after all.

The thing made a slurping noise, and then Noah heard the unmistakable sounds of its gnashing teeth and loud, quick gulps. It was eating Jackson. Noah trembled as he listened to it consume his friend. Then all sound stopped. His entire consciousness urged him to get up and run, but his body wouldn't comply. He was rooted to the spot. He opened his mouth, to call out and somehow shatter the invisible force holding him at bay. His whole body shook as his bladder emptied itself, leaving a dark stain on his pants. This seemed to spark something in his unseen enemy. A deep, penetrating growl emitted out of the mist. Noah was sharp enough to realise it was closer. Much closer. He didn't think – his body seemed to move on autopilot. Just a small movement in the wrist at first, then he was pulling the trigger of the gun, again and again. He fired a volley of shots and then was sprinting, faster than he'd ever run in his life. He had no idea where he was going, and he couldn't see far through the fog. Then he heard the sound he'd been dreading would come. The smack of large, running feet, gaining ground with each impossible stride.

Something grabbed him by the back of the neck, and he was lifted off the ground effortlessly. His legs kicked out at nothing and he twisted and squirmed, trying to face his attacker. He lifted his gun up and went to shoot over his head, but it was ripped from his grasp before he could pull the trigger. He was summarily dropped to the ground, and he spun onto his back. Nothing was there. He peered into the fog, knowing his foe couldn't be far. It had to be right there. The mist swirled around a black mass ahead of him and it slowly began to take form. Just for a moment, there was a flicker of eyeshine, the colour of burnt amber. The thing opened its mouth and Noah caught a flash of its yellowed fangs as it let out a roar. Then there was a flash of white, as he realised it still had hold of his gun. Noah had time for a singular, sharp intake of breath from the shock as the creature launched at him. With deadly precision, it brought its straightened arm over the top of its head, bringing the gun down onto Noah's skull like an axe. The fragile bone, flimsy flesh, and even the steel and polymer components of the gun, were no match to the assault. As Noah's face collapsed in on itself, it oozed streams of blood, fragments of smashed nose cartilage and skull, broken teeth, and pulped, minced flesh.

~

Bodhi trembled as he watched. The creature had attacked with lightning reflexes. It had launched itself like a spear at the first guard, so quickly he'd practically missed it. In a single flowing movement, the creature had body slammed the man with its shoulder, then, as he'd fallen backwards, its hand had swept him underneath its arm as it moved back onto two legs, running forward, and distancing itself from the other man. Bodhi had heard the man it held scream, and he'd looked at Katie again, urging her to keep quiet and still. They had ringside seats to the slaughter. For a moment, he'd had a nagging urge to rush down the hill, firing the shotgun. But he knew it would be a death sentence. Now, it was just about hoping they could go unnoticed and get out alive. He went back to the gruesome vigil. The creature now held the man, its thumb beneath his chin and the rest of its fingers gripping the top of his skull. Still striding forward, never losing its momentum, the creature took a few steps before driving the head in its hand into the top of a nearby stump.

The irony the cannabis farmers had probably felled the tree wasn't lost on Bodhi. The body of the man went limp, and the creature began to feed. It pulled an arm off the corpse and seemed to suck on the stump before it began to tear strips of flesh from it. He saw the cold, dark fragments of torn clothing fall away from what was left. Then the creature stood up and turned, as if it had forgotten its other victim.

Bodhi watched as the creature crouched and made its way towards the remaining guard. Bodhi knew it had excellent night vision, but it didn't seem to know if the guard could see it too. It approached carefully until it was within about fifteen yards of the man. Bodhi guessed this was just beyond how far a human could see through the fog. The sasquatch was playing it safe. Despite not being able to see it, the guard seemed to sense it, and Bodhi watched as he blind fired the gun. If he hit the creature, it didn't react, but Bodhi was pretty sure the aim had been about four feet off. Bodhi heard the growl from their vantage point, and it made him shudder.

His own experiences had been low key. They all knew what the doc had been through. Nobody had been upset about their federal shadows that day. In his homeland of Australia, where he'd investigated the native bigfoot known as the Yowie, the rock throwing and intimidation tactics had been as close to aggression as it had gotten for him. Over here in the states, he'd heard plenty, but seen less. Most of it had been at a distance. This was the best footage he'd ever captured. It was a pity almost none of it would ever make it onto the show or a broadcast. Nobody on the team needed to be convinced of the creatures' existence anymore, but the rest of the world did – only, it wasn't that simple. Someone, somewhere, way above his pay grade, determined that the world wasn't ready. And they certainly weren't ready for this. Bodhi waited until he was certain the creature was distracted and feeding, with its back turned to them.

"Time to go," he whispered to Katie. "Real quiet, real fast, okay?"

Katie nodded. She looked incredibly pale.

They made their way down the bank and back onto the trail. Bodhi kept the thermal biocular handy round his neck on its strap. They had gone about 500 yards when Katie suddenly reached out and grabbed him, her grip vice-like. He snapped his head in her direction, ready to scold her, but then he noticed her eyes, bulging, and the tremble in her arms. Then he felt it too. He froze as the hairs on the back of his neck stood on end. Raising the shotgun, he slowly turned around – his ears pricked for the slightest sound to come out of the silent, freezing fog. When none came, he raised the thermal camera and looked through the viewfinder. He gasped and took a step back. Back at the end of the trail, seemingly facing them, four figures stood, still as statues. Their bodies glowed greyish white against the darker background. One towered above the others, who stood behind it. There was no real way to gauge height, but he knew it was immense. He guessed somewhere between nine and ten feet. The creature raised its arms and stamped the ground as it let out a ghastly, reverberating roar that Bodhi swore he could feel in his gut and through the ground beneath his feet. Then he and Katie were running, as fast as they could and for their very lives.

CHAPTER TWELVE

WEED KILLERS

"You know the lay of the land in places like this... there is no police. There might be a sheriff's department somewhere, but they'll be hours away. Most of the time, it falls to the Game Wardens and Rangers to enforce the law. So, if you want to report something, it's to them," Tilly Miller, Seeking Sasquatch's Senior Producer, explained again to Katie Cash.

Katie rolled her eyes and waved her hand in the air, dismissively accepting what she was being told.

"Fine," she sighed. "Jason, how much of last night's footage can we actually use, d'ya think?"

Jason, the other producer on the show, shrugged.

"Remember, the only reason we have the toys we do, is because they're on loan from our gracious shadows," he replied. "They get full editing rights. But my guess is... not much. Certainly, none of the money shots, but maybe bits of it crawling forwards or standing up, with the quality watered down a bit. And not full frames, of course. It's with them now."

Katie nodded.

"Never seen one like this," Bodhi stated, shaking his head. "It's got a fucking hard on for killing, that's for sure. And what about the others we saw on the trail?"

"They were all together?" Joe asked, joining the rest of the Seeking Sasquatch team around a camp table.

"The one that... killed those men, it was on its own," Katie said. "We didn't know the others were there until we were way down the trail. I just got a horrible feeling in my gut and froze. Bodhi was the one that saw them. I just heard the roar."

"My guess is that they're a separate group from the

killer," Joe explained. "Hell, maybe we'll get lucky, and they'll do what the Army sometimes struggle to do."

Dr. Mary Beth Benoit joined them, completing the team's line up.

"You think they'll call the Army in?" she asked.

"They seem to show up sooner or later once they know they have a rogue," Joe shrugged.

As Tilly approached the team, she was still putting her phone away.

"Both the feds and the Rangers are going to head to the farm," she explained. "Neither can get there straight away. The feds are still wrapping up the last crime scene, and the Ranger said she was headed to check in with a logger, but it's nearby. So, for now, we just wait it out. No filming today gang. Smoke em' if you've got em."

~

Nina had decided to take one of the Ranger trucks for the follow-up visit with Patwyn Dalton. Sometimes, it helped to look official. However, the green and white liveried Chevy Colorado complained at the rough treatment, as she pushed its capabilities along the winding dirt track leading to Dalton's camp.

"He was itching to get hold of us yesterday, now he's not picking up the phone," Scott said, putting his mobile back in his pocket.

"Maybe he didn't recognise your number," Nina replied.

"Want to bypass him and head straight for this supposed cannabis farm?" he suggested.

He hid it well, but she picked up on the eagerness in his tone.

"Easy cowboy," she smiled. "That's a hornet's nest we don't need to poke without the help of our bureau boys, or at least Law Enforcement and Investigations. We're not the cops."

"Closest thing to it round these parts," Scott smiled, putting on an accent like an old movie, and glancing at the Benelli M4 tactical shotgun secured against the rear of the cab. "Plus, LEI won't get involved until we've checked it out first, you know that."

"Forest Service have only been carrying firearms for about a year. An itchy trigger finger isn't a desirable personality trait, you know?"

Nina drew up outside of Patwyn Dalton's cabin. She waited a moment, expecting him to come outside and meet them on the porch, as he'd done before. She cast her eyes over the damaged equipment, unmoved from the day before. With no sign of Dalton, she got out of the truck. Nina took a few steps, but then slowed and stopped. She looked around, frowning.

"What's wrong?" Scott asked.

"It's a little quiet, don't you think?"

Scott looked around, cocking his head sightly as he listened.

"No birds, no... anything," Nina added.

She walked briskly up the front steps and knocked loudly on the door.

"Mr. Dalton," she called out. "Nina Lee, Forest Service."

There was no reply. Scott seemed impatient as he shrugged at her. Nina shook her head and followed the deck around to the back of the cabin. She froze. The large, black-coloured bird tilted its head towards her, a piece of tattered, pink flesh gripped tightly within its large, broadly curved, black beak. It spread its wings and launched itself into the air, flying low over the back field, emitting muffled croaks of alarm as it went. Nina's gaze returned to the raven's meal. What remained of Patwyn Dalton lay in a slurry that ran across the decking. She forced herself to move closer, bending her neck and lowering her head. More than anything else, she could smell the blood. It was everywhere and it was easy to see why. She took deep breaths as she steadied herself, resetting her spiralling thoughts so she could make the required observations.

She took a few steps closer. Scott came around the corner of the deck.

"What's taking so..."

Nina turned in time to see Scott double over and vomit over the rail of the veranda, into the long grass the other side. She wondered, if he hadn't distracted her, if she'd be doing the same. It was understandable. She returned her focus to Patwyn Dalton's remains. By moving forward, she could now see the head. It looked like some kind of macabre, novelty cooking pot without a lid. The top was missing completely. Only the bottom half of the empty eye sockets remained, and the nasal cavity was completely caved in. Sharp, thin fragments of bone and flaps of skin were all that remained above the cheek bones. The jaw too was lopsided and broken. The way it looked, it was as if someone had ripped the top of the head off, perhaps poking out the eyes and gripping the skull like a bowling ball. She dared herself to get a little closer. What remained of the head was an empty cup. The brain had been completely removed. A bloody, brown, and pink pulp was all that remained.

She slowly worked down the rest of the body, taking mental notes. The unhinged, broken jaw revealed some loose teeth and an empty throat devoid of the tongue. That's when she noticed Dalton's lips were missing. If the skull had been intact, it would have been more obvious, but the head was so badly misshaped and damaged, it was hard to distinguish through the different trails of blood. The chest seemed unmolested, but the stomach had been torn open, violently. Parts of the bowel were visible, no longer contained by skin and sinew. She had no doubt faeces were mixed in with the other bodily substances and fluids staining the deck, darkening the blood, and adding to the stink. She had no interest in getting closer and seeing what remained of the internal organs, but her best guess was that the choicer ones would be missing. The legs were untouched and stretched out straight. Only the left arm was visible, and both the clothing and flesh beneath had been cut through by what she imagined to be long, raking claws.

"Guess that settles it about the bear," Scott said, trying to regain his composure.

"Head back to the truck and radio it in," Nina said softly. "we're going to need a coroner or medical examiner. The feds will need to know, and a few state troopers wouldn't go amiss."

Scott nodded, wasting no time in heading round to the front and out of sight. Nina turned her back on the corpse. She didn't know what to make of what had happened. The pure strength shown, yet almost casual nature of the attack, perhaps did imply a bear. The grizzly – Ursus arctos horribilis, a subspecies of brown bear that counted Washington State as one of its few strongholds, was a professional opportunist. They were known for eating everything from grass shoots to moose, making them neither picky nor against taking a human being occasionally. But bear attacks were incredibly rare. Grizzly attacks averaged one or two a year for the whole of the U.S. And grizzlies didn't favour brain and innards over prime, juicy cuts of meat like leg, or butt. And whereas territorial or defensive attacks often saw injuries to the face, she'd never heard of one where the skull had been cracked open.

Nina stood with her hands resting on the rail that separated her from the deck and the back meadow. She was deep in thought, staring out into the wilderness. Then her focus returned, and she noticed something. It was subtle, but from the elevated deck, she thought she could pick out where something had crossed the meadow, snaking its way through the grass and mud. Where the foliage had been pushed aside, it faced away from her, suggesting that whatever had made the trail had been moving away towards the woodland. She worked the trail backwards and found it led to the congealed soup of blood, faeces, and flesh that had dripped from the deck and down the steps, pooling at the bottom. She walked down into the meadow, then paused, looking around to see if Scott was returning. It was easy to feel exposed and alone given what they'd discovered. But her curiosity and instincts were compelling her to follow the trail. They rarely let her down, so she decided to follow them.

It wasn't an obvious trackway, and it snaked through the meadow towards the treeline rather than making a direct line towards it. She took her time looking for signs of a change in direction, or anything that might suggest that whatever made the trail was still hanging around. But other than a few bent blades of grass, the path she was following was almost invisible. Then, about twenty feet from the treeline, she stopped. Here, the meadow was swampier and damper. There was clearly ground water close to the surface. A slick of mud gave away its presence, appearing like a crack a few yards long in the meadow. Off to one side, there was a deep impression. Nina crouched, studying it. Only about half the print had been left in the mud, whereas flattened grass to the side hinted at the true size. Again, she looked up to see if Scott had returned. What she was seeing was making her doubt everything. She estimated the full track to be eighteen inches long and nearly nine inches across. Whatever had made it, had been heavy, compressing the mud down a good way – at least half an inch.

She took a moment to calm her breathing. She reminded

herself when bears walked on all fours, their hind paws often overlapped their front ones. The result wasn't unlike a large, elongated human footprint. But, although claw marks weren't always obvious, she would expect to see them in fresh, pristine mud like this.

"Lee, you here?" she heard Scott call.

"Over here," she replied, raising her hand but remaining crouched.

Scott walked over to meet her, oblivious to the trail Nina had so diligently followed in. He cut straight across the meadow.

"What does that look like to you?" she asked, gesturing towards the print.

Scott stared at it for all of six seconds before letting out a high-pitched whistle of surprise.

"That's a big bear," he exclaimed, shaking his head. "So, coroner is going to be a few hours at least. Troopers might get here a little sooner. We're on guard duty."

"To hell with that," Nina blustered. "You don't have to come with, but I want to follow this trail. Whatever made it, killed Dalton."

Scott nodded. "Look, I don't want to hang around here, but we can't leave him like that... what if somebody turns up, or comes looking for him?"

"We'll get hauled across the coals. Might even get suspended or worse," Nina shrugged. "But this is what killed him, I'm sure of it, and if it's a bear..."

"There's a good chance it's still hanging around," Scott remembered.

Scott remembered his training. The scene they had discovered showed all the hallmarks of a bear attack. There was a distinct sign of a struggle, and the kill had been brazened and messy. That made it unlikely to be a big cat. But more worryingly, most of the body was still intact. If a bear didn't cover up a kill, that meant it was likely to be nearby or intended to return frequently to gorge on its prize. There was even the possibility they had disturbed it as they arrived.

"We'll go back to the truck for the shotgun, and we'll cordon off the area with tape," Nina suggested. "But I'm not sitting on my ass for two hours. I'm going after it."

Scott nodded.

Ten minutes later, they were both at the treeline. Scott carried the shotgun, and Nina had unsnapped the holster for her revolver.

"Here goes nothing," she shrugged, and stepped into the forest.

Moving into the trees had been like crossing some invisible threshold. The morning had been bright and clear, but in the forest, it was an eternal twilight. There was a dampness that clung to the air permanently. Whisps of water vapour gathered into an ethereal mist further up towards the canopy. It wasn't thick enough to be fog, but it shrouded what lay beyond in a translucent veil. Nina smiled and took a deep breath. She was used to this. When most people thought of rainforest, their minds pictured the Amazon, maybe tropical birds, and sweltering heat. But this too was rainforest. A single glance would tell you that water was everywhere. It was everything in this landscape. The iron-coloured rocks had the sheen of the water that had carved and shaped them. Moss and lichen consumed everything it touched on the forest floor. Lush ferns crowded around the bottom of the Sitka spruce and western hemlock that made up the forest, whilst their branches hung heavy with vines and moss.

Unlike tropical rainforests though, which were filled with sound night and day, these woods were often eerily quiet, just as they were now. But they were far from being devoid of life. They were, in fact, teaming with it. In addition, the Olympic rainforest was a completely unique ecosystem. There was nothing else like it on the planet. She'd seen animals as large as the mighty Roosevelt elk and as unexpected as playful river otters within these woods, as well as the country's most dedicated predators. Mountain lion, as well as wolves, and both black and brown bear, were no strangers to the forest. Here, beyond the trails, it was her and Travis who were out of place.

It was strange how just taking a few steps into the trees made her instincts kick in. Without thinking about it, she had stood still, scanning the way ahead without moving her head. She had relaxed her body and her breathing, dropping her shoulders and her stance. Her peripheral vision strained hard, anticipating movement. Her hearing tuned out the thud of her heartbeat and the thunder of the blood in her veins. She squinted, narrowing yet sharpening her field of vision as she observed her surroundings – and reducing the reflective surface of her pupils at the same time. Humans, after all, had the forward-facing eyes of all predators, and it was often the physical characteristic animals recognised first. It had only been a matter of seconds, but in that same time, Travis had checked his watch, ruffled his hair, and scratched an itch on his shoulder. She had not needed to turn around to see him do this. Her senses had worked in unison to give her the information. Most people were oblivious to how much they moved and gave themselves away, with barely a minute passing by.

She remembered her father teaching her to track and stalk through woods that looked much the same. He had told her to be still rather than quiet. He had later explained this was because quiet was subjective. Everyone had their own understanding of quiet – from barely a whisper to almost raucous. Stillness was more absolute, and quietness was usually a more universal side effect. He had also impressed upon her the importance of following her instincts. One of his favourite sayings was that telephony had replaced telepathy. He hadn't meant mind reading or 'using the force'. It was more that people, including Nina as he often pointed out, were glued to their smartphones, and had lost a very special, real connection with the wild. The instincts that every animal counted on for their very survival had become dulled, perhaps even muted in modern humans. For most people, even though the forest still spoke to them, they could no longer hear it.

Her gaze came to rest on a dark streak that showed where the moss on a log had split, revealing the damp, rotting wood beneath. She moved in to examine it. The moss was flattened – crushed in fact. Mass and friction had been enough to stretch the sponge-like plant to breaking point, and it had torn like a piece of brittle carpet. The area that had been flattened down was similar in size to the print they'd examined. It wasn't hard to imagine their quarry had stepped up onto the log. Nina followed its example. The log was relatively wide and pointed up at an angle, resting as it was on a bed of rocks and other deadfall timber. It only elevated her a few feet, but it made all the difference. What had been an impenetrable forest just moments before, now revealed several ambling pathways through the brush. They were subtle, and clearly made by animals like deer and maybe smaller creatures like foxes or skunks. But they were visible. Nina looked down at the impression in the moss and gauged the direction their quarry had been going in.

She jumped down from the log and moved forward, instinctively lowering her upper body as she did. A glance behind assured her that Scott was following her, albeit less stealthily and enthusiastically. She didn't find another trace of the animal until she'd gone a further twenty feet. This time, the impact was more significant. The track was almost twice as long and about a third larger in width. She studied it for a second and looked back at the log before returning her gaze to the impression at her feet. The narrower end of the print was deeper – much deeper. Once more she scanned the vegetation between her and the log. She pieced together the scant evidence in her mind. Could it have leapt and landed here? That would rule out a bear. She checked twice for where front feet should have been if it was a grizzly. She was willing to accept she had missed some sign of its passage if she found even the slightest anecdotal evidence. But there was none. They were following something that walked on two feet and was extremely agile. That meant a human, and if they were running around in the forest barefoot, that most likely meant it was someone from the reservation. Or, at the very least, someone who was Native American. A shiver ran down her spine. She preferred dealing with animals over people any day of the week.

"Stay close," Nina instructed Scott. "We're following the most dangerous animal on the planet."

Scott nodded, understanding she meant a person.

He closed to within a few yards, flanking her as he did. He now had a wider point of view to cover her from. She was glad that despite all his gusto and bravado, Scott Travers was extremely competent. With him backing her up, she could concentrate on picking out the trail. She returned her gaze and concentration to reading the ground. For the next ten minutes, she worked forwards, then re-checked the ground they had covered. When she lost the trail, she retraced her steps and changed trajectory. Soon, she began to recognise a pattern. Whoever they were pursuing, they had some knowledge of covering their tracks. It became clear they were using fallen trees and rocks to traverse the landscape. This made sense, as it meant for quick, efficient ground coverage without getting bogged down in mud, or having to clamber over obstructions. By elevating their path several feet off the ground where they could, they could move faster and be less incumbered. But it also felt very deliberate. Something else disturbed her. When they came to patches of open ground their quarry would had to have crossed, the only impressions she could find were between three and five yards apart. A human would have to be running flat out to do that, with their feet barely touching the ground – cheetah like. It didn't add up. They continued to follow the track.

After about forty minutes, Nina noted they were approaching a ridgeline, one conveniently covered in trees to provide cover. The trail seemed to head straight towards it. They were now far beyond Dalton's cabin and over a mile into the forest. There were certainly no trails here, and she didn't recognise the surroundings. This was new territory for her, and she became more cautious as she moved forward. Instinct told her to approach the ridge quietly and to stay concealed. She dropped to a crouch, then to her stomach, commando crawling to the top. Travers stayed crouched and approached to her right. She held up a cautionary hand.

Nina lifted her head, only ever so slightly, gaining a view into the hollows that led down the other side of the ridge. Only her eyes and the top of her head crested the outcrop, and they were partially hidden by the foliage on the other side. She was confident she wouldn't draw attention, and that was a good thing. They weren't alone. In the morning light, the tight clusters of cannabis plants were easy to see, even under the camouflage netting that surrounded them. The landscape formed a natural bowl, and from her vantage point, she could see the undulating mix of channels and hollows that had been dug out of it. Each mini valley contained prolific fields of marijuana. At the centre of it all, she could make out some kind of camp. What immediately concerned her though, was the black, four-seater side-by-side and the four armed men that were walking back and forth. She could tell they were agitated and having a heated debate. The black smoke of a fire was rising from somewhere behind them, and a few seconds later, the unmistakable smell of burning flesh came to her on the breeze.

The men were all carrying what she assumed were automatic rifles. Something about their swagger said bad news. She knew this much product was worth killing for, and she was in no doubt they'd be willing to do so. Nina looked at Scott.

"Call it in," she nodded.

"Been trying to... not getting through," he shrugged. But I think we've got bigger problems."

He pointed to a lodgepole pine across from them. She saw it immediately. The camera was well hidden, but the low morning light caught the lens and reflected when she looked directly at it.

"They might not know we're here, but they're gonna soon," he implied.

"Let's start backing up," Nina said. "We're outnumbered and outgunned."

"We have an obligation," Scott protested.

"What we'll have, is an obituary," Nina replied. "Absolutely not."

Shouts rose from the men, and Nina and Scott risked a second peek over the ridgeline. Two of the men were still standing at the camp, but the other two were running in their direction.

"We have the high ground here," Scott suggested. "It's a better option than running".

Nina looked behind them. Her gut instinct said he was right. They could retreat, but they'd lose the small advantage they currently had. The men had already split up – evening the odds. But if they took to the trail, they could reunite at any point. And it was uncertain how far they'd have to go before they were back in radio contact with dispatch. Nina nodded reluctantly at Scott. He didn't need any further encouragement, and scrambled up to join her, shouldering the shotgun and taking refuge behind another pine. Nina flanked him, drawing her revolver. She scrutinised their position. The men were still a good five hundred yards from them, their pace slowed by their ascent. Not much cover was afforded to them, other than a few tree stumps that had been too big to remove when they'd cleared the land, as well as a few natural dips in the ridgeline and the odd boulder. Nina and Scott had a single line of thin-trunked pines to shield them.

When the men had traversed another hundred yards, she called out.

"That's far enough."

The men stopped and looked up along the ridge to where they thought the sound of her voice had come from.

"You're trespassing on private property, you have no right to be here," one of the men yelled. Nina could tell he was still trying to get a bead on their exact position – probably buying time.

"Nice try. You've set up shop in a National Forest. Forest Rangers – put down your weapons and back up," Scott shouted back.

"Wanna step out and show us your badge, Ranger?" the man nearest to them jeered.

They didn't seem like locals to Nina. The accent was more like southern California. They looked a little too slick and well-groomed for North Washington. Even the four-seater side-by-side was flashy. Her guess was these were the guys in charge. Which led to the question as to where the guards were. Her eyes darted to the thick black smoke that was billowing from beyond her line of sight.

Clean-up crew, she thought.

"I won't ask again, put down your weapons and get down on your knees, hands behind your heads," Scott commanded.

The second man, who stood slightly behind the one that had mocked them, moved quickly. He dashed to a tree stump, where he crouched and rested his rifle on it – an AR-15 of some kind. By the time he was looking down the scope, he was pulling the trigger. Both Nina and Scott flinched at the sound of the shots.

"Sounds automatic?" Nina shouted, in surprise as bullet spray hit about twenty feet downhill from them.

"Probably a bump fire mod," Scott yelled back. "Watch the comedian, he's flanking."

Nina had seen him too. As his partner kept them occupied with fire, the one who had asked to see Scott's badge had moved up. They were both now approximately two hundred yards from them. That changed the game – as the AR-15 rifles the men were armed with were now within lethal range – if they were competent shooters. She knew she could shoot competently at 125 yards, but Scott's shotgun was far more limited, even with the rifled slugs it was chugged with. Nina kept her cool and observed. She had no intention of leaving cover or taking a shot before the risk was worth it. She held the gun steady in her hand, down towards the ground. She gauged distance and the shooter's ability with each step closer. It soon became apparent that the advantage the cannabis growers gained through the bump mods made to their rifles, came at a price. They emptied their magazines, of 20 to 30 rounds she guessed, quickly. It also revealed they were amateur shootists, as they were surprised when they quickly had to reload. And she doubted they were carrying more than two spare mags each in their fancy vests.

As if to confirm, the shooting stopped and there was a longer pause than before, as the men moved up again. Nina heard the metallic ping of a reloading mechanism and watched as the comedian, as Scott had called him, looked down for a second to change the mag. He was now the nearest of the two. It was the best opportunity she was going to get. She sprang upwards, her arms tightening and straightening as she took aim. She allowed herself one step out of cover for a better view. She noticed the man tense as he looked up. It was an instinctive response she'd seen in every hunted animal; the senses picking up on being watched – that a predator was homing in. There was no decision to make, they had discharged weapons. She pulled the trigger, lining up the follow-up shot straight after. It wasn't needed. She'd hit dead on in the right-hand shoulder. He'd dropped his weapon and was already on his way to the ground. Then she noticed the movement from her left in her peripheral vision. All this played out in a matter of microseconds, but it seemed like an hour. The second gunner had changed direction and was headed straight for her. He was moments from pulling the trigger and killing her, and she didn't have time to respond. Scott exploded from the cover of the trees, working the pump on the shotgun as he fired at her attacker.

He missed, and as he fed the next round into the chamber, they both knew they'd lost the advantage. Nina was about three quarters through her swing to change position, but the man was quick. All he had to do was move the barrel a few inches upwards to line up on Scott, and then there was an eruption of noise and flame as the AR-15 discharged. The first few bullets went wide, but then a cluster found their mark. Scott's body twitched, as if electrocuted, as it felt the impact of the rounds. Nina felt her stomach drop, then a surge of anger. Her gun was lined up on her target now, and she fired. Much closer, she saw their assailant's chest turn red as he fell to the ground. Shouts rose from the camp below, but she was already on her feet and running towards Scott. She grabbed the discarded AR-15 from the man she had killed and threw the carry strap over her shoulder. She reached Scott and knelt on one knee beside him. The bullets had peppered his left shoulder, arm, and side. There was a lot of blood. She knew it was a risk, but she wanted to move him back into the cover, before the men below began to ascend towards them.

She slowly pulled him up by his good arm. Scott groaned, still conscious, but pale. She nodded at the treeline on the ridge just a few yards behind them, and he nodded, although the effort made his eyes roll into the back of his head. She scooted around to behind him, and thrust her arms underneath his, and began to drag him back. More shouts from below, seemingly louder, and closer, made her look up again. The other two men were moving fast. She was going to have to make a stand with the AR-15. But as she went to gently lay Scott back down, she heard something else. The low, fast whump of a helicopter. She was suddenly filled with dread, realising they had more support than she had ever imagined. A second later, a large, streamlined aircraft streaked overhead. She recognised it as an Army search and rescue helicopter – a Sikorsky Pave Hawk. Just as law enforcement came down to whoever was closest out here in the wilds, so it was for search and rescue – hence she'd seen them before. The helicopter went into a hover, and its open side door revealed soldiers clad in forest camouflage, and with their weapons trained on the encroaching drug runners. There was no warning, just a barrage of fire, followed by silence. Then the helicopter dipped towards the ground.

CHAPTER THIRTEEN

THE TEAM

Second Lieutenant Wade Garrick glanced at Master-Sergeant Amos Dugas, who was smiling.

"Best job in the world," he smirked.

Wade shook his head in mocking disbelief. "We're landing, try not to fall out," he added.

The Sikorsky set down, and Wade listened as the motor noise changed and began to wind down. The amber light on the pillar next to his head turned green, and he, Dugas, and the other six members of their team, made quick work of disembarking the aircraft. He and Dugas were the only ones to come from Fort Skookum. They had joined the others at McChord Airforce Base, from where they'd flown out. Not much had been said between them on the relatively short flight. Wade knew this was often the way with special ops teams. He guessed, like he and Dugas, the other six team members were likely made up of three pairs. They all wore gold and teal Special Forces insignias – of a dagger crossed with three lightning bolts, on their shoulder patches, obscuring their originally designated branches. Wade knew it was bad form to ask personal questions. It also gave him an uneasy feeling in his gut. Teams like this were often put together and encouraged to take little interest in each other for obvious security reasons. And because it was likely not everyone would make it back. He wondered if they understood what they would be hunting down, as he and Dugas did.

The soldiers acted naturally and quickly, their training

and experience apparent. Two checked the cannabis growers for signs of life whilst the other two pairs set up a perimeter around the landing zone. That left Wade and Dugas to head up the hill towards the Forest Rangers. As soon as they approached, they could see things were bad. Dugas went straight to the wounded Ranger on the ground, taking the Combat Lifesaver Bag from his pack. He stripped away the Ranger's shirt with his knife and set about cleaning the wounds, working fast to then add clotting powder. Moving him gently but as fast as he could, he then applied an emergency elastic trauma bandage. Even Wade was impressed at how quickly Dugas worked.

"It'll hold, but he needs a doc, and a hospital," Dugas informed them.

"Get our friends to bring a stretcher from the bird," Wade suggested. "We'll medivac him out."

Dugas nodded. He touched the advanced, subtle earpiece each of them wore to activate it and spoke the instructions quietly. Nina got the impression he didn't want her to hear.

"Thank you," she said.

She had stood back and watched as the soldier had attended to Travers. Her partner had passed into unconsciousness as soon as the clotting agent had been applied. Nina knew it was the pain, but she also knew that wasn't good. It was usually imperative to keep a trauma patient awake, regardless. They weren't just falling asleep, they were either going into shock or, worse, their systems, including the brain, were shutting down.

Nina was about to say something when her keen hearing picked up the sound of a vehicle engine. It was approaching from the other side of the cannabis fields, beyond the helicopter. The soldiers didn't seem alarmed, so she didn't ask. The sound of the engine cut off before it came into view. But a few moments later, two figures entered the camp. Even at distance, she recognised them as the two supposed agents from the Bureau of Land Management. She bristled but was distracted as two more of the soldiers joined them, carrying the stretcher for Travers. They transferred him with expert care and then began to carry him down. Nina, Wade, and Dugas followed them.

"Looks like you'll have a fair bit of paperwork to do," Wade offered.

Nina could tell he was trying to make conversation and lift the tension. She smiled, appreciating the gesture.

"And then some," she nodded. "Could easily be enough to get me fired."

"Or hailed a hero. You just shut down a major drug operation," Wade shrugged.

"You shut it down," Nina replied, shaking her head. "I shot two people, and my partner was seriously injured as a result of my decisions to follow... whatever it was we were following."

It seemed like a distant memory now.

"I think, officially, you'll find we were never here," Wade smirked. "I think that's what our friends down there are here to oversee," he nodded.

Travers was quickly loaded onto the helicopter. Dugas climbed in beside him, using the more stable platform to administer more first aid. He set up a drip of some kind, hung from the Sikorsky's infrastructure, and started checking vitals. Nina felt herself stiffen as Agent Cordell Jones approached her. Out of fairness to him, she could see he had cleaned up his act a little. His appearance was no longer grubby. Instead, he wore a mix of high-end outdoor gear and a tactical vest, belt, and boots. His swagger was still there, and confident, but it was somehow different. When the soldier who had spoken to her stood to attention and saluted the agent, she did nothing to hide her slight surprise. Agent Cordell Jones nodded an acknowledgement, and the soldier immediately relaxed.

"No need for any of that son, not while you're wearing those insignias," he huffed. "Ranger Lee, isn't it?" Cordell asked.

Nina nodded. She was wary, coiled, and ready to strike.

"Pretty impressive and ballsy to do what you did... your partner owes his life to how good a shot you are. We're getting him out of here right now. I can't tell you he's going to be alright, and I know you don't trust me. But I ain't try'n to get rid of you when I say I think you should go with him."

Nina looked from Agent Jones to the helicopter. She felt the slight tremble in her fingers and could feel how sluggish her thought process was. She fought it, recognising both as the first symptoms of shock. She nodded and headed towards the open side of the Sikorsky. Dugas offered her a hand as she clambered on board. She took a seat, pushing her back against the hard metal frame of the cabin. Jones appeared to her side.

"We followed its tracks in," Nina managed to blurt out, just before the rotor blades began to move. "I don't think your bear is a bear...".

Cordell nodded and half smiled. "I get that a lot," he replied.

He slapped the side of the helicopter hard. The

reverberating thud seemed to signal the pilot, who began to wind up the engine hard and fast. Cordell and Wade backed away as the exhaust whined and they began to feel the backwash. They watched the Sikorsky lift gracefully into the air, both meeting Nina's gaze as she watched them. Dugas was busy checking her harness, then the helicopter turned away and began to gain height and speed. In less than a minute it had disappeared, headed towards civilisation.

The remaining soldiers quickly rallied, gathering in a 180-degree formation around Cordell and Special Agent Gregory Smith.

"Gentlemen," Cordell acknowledged. "Each of you has either trained at Skookum with me or been stationed there. That means I don't need to explain why we're not here to shut down some redneck potheads."

"No, just the coneheads," one of the soldiers sneered, quietly though.

"What did your reccy reveal," Smith asked, his tone unforgiving and correcting.

"Two bodies back there being burnt in a shallow grave," the soldier replied, straightening up. "Hard to tell if they were vics of our target, but one's missing an arm, so I'd say there's a good chance."

"To the north perimeter, there's a bunch of dead critters," another of the soldier's piped up. He had short, blonde hair, and Wade had turned his head, recognising the Alabama lilt of the man's accent.

"And there's a trackway of sorts that leads through the camp from the south and exits west," the southerner's partner piped up.

"Baker, Campbell – you follow up on that trail and see

where it leads," Cordell commanded.

The two Alabama boys turned about and headed off without another word – although Wade noted their names for later. He liked to know who he was working with, regardless of policy. And in his experience, working as a team – as well as the urge to look out for one another, came a little easier when everyone was better acquainted.

"Parker, Jackson... our Hollywood friends encountered possible tangos the other side of that ridge to the East," he said, pointing it out, "see what you can find".

Another pair split off. Wade had studied everyone in the team. They were all young men, in peak condition. None had the cut of a greenhorn, meaning they were all experienced soldiers. The pair from Alabama – a redhead and a blonde, were Army like he and Dugas were, he was pretty sure of that. These two were well-built and stern looking. They gave off a Ranger vibe, maybe. For sure though, they had both seen service in the desert. They had the weather-beaten skin, sun-bleached hair, and the faraway look in their eyes he'd seen in all who'd toured in Afghanistan.

"Hicks, Dixon, you stay here, look pretty, and start on clean up," Cordell growled, glancing at the soldier who'd made the cocky remark.

The very fact he'd felt self-assured enough to make a snide remark in front of a commanding officer – FED or not, suggested special forces. Both had black hair, longer than the rest of them. There was a slick grittiness to them that made Wade think Delta Force, but he had no real way of knowing. All he could guess was, like him, they were officially volunteers. Nobody was being forced to be here.

"Garric, as you're down a partner, you'll come with me," Cordell added. "Everyone else, stay put."

Wade followed Cordell. Having just arrived, he was unsure where the agent was taking him. He wondered why the soldiers had been so quick and at ease with him giving orders. Usually, anyone in intelligence was treated with suspicion and they certainly didn't commandeer the respect to give out orders.

"Guess you're wondering why the Army's best are happy to do my bidding?" Cordell suggested to Wade with a wry smile as they walked away.

Wade nodded.

"You and your buddy, Dugas... you didn't have the pleasure of my time at Skookum?" Cordell asked as they walked.

"No sir," Wade answered.

"I don't wear a suit," Cordell replied. "It don't feel right after the uniform," Cordell explained. "My daddy was a Night Stalker. I made it as a Green Beret before this became my particular calling."

Wade could sense the sarcasm but knew not to interrupt.

"These things have a habit of either changing your life, or ending it," Cordell continued. "Once you know they're out there, it's a little hard to put it to the back of your mind. They're all dangerous, but most of them don't want anything to do with us. The ones that do, we call them rogues. I gather you've met the inhabitants of no man's land back at Skookum?"

Wade nodded, remembering the creatures. Amos Dugas had brought him up to speed as soon as their joining of the team had been greenlit.

"Why... why do they keep them alive and up there, sir?" Wade asked.

"That's above my pay grade," Cordell replied, honestly. "Super soldier programme maybe... species preservation – they're rare enough, I'm sure. It's kind of new. I doubt it will end well. You get the chance, I'd move on just as soon as you can."

Suddenly, Wade caught an overwhelming stench and snapped his head in the direction the wind carried it from. If he hadn't been distracted by the conversation, he was pretty sure he'd have been sick.

"This is what I wanted you to see," Cordell said, pointing.

Wade saw the shallow ditch and the bodies of the animals that lined it. Deer, a badger, foxes, and two black bears lay stiff and lifeless. The crows and jays that had fed on the corpses hadn't made it far and lay around the perimeter of the ditch.

"Are you saying one of those creatures did this?" Wade asked.

"Nope," Cordell shook his head. "I've heard you're as good a tracker as you are a soldier. You tell me what happened."

Wade held his breath and walked closer to the ditch. A cursory examination of the animals assured him that, beyond the ravages of the scavengers, they hadn't been touched. It was then that he noticed the ground around the pit had been stirred up significantly. He bent down to get a better look. The grass had been flattened down into the earth, compacting it. His finger traced the shape of a toe – albeit one the size of his middle and index finger put together. A series of impressions to its right were where he imagined a heel had come down, over and over again. Here and there, the impressions were more solid and shapely, once he knew what to look for. He circled the pit once, slowly. Then he stopped, gazing off back the way they'd come and towards the camp.

"It came here first, circling many times," Wade declared. "Its pace increased, then it charged off towards the rise over there."

"Very good," Cordell declared.

They walked in the direction their quarry had taken. They discovered the dugout cots the camp guards must have used. In the morning light, the clawed remnant of one sleeping bag was easy to find.

"No blood," Wade stated.

"Nope, our boy made a mistake. A presumption."

Wade looked around and back in the direction of the pit.

"It had been here before," he realised out loud. "He expected the guards to be there."

Cordell nodded, approvingly.

"My guess is that he spooked them, and they were a little less inclined to get under the covers."

"Why was it interested in the pit?" Wade asked.

"I try not to presume anything," Cordell shrugged. "That said, I honestly think it pissed it off. Some of the Indians, and a lot more of the hippy folk, like to think of them as protectors of the forest. I think that ain't worth spit. I think they plain just don't like us, and their tolerance is pretty low to start. Something like this is just an excuse to ramp things up to eleven.".

Wade nodded. It made sense enough, and he had to presume Jones knew what he was talking about. They made their way back to the camp, where the others were waiting for them.

"Report, Jackson," Cordell commanded.

"Looks like a family group came in from the East," one of the presumed Rangers replied. "They seem to have kept their distance. We lost their trail about half a click out."

"Yeah, they're not the ones I'm worried about," Cordell sighed. "At least not yet, that is," he added. "But you can be assured our boy has their attention, maybe deliberately so. That might just put them shit out of luck. Baker?"

The Alabama redhead looked around. "Our distinguished guest was continuing to head West when we lost his trail, also about half a click out," he replied.

Cordell took out a map from the side pocket of his tactical vest and studied it. To the west there was nothing but forest until further out, it reached private property. He'd scoped it out, knowing a reclusive, and very wealthy author lived there. The highly detailed, military 1:25,000 topographic map showed him a series of canyons and ravines that ran west towards the property. It offered cover, hidey holes, and a few escape routes along the way. But once past those, it had to keep heading west, if it wanted out. The plan was simple. Plug the exits. Corral the target. Put it down.

They all looked up as the Sikorsky thumped its way over a low brow of a hill to the North, making its way over the treetops towards them fast. When it reached them, it banked into a slow, pirouetting turn. Amos Dugas smiled and waved at Wade from the open side door.

"Right, now the humanitarian mission is done, it's time for the real deal," Cordell yelled. "Back to base, then game faces on."

CHAPTER FOURTEEN

AMBUSH

As the light began to fade, Wade could feel the usual build-up of excitement and tension in the team. Everyone was busy. The two pilots of the Sikorsky checked over the aircraft in every detail, whilst the aerial gunner cleaned and attended to the M134 minigun. The soldiers in turn were checking their own weapons and equipment. Parker and Jackson, who Wade presumed to be Army Rangers, carried M4 rifles with holographic reflex sites, a foregrip, and tactical lights added to the standard frame. Baker, the Alabama boy, carried a more standard looking M4 Carbine like Wade, but his partner, Campbell, was equipped with an M249 light machine gun. If there had been any doubt about the Special Forces potential of Hicks and Dixon, it was confirmed by their weapons. Hicks, the cocky one, carried a HK416 Carbine assault rifle, with a shorter barrel, an upgraded scope, and grenade launcher attachment. Dixon, he almost felt sorry for, with the 29lb MK 15 sniper rifle on his back, and an additional HK MP7 submachine gun for good measure.

Wade looked round as Dugas made his way over. Base, for now, was a campsite with cabins that the Forest Service had relinquished for them. What it lacked in the normal base facilities, it made up for with tourist-friendly beds, bathrooms, and more personal space than a military bunkhouse would ever have. The soldiers had kept themselves operation ready by checking and cleaning their gear and weapons, and building a significant fire in the centre of camp. When that was done, they'd set up a series of portable stoves on a cabin porch and fed themselves M.R.Es – 'Meals, Ready to Eat'. Chicken noodles with cornbread, crackers with cheese spread, M&Ms, and snickers bars. Not the worst by any means, but not exactly last meal candidates. He wondered how the operation was going to play out. As Dugas drew close, he noticed he had swapped out his M4 rifle for an M870 shotgun. They both had their Beretta M9 pistols too. The show of force, just in the chosen weaponry, suggested they were going up against a serious threat.

Dugas smiled at Wade and was about to say something when Agent Cordell Jones made his way from a cabin to the fire raging at the centre of camp, carrying a large supply box. The soldiers moved in on him as one, as he lifted the lid of the box, taking out what Wade recognised as a rifle laser attachment. It would fit any of the accessory rails of their assorted weaponry.

"Blue tracer lights," Cordell explained, handing out the devices, which were about the size of a mini-Maglite. "You'll only be able to see it in mist or when reflecting directly off a surface, but our hairy friends see it just fine, and they'll come a running."

Wade attached the optic to his rifle, as did the others.

"We'll be dropping you in, but here's where you'll be at," Cordell continued, taking a map from his back pocket, and folding it out. "Hicks, Dixon – if all goes to plan, you'll be shooting down range from the choke point formed at the top of this ravine," he pointed. "Parker, Jackson, you'll be covering this branching trackway to the south. Baker, Campbell, same goes for you with this one to the East.

Garric, Dugas – you'll be our point men. You'll set up a campfire, let off some rounds, make some noise."

"Bait, in other words," Wade offered.

"Actually, the hope is our boy will avoid you like the plague and move off. We've left something in the ravine to get his attention too. But, yep, he may take a liking to you and come your way."

"It's alright sweetheart, us big boys will come to your rescue," Hicks scoffed.

"That's two strikes Hicks, wanna make it a full house?" Cordell snapped. "Not everyone here pissed their pants first time they saw one of these things, now did they?".

Hicks stiffened but shut his mouth. Wade was impressed. Cordell clearly had the authority he claimed.

"Gear up. Collect the rest of your equipment from the Command Centre. Wheels up in ten," Cordell ordered.

The men headed for the deserted camp's reception office, currently acting as the Command Centre. Special Agent Smith was already there, speaking into a headset. He looked up as the soldiers filed into the front of the building. He pointed to the row of helmets equipped with night vision goggles laid out on the front desk. Wade waited his turn and picked his up.

"New toys," Amos laughed from behind, raising an eyebrow.

As the Sikorsky dusted off, each of the soldiers donned a headset. The flight wouldn't take long, but if anyone did want to talk, they could. A dull, dark red light flicked on in the cabin, signifying they were flying in stealth mode. The engines were using fewer rotations and less power, meaning they could drop out of the sky should anything go wrong –

like it had when they took out Bin Laden. That helicopter had been a prototype, but like that one, this one featured smaller, enclosed tail rotors to reduce noise. None of this passed Wade by as he glanced down again at the night goggles. They looked new and felt expensive. The operation was well funded.

"Know how to use those?" the tall blonde soldier named Parker asked.

Wade nodded. "Ranger, right?" he queried.

Parker nodded. "Most of the time, at least. You're based at Skookum right now?"

Wade nodded.

"Know why it's called that?" Hicks chimed in.

The other soldiers turned in his direction. He held the microphone of his headset to minimise the background noise.

"It's a Chinook word meaning monstrous, or powerful. These days, it's used almost exclusively in reference to those things. Especially when it comes to that base. It's a local name for them," Hicks explained.

"Where I'm from, they call these things the grassman," Parker added.

"Boogers in my part of town," Baker, the Alabama soldier chimed in. "Uglier, meaner, and a little shorter and spryer than the big fellows up this way."

"You've all come up against these things before?" Wade asked.

Parker nodded again. "Afghanistan. Our unit got taken out by one," he replied, nodding at Jackson. Four Rangers, armed, experienced in combat. It went through them like a knife through butter. They got enough rounds into it to slow it down so we could finish the job."

Wade stared. "You're saying there's more than one kind, and they're not just found here?" he asked.

"Anyone here been up against a Gugwe?" Dixon, Hicks' partner countered. He looked at Wade. "It's how Hicks and I got into this. One attacked our squad. We were on a war games exercise with the Canadian army. We were operating in the Saguenay Fjords National Park. Looked like the biggest, meanest baboon you ever saw. Huge fangs, muzzle – and so fast. Killed the other two members of our team and gutted one of the Canadians before they got us out. I'll never fire blanks again."

"Not what the girls say," Hicks smiled.

The rest of the team laughed.

"The civvies say there's four types," Hicks explained. "The Gugwe – what we saw, tends to be found in the North and East. Down south, they are more wiry and shorter – like a fucked-up chimp on steroids. The ones up here are the biggest and broadest of them all. In the Eastern states, they don't look too dissimilar, but again they're a little shorter and seem more humanlike in the face. Most of them avoid us, but if you're in the wrong place at the wrong time, they will not hesitate to take us down. Some, like the Gugwe, are hyper aggressive."

"I figure they're a little like us," Dixon added, "some are just assholes," he nodded towards Hicks.

Again, the other members of the team laughed, and Wade noticed how they all seemed more relaxed. His instincts had served him right as to starting up a conversation.

An amber light started flashing in the cabin and they all

stopped and began to check their gear. As the helicopter descended into a small clearing, Dixon and Hicks returned their headsets to the rail on the cabin wall. They were being dropped first, with the rest of the team following in reverse order. That meant Wade and Dugas were last. But that wasn't it for the helicopter. Once the soldiers were in place, the gunner was to drop primate scent lures over the area, to draw the creature in. The tracks and Agent Jones' instincts told them it was already here, but it wasn't known for sure. If the pilots caught it on infrared or in the spotlight, the gunner would try to take it down or direct it towards the soldiers. The rest of the team disembarked with knowing nods, and soon enough, the Sikorsky began to descend towards the ground at Wade and Dugas' drop off point. It was a trail head that led deeper into the forest. Wade was impressed with the pilot's skill and guessed, like the rest of the team, they were the best available. He'd picked out small gaps in the forest canopy, or in this case, a small, exposed rise. Hovering a few feet off the ground, surrounded by trees, even now the helicopter was relatively quiet. Wade and Dugas jumped and watched as their ride disappeared back into the night.

"Well, let's do like the man said, and get all cosy and comfy like," Dugas grinned. "Hope you brought the marshmallows."

Wade busied himself collecting firewood. Muscle memory did all the work as he watched the surrounding trees. He strained his hearing, willing himself to pick out the sound of something large moving through the forest, but he couldn't detect anything out of the ordinary. He circled back, and he and Amos spent some time splitting the smaller pieces into kindling. Dugas lit the fire with waterproof matches and kerosene from his pack. They stood by the fire and talked in fits and bursts, keeping their voices low and their eyes on the treeline.

~

Shartale placed his feet heavily on the ground. He stood, secreting his odour liberally and allowing the wind to take it. He knew the two males would pick up on it if nearby, and he had gone to a lot of trouble to get their attention. The trail he had laid was thick, yet not so deliberate to be obvious. He travelled some distance through the trees, this time stepping lightly, silently, and upwind. He froze and crouched, picking up a buzzing sound in the distance. He recognised the tools of man, just as he recognised his favourite stones. He remembered dropping one and it splitting as it hit the ground. It broke along the grain of the rock, revealing a defined, sharp edge. Since then, he had sought out similar rocks of the same kind, sharpening and shaping them against each other. He often stashed them in piles, in the territories he stayed in for longer. In this forest, the rocks were common, and finding one was easy when he needed to. Although they were ideal for delivering a crushing blow in ambush, up close, he relied on his brute strength.

He moved off through the trees again, only to pause as the wind changed. The others were in the forest, and he was sure they were on his trail now. He let out a grunt as he dropped to all fours and quickened his pace. As he made his way through the dark, he could trace the chemical taint – something almost certainly left by the humans. It did enough to excite him and interest him, but he was experienced and intelligent enough to distinguish it from something more natural. He stopped again, calculating his next move. Whereas the alpha would know, as he did, that the scent was a trap, he doubted the younger male would be so controlled. He began to sweep closer to the scent trail, hoping the others would follow.

~

Adotey caught the glance of his son, Cona, and lifted his head, signalling he should bank right. The young male grunted and obediently changed direction. They were moving quickly but carefully on all fours. Closer together, the two females followed – Katshar, Adotey's mate, and Fala, their daughter. The females could sense the agitation of the males; it showed in their quickened pace and their purposeful patrol through the forest. They were on the hunt, but not for food. They intended to face the intruder.

Without slowing their pace, the group began to climb a gently sloped ridgeline. They knew it gave way to a series of hollows and game trails on the other side, but it would also give them a good viewpoint of the surrounding area. Its highest point faced directly into the wind, and they intended to know the exact location of the intruder before they closed in. For now, he was frustratingly distant, at the edge of their senses. They knew he was in the area, but he was showing more caution than before. The trail had to be checked and validated regularly to make sure they hadn't gone astray. Adotey glanced again at Cona. The young male stood still as a statue, his face grimacing as his muscles tensed. He was on guard and agitated. The bond with his sister was deep and he knew why the interloper was in their territory. Just as he had, Fala had come into her adulthood. Adotey growled a warning. Almost hidden in the guttural sound was the command "lah", which meant calm. Cona didn't respond and continued looking out into the forest.

They were just about to turn away, when Cona snorted and rose onto his legs to his full height. He pushed his nose out into the wind and let his jaw drop, pushing the scent into the roof of his mouth for maximum effect. He sprang from the ridgeline, crashing into the branches of a Sitka spruce below. Limbs snapped with a resounding crack as he made his way to the ground. Adotey filled his lungs, ready to unleash a roar of disapproval, when Katshar clicked her tongue at him. He paused, looking in her direction, then he cocked his head. He could hear the faint, distant noises too. Adotey, Katshar, and Fala turned as one and began to traverse the ridgeline silently and swiftly. All the while, Adotey glanced out into the forest, picking up the scent that had pulled Cona away from them.

~

Shartale had stumbled upon the two humans by pure accident. His intention to loop away from the family and keep a distant tab on them had led him south. The humans were both male and directly ahead of him. Completely silent, they barely moved. In cover, they lay on the ground facing away from him and downwind. He was confident they did not know he was there. Shartale could smell the oil and grease on the metal objects they carried – and he knew the harm they could do. He had not moved since one of the men had stirred, crawling slightly forward. If the man had not done so, Shartale have likely given his position away, walking too close to them. But now aware of their presence, it gave him a temporary advantage. The others wouldn't dare approach him if they too picked up on the human's presence, if they successfully followed his scent this far as intended. However, he also couldn't allow the men to remain in his path or continue to be a threat.

Shartale slowly and silently reached up with one arm and lifted himself into the overhanging branches of the western juniper tree behind him. Its bulky trunk hid his form well, and its thick, strong, yet spongey branches were able to hold his mass without creaking or breaking. The spindly, evergreen leaves cushioned the sound of his movement even further as he moved higher into the tree and then further forward. He paused, happy with the distance and viewpoint he had, then launched himself into the air.

~

Parker turned his head slowly to Jackson, about to ask if he'd heard something, but it was too late. All Parker saw was a disproportionate, elongated, hairy foot come down on Jackson's neck with just enough force to break it. Before he could roll onto his back and level his weapon, Parker felt a huge pressure in the small of his back as thick, greasy fingers the size of sausages, wrapped around his throat with ease and crushed his larynx. He heard the crack of his own neck before everything went black.

~

Shartale pushed the bodies of the two men together. This meant they would stay warmer for longer, disguising any hint of death from the family, should they approach this way. By killing them without significant damage or drawing blood, the bodies would look relatively untouched and wouldn't rouse the suspicions of the others. Like his, their sense of smell was highly sensitive to blood. His own clan had hunted deer in this way, ambushing them and snapping their necks with their hands. It kept the meat fresher for longer and meant they could dismember the animals with ease and at their leisure. Prey that didn't fight back had many advantages. But Shartale had his reasons to hate and hunt the humans.

Shartale was a natural hunter, and as with most of his kind, his instincts and senses were sharpest at night. It was especially so for alphas, and his very size made Shartale an alpha. But he had grown up in a large clan of three families and there had been a hierarchy. The older males in his family, and the others, were the hunters. In return, Shartale was made a sentinel guard. It was a position of privilege and came with significant responsibility, and he was often presented with prized food and objects in thanks. But the role wasn't one suited to Shartale. He often grew tired during the day whilst the others slept, and he grew irritable and bored watching and patrolling the borders of the territory. His muscles ached and groaned at not being able to run down prey. The clan was so large that it rarely encountered threats in the form of more of their kind. However, his ingrained hatred of canines meant he hunted down and killed any wolf or coyote pack that dared to enter the territory. But these moments were few and far between, and soon, all the local packs had learned to give the regions he patrolled a wide berth.

The larger, brown-coloured bears were also given no quarter. They were opportunists and would take the clan's young if they had the chance. Of the big cats, he was more tolerant. They preyed on the smaller deer and did not compete directly with the clan for food. He also encountered them less across the territory and they seemed to instinctively recognise his kind as alpha predators, rather than challenge their standing as the other carnivores did.

It was when the sun was high and the air at its warmest that Shartale found it hardest to be vigilant. The day he'd first encountered humans had been like that. He remembered feeling hot and agitated. Nothing had disturbed his vigil from the ridgeline, meaning he had no reason to move or stretch his complaining limbs. Then he'd heard them, off in the distance. Not wolves or coyotes, but dogs. He knew of dogs. He'd seen them at human encampments but had never encountered them – having always kept his distance, as he had learned from the elders. They had never come into the clan's territory before.

Shartale had moved off, quickly closing in on them, just as he would with their wild kindred. Each stride took him further from his position, where he watched over the grass nests of the others in the meadow below. They had killed several elk the night before and were sleeping heavily. Although a wariness of humans had been effectively communicated to him by the others, he had no reason to think of them as a direct threat. And he had not yet learned the presence of dogs in the forest meant humans too were nearby.

The dogs were easy to find. They were loud and excitable. As he drew near, they showed little of the ferocity of their wild cousins, cowering, and whimpering when cornered. He dispatched them with ease, snapping their spines or crushing their heads with devastating speed and strength. His many hunts and patrols had honed his skills. It was as he drew close to the final dog that the shots had rung out, thunder cracks of sound that ricocheted across the valley from the direction of the meadow. For the first time in his life, Shartale had felt fear and dread.

He had raced through the undergrowth, back towards the meadow. His body was a machine as muscle and instinct guided him. He had never run so fast before or since, an unstoppable force. He could smell the blood of his kin in the air as he approached. Fear turned to rage as he burst from the trees. He had ignored the bloodied, brown bodies and instead had focused on the group of four humans that had gathered around them. It was clear he had taken them by surprise. They didn't have time to raise their weapons as he reached out for them, his arms engulfing them in a murderous embrace as he leapt. Three of them had died almost instantly. He lodged his fangs in the skull of the man directly underneath him. Another, he crushed the life from as he squeezed his fingers around the man's neck. With his other hand, his claws had gutted the man knocked aside by the initial charge. That left one more.

The man was pinned beneath him and unable to move. Shartale raised himself up with one arm, releasing the grip he had on the dead man's throat. Shartale had looked directly into the remaining man's eyes and had seen the fear there. It had been the moment he realised that humans weren't a threat in terms of strength, size, teeth, or claws. Shartale caught the movement in his peripheral vision as the man went for the metal object tucked into the coverings around his waist. It was smaller, but Shartale recognised it as "vahk" – objects of thunder that his kind had grown to fear, like the long sticks the humans carried. The adrenaline surging through the human's body made him reek, but it also made his movements clumsy and slow. His hand shook as he tried to yank the vahk loose. Shartale knocked it from the man's hand with ease. Still bent over the man, with one hand on the floor, Shartale hooked the man with his free hand and claws through the soft patch of skin beneath the jaw. Blood spewed from the man's mouth as he garbled and gurgled. He tightened the tendons in his fingers and two claws burst from the man's mouth. Shartale rose to his feet, lifting the man with him. He grunted, wrinkling his nose in disgust as he observed how powerless the man was. With the simplest effort, he ripped the man's jaw from his face and let him fall to the ground. The man crawled on his belly, whimpering and in shock. Shartale's foot found the base of the man's spine and he began to push down gently yet relentlessly. He didn't stop until he had heard the bones begin to splinter. Shartale was a natural killer. He had learnt the weak spots of all his prey and every enemy. And from then on, he had always viewed humans as both. He sat in wait, knowing both the humans and the others would come to him.

~

As the family pursued Cona through the trees and brush, Adotey felt the fear and anxiety building in his chest. Both the females were secreting strong, drifting wafts of scent from glands underneath their armpits, to try and counter the effect of the aroma enticing Cona to ignore all danger, but it was to no avail. Adotey slowly felt the small amount of control he had over his son ebbing away faster with each quickening stride. He looked behind at his mate. Her wide-eyed expression mirrored his own and spurred him on to risk things further. He leapt high at full speed, throwing his arms wide and above his head, losing no momentum as he brought his fists and feet to the ground. He came to a complete standstill, decelerating in an instant. The effect was like a cannonball, the explosion of sound echoing out into the night. It was drowned out by the savage, possessing roar that erupted from Adotey's throat. Then, almost imperceptible, a low, menacing growl eclipsed it and began to grow in strength. The very air seemed to vibrate as it resonated through the forest.

A moment later, Cona stopped dead in his tracks. He spun around, shaking his head as he swayed to and fro, suddenly unsteady on his feet. He grunted, as if hurt, but what he felt was betrayed – a new sensation and emotion for him. In their language it was called "sharkaah", or the dark voice. It was a vocal weapon, used to stun and disorientate their prey. And although it was not forbidden for use against each other, it was considered disrespectful. Doing so often meant an open, confident challenge – one where no peace was sought or wanted. In this case, his father had sent a message out into the forest that his son was not worthy of respect and was a challenge not to be taken seriously. Cona knew that no female would pay him interest now. Which is why he was confused when the strong, pheromone-laced scent continued to come to him from up ahead. In fact, it was stronger now than ever. Closer. But having stopped, his intellect had time to override his biology. The chemical traces were too pungent and somehow off. He now understood the actions of his father and turned his head to acknowledge his blunder. That was when the scent of the two humans reached him. He rose to his full height and turned in the direction he knew they were approaching from. As his father reached his side, they both let out a warning growl. Hidden within Cona's was a mournful wail that told his father he recognised the trap he'd led them into.

~

Baker flinched at the sound of the growl and immediately raised his rifle. Campbell already had the light machine gun up, as he found it easier to carry with the stock resting on his belt. Both acted at the same time, reaching along the tactical mounts to turn on the blue tracer lights. Baker also pulled the night vision goggles down from his helmet and rested them over his eyes as he flicked them on. The world around him burst into view as a myriad of sharp, contrasting hot white and duller greys. He slowly panned from left to right, looking for what he knew was out there. The pheromones had been placed throughout the hollow and upwind. But the growl had taken him aback – the creature was much closer than he had thought possible.

In his first sweep, he missed them. But during his second, he noticed the faint, ghostly glow of the two creatures. He let out a gasp of surprise when he realised, they were, in fact, standing behind two much larger creatures. Then animals he was more used to – boogers as he called them, were much leaner and wirier than what stood ahead of him. Most of the boogers he had come up against were not much over six feet, although he knew they could get bigger. But these things were nearly twice the size and easily twice the breadth. Baker knew that many people, including some of his commanding officers, took him for a simple, uneducated, albeit somewhat cocky redneck. He knew part of that was the national – even international prejudice, that seemed to come with a southern accent. Especially if you were Cajun. But he was well read and had joined the army from college.

He'd done his homework on the creatures too. He knew they had the ability to partially cloak their thermal signature and that their thick hair also naturally absorbed heat – but this was the first time he'd seen it. The two larger creatures to the front were barely visible, even now. Just an outline against the dark. The two smaller creatures behind were still hot from moving and easier to see. He could make out their facial features – the broad, simian-like nose, the heavyset brow ridge, the broad mouth flanked by tight, narrow, indented cheeks. And the eyes – seemingly unnaturally too far apart. Through the thermal, they appeared as dark, empty pits. That were looking straight at him. It was unnerving. The animals knew he and Campbell were there, that wasn't so out of the ordinary. But how, in the dark, and at such a distance – nearly five hundred yards, could they seemingly be looking straight into his eyes.

"You see 'em," Baker whispered.

"Yep," Campbell replied, having turned on his own goggles. "Let's see if these lasers are worth a damn."

Baker and Campbell switched the blue tracer lights to a fast pulse setting as they'd been shown. The impact was immediate. There was a startled whoop, followed by a high-pitched, frenzied scream that made Baker want to cover his ears. Baker stared down the barrel of his gun, which appeared black against the landscape, painted grey by the goggles. He wondered what it could be about the lasers that aggravated the animals so much. He watched the creatures examine each other with apparent alarm, looking at each other's faces closely and then snapping their heads back down towards his and Campbell's position. Then he saw it. He noticed the eyes now reflected bright and white in the goggles. Curious, he lifted the goggles from his face. The fact that the creatures were somehow drawn to the laser light was undeniable, as he could see their eye shine following the beam from Campbell's gun. It reminded him of his girlfriend's kitten, who would sometimes try to catch the spot of sunlight reflected off his watch. A simple flick of the wrist could send the cat scurrying from one side of the room to the other. But it was more than that. For now, even without the goggles, he could see four sets of red, seemingly glowing eyes in the dark. He now understood their unease. Something in the blue tracers made their eyes react, making these unseen, apex predators visible in the dark. Watching them, he knew it was more than eye shine and mere reflected light. Something biological or chemical was going on in there. And the creatures didn't like it.

As if to confirm his thoughts, a more savage and aggressive roar pierced the night air, followed by total silence. This was something he'd experienced before. He couldn't hear the animal coming at them, but he could feel it. Strong, distinct impact tremors that increased in strength and frequency, rippling through the ground towards them. It was another thing that made no sense – how an animal that could take on a grizzly could move so silently. As he went to flip the goggles back down, Campbell let rip with the light machine gun. The allegretto rhythmic pulse of the ammunition let Baker know the gun was set to rapid, sustained fire – sending out a restrained 200 rounds per minute, compared to the 1,150 rounds per minute it was capable of with the right settings and ammo. But as it was, it enabled Campbell to keep the 5.56 NATO cartridges on target and with minimal spread. Baker raised his own rifle and sought out a target.

He was just in time to see the creatures split up and enter the treeline. The largest, although moving fast, had a distinct limp.

"Think you clipped the big boy," Baker said, placing a hand on Campbell's shoulder.

"Time to move," Campbell replied. "Let's get them to the party."

Baker and Campbell moved fast, in fits and bursts, each covering the other as they made their way back along the trail.

"Calling all interested parties," Baker said, touching his earpiece. "Bringing four tangos from the rear to the rendezvous, over."

"Receiving," came Hicks' cool, collected response. "Reception's ready and waiting. Bring them on in."

~

"Hey," Dugas cackled as he turned towards Wade. "Didn't Jones say those weren't the ones we needed to be worried about?"

"I think you'll find his exact words were 'not yet'. I imagine that's changing, right about now," Wade replied.

"Wanna move up the trail and get a look-see?" Dugas suggested. "They should go right past that opening up yonder."

Wade followed Dugas's nod towards where they had turned down the trail. It was a good six hundred yards from their position. He shook his head.

"Too far off point, we stay here until we're told otherwise," Wade explained.

Dugas smiled ruefully, then turned his back towards the

fire.

"We already had our fun back on base," Wade added. "Let someone else get some tonight."

~

Baker and Campbell maintained their pace and vigilance as they moved forward, all the while knowing they were being flanked by the creatures as they slipped from tree to tree, disappearing into the darkness beyond. Baker could feel his heart thumping in his chest. He was amazed at their intelligence as they seemingly tested the boundaries of both the lasers and the night vision goggles. The creatures reacted instantly with every turn of his or Campbell's head, leaving him in no doubt they could see them both just fine. And now aware of their eye shine, they deliberately stayed at a distance and rarely looked directly at the soldiers. Only the guttural, threatening whoops and growls gave them away. Again, Baker noticed how different they were to the animals he knew as boogers, which made more chattering, chimpanzee-like calls. These things, on the other hand, reminded him of the gorilla soldiers from science fiction movies he'd watched. He knew they were trying to intimidate him and Campbell, hoping they'd make a mistake – like wolves hunting down deer. It had been a long time since he'd felt hunted, and he didn't like it.

He was certain Campbell had wounded the one that was limping. The creatures moved so fast, he hadn't been surprised that perhaps only a few rounds had found their target, even from the machine gun. The two soldiers were moving at their maximum speed with weapons and a light pack, but Baker guessed it was no more than a light jog for these things. Even if one was wounded, it hadn't retreated or panicked like other animals might have. Instead, it had the intelligence and patience to adapt a plan of attack and form a counter strike that gave them the upper hand. It was another thing that unnerved him and differentiated them from the rest of the natural world, as far as he was concerned.

Baker took point, switching past Campbell with a blistering stride. He'd always been fast. Campbell was beginning to show signs of struggling to keep up. He gave his partner a quick glance to check he was okay, and to show he was about to slow the pace a little. Campbell caught the movement of Baker's head and cocked his head with a smile. Taking the focus from his feet for a mere second was all it took to unbalance him, and Campbell tripped, face planting into the ground and even sliding a little way, like he'd just made third base in time. The heavy machine gun went down barrel first into the trackway, the secondary carry handle scraping along Campbell's forearm viciously enough to open a nasty gash. Ever the professional soldier, Campbell ignored it, and began to pick himself up, with an acknowledging smile.

The trees and scrub behind Campbell exploded. A vast, black form streaked across the trail, a monstrous arm reaching out for the soldier and connecting. The next moment, Campbell was flying. His momentum was violently halted as his back struck the sprawling trunk of an elderly oak across the trail. He flopped to the ground, lifeless. As soon as Campbell had gone down, Baker had raised his one weapon, but even he had been unprepared for the creature's speed. Baker squeezed the trigger of the M4 Carbine, which spewed out the same rounds as Campbell's machine gun. Baker saw a puff of red mist spray from the very edge of one of the buttocks as the creature turned. Even this close, he'd barely clipped him. The growl that hit him in his chest seemed to play out in slow motion, whilst the creature moved as if sped up. He was struck violently across the face in a downward swipe, by what he didn't know – but it drove him to the forest floor with little resistance. He fought for breath, wheezing hard as he struggled to take in air. As he blinked, he watched the hulking shadow take form as it towered above him. Baker closed his eyes.

When he opened them again, the creature was gone. He'd heard nothing as it departed. What had made him open his eyes was the groan emitted by Campbell. Baker found his feet, still wheezing. He stumbled over to his partner and knelt beside him.

"Think you can make it?" he asked.

"Just get me up," Campbell pleaded.

Baker stuck his arm underneath Campbell and hauled him upwards. Both let out a short gasp of pain that came with the exertion. Baker placed Campbell back against the tree, albeit standing this time. He unclipped the torch from his rifle's tactical rail and switched it on, intent on giving Campbell a once over. His helmet was missing, and he now had a nasty gash on the back of his head to match the one on his arm.

"Take a deep breath for me," Baker instructed.

"No need, I can tell you my ribs are busted just fine," Campbell wheezed. "I can't stand up straight. But it only hurts when I breathe, talk, or do anything at all."

"Lucky you're a lazy S.O.B most of the time I guess," Baker quipped.

"You ain't looking so suave yourself," Campbell nodded. "Your mouth looks busted up pretty bad."

Baker hadn't noticed, but he could taste the blood. His shoulder felt sore and stiff too. He guessed Campbell had all manner of torn ligaments and contusions he couldn't see, just to add to the mix. He looked around into the darkness of the trees. He realised his helmet and night vision goggles had also been knocked from his head, and he began to look for them with the torch. They were a few feet away. As he went to reach down for them, a menacing growl of warning sounded out. Baker spun around. It had seemed to have come from right behind him.

"Let's just walk down the trail, nice and easy like," Baker whispered.

Campbell nodded in reply. Baker moved to his side, supporting his partner as they began to take slow, laboured steps back along the trail. They both took fervent glances into the trees on either side as they went. Every thirty or forty yards, a deliberate twig break, or perhaps a raspy intake of breath would let them know that they had not lost their pursuers.

"Guess they like Cajun food, huh?" Baker half laughed.

Campbell shook his head.

"Thought you did your research. They ain't hunting. This is territorial," Campbell wheezed. "We're being escorted off the premises."

Baker nodded in understanding. "Then let's hope they're too busy with us to notice the reception up ahead."

The crackle in his ear made Baker cock his head to the left.

"Got you boys on the drone's thermal," came Agent

Jones' gruff voice. "Keep going. Hicks and Dixon are up ahead. You're leading them straight in. Do me a favour though?"

"What's that, sir?" Baker replied.

"Don't look behind you," Jones said stoically.

Baker could tell he wasn't joking.

"Shit," spat Campbell.

"How close, sir?" Baker asked.

"Close enough for you to be going steady," growled Jones. "Just keep going like nothing happened."

Baker and Campbell continued up the trail, supporting each other as they went. Each step was taken with care to prevent another fall. And both were tensed, ready for the next charge from the creatures flanking them, or the crackle in their ear mics that would signal them to drop to the forest floor. It was the latter that came first.

"Hit the deck", came the simple command from Hicks.

Their actions weren't as immediate or as well executed given their injuries, but it was quick enough. Both soldiers closed their eyes and controlled their breathing, playing dead as they had been told in their individual briefings.

~

Uphill and upwind, sprawled on a ledge some 900 yards further up the trail, Hicks looked through the rifle scope attached to the MK 15 sniper rifle and waited for Dixon to confirm. They'd spent some time observing the area and picking out their spot. It gave them an unobstructed perspective down range – nearly 1,300 yards along the trail in all. They had split their field of view in two, establishing two sectors right to left. These sectors were then sectioned into inner fields, front and back, nominated alpha and bravo respectively. In short, this gave them four areas to narrow down a target in. They'd then spent some time identifying landmarks and other key features of the landscape to help them zone in on their quarry, wherever it was within the 52,000 square yards between them. Dixon was equipped with a FLIR Recon V thermal binocular, whilst Hicks relied on a FLIR MilSight S140-D thermal weapon sight, sitting forward of his rifle's standard scope. Dixon had the wider field of view and would instruct Hicks where to look.

"Go to glass. Target is two bravo, seventy yards and closing on VIPs," his partner whispered.

The communication signalled that Dixon had spotted the target in the rear of the right-hand sector, and that Hicks should be looking down his scope. Hicks moved the rifle ever so slightly in that direction and complied.

"Contact," Hicks confirmed. "Target has now stopped moving and is fifty yards from VIPs."

"Confirmed," Dixon replied. "Check parallax and mil."

Hicks crisped up the image in his scope by threading the rifle's parallax knob a few notches. He then canted the scope, placing his reticule at the top of the target.

"1.13," Hicks replied, confirming the mil.

"Affirmative, check level and hold over."

Hicks made a mental note that he hadn't over-canted the scope and he was looking straight through from a level position. He started to let out his breath slowly and took up the slack on the trigger.

"Left, point two," Hicks added, letting him know there was little or no windage to worry about.

Hicks squeezed the trigger. The crack of thunder announced that the 50. BRM cartridge had erupted from the barrel and was about to hit its target. At 900 yards per second, it would take less than two heartbeats to get there. Which is why Hicks was shocked to watch the creature turn. He missed. At least at first. The creature he had been trained on – the largest – had somehow sensed the incoming shot and turned away in an instant. But the animal behind him had not been so lucky.

Both the soldiers watched the bullet strike the creature in the throat. Dixon had the better view through his larger scope. He tensed. As the animal went down onto its knees, it placed one hand on the ground as it held the other up to its wound. It looked incredibly human-like. Its biological defences kicked in, and its heat signature quickly began to fade from view. For the two larger creatures to the front, it was the opposite. They began to glow brighter. The other sasquatch surrounded the injured one. Frantic, screeching chattering sounds erupted into the night air.

"Shit," Hicks uttered, his eyes wide, yet staying on target. "How the fuck did it do that? It's like it knew."

"If that's a female... and I think it was, playing dead ain't gonna cut it for our boys," Dixon replied. "Campbell, Baker, this is Dixon," he said, touching his earpiece. "Evac now, double time. Mission is Charlie foxtrot."

"Clusterfuck. You can say that again," Hicks swore under his breath.

~

Adotey looked at Katshar as blood filled the space between her fingers. She gripped her throat tightly and wouldn't let go. Her daughter, Fala, sat crouched beside her, swaying back and forth as she supported her weight on her knuckles. She made cooing noises of support, but her eyes flashed in panic to her father and brother. Adotey stood over his mate, taking deep gasps of air as he watched over her. For a moment, their eyes met, then hers rolled into the back of her head and her hand fell away from her throat. Her last breath was ragged and gargled through the bloody gaping hole in her airway. Adotey raised his hand, as if reaching out for her, to entice her to stay. His eyes snapped to Cona. Already injured, and with his mate dead, he could not risk facing the humans again out in the open, and he was worried that with Cona's blood already up, he would not be persuaded to retreat. But the roar he was expecting came from Fala, who launched forward, her mouth agape and her teeth bared as she barrelled towards where the humans lay on the ground ahead of them.

One of her intended targets rolled onto its back and raised the metallic object they all knew to fear. A burst of light and deafening sound erupted from it, and Adotey's night-sensitive eyes were temporarily blinded. When his vision returned, his daughter lay on top of her attacker, panting for breath. As the other human began to turn towards Fala, raising a similar weapon, Adotey leapt. He ripped a branch from a tree and waved it in front of him, landing beside the man. He reached down and plucked the weapon from the attacker, crushing it in his hand and discarding it. He continued to swing the leafy branch back and forth, creating a visual barrier between his family and the other humans he now knew were further up the trail. He grunted a command to Cona, who obediently went over to his sister and picked her up in his arms. Adotey backed away until he reached Katshar, then he discarded the branch and picked up his mate. As he turned to his side, he met the gaze of the men with an open-mouthed grimace that revealed his four fangs and a stare that promised them death.

Adotey and Cona carried their burdens back through the trees to a fork in the trail. Cona looked at his father as Fala made soft moaning noises. As they changed direction, Adotey growled as he picked up the human scent again and saw the fire ahead of them. He turned, flanking the clearing up ahead and moving quicker now, hunched over, and cradling the body of his dead mate in his arms. Cona followed his father without question. He could smell both the blood from his wound and the powerful scent he was secreting. The alpha was preparing for a fight.

The humans did not appear to notice their flight, nor that their camp and fire was set up not far from a small inner lake. Each of them could smell the water and were drawn to it now. A slither of moonlight reflected off the snow-capped peaks to the north and illuminated the clear, turquoise waters a little way. Several trees had fallen close to the shore, their branches shed and scattered along the stony beach. Cona stopped and gently lowered his sister onto the soft clay that lined the upper bank. He sank down behind her, letting her back rest on his chest. He could feel her ragged breathing and the tremors that reverberated up her arms and along her shoulders. They both watched as their father laid their mother on the stones and placed a smooth, flat, bluish pebble in her mouth. He then lifted her in one fluid movement and waded out into the water. He didn't stop until it reached his shoulders. Cona squeezed his sister as he felt her heartbeat falter and she began to rock and squirm, half growling, half screaming as they both watched their mother disappear beneath the lake's surface. Then, Cona felt his sister slip away too, released from the pain of her wounds and what they had been forced to witness.

As Adotey turned, he watched Cona repeat the ritual and wade past him, carrying Fala. When she too had been committed to the lake, he and Cona lifted their heads and howled long and deeply. It was answered by a roar.

~

It was Shartale who let out the roar as his frustration got the better of him. He had watched the humans and the sasquatch as they sought each other out across the forest. Keeping to the trees, he had kept track of them all, by scent alone where necessary. Two of the humans, who hadn't moved far from a fire they'd built, hadn't been hard to find. The loud booms of a weapon carried by the humans had given away the location of two more, further into the forest. And he had intercepted and killed the pair he'd discovered to the south. But now, in a few short moments, his cunning had been undone by fate. The two male sasquatches lived, and the females had died. From the scent carried to him on the breeze, he knew his rival had been wounded. But his main reason for invading their territory in the first place had now been violently extinguished. His gaze lifted to the sky, where he could detect a small electromagnetic field of disturbance. With his head raised, he could now pick out the sound too. A low, quiet buzz. Something unnatural, and therefore human. He snarled at it in disgust and leapt from the tree, crashing to the ground with no attempt to hide his location or path of direction.

Immediately, the two male sasquatches were aware of his presence. He moved quickly but with purpose. It was clear to them that he wasn't heading directly for them. They therefore watched as he appeared out of the treeline and crossed the shoreline of the lake further up from them. It was another gamble. He was close enough now that he would be unable to evade them, and he risked their joint attack. But his roar had not been aimed at them and they knew it. He stopped, turning to face them for a mere moment. He let out a machine-gun-like rapport of chatter.

"Nahlzeei, da goo, nahookos, bee'l, eldoohk."

The larger of the two sasquatches smacked his left shoulder with his hand, in a gesture of understanding. Hunters, in pairs, hidden on rocks ahead. Shartale passed his hand over the back of his conical head, indicating they should look up. They did, finding the source of the sound as he had done. The smaller of the pair growled his dislike of Shartale's collaboration, but the larger one quieted him. Shartale curled back his lips, amused, but also revealing his fangs should they give in to their desire to attack.

"Aoe," the wounded one, commanded, meaning "no".

Then, moving as one, the three males turned and entered the forest, heading along separate lines of trajectory towards the same destination.

~

Jones watched the view screen of the drone as the sasquatch disappeared again. They were on the attack now, covering their trail and hiding their thermal signature. They would be difficult to trace via infrared for several minutes again now. He talked to the pilot of the Sikorsky on the radio and told him to turn around and head back. He had watched the operation play out from the viewer of the drone, a military-grade machine with advanced range – which the helicopter helped extend even further. But now the operation had gone south. Three male sasquatches were on the attack, and very little could stop that kind of force. Parker and Jackson were not responding, meaning Jones automatically assumed the worse. That left two men per sasquatch, and even armed as they were, those were odds he didn't like. Especially as Baker and Campbell were already compromised. There was also something about this rogue sasquatch that had presumably killed his men and others. It seemed to know their tactics, making Jones suspect it had encountered humans before. Maybe, it had even come up against a team like his before. He knew there'd been others. And nobody knew how long they lived. These things could have been squaring off against the likes of him for generations and nobody would know. There was no plan now. They just had to get in there and get their men out, before it was too late.

"Wade and Dugas first," Jones instructed the pilot over the radio. "Easier to land the bird on the trail. Hopefully, Baker and Campbell will have joined them by the time we get there. We'll advise Dixon and Hicks to relocate for an easier pick up once you're closer."

Jones watched on the drone's screen as the pilot banked the big Sikorsky hard and turned it back towards the inner forest. Jones tapped the follow button on the drone's controls. It obliged but showed signs of struggling to keep up with its much larger counterpart. It made a straight line for the aircraft as it continued to bank, then darted down towards the campfire below. Jones watched on the monitor as the helicopter landed, its open troop door facing down the trail and the aerial gunner positioned opposite, staring straight into the trees. As Jones scanned with the infrared, he was glad to see Baker and Campbell slowly making their way along the trail towards them.

"Move your butts," he yelled through the earpiece. "Wade, Dugas, that goes for you too."

Jones watched the men by the campfire get up and double time it towards the chopper. That's when he noticed the rotors were winding down. He turned back instantly and grabbed his mic.

"I didn't say shut down, damn it, you'll need to jump that LZ ASAP," Jones screamed with rage.

Moments later, Jones watched the reassuring whump of the blades getting back up to take off speed. That's when Wade and Dugas reached the open door. They hauled themselves in and turned around, waiting on Baker and Campbell. They were nearly there.

"On their six," the pilot yelled, pointing through the windshield.

Wade thrust his head out of the troop door and offered his hand to Dugas, who huffed as he threw the shotgun over his shoulder. Wade leaned out further, his other hand hovering over his pistol, still in its holster on his hip. He saw the movement of the trees as the large male sasquatch stepped out onto the trail just over two hundred yards down. It swayed back and forth, but Wade picked up on its imbalanced stance, favouring its left leg. This was the injured alpha from the family group.

Jones continued to watch through the drone's viewer screen. Up until now, the alpha and the family group hadn't been a target – or at least not their main target. But Jones knew that these animals more than held a grudge. They would neither forgive nor forget. With both the females killed in the crossfire, each of the males would now be considered a valid target. These were the ones that would eventually target humans, either as prey, or as an object to vent their wrath upon. He'd seen it happen before and it wasn't pretty. Even with the goggles, he knew the team would only be able to barely see the creature.

Wade was thinking the same thing, and about grabbing Dugas' gun and turning on the blue laser, but he had a feeling that the moment he turned his back, the creature would disappear again into the trees. That's when it occurred to him that was the whole idea. Just like sharks, it was the one you didn't see that got you. Wade spun on his heels, back towards the open door on the other side of the helicopter. The gunner, still poised over the M134 minigun, must have noticed the movement in his peripheral vision and turned.

Rookie error, Jones thought, his apprehension building.

As if on cue, something burst from the treeline opposite and barrelled towards the helicopter. With both the gunner and the gun in his way, Wade caught a momentary reflection of eyeshine, a blur of movement, and then a hairy arm and hand plucked the gunner from the open doorway. Wade and Dugas both turned and raised their weapons, but they were met with nothing but empty blackness. Then the gunner screamed, his absolute terror made abundant to them. It was cut off abruptly with a wet, cracking sound. Moments later, the gunner's head, still encased in its helmet, was propelled back through the open troop door. Blood and a few fragments of windpipe spilled out onto the cabin floor as it rolled across the metal plating. The eyes had rolled back into the head and the jaw fell open as it came to an ungainly halt on its side. The tongue flopped out grotesquely and unsupported, phlegm and foam still dripping from it.

The pilot took matters into his own hands and lifted off – straight up and fast, whilst Wade scrambled over towards the minigun. He let off a few bursts of unaimed fire into the brush, then turned back towards Dugas.

"Light em' up boy – you might not hit anything, but it'll deter them from trying to jump to us," he declared, turning his attention back to the minigun.

"They can do that?!" Dugas yelled, moving into position at the opposite door and raining fire down towards the brush. Wade was sure he saw a void in the darkness pass beneath them, then it was gone.

"Hicks, Dixon, get to LZ Charlie, lift off in sixty seconds," Jones commanded through their earpieces.

The helicopter climbed to just above the treetops and then banked steeply away over the canopy. Wade scanned for glimpses of the forest floor below. When the trail or a clearing did come into view, he couldn't be sure if the shadows passing across them were real or imagined now. He continued to let off short, erratic bursts of fire from the minigun, as Dugas did from the other side with his rifle. Suddenly, the nose of the aircraft rose steeply and the passengers inside the troop compartment instinctively reached for the netting and handholds in the upper parts of the cabin. It brought all gunfire to a temporary halt. Wade swore, as his loosely worn helmet fell from his head and disappeared into the darkness. Looking out, he saw they were climbing the escarpment where Hicks and Dickson should be waiting for them. Reaching the top, the pilot expertly pivoted the helicopter 180 degrees, bringing the open troop door round to face both the steep side of the escarpment that led down to the forest, and the flat piece of rock at the top.

Wade glanced left and saw two figures emerge from the treeline. He held his breath for a moment, then realised they were human. Hicks and Dickson jogged towards the hovering aircraft with their heads lowered. Wade could see Hicks was slowed by the weight of the big rifle he carried, but he was doing his best to keep up with Dickson, who was moving fast and reached the open door first. Wade threw out his arm to help him onboard, then did the same for Hicks. Just as the special forces operative manoeuvred towards the cabin, his feet on the aircraft's landing skids and one arm locked around Wade's, there was a small explosion and both men were peppered with what felt like BB pellets. Dust, like cement powder, hung in the air, and for a moment both men were confused at what had just happened. The helicopter groaned, and a shudder rippled along its metal hull.

"Something hit the rotors," the pilot yelled through the earpiece. "We're okay, but don't let it happen again."

Wade glanced at Hicks, who was looking down. His face was ashen. Wade followed his gaze. His jaw fell. There, at the bottom of the escarpment, two of the creatures stared up at them. Then one leapt into the air, its arms outstretched, and its body flattened. As its fists hit the rockface, its broad, flat feet smacked into the stone, propelling it upwards in muscular bounds. Wade noticed Hicks had clipped himself into the cabin of the helicopter and was leaning out of the open troop door. The MK15 sniper rifle pointing straight down. There was a flash of light, then a thunderous boom as the weapon fired. The scream from below was so loud, Wade heard it even above the noise of the helicopter's engines. He joined Hicks at the door and watched the large dark mass crash back down the rockface. The other had disappeared. For now.

"Don't we need to retrieve the body?" Dugas asked.

Wade shrugged, looking at the injured Baker and Campbell, and then at the pilot for any kind of confirmation.

"No can do," the pilot confirmed, "that was a good-sized rock that hit the rotors, and my elevation and rudder controls are a little too sluggish for comfort. We're heading back."

"Forest's secure, and we can check back in daylight," Jones assured the gathered soldiers over the radio. "They took two of our pieces off the board tonight, and we returned the favour. But dancing with two male, extra pissed-off sasquatch in the dark compromises us more than I'm willing to allow. We'll come back at first light to retrieve Parker and Jackson. If Hicks shot straight, we may have something else to bring back that'll give any taxidermists in town a heart attack."

~

Adotey crashed and flailed down the escarpment. His vision blurred as he twisted in the air, and each contact with the rockface drove the air from his lungs, silencing the screams and roars that wanted to burst from his chest. His arm and shoulder on one side were useless, unable to resist the tug of gravity. He landed badly and face down, but quickly rolled onto his side. He used his good arm to raise himself into a sitting position. He took raspy, gargled breaths and as he looked down at his fingers, he saw his own blood shining black in the moonlight against his skin. He pushed out his mouth and lips and made soft oohing noises. He closed his eyes as he turned his head, letting his cheek rest against the cool of the rockface. He opened them again when he heard movement close by.

Shartale took a step out from the treeline and met Adotey's gaze. He walked closer, dropping to all fours as he neared. A wicked grin spread across his face as he saw Adotey's wounds. Then he stopped. He looked up at the metal beast the humans travelled in through the air. It was turning and moving away. Rolling his mass from one side to the other on his knuckles, he raised his nose into the air, checking for the scent of Adotey's son. He was close, but not close enough. Shartale looked into Adotey's eyes and grunted, glancing up again at the humans and their machine. He pressed his hair covered thumb into the centre of his throat. In that moment, Adotey knew two things. First, Shartale was about to kill him, and second – he would seek out and kill the humans to avenge the death of the females.

Shartale looked down at Adotey's injured arm and gently ran his thick fingers along its inside. His claw found the old scar, and he lay it along the length of the damaged tissue. He remembered giving Adotey the wound when they had both been younger. He had been fully grown and Adotey still an adolescent. Adotey huffed, almost impatiently. Shartale dropped his gaze, then slammed his elbow into Adotey's throat, brutally crushing the windpipe and tearing the larynx. The twig-like snap of cartilage also meant Adotey's hyoid bone had been shattered, though Shartale only knew his killing blow had been effective. For a moment, Adotey's eyes widened in shock as his body was denied air, then they rolled into the back of his head and his body slumped. Shartale watched and waited, having known his kind to feign death, but it only took a few moments before he was certain. He turned as Adotey's son rushed from the treeline to their position.

Shartale stepped back, allowing Cona to examine the body. He knew his killing blow could not be distinguished from the wounds Adotey had acquired from his fall. Those, however, were eclipsed by the gaping, bloodied wound in Adotey's chest, left by the weapons of the humans. Shartale bowed his head in respect and stepped back further, still on all fours. He watched Cona sniff at the wound and then turn his head to the retreating humans, still visible in the night sky. Now, as their bodies cooled, Shartale could tell that both he and Cona were injured. They too had been stung by the weapons of man. He needed to rest and heal, and he couldn't risk a confrontation with the son of Adotey. He looked up once more at the metal contraption as his open hand sought out a rock. He found one of appropriate size and shape, and lifted it, carrying it with him in his upturned palm. Shartale let out a growl as he barrelled forward, using the full extension of his arm to swing the projectile up and away from him. It catapulted from his hand with deadly precision, arcing high and then dropping onto its target. It hit the tail end of the thing in the sky, and both he and Cona watched as a burst of flame and a billow of smoke erupted from it. It made strained noises like a wounded animal as it began to drop from the air. Its flight was strained. Slowly and steadily, it began to dip back down towards the forest.

Cona turned to face Shartale. There was little to disguise his hate.

“Niha,” Shartale growled, raising his head in the direction of the falling metal bird.

Cona sucked in air. The word meant ‘gift’ in their language. He stood for a few more moments, as if considering his options, then he dropped to all fours, sprinting back towards the forest and the humans. Shartale watched him go, then headed into the treeline to the north, following a new scent that lingered in the air, promising both food and shelter.

CHAPTER FIFTEEN

MONSTER TRAP

Lucas Christian walked out onto his observation deck, three stories above the ground floor of the lodge-style mansion he called home. He watched the distant helicopter through the Swarovski ST Vista scope, mounted on a carbon fibre stand that was permanently fixed to the deck. Completely weatherproof and capable of turning 360 degrees, the $12,000 instrument was suddenly earning its keep. Even in the dark, the 30x magnification gave him an excellent view of the aircraft's struggles, and he was in no doubt it was going to crash land somewhere in the forest. And all his research suggested what they were hunting would flee in the opposite direction, onto his land. Straight into his trap.

At a casual glance, the pristine forest and wilderness stretching out behind the house was completely natural and untamed. But this was far from the reality. Ravines, creeks, drop aways, and densely packed brush had been used to create a series of bottlenecks. Within this maze were pitfall and deadfall traps crafted with expert care. They were reinforced with steel lined cages and titanium alloy netting. And as soon as one was triggered, the dogs would be released from their compound, cornering and maybe subduing their quarry. But as powerful and significant as the Tibetan mastiffs under his command were, he knew better than to rely on their strength to bring down his intended prize. For that, he had turned to something more certain, and illegal. Each trap was also equipped with an automated venting system that would release a mix of Neothyl and

Fentanyl. With his books incredibly popular within the Russian federation, he had been able to secure the canisters with relative ease. Fortunately, he had put his plans in place long before recent events would have made it difficult for his diplomat friend to have brought them into the country.

In the Siberian north, what the Americans called bigfoot, the Mongolian, Turkish and Chechen Mountain people knew as Almas, or the Almasty. As with many aboriginal peoples, these creatures were feared so much that their very name couldn't be mentioned. Instead, they referred to the animals as Akhai – which loosely meant "uncle", or "brother". As Lucas' diplomat friend had explained, the name was a little tongue-in-cheek. Kirill Volkov, who he'd met at a Russian literary gala, had claimed to have seen the animal itself in his youth, and it had not been friendly. He and two friends had come across the creature by chance, whilst out fishing on a vast frozen lake. It had pursued them back to their village, claiming one of the boys and disappearing into the forest with him. Volkov had said neither the creature or his friend were ever found.

Lucas' research had led him to believe that the creatures existed on every continent except Antarctica – at least as far as it had been explored. Bigfoot had a Canadian cousin called the sasquatch. Although the names were now somewhat interchangeable, the sasquatch was a creature known by the Salish and Sts'Ailes first nations. The Chinese called their giants of the forest the yeren. Australian Aboriginal people knew them as the yowie. Nepal and Tibet had no fewer than three supposed species of yeti, the largest of which was the original "abominable snowman". In Indonesia, the Orang Pendek had been tracked by legitimate biologists in the region. Then there was the Mande Barung of India, the Mapinguary of Brazil, Barmanou of Pakistan, and even the Woodwose of Britain and Europe. American troops serving in Vietnam brought home stories of the rock apes. And within the United States itself, they had numerous local names. Some were individuals, such as Old Yellowtop. Others were state celebrities, like the Ohio grassman and MOMO – the Missouri Monster. From Texas to Alaska, it was a case of bigfoot by any other name. But despite their abundance, they remained unproven flights of fancy to most. Tonight, for the first time, he wondered if the chance of providing the world with the proof it demanded was finally within his grasp.

When he had first started writing his novel, nothing could have been further from his mind. His elaborate plans and ideas for traps were intended as a publicity stunt. But his research led him to seek out those who said they'd encountered the beast. And his instinct led him towards a conclusion: monsters were real. It was hard to dismiss the stories he was told. He remembered how a grizzled, cigar-chomping trucker with the prison tattoos to match, had broken down and cried like a baby as they'd talked. A brilliant heart surgeon, whose steady nerves had performed revolutionary operations, couldn't control his trembling hands as he retold his encounter. Lucas had become convinced they had experienced real trauma.

He'd also spoken to a longstanding college professor, who had devoted her entire life to tracking the animal. Lucas now owned several original and highly valuable footprint casts himself, mounted on the wall in his office. He always did this, he reminded himself. He would become obsessed with his subject matter, allowing it to take over his living space. With each new project, his office would slowly be redecorated with new objects of fascination, paraphernalia, and items intended to inspire or aid his research. It gave a realism to his work that his readers enjoyed very much. And it made him a useful consultant when they were made into movies. From vampire hunting kits to photographs of fairies – many of his possessions had ended up as props in the films of his books. In turn, that had made them even more valuable at auction once he had no need for them. Some items though, would remain his property for all time. But not the body he intended to procure tonight. No, that he would give to the world.

Lost in his thoughts, he hadn't noticed the forest grow quiet. The helicopter had disappeared, no doubt now grounded. He felt unnerved and decided to withdraw inside, to the safety of his study. From there, he would rely on the network of hidden cameras and other equipment that had been meticulously hidden throughout the forest. These weren't the off-the-shelf game cameras you could buy in any hunting store. Each one had been built into the cover of the trees and brush, seamlessly blending in with their surroundings. He had infrared and ultraviolet cameras also concealed throughout the verdant corridors that led to his traps. Keeping so many cameras operational 24/7 was ineffective in terms of the cost in both time and money, so each zone was split into sectors with seismic sensors buried along the pathways and motion detectors connected to the corridors of trees. Once triggered, the cameras in that sector would automatically become active. But even then, only an animal with a mass of 300lbs or more could trigger the sensors. As with everything else, they'd been built to his specification. Now, he would find out if his significant investment had been worth it.

His thoughts were interrupted by the gate buzzer sounding on his intercom. He frowned as he walked over to the desk and sat down. As the buzzer sounded again, he brought up the security controls for the whole property and zeroed in on the camera at the main gate. He recognised the python green Porsche Macan SUV and the driver impatiently staring him down through the screen. After all, he'd bought the vehicle and married the driver – although that hadn't lasted long. The Porsche was a running joke, part of the divorce settlement he'd offered. The colour was far too lurid for her personal tastes, and he'd taken some pleasure in picking it out. Ironically, her renowned good taste could be seen throughout the house in its furnishings and textiles. But just as he did his novels, he had researched his prospective partner before marrying – and his findings led to him insisting on a prenuptial agreement. It hadn't been her first affair that had clinched it for him, or the second. It was the third. The three-strike rule had served him well throughout life, and it had been time to finally admit his friends and family had been right all along.

That didn't mean he didn't still love her though. He knew he did. And he understood why others would. Josie-Mae Kesnann was a strikingly beautiful woman with hair the colour of French roast coffee, brought out by toffee-coloured highlights and eyes that flicked from olive green to hazel, depending on the light. She was slight and petite, yet curvaceous and well framed. The sight of her in a figure-hugging dress was enough to take his breath away. She didn't have the height to give her what the world would call great legs, but they had a sexy, subtle contour. One that encouraged the eye – his at least – to travel up the hem of such a dress and hope she would turn in just the right way. She never had need for heavy makeup or audacious jewellery, as she had all the right stuff already going on. It had never been about him not loving her. It had been the realisation that she didn't love him.

He had at first been drawn to her naivety and vulnerability. He'd felt compelled to protect her. Show her a world that was filled with wonder and beauty, compared to the ugly one she knew. Her past was one of abuse, of being used, and of being treated like an object to be owned or paraded around like a racehorse. It was why she hid her kindness and gentleness with the temper of a rattlesnake and the venom to match. Its why her warm, giving heart could freeze over at a moment's notice in an act of self-protection. And it was why, no matter what, she felt compelled to return to men who treated her with contempt. Her conditioning had been so thorough that the genuine love, warmth, and protection he offered unnerved her. She found it hard to ever believe such things truly existed.

He remembered how they'd first met. She'd come to a book signing of his in San Francisco – where he lived at the time. He had always wondered if she hadn't been attractive, would he have noticed she had been crying. Whether it was because he was a little old-fashioned or wanted to live up to the prescribed aesthetic of being an author – he always carried a pocket watch and a handkerchief in his check-patterned blazer. The pocket watch had indicated his time at that bookstore should have ended over an hour ago, and when he looked past the woman in front of him, he realised they were closing up. So, he had felt no guilt in offering the handkerchief, a free copy of the book, and a Starbucks of her choice. And it had been whilst sipping their drinks that he'd discovered that the latest in a string of bad choices, had stolen from her and left her in financial ruin. Helping her at first had just been a random act of kindness for a fan – she'd professed to buying all his books and seeing the films. He'd found her insights on both his writing and their big screen outings refreshingly honest. And he'd felt a great swell of pity when she had confessed that coming to the book signing had been the only thing that had stopped her from trying to drive off the Golden Gate bridge that morning.

His feelings, and that need to look out for her, had never left him. And it meant that he had still been generous in the settlement, despite the prenup. He would be hard pushed to say they were friends. Their connection was something deeper and more dangerous than that. The same forces that could destroy them, as they had done before, also drew them towards each other repeatedly, like runaway trains on a collision course. It turned out they needed each other, not romantically, but simply because each knew the raw, honest versions of themselves that nobody else ever saw, or perhaps would even accept. And that was enough. But tonight, just like it had often been in their marriage – her timing was off.

"Josie, this isn't the best of times," he declared apologetically into the intercom.

"I've just driven from Seattle. You think I'm turning around?" she replied.

"You could have called ahead," he grumbled. "What if

I'd been out?"

She stared into the camera in silence. Her smirk and the raised eyebrow did all the talking.

"I'm right in the middle of something. Drive up to the house and come straight inside. Don't dawdle," he commanded.

"Yes sir," she muttered.

He pressed the buzzer, and the gate began to slide open. He turned back to the larger screen to his right and studied the myriad of camera images that filled it. The system was in its default mode, showing looped images and screenshots. Nothing had been triggered yet. He heard the front door open, and he was on his feet, headed for the staircase as soon as he heard it close again. He moved quickly down the three flights of stairs. He rounded the final turn of steps and strode past his ex-wife determinedly.

"Err... hello," Josie laughed.

He waved his hand in the air but glanced back at her suddenly. His keen observations noted the few dark speckles that dusted her cream-coloured Givenchy hooded coat. Droplets of water also coated the aluminium shell of the Montblanc cabin trolley she had pulled in behind her.

"Is it raining?" he asked.

"Seemed to have just started," she nodded.

He continued over to the security panel by the front door. He punched in a code and the green blinking light in its top right-hand corner changed to a constant red. There was a distinct thud as mechanics whirred within the double front doors and locked into place. The sound was echoed throughout the house as windows and doors became secured.

"Something wrong?" Josie asked, her humour evaporating.

"Let's just say I don't want any more uninvited guests tonight," Lucas said quietly. "It looks like you came prepared to stay – so I presumed, and I'm locking up behind you."

"Uh-uh," Josie shook her head. "What's going on?"

There was a booming, joyous sounding bark and they both turned as the pair of Tibetan mastiffs trotted around the corner from the kitchen.

"Boys!" Josie cried with glee, dropping onto her knees.

The enormous black and tan dogs looked to their master for approval. He laughed, seeing their resolve and obedience was about to break. It was the only signal they needed to gallop over to Josie and swarm her with happy licks and roughhousing paws and flicks of their tails. She laughed uncontrollably as she playfully fought them off.

"They're working tonight," Lucas said, sheepishly. "As am I."

She glanced up with a questioning look.

"Look," she sighed. "I came up because I want to talk to you about moving to Portland. I also have an idea about maybe starting my own business. We could sell the Seattle house. I don't need a two-million-dollar home..."

Lucas raised his hand, gently, in surrender.

"I'm honestly not against a conversation or supporting you, but can we talk about it tomorrow? I really am in the middle of something."

"What have you got going on?"

"It's complicated... you know I'm writing that sasquatch thing. Well, I think the move here and everything else is about to pay off. I think..."

"You've found bigfoot?" she interjected, narrowing her eyes. "Wow, Discovery couldn't do that in nine seasons and god-knows how many TV specials."

Lucas shrugged. The dogs padded back towards the kitchen, and he followed them. The canines pawed anxiously at their doggy door, which was now locked shut. Lucas punched the wall switch, and the pneumatics huffed as the steel panel slid open. After they passed through, it closed and locked again automatically.

"It might be nothing, but I need to concentrate for at least a little while. Why don't you get comfy in the guest suite, and I'll come find you later? I'll make some pasta or something, or you can raid the fridge and larder."

Josie nodded, a wry smile still on her face. She followed him as they made their way up the stairs. At the top, Lucas turned right towards his study. To the left was the guest suite, but Josie paused, peering in after him. She left the cabin trolley in the hall and walked over to him. He sat in the green leather chair, which was designed to give excellent back support – if you didn't hunch and slump forwards as Lucas now did. She placed her hand gently on his back. His computer had three screens, and his gaze was fixed on the one to the far right, the largest. It was filled with CCTV images, two of which had a red blinking light next to them. She suddenly glanced out through the security-glass panelled windows that overlooked the forest to the rear of the property.

"What's out there?" she asked.

Lucas detected the slight anxiety and fear of the unknown in her voice.

"I don't know yet," he said. "It's most likely to be a big black bear, or a grizzly. If there's a momma mountain lion with some sub-adult cubs passing through, they'd be enough to trigger the system collectively. Whatever it is, it's nothing to worry about. The dogs will make more than enough noise if they get a sniff of anything. I just need to get some images of it. Even a blobsquatch will be enough to get the marketing machine rolling towards the next hit."

Whilst he knew that wasn't strictly true, he had no intention of letting her know he was planning to capture a creature. Animals were the only thing that brought her true happiness, and she was completely anti-hunting. If he even hinted at the idea of trapping something, which might cause it stress or pain, she'd turn more dangerous than the animal itself. He could see she was less than convinced as it was.

"I'm going to run a bath. Do you think you'll be able to concentrate in an hour?" she asked.

Lucas smiled. Patience was a virtue, but not one Josie-Mae possessed.

"No promises," he said. "But if nothing's taken the bait, I'll give you my undivided attention."

"Bait?" she asked, snapping her head in his direction.

Lucas cursed himself for nearly giving the game away.

"A figure of speech," he explained. "I just mean if I don't catch anything on camera".

She paused, staring directly at him, trying to get a read. He felt like a deer caught in the headlights. His mind raced as he suddenly thought how he might look guilty. She knew all his expressions and tells. It was like when a cop car appeared behind you; you drove worse and perhaps even suspiciously, because you suddenly weren't your natural, relaxed self behind the wheel. But apparently, she either saw nothing or was too bored to make anything of it. She simply raised her eyebrow in the dismissive but not unkind way he was so familiar with. She disappeared back out the door and headed for the guest suite on the other side of the corridor. A few moments later, he heard running taps, and he turned back towards the screens.

At first, all seemed quiet. Then, he noticed movement on one camera. It came from the interior branches of a Pacific yew. He squinted as he tried to make out what it was. The large eyes seemed to glow in the infrared flare of the camera, but as it moved its head, the creature revealed itself. The great gray owl hunched itself, its wings folded tightly over its back as it craned its head forwards. With one foot and leg firmly rooting it to its branch, it raised its other into the air and clawed slowly at the darkness with the four talons of its toes. The bird was stretching, as if just woken. Lucas knew that bright, piercing yellow eyes were searching the night forest for prey. Only they weren't. The owl shifted its weight back and forth slowly as its head remained in a fixed position. It was watching something. Something large and brash enough to get its attention and disturb it. That's when the next set of seismic sensors sounded their alarms. As if it had heard them, the owl launched from the tree, shooting upwards as it let out a booming call of warning.

Lucas turned back to the computer keyboard and tapped in his instructions. A digital map of the forest beyond the house blinked onto the central screen. His eye was drawn to the flashing red beacons that lay along the corridor leading from the outer perimeter and into the maze he had created. Whatever this thing was, it was being cautious. According to his Russian friend, the creatures could distinguish between the foreign, manufactured scents used as pheromone lures and the real thing. This wasn't so unusual in nature, which had taken the time to develop some of the most powerful and sensitive noses over millennia. Many animals, from big cats to turkey vultures, investigated such lures once out of interest, but never paid them much due after. In any case, Lucas had decided to stick with the temptations that worked best – the genuine call of fresh meat and clean water. The water was provided in a small creek that ran downhill to a collecting pool, where it was constantly refreshed and recycled by pumps deep within the natural well. As for the fresh meat, he tapped a new set of instructions into the keyboard, glancing quickly behind him. This was the part Josie would not approve of.

He glanced at the large screen to his right, showing the individual camera feeds. As the one he was operating went live, it automatically became the largest segment on the screen. Lucas watched the hidden door of the fabricated cave open. From within, a small, black and white feral hog stepped out into the night air. The door behind it closed again, and it let out a squeal of panic as it's temporary home, and the comfort and safety it offered, were cut off. He thought back to the reports of the Fouke Monster – a creature that had terrorised a town in Arkansas during the late sixties and seventies. One smallholder had told the journalists and TV crews willing to listen, that he had stepped out onto his back porch only to see the black-haired bigfoot nonchalantly disappearing into the swamp, with a prize hog held securely under each arm.

Feral pigs held less favour than those two unfortunate

swine. Although only just becoming known in Washington state, the invaders were already unwelcome. They were considered deleterious exotic wildlife by the authorities, and it was illegal to import, hold, possess, offer for sale, sell, transfer, or release them as a result. By acquiring several for his needs, he had therefore broken a minimum of three state laws. But for some reason, he felt he was contributing to the state ecology rather than causing it harm. Although isolated populations of feral hogs had been eradicated from Puget Sound and Gifford Pinchot National State Forest, reports persisted. A population of hogs in Oregon had been reduced from over 4,000 to a mere 200, but a steady stream of newcomers from California propped up the numbers. It wasn't hard to fathom that a few were slipping further north.

The spread of feral hogs across the United States was estimated to have caused over $1.5 billion in damages to crops, wildlife, and precious local ecosystems. They also carried more than two dozen diseases and parasites that were harmful to both humans and livestock. America had declared war on the pig – but it was hard to say who was winning the fight. After decades of selecting bloodlines for their robustness, size, disease immunity, and an ability to find nutrition in almost anything, it was no wonder their ability to survive defied the odds. Ranchers and Forest Rangers alike wanted to take things into their own hands. So, Lucas had little trouble influencing a small number to give up a few they'd found on private hunting parties. He funded their progress and in return, promised the pigs would never leave his land alive. He focused his attention on the cameras and the forest behind the house, waiting to make good on that agreement.

The hog was not pleased at the prospect of being alone in the dark. It let out a squeal of indignation as it rammed its head against the sheet of rock that blocked its path back to safety. It grumbled in high-pitched grunts and belches as it turned around. Finding only one route, which led downhill, it trotted obediently along it. The sound of a bough breaking some way off in the canopy behind it, caused the animal to stop. It tentatively raised its head and sniffed the air. It raised a single trotter into the air as it paused.

The snap of another branch rooted the pig to the ground. It lowered its head and Lucas could see it clearly trembling in the pixel perfect night vision feed. It turned towards the woods behind it and stared into the darkness. The bristles along its spine rose in unison, then it let out a squeal and bolted down the only path afforded to it. From the gloom beneath the trees came a roar that Lucas heard through his computer screen, and distantly as the blast of sound hit the insulated glass of the study windows. A blur passed across the camera, then the map of seismic sensors on the screen lit up like the fourth of July. The creature was on the ground and following the trail that had been so carefully laid out for it.

Lucas watched as the network of cameras came alive, automatically activated by the activity. Now on the ground, the creature would find it difficult to return to the trees. They had been cleared of their lower boughs and branches. Steep, sheer walls of rock and impenetrable brush laced the narrowing corridors that led on to an unseen destination. Perhaps culmination was more precise, as all roads led to a singular end. The pig dashed obligingly along, the stress of deciding which way to go mercifully removed from the equation. A blur, blacker than the surrounding night, passed in front of a camera. Lucas quickly activated the slow-motion capture settings for the cameras ahead. He checked that recording and back-ups were also turned on. In the eventuality that he was unable to capture the creature physically, he still intended to do so digitally – but in unequivocal clarity that couldn't be contested. But, as he had said to Josie, even something questionable would be enough to stir the pot and market the book series he had planned. Just as with the forest outside, he had every angle covered.

When Lucas looked back to the camera screens, he saw the hog had come to a shuddering stop. Ahead of it was a dead end. Retreat was the only option allowed to it, and it knew better than that. The wild pig took a few tentative steps forward and Lucas held his breath. Suddenly it whirled around, facing back up the trail. The squeal it emitted was of sheer terror, and it sprinted back and forth. For a moment, something appeared on the screen and obscured the hog, then it was gone. In its stead, a chasm had opened where the forest floor had been, and Lucas realised that his trap had been sprung. It had worked. A few moments ago, he had feared the weight of the pig would trigger the mechanism prematurely, but his calculations and preparation had now paid off.

He watched as the trap doors began to close. Moments later, an amber light flashed on the system's digital dashboard. Now, he had a decision to make. Contained, he could attempt to keep the creature alive. Or, with one click, he could release the Neothyl and Fentanyl in a large enough quantity that its death would be certain.

The complex technology and natural landscape barriers he had created needed significant maintenance. For this, a series of access tunnels and utility spaces had been built underground, connecting the intersecting points of the maze he'd designed. He had often referred to it as "the colosseum" when he had first dreamed it up. Arguably Rome's most famous landmark, its main arena had once been fed by a myriad of service tunnels, animal cages, prison wards, infirmaries, and even kitchens. The forest above was his own personal arena, and just as with the real colosseum, it was designed to keep things inside. But to do so required technology, and power, and infrastructure. At first, he had envisioned something simple – like the tunnels of WWII and Vietnam. But it had soon become clear that to have any chance of containing the quarry he pursued, it would need a more modern and secure approach. He'd then turned to several companies that manufactured readymade bunkers. Over time, he connected them with steel and concrete reinforced corridors and adapted them to his purpose. They served as nerve centres from where the generators and cabling could be housed, as well as providing easy access for servicing some of the cameras and other equipment. This included the titanium-walled trap that had just received its intended guest.

~

Shartale's fingertips had just brushed the underfur of the hog when the ground gave way beneath him. He plunged into blackness, face first. Instinct kicked in and his arms and legs shot out to his sides, reaching to their full extent. Although ready for the impact with the ground, it came so quickly that his chin still shot downwards and the whisps of his beard-like hair tensed and recoiled as they sensed the proximity of the floor. Although there was loose soil and sand here, he felt and heard the metal buckle under his mass. He looked up, just in time to see the starlight above the forest canopy disappear. His sensitive hearing detected the whirring mechanics, and he instinctively understood the thing was humanmade. But there was enough time and light for his retinas to expand, giving him a sense of the space he found himself in.

Furthermore, he understood its function. He used hidden drops created by the natural landscape to goad his prey into, cornering them and often disabling them, if not killing them outright. This was more sophisticated, but the premise was similar. Shartale realised that here, where no landscape feature provided a drop, one had been created. As he dug for grubs and groundhogs, this hole had been dug from the ground and covered. He was excited to learn something new that could benefit him. He could attempt to copy and use the same hunting technique. But first, he would have to escape the trap.

Resting on his outstretched fingers and toes, he sprang up onto his feet. He detected movement in the far corner and tilted his head in that direction. His eyes widened in their search for light. A very faint, horizontal strip directly above him provided all the illumination he was going to get. But it was enough to distinguish the frozen shadow that huddled in the corner. Looking in its direction, the hairs lining his ears pricked, and he listened to the hog's laboured and hurried breathing. Robbed of direct sight, his other senses kicked in, and he caught the scent of blood. The pig was injured. The fall had been sudden and unexpected for

Shartale, but not significant enough to be of consequence. But for the bait he had chased into the trap, it had been more than one of its forelegs could take. The bone had shattered and broken through the skin. In the darkness, the hog only knew it shared the pit with Shartale. It could not see the terrible grin he wore as he tensed for the spring.

Shartale's attack was sudden and vicious. He lurched forward and snatched up the pig by its rear legs with one hand, swinging it around with devastating force. Its head smacked into the steel side of the pit with a jarring crunch. Just to be sure, Shartale held the hog by its back legs, his arms outstretched as he manoeuvred it against the wall. He jammed its head against it. The animal made no sound and Shartale could smell the blood that dripped from its mouth and nostrils. But pigs were intelligent, and he'd encountered several with tusks. They needed to be dealt with quickly. He brought his foot down on to its neck with a thud that resounded through the small space. There was a loud, singular crack and all remaining breath and life expunged itself from the hog in a squeal-like whine of surrender.

Expertly, Shartale twisted and tore the rear haunch from the pig, using his canines to sheer the flesh from the skin. He gulped down the rich globules of fat that lay in between, savouring the greasy texture and the taste. He knew it was an important food for restoring some of the energy he'd lost. But now, he thought of another use for his prey. Using both his fingers and his teeth in unison, he began to separate the long bone through the centre of the haunch from the remaining muscle. As he did so, his gaze would routinely rise to the narrow crack of light above him. It took a few moments, but he was soon able to rip the bone out completely. With no stones to aid him, he set to work splintering its thinnest end with his teeth. When he had worked it into the sharpest point possible, he spent more time sucking the ball joint clean of sticky blood and jammy flesh.

Shartale knew his prey, down to the bone. And this one was strong and compound. It would not break easily. With the weakest point reduced and refined, it would withstand a heavy impact at the thicker end without breaking. Now, he just had to climb. He stood up to his full height and stretched out his arms. The sensitive, leathery tips of his fingers couldn't quite reach the walls on either side of him, but they were close enough for him to sense they weren't far. Their metal casing carried a small amount of natural static charge that made the hair on his knuckles raise up. Shartale made a small, test leap and planted a foot against the wall behind him whilst his free hand found the wall in front. He made a quiet, "ooh" sound, pleased with himself as he remained suspended off the floor. He did it again, using his powerful lower leg and ankle muscles to propel himself upwards. He was now higher than he stood, which put his six-foot arms within reach of the pit roof. Using his entire arm and his clenched fist the size of a cantaloupe as a pendulum, he swung it straight up with pinpoint precision. He rammed the bone shard into the slit where the light was penetrating and let out a roar of triumph as it held. But he didn't let go. Gripping tightly, he wrapped his fingers around the ball joint of the bone. Without releasing his foot from the wall completely, he tested it to see if it would take his weight. There was a slight give, and he instantly took off the pressure and placed his foot against the wall with his full force. Using his palm, he growled as he punched at the bone, shifting its angle, and driving it further into the crack. He felt a little breeze of air greet him from the effort.

That's when he heard something begin to whir back in the darkness below him, and a new and strange scent came to him.

~

Lucas Christian watched in astonishment as the creature killed the hog and began to eat it. The infrared footage was crystal clear. When he released this, nobody was going to say it was a hoax, surely? But, in his heart, he knew that even this would not be good enough. If Hollywood could bring dinosaurs back to life, a man of his means could use those same digital effects to feed a hungry sasquatch, especially in the "convenient" night vision setting. He knew most people would only be convinced of its existence by a physical body, or a "type specimen" in scientific terms.

Yet still, his finger hovered over the button to release the gas. What he was witnessing was incredible. The power of the animal, the intelligence it showed. And the grin he'd seen it wear when it realised the pig was within easy reach. It knew what it was doing, and it enjoyed it. At first, Lucas hadn't realised what the creature was doing as it went about dismembering the hog. He figured that it had nowhere to go, so it was using the time to butcher its prey more effectively. He knew big cats regularly broke open bone to feed on the fatty marrow and wondered if the sasquatch was doing the same. He initially hadn't noticed the creature fashioning the bone with its teeth, but he had grown suddenly tense when it had begun to scale the walls with such ease. He had underestimated the potential size of these creatures. In just a few seconds it was within reach of the roof, and only then had its plan become clear. As it swung with such grace and purpose, he could see why many eye-witnesses had likened the creature to an Orangutan, or its giant extinct cousin, Gigantopithecus.

But, as he turned to look at the museum-quality replica of a Gigantopithecus skull that was displayed on a column by the study door, he could see that, whatever this animal was, it was quite different. Although a comparison to the size could be made – approximately five times that of a modern human, the teeth he'd seen flashed in that wicked smile were quite different. In the Gigantopithecus skull, the canines were broad and blunt, despite the pointed shape. The bottom canines were almost flat. Whereas the trapped animal possessed a set of splendid, fang-like teeth that sat prominently in the corners of the mouth. The skull in his study also showed large, round but relatively close together eye sockets. The creature currently trying to break out of the trap also had large eyes but spaced apart much further, to the point that it looked odd. Besides, they were more almond shaped – more human perhaps. Just looking at the Gigantopithecus skull, complete with its sagittal crest, you could see its ape ancestry. But this thing, on the screen in front of him, was different. It didn't hunch over, and it didn't walk on its knuckles. It walked upright. It was no ape. But it also wasn't human. No wonder people called it a monster.

His eyes went back to the screen. As the creature's broad, flat feet hit the trap doors with all the force its pendulum-like swing could muster, Lucas watched as they visibly shifted and rose. The momentary flash of ambient light they let in showed up as a green flash across the screen. He panicked and pushed the button to release the gas without further hesitation. A red warning light showed on the monitor, as the gas started pumping into the chamber.

~

Shartale grunted as he paused, taking in a deep breath. He heard the hissing sound coming from the corner of the metal wall. As he scanned the floor below him, the same biology that game him such excellent night vision enabled him to see traces of the gas as it began to build up below him. He could detect no odour from it, yet he instinctively recognised it as a threat. From swamps to the rivers of molten rock he'd occasionally seen from afar, he knew gases that hung heavily in the air were to be avoided. He held his breath and tensed his legs against the back wall, suspended with one hand gripping the hog bone imbedded in the unnatural roof of the metal cave. With all his might, he swung again, knowing what he must do.

In one fluid movement, this time, as his feet hit the panels, his fingers drove upwards towards the crack that appeared as his mass slammed into the ceiling. They found the gap, but it instantly began to close on them, gripping them as if they'd been crushed in a rock fall. He howled with the pain and then roared with rage. He dangled helpless, struggling, and fighting the urge to take in another breath. The gas may have been odourless, but he had tasted it when he had opened his mouth to vent his fury. It was bitter and dank, and he had to fight the urge to vomit. He now knew its insidious nature without doubt. He lifted his legs one final time and braced them against the wall. With his fingers trapped between the gap, he no longer had need of the grip provided by the hog bone. He let go of it and prepared to swing again. He pushed off. This time, he changed his trajectory slightly, arching his back and bending his knees so that the sole of his heel met flat with the ball-joint end of the bone. At the same time, his free hand sought the same gap that he knew would appear momentarily. Again, it closed around his fingers, but this time, he had found deeper and better purchase. Through the pain, he felt the breeze brush over his exposed fingertips. Running out of breath, he slowly placed his feet on one of the panels and began to heave with all his remaining strength.

Nothing happened. He strained as his eyes widened with panic, something he had not felt for years. He could not hold his breath any longer and would have to inhale the toxic fumes that had now built up all around him. Then the panel shuddered, and he felt movement. His ears pricked as something pinged away from him and there was another sharp explosion of gas. The panels began to lift, and he exerted more pressure. Using the last of his strength, he kicked them open, revealing the night sky above. He threw out his right arm, scrabbling for a purchase that would prevent him from falling back down into the pit, where he knew death would claim him. His fingers wrapped around something solid – a branch or root, and he flung himself upwards and out with desperate tenacity. In a moment, he was free of the danger presented by the pit, and he rolled across the solid ground onto his back.

For a moment, he lay there, replenishing the oxygen his lungs burned for. He could hear his own blood thundering in his ears as it sought to replenish strength to his aching muscles. He lifted one of his hands above his face. They were bloodied and misshapen. With the same curiosity and perhaps naivety he'd shown as an infant, he touched the broken finger with his other hand. It was instinct that drove him to straighten it out and restore it to its original shape. But instinct had not told him of the pain that would come as he did so. He roared and sprang to his feet. He swayed to and fro with immense agitation. The need to dispense punishment and wraith was now uncontainable. He circled, penetrating the darkness with an unforgiving, relentless gaze. Then, to the south, he saw the lights. A human dwelling. Within it, he would find the one that had nearly captured him.

~

Lucas stared at the monitor aghast. He was stunned at how quickly and easily the creature had overcome the trap. His finger still hovered over the keyboard, eagerly awaiting commands from the brain. But his mind raced. As he forced himself to think, he knew what he had to do. The dogs were well trained, and this is what he had been preparing them for. He even suspected it was something they were destined for. But he wasn't heartless. He didn't want to sacrifice them or expose them to suffering. However, the creature was clearly injured and had been exerting itself for some time if the presence of the military helicopter from earlier was anything to go by. It must be tired and close to exhaustion. He doubted it would be able to hold off the dogs for long. He had gone to great lengths to see their holding area was well ventilated, masking the scent of the dogs or even removing it entirely. One thing was clear from his research. The creatures did not like dogs, and the feeling was mutual. He'd gone to the lengths he had to prevent any potential sasquatch avoiding the property if it knew large, aggressive dogs lived there. Smaller dogs and pups were seen as prey. Larger dogs – canines and coyotes were a threat to food sources, or perhaps even young sasquatch. He didn't really know for sure why the two species were so adversarial. But he knew that when thrown together, neither his dogs nor the creature he'd hoped to find here, would back down from a fight. He pressed the button on the computer's touch screen that opened the kennel's outer run door.

~

The two dogs paced impatiently. Jetsan – whose name meant "King" in Tibetan, was the larger of the two, but not the dominant one of the pair. Since their earliest days together as pups, Ariel, had been the decision maker. Not only did his name mean "Lion of God", which suited a dog known for its rugged mane, but it more than matched his character too. Tibetan mastiffs were a relatively rare breed, and their similarity in colour and size was not by chance. They shared the same father, a huge, 195lb stud said to have lion's blood in his lineage. This was, of course, not true. But it did mean they were both pure bloods; thoroughbreds descended from the same dogs that once demanded price tags of one million dollars or more. It had only been a few years since freshly minted Chinese tycoons had highly prized the dogs. The fad had quickly led to diluted bloodlines and even crossbreeding. The prices had dropped almost as quickly as their popularity, as the tycoons turned their attention to more stable status symbols like sports cars and waterfront property. Lucas had made quite the deal when he had taken them off the hands of a disillusioned breeder in Hong Kong. The dogs though, were worth every cent of their previous dollar value. They were fierce, loyal, intelligent, independent, and stubborn. They also showed incredible empathy and were easily upset or thrown off kilter by human moods. Training was therefore difficult, as they often sulked if over disciplined. But Lucas had seen to it that they had the very best, bringing out and even amplifying their natural guardian nature.

Ariel was just beginning a return stretch along the front of the kennel run when the metal gate groaned and slowly slid open with the shrill sound of moving parts in need of grease. Ariel stood to attention and studied it, then turned to look at his half-brother, who walked over to him. Ariel took a step forward, then another as the strangest scent was brought to him on the wind. The dog did not understand fear in the same way other animals, or even other breeds might. It knew the creature it was scenting was a predator, and he knew that it was injured. He could smell the blood. But more than that, he could already pick up on its intent. This creature, whatever it was, was a threat. And it couldn't be tolerated. With rumbling growls, the two dogs dashed from the kennel run and headed for the intruder.

~

Shartale charged towards the human dwelling with a murderous roar. His call to war was answered by raucous barking that immediately began to close in on him. He had not been aware of the canines. A growl rose into his throat and stayed there, sending a deep rumble of sound into the surrounding forest. It sent reverberations down his spine and through his aching muscles. For a brief, singular moment, he considered fleeing. He could retreat to the trees and return for his vengeance another time. But the pain in his foot and in his fingers willed him on. And in the time it took for him to decide, the dogs were on him.

~

Ariel came to a shuddering halt as he turned the corner of the path. His senses were on fire and every one of them was telling him the creature he sought should have been standing there, in front of them. The scent was strong in the air, as if pouring directly from the animal itself. Ariel gave a low, rumbling growl of warning which veiled his sense of unease. It was not unusual for an animal they came across to flee as soon as they showed interest, but this was different.

The canine brain had evolved over time to put significant focus on the processing of scent. In the case of many domestic breeds of dog, the grey matter dedicated to analysing smell was over 40 times greater than in a human. This was no different for Jetsan and Ariel. In the base, primal, instinct-led depths of their olfactory centres, they could tell the different between an odour emitted in fear – which would usually excite them and spur them on, to one secreted in warning. This was the latter. And even then, they knew it was something elevated beyond the stink of a skunk that acted purely defensively. The scent that laced the air so thickly now came with the same weight of warning as the heavy rattle of a diamondback. Both dogs knew that moving forward came with deadly risk. But it didn't stop them.

Ariel was smart enough to hold his ground, but Jetsan was impatient. As one of his great paws moved forward, it was met with a corresponding snap of a large branch in the trees above them. Jetsan immediately lowered his head and crouched, barking furiously as his eyes searched the shadows. A moment later, a bough crashed down on top of the dog. Jetsan leapt just in time to avoid his skull being crushed, but still received a heavy blow to his side that knocked him to the floor. Ariel's size and shaggy coat belied the speed of movement he was capable of. His flumed tail whipped back and forth as he shot forward, with barks that were more like roars as he moved in to instinctively protect Jetsan, who was getting back onto his feet.

~

Shartale watched from the fork of the tree, where he remained crouched and still. By ripping the bough from the other side and hurling it at one of the dogs, any movement he now made would be exposed. Usually, the combination of his secreting glands and intimidation display was enough to drive away bears, let alone dogs. He had expected them to whimper and run, not close in on him. He glanced past the dogs to the lights of the dwelling. There was no further tree cover here – to reach it, there was no alternative other than to get past the dogs. He grunted in frustration as he dropped forward, one extended arm reaching up for a branch hold to control his descent. Then he dropped to the floor, directly facing the two canines as their hair bristled and their barks became a frenzy of warning.

~

Lucas watched via the monitor, holding his breath. Ariel and Jetsan instinctively edged away from each other, each holding a guttural growl in their throat that warned the intruder not to come closer. It was loud enough to be picked up by the camera's microphones. The dark form stood slightly crouched; its knees bent. Yet it still towered over them. In the veil of the night, underneath the canopy of the Western Hemlock that marked the path back into the forest, no eyeshine could be detected. The three animals stood in an uneasy deadlock, each feeling the penetrating stare of the other, waiting for the stalemate to break.

What neither party knew was that this confrontation had possibly played out over a thousand years, far way on a different continent, between their ancestors before them. Dogs of this type were believed to be the forbears of almost all the large, modern working breeds – from mountain shepherds to the St. Bernard. Before the 1800s, Tibet was virtually unknown and unexplored by the Western world. But Lucas knew the breed was ancient. As far back as 1100 B.C, Chinese records spoke of a large, ferocious dog of the Himalayas, known locally as Do-Kyi – the tied dog. The formidable animals guarded homes, families, flocks, and herds, often chained, or tied to a post where it could carry out its work. It was thought that their ancient lineages were what gave them such an unrivalled understanding of their human counterparts. Perhaps their ability to bond so deeply, and to be so personable, came from millennia of being by our side.

But it was what had been discovered in their recent history that had drawn Lucas to the breed. By the time the West did come to the Tibet, the mastiffs had become almost sacred, working as guardian animals that traditionally protected monasteries. The dogs were believed to have the souls of those monks that did not make it into Shambhala and were instead called back as warrior spirits. They guarded the sanctity of Tibet's holiest places. Which begged the question – from what did these fortress-like encampments need protecting from? A potential answer lay in the breed's own temperament and characteristics. Tibetan mastiffs were protectors, not killers. They were bred with incredible strength, combined with a temperament that included intuitiveness and fearlessness, but also gentleness towards humans, as well as patience and loyalty. Most intriguingly, Tibetan mastiffs were known for putting on some of the most terrifyingly intimidating displays of aggression, only to return to slumber the moment a potential intruder or threat walked away. These were not shepherd dogs. They had singular purpose. To make enough noise and put on a show of force that would make anything think twice about approaching.

Lucas had surmised that, formidable as Tibet's known predators were, the development and almost religious awe that surrounded the dogs was overkill. The two largest predators in Tibet were rare nomads – the blue bear and the snow leopard. Even in times when their numbers would have been more plentiful, these predators would have attacked the herds of livestock on the mountains, as did the wolves. The mastiffs were not suited to herding and flock guarding in the same way as other breeds. Their use was solely reserved for protecting the livestock and those that shepherded them when they returned to the monasteries.

In his travels, Lucas had heard whispers of why the dogs were bred so large and so strong, and why they were so revered by the monks that called them friend. They kept guard against the predator that came in the night, one capable of scaling the walls of the most fortified stone encampment, and returning back into the night with a bullock, calf, pig, or even an unlucky nun, child, or shepherd's wife under one arm. In Tibet, they were known as the Yachê – meaning "rock bears". But from the earliest part of the 19th century, when the western world was introduced to such creatures, they became known elsewhere as the yeti, or more fragrantly, as the abominable snowman. Lucas was sure, beyond the myth, propaganda and folklore, the Tibetan mastiff had truly been developed to stand between man and the monsters of the Himalayas. And now, here in the forests of Washington state, they were doing the same.

~

Shartale somehow sensed these dogs were different to any he had encountered before. He neither moved nor took his eyes from the canines in front of him. His instinct tugged at his consciousness, compelling him to flee and retreat. Somehow, he knew the dogs would not follow. Even if they did, once he was in the trees, they would not be able to. He turned, his shoulders dropping as he made the decision to flee. The dogs picked up on his change in body language and halted their barking as they waited for his next move. He swivelled his foot, preparing to turn away completely. And as the bulk of his weight moved from one side to the other, a ripple of tormenting pain shot through his foot and ankle. Hidden in the tree and standing still as he had been, the injury to his foot had bothered him less. But in an instant, he was reminded why he was so determined to reach the human dwelling. Inside it lived the source of his pain and weakness. The trap maker. It was a threat he could not tolerate. He stopped mid-turn and let out a final, savage snarl of warning at the two dogs.

The three combatants leapt at the same time. No signal or warning was given. The agility of the dogs surprised Shartale. He only had time to turn his body and shield one arm, enabling him to glance the incoming canine missile off his shoulder. The other dog found its mark, its jaws large enough to slip either side of his hand. It bit down with incredible force, making him roar with the pain. The dog tensed its shoulders and began to heave backwards, sporadically shaking its head as it did so. Shartale's other arm was already swinging round to grab the dog's head, but with his focus distracted, he didn't see the other dog as it leapt a second time. It caught him by the wrist of his free arm and immediately began to pull down and backwards, joining its companion as they tried to force him lower and off balance. Shartale roared and threw himself back, but the dogs clung on. For a moment, the pain caused him to lose his mind, and he was driven into a frenzy of panic as he tried to shake them both off. He lifted one dog, then the other, roaring into their faces. Their constant movement and their strength made it difficult for him to manoeuvre them, although his efforts lifted them from the ground several times.

As Shartale began to tire from his efforts, his clarity began to return. He growled as he gathered himself. He expelled the remaining air from his lungs, then threw his arms high into the air, as high and as fast he could. The dogs hung on, but now dangled from where they had locked their jaws onto his own body. Shartale could already see that the dog that had sunk its teeth over his wrist was already losing its grip, its own weight working against it, as its shaggy tail draped across the floor. Shartale suddenly ducked down and to the right, letting the dog that had his hand in its mouth touch the ground again, as the dog chewing on his other wrist was hoisted even higher into the air, albeit momentarily. With lightning quick reflexes, Shartale flung the dog through a wide arc, using the full length of his arm to do so. It smashed into the rocky path where they battled. The impact was enough to force the dog to release its grip and Shartale followed up with a swift rear kick that sent the dog flying back into the scrub behind. Now, he turned his full focus back to the dog whose teeth were buried deep into his hand. He could feel his own blood making his fingers slippery. But this dog was smart. Realising that it was now vulnerable, it quickly let go and leapt back and once more took up its ceaseless barking and baiting, bobbing forwards on its front legs but mindful to keep just out of Shartale's reach.

Shartale's eyes darted to the bushes, as the second dog limped from the scrub, back towards them. Its growl had become more menacing and threatening. He recognised the same processing of the pain he'd experienced, steeling himself towards a fight and wanting to hurt the thing that had hurt him. He was surprised by it, momentarily gaining a new insight and respect for the animals he instinctively hated, and more than occasionally consumed. He perhaps understood more now, why the humans and they so easily aligned. But it was also something he could use to his advantage. Goading this dog into a mistake would be easier now, and it was already injured. He adjusted his weight and footing, only slightly, so he was turned more in its direction than towards the other. Its growls were replaced with fierce barks filled with murderous intent as it rushed forward. It did not show the caution its partner did, and it paid the price. Shartale leapt backwards but was quick enough to catch the dog by the scruff of its neck with one hand. He spun on his injured foot, catapulting the canine into the trunk of the tree he'd stalked them from. The dog emitted a cry of pain with the impact, then fell to the floor in a heap. It lay motionless, and Shartale turned around, once more able to give his full attention to the more dominant dog.

As he'd sensed before, this animal was more astute. Confident but cautious. It growled a vicious warning as the hair of its mane bristled and waved back and forth as the dog shook with rage. Shartale began to edge around the dog, but it instantly followed his every move whilst keeping out of reach. Eyes locked, the combatants slowly began to circle each other. Then Shartale constructed a new plan. He began to backtrack up the trail a little way. He had to feint forwards several times to encourage the dog to follow him, but eventually, it did. Shartale didn't stop until he felt the cold metal of the pit trap's door touch the heel of his foot. He stooped low and let out several groans as he dragged his most injured foot. The dog growled and barked as it rushed forwards and then jumped back, always cautious to keep its distance. Shartale wondered if the dog could sense his deception or had noticed his momentary stop, as his fingers felt out the edge of the damaged trap door. He continued his ruse, letting out a huff as he collapsed, with his feet now touching the safe ground on the other side of the trap and his arm stretched out, gripping onto the door's edge. He let out deep, laboured breaths as he lay on his side, watching and waiting for the dog. It growled and lowered its head, but Shartale saw it also tense its legs and shoulders. The dog was smart; it knew it had to strike to kill. It would leap for his exposed throat.

Nothing Shartale did could tempt the dog to commit to a

charge. It darted in and out with furious barking, but always kept a safe distance. Shartale recognised that just as he was, the dog was trying to goad him into making a lunge and a mistake. It wanted to make sure he was in a position where he couldn't get up easily and was off balance. Shartale was tempted to give the dog what it wanted, a stand-up fight to the end. But then, biology played a deft and final card. Shartale breathed fast as hormones coursed through his bloodstream, directed from his apocrine glands to his bladder. Almost instantly, a stream of urine burst from his semi-erect penis and hosed the dog. It was an insult the collected, shrewd canine couldn't abide, and it leapt forward with savage intent, straight at Shartale's throat. Shartale moved with the same, sure, calculated speed, lifting the trap door by its edge with his fingertips. The dog's aim was true, but so was Shartale's. The canine slammed into the underside of the open steel door and gravity did the rest. Its front paws were just quick enough to scrape hopelessly on the metal as it fell downwards. Shartale barged the door with his shoulder as he rose to his feet. As it slammed shut, his gaze returned to the path that led back towards the dwelling.

~

Lucas watched the monitor with despair. He glanced over to the luxurious, wood-panelled gun cabinet he'd had installed in the office. Quickly, he got up and went to it. He punched in the code, and the cushioned door swung open, revealing the two firearms he'd bought for this worst-case scenario. The gun store clerk had been quick to recommend the Blaser R8 Selous rifle, in a 458 Win. Mag calibration. This almost certainly had as much to do with its price tag, north of

$20,000, as it did its big game stopping power. Lucas' hands were shaking as he took the rifle out and loaded it. He then reached down for the smaller handgun – a Dan Wesson Kodiak 10mm pistol. He'd bought it because he liked the tritone finish, as well as on the recommendation of the store clerk again. It offered serious stopping power with manageable recoil. No doubt the clerk had picked up on Lucas' novice shooting level. He checked the monitor again and then pressed a button on the computer. The armoured doors to the balcony slid open again, and he stepped out into the Washington night air, shouldering the rifle.

~

Shartale felt his strength beginning to ebb as he staggered forward, dragging his wounded foot. He stepped over an ornate stone planter that marked the rear of the dwelling. This space felt more human, more alien. Here, there were straight lines and flat stone surfaces. As he walked over the slabs, he left streaks of blood in his wake. Usually so careful to hide his presence, it did not bother him now. The rules had changed. He had no clan to protect, and the human knew he was there. Shartale raised his arms and brought them thundering down against the glass walls of the dwelling, but they did not give. He charged at one, with no effect. He had never encountered a dwelling like this. The ones he'd seen before were not so well guarded or so strongly built. He'd often watched through the easily breakable transparent panels. More than once, he'd been seen. More than once, he'd found them open or easy to access. Little round knobs, or thin, straight slips of metal could be manipulated to cause the sides to split and open. The humans used their fingers and thumbs to grip them, and he had watched and learnt. But not here.

He ran his fingers and palm over the rough, hewed stone that made up the dwelling's walls. There were no handholds or crevices for him to find here. He instinctively hid from the bright, artificial lights that burned around the perimeter. Not for fear of being seen, but to protect his night vision. He crouched against a corner in the shadow of two walls that met at an angle. His gaze wandered up the smooth surface, pausing momentarily on several panels of dead wood that supported vines of jasmine and honeysuckle. He shifted his bulk, giving him a better view. The powerful muscles in his neck gave him incredible jaw strength, as well as protecting the throat and top of the spine. This was necessary, as when forced into a fight, his kind often focused on the throat and head. They knew to take advantage of any biological weakness. Their kind had few, but the eyes and throat were more vulnerable than other parts of their bodies. A strong bony brow ridge, buffered by fat stores for shock absorption, offered some protection for their eyes. But the neck muscles that protected his throat restricted the movement of his head. Often, to look at something, he would have to turn his shoulders to get an optimised view of it. Having done so, his eyes fell upon the broad, dull, metal pipe that was attached to the dwelling, higher up, but opposite the panels of dead wood.

As he stepped out of the shadows, the wind changed. He immediately froze. He turned his shoulders in its direction, lifting his nose into the air and his gaze upwards. There, far above him and beyond his reach, he saw the man. He recognised the tubular metal stick that the human angled down in his direction as a vahk – a weapon. He was beginning to understand these weapons had different looks and capabilities. Over time, the weapons had become more deadly too. Even in his lifetime. Like the ones the other humans had in the forest. They were noisier. The little metal stones they seemed to throw were lighter and did little damage on their own – but they launched multiple stones in quick succession. They wounded, perhaps even killed through attrition. The longer vahk seemed to only be able to launch one metal stone at a time. He had dug such a thing out of a young alpha, back when he'd been part of a clan. But as he'd seen back in the forest, these too had grown in power over time.

Shartale bared his teeth. All his senses were fixed on the man poised above him. His predatory instincts enabled him to read the body language. The human was scared. The wind brought the scent of the man's sweat. Within it, he could sense the chemicals and hormones that came with fear. And although faint, his ears heard the metal scraping against the stone. The man trembled. And he hadn't yet used the vahk. He heard a metallic ping and sensed the man suddenly tense. Then he knew the metal stick would unleash its crack of thunder soon. But he also realised how this weapon worked. It had to be lined up to hit him. He flashed his teeth again and roared, but it was drowned out by the burst of fire and sound that leapt from the end of the weapon. Shartale had already stepped back though. He looked down, as the flat stone where he'd been standing exploded into several pieces. Then he leapt, grabbing for the panels of dead wood, and launching from them over to the metal pipe. He scrambled upwards with furious speed, not stopping until he reached the steep side of the dwelling's roof. He turned to look back, knowing he was now beyond the reach of the man and his weapon. As he began to traverse the smooth surface, which reminded him of a shale slope, he suddenly saw a dim glow of light coming from further up. He made his way towards it.

~

Lucas trembled as he watched the creature disappear over the edge of the roof. Then he took a deep, sharp inhale of breath in renewed terror. It was only now that he remembered Josie-Mae... and the skylight above the guest bathroom.

CHAPTER SIXTEEN

BLOOD BATH

Josie-Mae Kesnann lay back with her head against the rim of the thick-walled, stone bath. It was filled and nearly overflowing, with a creamy, floral bubble bath covering the top. The temperature was so hot she barely moved. Only occasionally would she turn or bob her head as she listened to her music through the expensive waterproof earbuds Lucas had given her. She'd said she wanted them for jogging and hiking, so they needed to be sweatproof. She let her long, brown hair half dip and submerge in the water. She hadn't decided if she'd wash it yet, and if she did, she'd take her earbuds out. But for now, she was letting the moisturising oils of the bath cream warm and refresh her skin after the drive over.

She slowly blinked her eyes open and looked towards the door. She was sure she'd heard something. An ominous bang. She sat up a little, sending a gentle ripple down the length of the bath. For a few seconds, she watched the door, waiting for Lucas to come in. It wouldn't be the first time he'd thought up an excuse to see her naked. She didn't mind. It was payment of sorts. And when she wanted and needed sex, she wouldn't complain about his attentions. Especially when she had something on her mind that needed his support, or his wallet. But the door never swung open, and she heard nothing more. She leant back and nestled her neck against the rim of the bath, settling back into the comfortable soak she'd been enjoying. She was just about to close her eyes again when her gaze flitted to the skylight above. Often, with the lights low – as they were now, she'd be able to see starlight or even the moon depending on the time of night and year. Strange how tonight, she could see nothing but darkness. It must be cloudy after the rain earlier she thought. As her eyelids half closed, she sat bolt upright and sent a wave of water over the side. The movement had been small and in her peripheral vision more than anything. But it had been there.

She cocked her head slightly, listening. Was something scraping against the tiles up there? Her head snapped upwards again as she heard a faint tap, as if something had struck the glass. Like a bird's beak, or a small pebble. But they were nearly four stories up. There simply couldn't be anyone, or anything on the roof. She decided that any relaxation the bath now offered her had vanished, and she gripped the sides of the deep stone tub as she stood up and reached for her towel. Above her, the skylight exploded into a thousand pieces and rained down into the room. Then something dark, hairy, and writhing hit the floor. At first, she thought it was a bear, but then, slowly, it began to stand up.

~

Shartale had scaled the roof with relative ease. His feet spread wide and pressed flat against the tiles, despite the sharp angle of the slope. When he had reached the source of the light, he had been surprised to find a transparent pane, just like the ones he'd peered through in the sides of dwellings before. He pressed his face close. The space below was dim, but he could still see. Part of it was illuminated by singular flames that burned small and in isolated areas. This made him cautious, but as he watched, he realised the fire was somehow contained and did not spread. Then he noticed the movement.

The human female uncurled her naked form and sat up. She was half submerged. But Shartale saw her breasts, pink and flushed by the water. Her legs unwrapped and sent a cascade down her skin, making it shine in the reflected light of the small flames surrounding the water. Shartale's quick, calculating brain caught up with him quickly. Just as he recognised the family groups that made up the clans of his kind, he realised the humans had similar relationships. He'd seen this for himself. Those he watched moved with their partners and their young. And they lived with them too. He'd seen them gathered together, as he had observed unseen from outside their dwellings. This female was with the one that had tried to harm and catch him. In his excitement, he pressed against the panel, and it creaked a little with the effort. Shartale grunted in glee and leapt into the air. He smashed through the panel with ease, dropping to the floor below.

~

Josie-Mae opened her mouth to scream, but no sound came out. Her entire body trembled as she stepped backwards. No longer aware of her surroundings, she tipped over the edge of the bathtub and fell sharply backwards, crashing into the tiled floor. The towel provided some cushioning, but she still smashed hard against the ground. She smacked the back of her head, and her elbows slammed into the stone. But it was enough of a jolt to prevent her from slipping into shock, which she had been in danger of doing. She pushed herself up onto her elbows and scrabbled backwards with her feet. When her back hit the wall, she began to push herself upwards. As she did so, the thing on the other side of the bathtub came back into view.

It stood at almost twice her height; its head bent to avoid hitting the ceiling. Its eyes were fixed on her. Still unable to process what she was seeing, she stared into them. Small, perfectly round pupils surrounded by a round iris of burnt orange. Almost the entire almond-shaped eye was black, and she only saw a slither of white when its eyeballs moved towards the door and slowly back to her. She had once campaigned to have several chimps rescued from a life of scientific research. When she and Lucas had secured their release, they had been transferred to a sanctuary. They had looked very different to the apes she'd seen in zoos before. They were grizzled, weathered animals that had a hard life etched into every muscle and wrinkle across their faces. But even they didn't compare to the hideous creature before her.

Its eyes were set too far apart, and loose, charcoal coloured skin piled downwards from the centre of its heavy brow ridge to its nose, falling either side. Below the brow ridge, down to the upper lip, the face was free of hair. Thick plumes of cinnamon and silvery hair sprouted across the brow ridge, growing thicker as her gaze moved upwards, into slick, oily, darker, matted clumps. Overall, the creature was dark in colour, but its broad facial features were accented with lighter strands. In the limited light of the candles, it could almost be said to have a beard and sideburns, with a moustache that blended into its hairy cheeks and fell either side of the jaw. A jaw that opened to reveal upper and lower canine teeth that met in a scissor-like bite, with broad yet sharp incisors in between. The tip of its purple-coloured tongue dashed across them as its wide mouth set into a grin. Josie-Mae shuddered. The thing swayed back and forth on its feet. The rest of its body – bulky and muscular, was covered in a more uniform, dark-coloured hair, similar in colour to the purest of dark chocolate. As she allowed her eyes to dart from its predatory gaze for a moment, she noticed the unsheathed, semi-erect penis – stark and pink as it dribbled urine. Josie shuddered.

When she had first seen the chimps released into the sanctuary, her empathy for them had almost led to a deadly mistake. She had tried to touch one of the females through the mesh cage of the entrance tunnel – wanting to reassure it that things were okay. The sanctuary's zoologist had been just quick enough to save her hand. It was then that she had been introduced to the darker side of apes. Orangutans that held down females as they copulated, despite their screams and protestations. And chimpanzees that became so excited whilst hunting other monkeys, they became sexually aroused. Josie knew this was what she was now seeing.

As if it had made up its mind, it moved forward, its arms swinging from side to side with more animation now. Josie picked up the first thing she could find – a candle and threw it at the beast. It leapt back, colliding with the wall as it tried to escape the flame. It hit it in the arm, scorching a few hairs and spilling hot wax before spluttering out. It growled, grabbing the candle, and throwing it into the bath. It seemed deliberate, like it knew how to extinguish fire. Then, as if bored with the game now, it took one, lightning quick step and reached for her. There was nothing she could do. It knocked her to the floor with a swipe of its hand, then it was on her. She looked up as its head raced downwards, sinking its teeth into her left breast. She screamed as it used the leverage to lift her from the floor, only to slam her back down against the hard stone. Its engulfing hand pushed her head to the side as it gurgled, as if with delight, as blood filled its mouth. Claw-like nails dug into the side of her face and raked against her cheek, opening a ragged gash.

She felt a pressure on her abdomen that drove the breath from her chest and made her feel like her diaphragm was about to implode. She opened her eyes – not aware she had clamped them shut. One of the creature's sausage-sized fingers was being jammed into her belly button. Her eyes widened as she let a high-pitched scream escape from her lungs. As if this angered the creature, its head lunged again, this time biting into her shoulder. She felt her clavicle resist momentarily before she heard it snap. The searing pain of the teeth tearing through her flesh was intense, almost mercifully overshadowing the agony of broken bones. Then, the creature went back to probing her naval.

As her consciousness became erratic, a prologue to shutting down altogether as the pain, fear, and blood loss overwhelmed her, a flash of a TV interview with Jane Goodall – a celebrated primatologist and anthropologist, played in her mind. She had been one of the first scientists to discover the predatory nature of chimpanzees. Up until the 1980s, when Josie-Mae had been born, they'd been thought of as peaceful fruit eaters. Goodall had observed chimpanzees often hunted other primates – monkeys especially. Once they had caught their prey, they preferred to dispatch them in two ways. Either a bite to the head, or through disembowelment. In her last few moments, she looked down and let out a cry as her skin met the point it could resist no more and split. The creature widened the tear by forcing its fingers into her abdomen. Josie-Mae blinked slowly and for the last time, as the thing took out parts of her small intestine and transverse colon, biting them apart and chewing on them. The tearing of her insides killed her in moments, and exposed her stomach, liver, and heart as the beast ripped them from her body.

~

Lucas burst into the guest suite but skidded to a halt immediately – unprepared for what he saw. Almost nonchalantly, the creature turned, still crouched over Josie-Mae's body. It didn't move. The bloodied heart of his ex-wife and the woman he still loved was held in its mouth. It gulped it back, lifting its head to swallow it whole. Then it stood up and was coming for him, without warning. His hand trembled as he pressed the single-action trigger of the pistol repeatedly, sending multiple rounds into the creature, but it didn't stop.

Lucas stumbled backwards. He was saved by the creature having to stop mid-charge, encountering a doorframe too small for its bulk. It was the momentary pause Lucas needed for his sense of self-preservation to return. He spun on his heels and sprinted back up the corridor, darting into his office. He heard the roar behind him and the sound of cracking timber. Then came the monstrous thuds of sprinting steps eclipsing his own. Lucas didn't stop, passing the frame of the bookcase and smashing his hand into the large green button on the wall.

As the door of the panic room shut with pneumatic speed and precision, Lucas turned. He gasped, realising the bigfoot had almost reached him. It snarled as it leapt, its jaws open wide, and its arms outstretched to snatch at him. Then, it disappeared behind the thick, titanium plating. He heard it slam into the metal on the other side. For what seemed an eternity, he listened as it pounded on the door. Then, unsatisfied, it went about destroying his office. Sharp bangs and the sounds of splintering wood could be heard over the creature's grumblings. Occasionally, when hurled against a wall, the sound of glass or ceramics smashing hinted at the beast's commitment to thoroughly annihilating the space on the other side of the wall.

Lucas sunk to the floor, cradling his bent knees with the gun still in his hand. He trembled, openly sobbing as he thought about Josie-Mae, murdered, and devoured because of his single mindedness and obsession. It was much later, as police and forest rangers tried to batter down the front gate, that he realised the creature had left.

CHAPTER SEVENTEEN

CRASH LANDING

Whatever hit the tail rotor had been blunt, heavy, and hurled fast enough to shatter it. Each of the soldiers in the rear cabin felt the judder that reverberated down the helicopter's chassis. Wade thrust his head out of the open side door but pulled back instantly, as thick, heavy smoke billowed into the cabin. The chopper groaned and then careened sideways. The pilot was trying to maintain control of the aircraft on the way down. Without a tail rotor, there was no question of them staying in the air. Right now, the chopper wanted to give in to gravity, and pirouette and plumet to the ground. There was a flash of flame from the side of the Sikorsky, then they were falling. The helicopter scraped along a rockface it was unable to climb above, splintering the blades of its main rotors as it did so. It then nose-dived towards the trees, head down and fast. Wade hung on to the netting and handles around the cabin – the only things preventing him and the rest of the team from being thrown from the aircraft. All Wade could do was stare at Campbell, strapped to the stretcher, and hoping it would hold. His fears were confirmed as their eyes met, the g-forces of the uncontrolled dive ripping him, and the carrier, loose. One moment he was there, the next, gone.

Metal screamed, or one of the others may have, then they smashed through the canopy before the slender nose cone of the helicopter connected with the rocky ground. It bent and buckled, then the aircraft slid onto its belly as parts of the cabin twisted around them or tore loose from the frame. They ploughed through the dirt like a derailed train, before coming to a stifling halt. Caught at an odd angle, what was left of the helicopter jilted to its side and finally came to rest at a near-perfect 90 degrees. Thrown loose by the initial jolt of the crash, Wade slowly blinked his eyes as he regained his senses.

His head hurt, but his vision wasn't too foggy to miss the blood that smeared his arm. His alertness shifted up a gear when he suddenly smelt fuel. He could feel heat and heard the sparking of electrics. Behind it, in the background, was the crackle of flame too. He rolled over and let out a grunt with the pain. He knelt, his hands scrabbling for something to hold onto and right himself. The armrest of a sideways-slanted seat attached to the rear wall of the cockpit sufficed. He looked back down the aircraft and realised he could see the night sky.

"Impact tore out the side like tinfoil off a TV dinner," Hicks croaked, pushing himself up off the floor. "Campbell's gone."

Wade nodded.

"Baker?" he asked.

"Here, but not against being shot, all said and done," came a pained reply from down the cabin.

They both looked around and saw Dugas helping Baker to his feet. Wade nodded at his partner and looked Baker over. The soldier was limping, had a significant bloody gash to the side of his head, and seemed to be cradling his left hand. When Wade saw the fingers, he could tell they – and the wrist, were broken.

"Dixon, you here?" Hicks yelled out.

"Wipe away your tears, you ain't got rid of me yet," came the disgruntled reply.

Dixon half fell, half lumbered into view from behind Wade.

"What about our fly boys?" Hicks asked.

Dixon shook his head. "That's what I was checking on."

"We need to ex-fil this aircraft, now," Wade commanded,

there's fuel in the air and we're about to become barbecue. Hicks, Dixon, you're furthest back, sweep for usable items, weapons, and anything we'll need on your way out. Dugas, you and I will get Baker over the rough stuff."

With some sense of order restored, the soldiers made quick work of scrambling outside and putting some distance between them and the twisted wreck of the Sikorsky. Wade and Dugas supported Baker as they scrambled from the open side of the aircraft and quickly made their way down a gentle slope of scree and loose dirt. When they looked back up, Hicks and Dixon were on their way down, carrying two large duffel bags and at least two weapons each. As they joined them, a bloom of flame erupted from the wreck, backlighting them in an eerie orange glow.

"Two assault rifles, a shotgun, and my HK," Hicks confirmed, putting the weapons down on top of the duffel bags. "Two standard packs – water, first aid, radio plus a backup, flairs, and all the ammo we didn't use for round one. My HK and one of the rifles have a flashlight. Only the two assault rifles have the lasers still attached, and they've been knocked to shit. Might work after we've let them stabilise for a while. Didn't see any of our night vison gear left."

Wade had guessed as much. The night vision goggles were heavy and cumbersome and they were already down at least three pairs. And as soon as you were in a lit area, like the helicopter cabin, they flared and were pointless. He presumed the others had placed theirs under their seats. It was a natural enough place for any head gear once an op was over. They, like everything else loose in the cabin, had been thrown from the helo when the side was ripped off. As for the lasers, they were incredibly delicate, and only the slightest knock could throw them out.

"Take my sidearm," Dixon suggested to Baker, holding

his Sig Sauer P320 M17 pistol in the air, "there's three mags, so you're good. I'll take one of the rifles – and Hicks will keep me covered anyway."

"We'll all keep each other covered," Wade interjected. "No splitting up this time. We watch each other's backs."

Everyone nodded in agreement.

"Speaking of covering our backs," Baker spoke up, "we're going back for Campbell, right?"

"Affirmative," Wade nodded.

"I ain't saying we shouldn't," Hicks warned, "but it means leaving the crash site – where anyone looking for us will come. And it's all of us or none of us, like Wade said. So, if you're gonna object – now's the time."

"I can make it, if that's what you're worried about," Baker protested.

The soldiers stood in silence, watching each other's faces for any hint this wasn't going to happen.

"Okay, move out," Wade ordered.

"Finding the trail shouldn't be too hard," Dugas jeered as he picked up the shotgun and loaded it with ammo from the bag.

Wade looked back and past the wrecked hull of the helicopter. The trail of destruction it had left, whipping through treetops, and bouncing off the escarpment, as well as glowing cinders of burnt debris and foliage, was visible even against the inky night sky of the forest. Wade picked up an M4 assault rifle and resupplied his ammo.

"Dixon, try the radio as we head up – no use waiting 'til we get there," Wade suggested.

Dixon nodded.

The soldiers moved along the base of the escarpment. Hicks and Dixon covered the rear, whilst Wade and Dugas took point. Baker stayed in between them, with only the forest to their left to cover – the wall of rock to their right cutting off any potential line of attack. They had followed the base of the ridge for about 600 yards when they found the stretcher. The metal poles were bent, possibly from the impact. But the simple fabric material that formed the carrier was bloodstained and bore four distinct slashes. There was no sign of Campbell.

"Baker, reckon you're our best tracker," Hicks suggested. "Wanna take a look around and see if there's any sign?"

Baker nodded. They all could see the solemnity on his face. He took a step towards the forest. As if in response, an echoey, strained, scream of pain floated out of the darkness within the trees.

"That was Campbell," Baker declared, swallowing hard.

"Well, he didn't get up and walk out there on his own," Hicks warned. "Something else is out there with him. Maybe more than one something."

"Tough shit for us, I guess," Baker snapped. "We ain't leaving him."

Hicks nodded and smiled. "Atta boy."

Wade was impressed by how the team seemed to move as one into the trees. It was the difference between rookies and professional soldiers. Each one of them instinctively covered the man next to them. When the call came again, they stopped only momentarily to ascertain the direction, before splitting into two groups and moving in as a pincer movement.

Wade was the first to see Campbell. He held up his hand in a tight fist, bringing the soldiers to a hasty stop. He signalled his line of sight with two hand gestures. Hicks and Dixon headed to the right of where Campbell's cries had led them to. Wade, Dugas, flanked to the left. Glancing over to Hicks, Wade could see the special forces operative had the snub-nosed barrel of his submachine gun trained on Campbell, just as his own rifle was. The others had a clear line of sight to their rear and sides.

Campbell was on his knees in a small clearing ahead of them. His buttocks rested on his half-splayed calves. His torso sagged downwards, like a precarious melting tower of gelato. Gravity was doing all the work of keeping him upright. His chin rested on his chest, the jaw open and loose. His eyes were open, but they were vacant and blank. The uniform and body armour he'd been wearing had been shredded, and they could all see the jagged, frayed slashes across his chest that had bloodied his clothing.

"He's gotta be dead, right?" Dugas whispered into Wade's ear.

Wade's eyes met his without moving his head. He knew Dugas didn't want Baker to hear. But if they were all looking at the same guy, and if the other soldiers had seen the same dead bodies he had, then they all knew Campbell was gone.

"Dixon, any luck with the radio?" Wade asked.

"Thought I got a signal a second ago, I'll try again now," Dixon replied.

"This don't smell right," Hicks said. "Baker, I'm sorry about Campbell. But him out there like that... we're sitting ducks."

"If he's dead, then whose voice did I hear?" Baker challenged. "At least let's check the man's pulse."

Baker went to take a step forward, but Wade slapped a hand across his chest.

"Stand fast," he warned. "Hicks is right. Everyone back up, slow."

Hicks and Dixon turned 180 degrees and began to cover the retreat. Wade and Dugas took two steps back, still facing Campbell. Wade reached out for Baker's shoulder, pulling him gently with them. He was thankful he complied. Then they all froze in their tracks.

"Huuuuuuuulp," came the whisper on the wind.

Baker's head snapped back towards Wade. He could see the confusion on Baker's face. Wade's own eyes darted back to what he knew was Campbell's corpse.

"Baker, buddy, we both know there's no way that's Campbell, right," Wade said quietly.

"Huuuuuuuulp," the call came again, louder, and more aggressive.

Wade was paying more attention this time. The voice was deep and resonant, like it had an echo. Oddly, it also sounded ill. Like when you spoke to somebody with a heavy head cold. Things came out muffled and garbled through mucus.

"We don't know that for sure," Baker argued. "It can't be one of those things, they can't talk."

Baker raised his gun to his shoulder again. Wade could see from the look in his eyes that he was unsure – torn. The voice from the woods was feeding into a deluded hope that Campbell was somehow alive. Wade looked around as Dixon made his way froward, extending the radio towards Baker.

"Something you might want to hear, buddy," Dixon said softly.

Baker took the radio and held it facing him, so Wade could also hear. Wade nodded his appreciation.

"Son," came the drawl of Agent Jones through the hiss and crackle of static. "I know what you're going through, I do. Campbell was a good man, but that's not him calling to you out there. One of the native words for these things translates as 'ventriloquist'. It's a bad interpretation, but you get the gist. Stand down, son. Backup is on the way, but I need you boys to stay together and not do anything stupid. And I'm afraid, what you're about to do is..."

"Stupid," Baker acknowledged. "These fucking things."

"Amen brother," Dugas grimaced.

Baker handed the radio back to Dixon, who tapped the side button twice to acknowledge the conversation was over.

"We're out of fly boys," he explained, "but they're sending in a ground team. Until then, we're on our own. Radio kicked in just as we moved up," he added in explanation. "There's a lot of iron deposits in the granite, so we couldn't get a signal back at the crash site."

A deep, penetrating rumble of a growl echoed out of the trees.

"We find high ground, dig in, and don't get dead until backup arrives," Wade suggested. "And I suggest we find it in the opposite direction of that."

The soldiers began to move back steadily, in the same formation they'd previously adopted, until the clearing and Campbell were out of sight.

~

Agent Cordell Jones looked up as the black, unmarked, Dodge Durango pulled into the campground. He didn't have to wait for the door to open to know Major Clarke was in the rear passenger compartment. Cordell often thought it said a lot about a man who chose to ride in back when there was a spare seat up front. He put down the pack he was halfway through putting together, next to the FN SCAR-H heavy assault rifle he had just loaded. By the time he looked back up, Clarke's driver had already opened the rear door and the Major was striding over to him. He looked about as happy as Cordell himself felt about the situation.

"Just what kind of a fuck up of an operation is this, Jones?" the Major snapped.

"There were three of them Nathan, they're god-damn lucky to be alive," Cordell replied, going back to preparing his pack.

"It's Major Clarke," the soldier growled.

"Well, I'll be, I always thought you were a major asshole,

sir," Cordell shrugged.

"Just once in a while you could drop the whole 'answer to no-one' charade," Clarke glowered.

"Who said it's a charade?"

"What's your back-up?"

"You're looking at it," Cordell shrugged.

Clarke seemed to suddenly calm down, realising Cordell's intentions.

"Military search and rescue are en route from Whidbey Naval Station," Clarke explained.

"That's the damn problem," Cordell sighed. "Because we can't use civvies, the cavalry is nearly an hour away. They're in the hot zone, and they need backup now – or we're back to square one."

"Ever had one do this before?" Clarke asked.

Jones shook his head, his eyes darting over the map.

"It led the family group right into the firefight... I'm pretty sure it knew what it was doing too," he said. "My guess is it slipped away in the confusion and left them to it."

"Why would it do that? Why would it be so willing to sacrifice others of its kind?" Clarke asked. "That's not what I've been led to believe they're like."

"Don't be so sure," Jones replied, shaking his head. "We often compare their societies to those of gorillas, because that's what they look like to us," he explained. "But in truth, they're more like baboons or chimps. Not quite as peaceful as you'd think, with a lot of dominance behaviour and fighting for females, territory, and hunting ground especially. I wouldn't put it past our rogue to have used our guys to try and even the odds a little."

"So, where'd it go?" Clarke asked.

Special Agent Gregory Smith appeared in the doorway. He looked flush and out of breath.

"An automated alert was just sent out to the emergency

services from a panic room, some rich guy's place out in the sticks," Smith explained. "It's north of where the helo went down. There isn't a sheriff's department or patrol for miles, so the Forest Service is responding. I think we need to get in on that, in case our boy is making house calls."

"That might well be your answer," Jones sighed.

Major Clarke looked at Smith for a second, then back to Jones.

"Why don't we kill two birds with one stone, so to speak," Clarke suggested.

The two agents looked at him for an explanation, not following his train of thought.

"You've grounded the TV crew, who have been running interference as usual," Clarke expanded. "Let's give them something to do. They can meet up with the rangers, and they can hit that part of the forest and perhaps tempt out your rogue – who we know is likely injured. If they make contact, the squad comes a running," he shrugged.

"Could give us eyes on the ground at both locations," Smith offered.

Jones stroked his beard with deep, gauging rakes of his fingers, still looking down at the map.

"Alright," he admitted. "But not the doc. She's not ready for this kind of thing again yet. She can go in with the rangers to the house. The rest of the crew hit the forest, whilst I go in to back the boys up. Agreed?"

Clarke nodded with a smile. Smith was already disappearing out of the door, a phone to his ear. Jones picked up his pack and the rifle, following him closely. He turned back to Clarke when he reached the door.

"Soon as that search and rescue get here, you get them in. No delays, no observation, no bullshit," Jones growled. "You get them, and me, out. I'll know if you pull anything – and I'll take it personally."

"You have my word," Clarke replied, holding up his hands.

Jones stared at him, another threat on the tip of his tongue. But he realised it was pointless. He walked outside and headed over to one of the surplus ATVs. He chose a four-seater CAN-AM Maverick with a half black, half forest camo paint pattern. Its advanced roll cage would give the squad something to hang onto if they had to exfiltrate in a hurry. He was sacrificing carrying capacity for speed and agility. He threw his pack on the front passenger seat and secured his rifle. Then, as a precaution, he took out his sidearm – a Korth NXR. 44 Magnum revolver. It was a precision, German-made gun capable of incredible accuracy. He made sure it was within easy reach, loosely held in the side pocket of his pack as it faced him. He checked the map, then hit the lights and turned the engine over before gunning down the trail that led to the old logging roads and the dark forest beyond.

Clarke watched him go.

"Let's see what your boy can really do," he smiled to himself. "Showtime."

CHAPTER EIGHTEEN

HUNTERS HUNTED

Wade and Dugas covered the rear as the rest of the team retreated, heading east through the forest. Dixon, who had once been a cavalry scout, had never dropped the habit of carrying graphics with him – a small, foldable map that was always in his back pocket, with key landmarks highlighted in code. He'd suggested there was a trail in this direction, which ultimately led to a logging road where they could meet Jones. That put Dixon on point, leading the way. It was also surmised that if civilisation lay in that direction, the terrain may be more accommodating for a helo to land. But so far, that wasn't proving to be the case. As they moved, they looked for a suitable place to take a stand or hole up, but none appeared. The trees were just as thick and foreboding as back at the clearing. Hicks was within arm's reach of Dixon, covering him as he made trail. As before, Baker took up the centre position, flanked closely by Wade and Dugas. They moved quickly and silently; weapons raised.

Dixon was looking down at the map when they all heard a sharp, sudden snap to their right. He didn't know for sure, as he couldn't see anything, but Wade thought it sounded like wood being splintered by force. Like when you ripped a branch off a tree. He looked down the sights of the rifle, slowly moving the end of the barrel back and forth as he strained to catch a glimpse of movement. His ears were pricked and listening for the slightest rustle of leaves, or the sound of something brushing past the lush ferns he knew littered the forest floor around them. But they were surrounded by eerie silence. It was almost as if the creature knew they had lost their advantage of seeing in the dark. Not a single pair of goggles had survived the joint disruption of the attacks and the crash. Now, it was just their training and their instincts.

Dugas suddenly whirled around, his gun trained back the way they'd just come, and catching Wade by surprise. He looked at his partner for an explanation.

"I swear something just passed behind me," he whispered. "I felt the air move... didn't hear nothing though. You?"

Wade shook his head.

"Was probably just the wind," Wade shrugged.

It was impossible to trace the direction from where the high-pitched whistle came from, but it was violently loud. Wade saw Baker wince as the call continued, only for it to suddenly change down an octave and begin to fade. It was followed by a soft, moaning cry that seemed to hang in the air around them. Although mournful in sound, it had an ethereal aspect that was also sinister and threatening. Wade recalled how what they thought had been Campbell's call for help had sounded off too.

"That the wind too?" Dugas grinned.

"Don't know, why don't you go check," Wade suggested, returning the sarcasm.

Suddenly, to their left, there was a loud, distinct crack as wood splintered. It was followed by a groan and a rush of wind that accelerated and came nearer. It was the sound of a falling tree. Wade grabbed Dugas and pulled him back as the pointed top of a large fir crashed across their path. Wade raised his rifle again as an immense shadow passed the other side of the fallen tree, but it was already gone. Then, back to their right, they all heard Baker scream. Wade and Dugas scrambled over the fallen trunk – which was well over half a foot in diameter. As they came face to face with Hicks and Dixon, they realised Baker was indeed missing. No ventriloquist tricks this time.

Wade looked to the ground, finding Baker's pistol there.

"BAKER", Dixon yelled at the trees.

There was a short, raspy, gurgled sound in reply, but much more distant this time. Whether it was their teammate, or the creature, was indistinguishable. Wade turned to see Dixon using the flashlight on the rail of his rifle to examine the fallen tree.

"Trunk and roots are healthy – this didn't happen by accident," Dixon explained.

"It ambushed us," Dugas spat.

"I can't believe how fast it moved," Hicks declared. "By the time I'd turned, he was gone."

"It targeted the weakest among us and took him out," Wade added. "It knew what it was doing."

"What do you want to do?" Dixon asked Wade.

"Stick to the plan," he replied. "I know it goes against our instincts. But we know what these things can do. This team has had its number halved in a matter of hours. It knew we would look for Campbell. I guarantee it wants us to go look for Baker. Chances are Baker is already dead. If we go look for him, we probably end up the same way. It's got more chance to pick us off if we're spread out – which is the only way we'd find Baker. We get to the backup, then we come back in and get both Baker and Campbell home. But we can only do that if we're alive."

Wade could see that nobody liked their choices, but eventually, Hicks and Dixon nodded. Dugas placed his hand on Wade's shoulder and raised his head in agreement too. For a moment, they all faced the trees in the direction the creature had gone.

"Beginning to see how Jones got to the point where he hates 'em all," Dugas swallowed.

Wade nodded. Dixon checked his graphics again and began to lead them off. As soon as they were on the move again, they were aware of being shadowed. It was further off now. But it let them know it was there with branch snaps. Occasionally, what sounded like muttering drifted on the breeze to them. They couldn't make out any words, but the tone was hard to miss. It was angry. Frustrated maybe that they hadn't taken its bait, twice now. Suddenly, Dixon held up his fist and they all came to an immediate stop again. Brazenly, the sasquatch charged through the forest to their right, quickly accelerating past them. Then there was silence again.

Wade watched Hicks. The special forces operative had his eyes closed, using his ears to follow the sound of their uninvited shadow. The barrel of his sub-machine gun swung left as he tracked its movement. He opened them again as soon as it stopped. Wade tried to follow his line of sight out into the darkness, but there was little point. Wade made a mental note to recommend all weapons issued to the squad were fitted with red flashlights to their accessory rails going forward. Again, he cursed himself. He had been too reliant on the technology they had been issued with and not thought more practically. Now, they were paying the price for not having a backup. And one thing was for sure; the thing stalking them had more than adequate night vision.

They all turned as what sounded like a charging grizzly thundered through the brush behind them.

"Anyone got any bright ideas?" Hicks asked.

"We're easy pickings sitting tight like this," Dixon chimed in.

"I say, next time it does a mock charge, we rush it," Dugas suggested. "Throw it off its game".

"Looks like now's our chance," Wade nodded towards the trees.

The noise was closer and louder this time. Trees snapped and popped. Tremors ran through the ground beneath their feet. And over the top of all of it came a screaming roar that never seemed to end. Wade had already noticed that no other living thing in the forest dared move or make a sound. Then, just as before, it stopped. The growl that lifted into the air seemed to surround them. Wade watched as Hicks slowly turned his head from side to side. He knew he was trying to use his peripheral vision to detect movement. It was reassuring that even someone with Hicks' experience and background had been unable to determine from which direction the sound had come from.

Wade looked down at his rifle and decided to try the blue laser light again. He knew the instruments were sensitive to disturbance, and the violence of the crash was more than enough to render them useless. But still, there was no harm in trying. He switched it on, and it blinked and faded a few times. In quiet frustration, he hit it with the side of his hand. Immediately, the light flashed on vividly and steadfast. He smirked and laughed to himself at the irony. Works every time he thought.

Something crashed to the ground from the trees above. It was as if somebody had dropped a family car through the canopy. He swiftly swung the rifle upwards and moved the barrel from left to right, trying to catch the creature. If the laser had the same effect on its eyes as before, it would lose its advantage of being unseen in the dark. There was a thud, and then another, and another. The noise sent a shudder down Wade's back. It was the sound of monstrous, bipedal footsteps racing towards them. He searched the darkness for their source, expecting the hulking form to appear out of the gloom. But nothing came and they suddenly stopped.

"Ready?" Hicks asked.

The men nodded, each placing a hand on the shoulder of the man in front of them. As Dixon's hand hit his, Hicks burst into a run, his sub-machine gun raised and its barrel darting towards the shadows of the trees. Dixon followed suit, sweeping his gaze left. Dugas covered their right and Wade brought up the rear. They were moving as one and at high speed, attempting to catch the creature off guard. As Wade watched the blue light of the laser pass through the forest behind them, it made contact for a fleeting second with a giant, hairy torso, side on to him, as it crossed their six. He instantly lifted the barrel, searching for the face, but an arm with loose-hanging clumps of matted hair was held up to block the penetrative beam. The creature had learnt not to make the same mistake twice. Wade squeezed the trigger instead, sending off three rounds in rapid succession after the beast. The rest of the unit turned as he did so, instantly joining the firefight as more bursts of automatic fire from the rifles and the blasts of the shotgun followed the bigfoot back into the forest. Just as quickly, they silenced their weapons and looked on into the surrounding trees.

"Think we got it?" Dugas asked.

Wade shook his head. "Too fast. But I think we gave him something to think about. He's gotta decide if the fight's worth it."

A roar, which reminded Wade of a T. Rex in the movies, hit the squad as deftly as a punch to the gut. Wade was surprised to see Dixon stagger back, then drop to one knee. His eyes were rolling into the back of his head, which, close as he was and in the thin moonlight afforded them, Wade could see was awash with blood. It looked glossy black against his skin. As Dixon collapsed onto the ground, Wade saw a flat, sharp-edged stone that seemed out of place, off to the right. It too looked wet and shiny black on one side. Almost in disbelief, Wade snapped his head right. It had thrown the rock at Dixon with pinpoint accuracy. He realised they weren't the only ones with weapons.

Dugas sprinted over to Dixon, who was laid flat on his back. Hicks covered him whilst he took a closer look at the wounded soldier's head. The stone had landed a glancing blow, opening a long but not deep cut that started above the left temple and ended behind the ear. The earlobe was turning purple with bruising and Dugas could see the reddened scratches the stone had left as it deflected off the side of Dixon's head. There was a lot of blood, but it was already beginning to clot. And Dixon was beginning to come round. Still, Dugas fished into one of his vest pockets.

"This ain't gonna be precision work, but it'll get the job done," Dugas jested, holding up the small bottle of superglue.

He gripped the side of Dixon's head, whose eyes shot wide open as soon as the wound was touched. Dugas applied the glue quickly and messily, forcing the skin on either side of the cut together. Dixon was more animated now, and Dugas pinned his nearest arm down with his knee. He waited a few more seconds, then, satisfied the glue had set – or at least would hold, he relented and helped Dixon to his feet.

"Cajun surgery," he grinned, "you're welcome".

Still groggy, Dixon stumbled forward slightly. Dugas read the body language and knew the man wasn't going to fall, so didn't insult him by rushing to his aid. It took a few moments, but he noticed Dixon's eyes sharpen and he stood up a little straighter.

"Thanks," he said. "What hit me?"

"This," Wade chimed in, holding up the rock.

Wade went to pass it to Dixon when another roar erupted from the trees behind them. He watched Hicks raise his gun – seemingly straight at him. Dugas was turning, thrusting Dixon's pistol back into the wounded soldier's hand, whilst slipping the shotgun from his shoulder and twisting round in Wade's direction. Instinct kicked in and Wade dropped to the ground and rolled. As he glanced sideways, a foot broader and longer than his head and neck combined, smashed down into the earth beside him. The skin was pinkish grey and had the appearance of cracked leather. Clumps of long, cinnamon coloured hair clothed the top of the foot and the ankle. The anatomy was recognisable, but monstrously deformed and oversized. The round bony protrusion above the ankle reminded him of his own feet, but this was the size of a tennis ball. Then Wade's gaze continued upwards.

It was only for a brief second, but for a moment, ten feet above him, black hued eyes and their mahogany-coloured pupils looked down in hatred at him. Wade heard no sound, even though he saw the impact of three bullets hitting its pectoral muscles. It didn't even look up. Then, as if disgusted by Wade's continued existence, the creature kicked at him with the side of his foot, shunting him aside as it raised its arms and faced its attackers. The back of Wade's head hit the ground with a thud, and he felt dizzy and then sick. He flailed, trying to right himself and get to his feet. As he dragged one foot out from the other, he made it into a kneeling position, just as a canister landed beside him, spewing a thick, green gas. He looked at it, confused and blinking slowly. Then it hit his lungs and he couldn't see anything as he started to cough violently. The next thing he knew, he was being lifted up and half dragged, half thrown through the smoke and into the trees.

His eyes were streaming, and he knew better than to wipe at them. He was with it enough to have recognised the tear gas. The next voice he heard was Agent Jones.

"Sorry kid, didn't realise you were lying there until it was too late."

Wade felt pressure on his shoulder as he was directed downwards. His knees bent instinctively, and his butt hit the pad of a seat. He realised he was sitting in a vehicle of some kind – probably a side-by-side from back at the camp.

"Haven't got time to give you anything else, put your head back," Jones demanded.

Wade knew what was coming next, but the cold stream of water that hit his face was still a shock. The canister was then thrust into his hand.

"Guessing you could do with a drink too if you got a lungful," Jones said. "Buckle up or hang on to something everyone, it's gonna be a bumpy ride."

Wade realised he was talking to the rest of the squad. He wasn't going to try and open his eyes yet, but he heard the others clamber aboard. He turned his head, registering he was in the back and Jones had climbed into the driving seat. A warm body crashed into his side. He didn't need to guess who it was – he could sense Dugas' sarcastic grin from where he sat. In the passenger seat in front of him, he could smell blood and knew Dixon was riding shotgun. He heard somebody climb onto the back of the rugged vehicle. The heel of their boots swung into his back before securing a footing on the metal frame.

"Go, go, go," came Hicks' cry a moment later. "Tango, seventy yards. Holding back for now but think he's getting worked up for something. Get us out of here."

"Might I suggest you try shooting the fucker," Jones yelled back as the engine roared into life.

As the vehicle lurched forward, Wade was thrown violently to the side, and he felt Dugas' hand grab him by the shoulder and reel him back in. Moments later, the seat harness was thrown around his shoulders for good measure.

"You just sit tight, Stevie Wonder," Dugas chimed.

Wade heard Dugas scramble up out of his seat – presumably to help cover the rear with Hicks. There was a sudden burst of automatic fire from Hicks' submachine gun, followed by two blasts of the shotgun.

"It's in the trees," Hicks yelled.

"Shoot where it's gonna be, not where it's at," Jones

growled back.

The vehicle swerved again, and Wade heard the engine whine in protest as they left the ground momentarily and smashed back down, changing direction as it did. He decided to try and open his eyes a little, as keeping them closed was making him feel nauseous. The ATV veered right and left repeatedly, and as Wade's eyelids forced themselves open a little way, he could see the dark blur of the trees they were weaving in between. There was another blast of the shotgun, and Dugas cursed under his breath. He fired again, and Wade heard cracking wood and the roar of the creature. He tried to twist around in his seat, as a huge branch and a dark form hit the ground like a meteor.

"Didn't get him, but got the branch he was aiming for," Dugas grinned.

The silhouette rose and broke into a run as another roar erupted from behind them. Hicks let loose with another volley of automatic fire.

"Aim for the head, the feet, or under the arm," Jones yelled, "or you're just pissing it off."

"The feeling's mutual," Hicks yelled, lifting his gun again. "Fuck, I've lost it... wait, I think it's still shadowing us on your left."

Jones snapped his head in the direction Hicks indicated. He saw nothing, and Dixon smacked the dashboard, pointing ahead. Wade looked up too. His vision was slowly improving, and saw what Dixon was pointing at. The old logging road they had been headed for was coming up. They were headed straight for it at a ninety-degree angle. There was a slight rise from the forest floor to join it, then they'd be past the trees and running alongside a clearing next to the road. Jones yanked the steering wheel hard, and the bulky all-terrain tyres bit into the dirt, doing all they could to find balance between momentum, grip, and gravity.

They hit the rise and began to turn sharply. Wade glanced out to the side and watched, confused for the briefest of moments as the darkness took form. Then it was there. The creature's face was distorted into a display of focused, savage rage. It wasn't charging directly at the vehicle, but was on a side-on, intercepting course. Wade saw it open its mouth as a roar sprang from its throat. There was no time to do anything, no warning he could give. With perfect timing, the creature's watermelon-sized shoulder slammed into the rear quarter of the ATV as they made the turn. The side-by-side sprang into the air as if it had been hit by an eighteen-wheeler. Wade closed his eyes and hung on to the safety harness. There was a jolting, jarring impact as the vehicle rolled, first onto its side, then once more until it sat on the trail upside down and half crushed.

Wade fumbled for the release on the harness. As he hit it, he dropped from the seat and the top of his head hit dirt. The metal frame of the ATV provided rigidity, but not a full roof. He crawled out into the open and tried to get to his feet. He felt drunk and recognised the effects of a concussion. He staggered forward, resting his hand on one of the upturned tyres to steady himself. He felt something grab his leg, and he jumped, frantically looking around for a weapon. Then, as he glanced down, he saw Dixon crawling from the passenger front seat, using the purchase he had on his leg to pull himself clear. Wade leant hard into the ATV, providing Dixon with the frame of his body to haul himself up. Jones came round from the other side of the ATV, his face smeared with dirt and blood. He held a large revolver in his hand, and his eyes darted to the treeline.

Wade looked to his left, hoping to see Dugas come round from the other side. Then, he remembered Hicks had been on the back.

"Others?" he managed to croak at Jones.

"Your pal's out cold," Jones replied. "Hicks... I don't know."

There was a flash of orange and then a burst of rapid gunfire from somewhere behind them. Wade was impressed with how quickly Jones and Dixon swivelled into position and raised their handguns. Wherever his rifle was, it wasn't to hand. There was only a split second of silence before the two soldiers were emptying their guns with loud, explosive fire. Wade wanted to see, and he willed himself to stand up and turn around. The only light afforded them came from the moon above and the half-broken headlights of the ATV, but it was enough. Wade saw the outline of the creature, like an ogre out of a fairy tale. It was standing up straight, one arm stretched out in front of it, raising something up off the ground. Wade realised with horror that it was Hicks, who was dwarfed in comparison. The beast had its hand wrapped around the soldier's throat, who was kicking his dangling feet and grappling at the bigfoot's arm. Wade felt his legs begin to give from under him as the gunfire came to an abrupt halt. Jones and Dixon were reloading.

He slumped back to the ground, his back against the upturned ATV. He was breathing with his mouth open, taking large gulps of air as he thought to stave off going into shock. Wade looked upwards, noticing the stars for the first time that night. There was no light pollution here, and they lit up the sky in their thousands. His attention was drawn to a particularly bright one to the west, and he focused on it. He thought it wasn't a bad view if it was going to be his last. There was no fight left in him now, probably due to blood loss and fatigue. He didn't have a weapon. A week ago, he didn't believe in bigfoot. Now, he was about to be killed by one. He guessed that wouldn't be on the gravestone, or the coroner's report though.

Wade looked with disbelief as the star he was watching began to descend, to the point it was just above the treetops. Then, even more alarmingly, the star split in two and began moving towards them. Suddenly, his ears were filled with thunderous noise. It took longer than it should to realise that he was watching two helicopters descend. One was much larger than the other. Wade identified it as a Sikorsky King Stallion – a heavy lift aircraft. The other looked like a black hawk, but a second glance revealed it to be a new variant known as the Jolly Green II, built for search and rescue. Both looked modified and were painted matt black. They passed close and fast. Wade watched as the creature dropped Hicks and charged towards the trees. But for once, the creature had been caught off guard. The big King Stallion passed over the soldiers, its rear troop door open. Wade saw what looked like a harpoon sticking out. There was an explosion of light and sound as it fired, jettisoning a huge, weighted net that fell over the creature with perfect precision. It snagged under its feet, and it fell to the ground.

The Jolly Green II was touching down, and Wade joined Jones and Dixon as they helped Hicks back to his feet. Up close, Wade could see Hicks' throat and the sides of his neck were red, and his eyes looked desperate and bloodshot. The creature had been choking the life out of him, and it had been doing it slowly enough to watch. It was probably the only reason Hicks was still alive. Together, they made their way towards the helicopter as the rotors began to wind down. Jones made sure Wade, Dixon and Hicks were all secured inside before they all turned back to watch was happening on the other side of the clearing.

From the slightly elevated position of the cabin seats, Wade could see the King Stallion was also landing. The net that had caught the creature was now enveloped in a thick, descending fog of putrid brown smoke. The breeze was light, but Wade could smell it from where he sat. Some form of knock-out gas he guessed. The operatives from the King Stallion were all dressed in black too and wore gas masks over their faces, and the same kind of night vision goggles Wade's team had been equipped with earlier. The big helicopter's rotors were still whirring, and the men in black worked fast. They quickly connected the net to a winch inside the helicopter. The rear troop door was fully descended, and Wade caught a glimpse of the King Stallion's insides. Closest to the rear door, a row of seats lined the wall on each side. From them, a familiar figure stepped down the ramp. Removing his gas mask, Major Clarke gave a simple nod in their direction. Wade peered past him, into the forward section of the aircraft. A huge metal wall separated the rest of the cabin – which the net was being winched towards with utmost speed. Wade had never seen anything like it before, but instantly knew what it was. A holding cell for something very large, and very strong. The pieces of the puzzle suddenly fell into place, and he realised he now had the answer to a question he'd been pondering ever since that night back at the fort. The creatures he'd encountered on that patrol weren't there by accident. They hadn't surrounded the base or moved in on it like the displaced animals he'd taken them for. They were being shipped there, perhaps from all over the country. But the answer only led to another question. Why?

~

Major Clarke eyed his prize through the tiny viewing slits of the titanium cell that took up the forward aspect of the modified Super Stallion helicopter's rear compartment.

"Sir, the second target has made contact with the bait, but its whereabouts are now unknown," one of the soldiers, explained, approaching him from behind. "The other helo is headed there to provide assistance."

Clarke nodded, glad that Jones' team would have something to keep them busy and off his back for a while. He turned around to see Commander De León, one of his best. This team were his specials – those that had survived countless incursions with the creatures and completed a minimum of three retrievals. He used them purely for captures, but he was already considering Hicks and Dixon to join the team. Wade was showing clear potential too, especially in leadership.

"Been a long time since we had one give us this much trouble," De León suggested. "You don't think it's... one of the others, sir?"

Clark snapped his head up quickly and assertively, then, he turned back to the holding cell and looked in again, as if deep in thought.

"No," he declared. "It's not one of them."

CHAPTER NINETEEN

BAD MEMORIES

Nina opened her eyes drowsily and glanced at the vibrating phone, sitting on the cabinet next to the bed. She fumbled for it, her motor skills still not quite responding in perfect unison with her brain. Picking it up, she looked at the screen; it was her boss, Marty. Although she'd been expecting the call, she was surprised to get it so soon. Travers was fighting for his life in a hospital bed because she had left a crime scene. There was only one way this was going to go. She pushed herself up, having collapsed face down on the bed before falling asleep, still in uniform. She swung her legs round into a sitting position and touched the screen to answer the phone. She was suddenly shocked to see Marty's face staring back at her, having failed to realise it was a video call.

"Sorry to disturb... I know it's been a rough and demanding couple of days," Marty said.

She could see he was in his office at HQ. Her eyes darted to the time stamp displayed at the top of the screen. It was three minutes to midnight – ironically the same as the doomsday clock. She hoped that was just a coincidence.

"I understand you went out to see Lucas Christian the other day," Marty continued.

She nodded, confused as to why that tidbit of information needed confirmation at this hour and before she was sacked, or worse, arrested.

"An automated alarm from his panic room has been going off for nearly an hour now, and we've been asked to go check in. I thought you might wanna do it, given the circumstances, and if you're up for it?"

Nina nodded again, slowly comprehending her worst

fears were not being realised – yet.

"There's something else," Marty added. "I know you also signed off the permits for the TV people. One of them, the Doctor, is gonna go in with you. Apparently, she has some trauma experience and might be of help."

"Is he being robbed, or is it a monster in the woods?" Nina jeered.

"They'll be with you in a few ticks, so get yourself ready," Marty replied, ignoring the jibe.

Nina guessed that as before, the orders were coming from elsewhere. The screen went blank as the call ended, and Nina put the phone back on the bedside cabinet. She got up, picking her gun and holster off the bed post and putting it back on. Across from the bed was an old, yellow-painted wardrobe with a mirror panel fixed to one of the doors. It had aged well and was showing signs of desilvering. Nina kind of liked it, and similarly to most other things in her father's cabin – it leant it character. The walls of the room matched the yellow of the wardrobe, with pink, floral patterned curtains framing the window as a stark contrast. She couldn't remember when she had last opened them. The room had been decorated for a little girl, and it hadn't changed much since she had returned to live with him. She needed to do something about that, but now wasn't the time.

Nina decided that her shirt wasn't too crumpled and wouldn't make her look too much like a hobo, at least not in the dark. She went into the bathroom and splashed some water on her face. When she stood back up, her father was standing in the doorway.

"Going somewhere?"

"Sorry, doing cop work again as they can't get up here," she explained.

Robert Lee fixed his daughter with a knowing look.

"When you get back, I think we should talk," he said.

"Dad... I don't want to be disrespectful, but I've got enough on my hands with nearly being killed by a drug cartel and the sheriff's department only ever coming up here to give campers parking fines, whilst leaving their dirty work for me."

"No drug cartel killed the logger," Robert warned.

"Fine, we'll talk about America's myths and legends when I get back, which will likely be three in the morning..."

"We can talk in the morning," Robert said softly.

Nina rolled her eyes but nodded. "Please don't wait up, I mean it, I'm gonna be late."

"I'm going to bed right now," he smiled. They both knew he was lying.

Nina took a coat from the pegs by the front door. There was no hall – just an open plan sitting room. Her father's bedroom was the only room upstairs. Like hers, it had its own bathroom. There was a kitchen the other side of the staircase on the ground floor, and a corridor that led to her room at the back. It was very simple, but her father worked hard to keep it in good condition. In a way, she was glad it hadn't changed too much since her childhood here. At times like this, it offered comfort and familiarity whilst she was still finding her feet.

She opened the door and put on the coat – a faux fur-lined arctic smock. She smiled as the black wolf, Achak, trotted round from the other side of the porch veranda. He butted his head against her leg in a soft growl of affection. She scratched between his ears, which twitched and then pricked up to their full height. Nina looked up, then heard what he had. A big engine was working hard as it made its way up the reservation's main, but still unmade road. Moments later, the big white Jeep that Travers had called the Wendigo, came into view. Nina could see Doctor Mary Beth Benoit was behind the wheel as it drew up.

"Go on," Nina whispered to Achak, who growled, but obediently disappeared back behind the house.

Benoit had the window down and looked at her in surprise. "Was that a..."

"Wolf, Nina replied, waving it off, "I get that a lot."

Benoit nodded at the empty passenger seat upfront, indicating she should get in. Nina walked around the truck and obliged. As she climbed in, she noticed Bodhi Prince and Katie Cash were sitting in the back.

"Hitching a lift," Prince grinned. "Joe's back at base, whilst we investigate from two different angles; you guys at this house that's been attacked, and us at ground zero in the forest."

Nina stared at them in abject disbelief.

"So, let me get this straight..." she started. "You think some kind of giant, undiscovered animal has taken up breaking and entering, and you want to be dropped off in the woods to go look for it?"

"It's kind of what we do," Prince shrugged. "Besides, we're going in with more than bad language," he added, tapping the Taurus revolver he'd been carrying when they met.

Nina shook her head. She was too tired to argue, and they had already proven they had friends in higher places than she cared to reach. If they wanted to get themselves killed, it was on them. She stared out of the window, angry with herself because she knew she wouldn't feel that way if something happened. She would feel responsible. She turned back to Bodhi and Cash.

"Look, I ran into a drug gang today, clearing up a site not far from here," she explained. "Any sign of trouble, and I mean any sign, get on the radio."

"Didn't know you cared," Cash, the blonde self-appointed leader of the Seeking Sasquatch team replied.

"I care about the paperwork," Nina sighed, half meaning it.

Nina went back to staring out of the window, preferring the silence to trying to make conversation. Her energy felt drained enough without the fatigue that would come from feigning interest in what they were doing. A few miles further in, Nina noticed they were winding along an old logging road. Bodhi Prince sat up, more alert and repeatedly glancing from his phone screen to the window.

"There should be a trail head coming up on the left," he indicated to Benoit. "Might as well make it our stop".

Benoit slowed the truck and began peering through the glass.

"It's okay, I know the one he means," Nina said. "We're not quite there yet. It's about three hundred yards, on the left like he said."

Sure enough, a little further on, they saw the wooden post with a green marker that indicated the trail. With the Wendigo's light bar and spotlights ablaze, it was easy to pick out. Benoit rolled to a stop as Bodhi Prince and Katie Cash climbed out of the truck.

"Give me a minute," Benoit said to Nina, also getting out but letting the engine run.

She left the driver's door open, and Nina noticed that the temperature had dropped. She craned forward and looked up, noticing that what had been a clear star-studded sky earlier, now featured some dark streaks of cloud. She turned around in her seat, as she heard the pneumatic jacks of the modified tailgate lift and then open the back. The truck sat high on its off-road suspension and chunky all-terrain tyres, putting her at eye level with the three TV personalities, as they began taking equipment out of the back. Benoit was helping them put on flexible, canvas material harnesses that housed GoPro cameras and lighting rigs on stalks that extended from their shoulders. This was in addition to the chunky, army-style packs they carried on their backs. Benoit helped Prince and Cash check their equipment, including the radios sitting in their harness shoulder pockets. They were positioned so they were close to the wearer's chest and within easy reach. To a certain degree, it did look like they knew what they were doing.

Nina watched through the rear-view mirror as Prince lifted a metal cover that lined the truck's trunk. When he shut it back down, he did so with one hand and was manoeuvring a modern looking shotgun with the other. He lifted it by the strap and Cash helped him slip it into the seemingly purpose-made holster sewn into his pack. He checked he could reach the handle from behind his head and grinned. Nina thought about saying something but decided against it. The one thing the last few days had shown her was the forest was not a safe place to be, and she wasn't going to nit-pick about weapon permits. Given it was so late it was early, she doubted they'd stumble across any hikers by accident. She knew the trails were closed and the area was as good as shut down, she just didn't like being unable to account for the unknown. You just never knew who might ignore the rules and go for a stroll. Or worse, just as the crew was, go looking for something. Then there were the veterans living off grid in their shelters, and as she'd discovered, the illegal cannabis growers, not to mention moonshiners, or even the ginseng and mushroom pickers. There were more things to worry about in the woods than just a potential monster.

She put those thoughts at the back of her mind. She did not linger on the possibilities of the existence of a creature. She could not understand why it made her so uncomfortable, or why elder folk like her father were as equally accepting of it as she was opposed. One thing was clear, there was no murderous bear out here. The federal and military presence she'd encountered made her think that there was a killer in the woods, but most likely, a human. Perhaps a serial killer on the run, or just some armed lunatic. She tried to remember if there had been any mass shootings on the news – nearby enough for the mountains and forests of Washington state to offer refuge to someone fleeing the authorities. She couldn't recall any, but admitted she was too tired to be at her cognitive best. She began to wonder if she should even be out here, as Benoit climbed back into the truck. As if flicking a switch, she came back to life in an instant and wound down the window.

"Check in every twenty minutes with both us and Joe at base," Nina commanded. "I don't think this is a run-of-the-mill night for any of us," she warned.

Bodhi Prince nodded and gave her what she guessed was meant to be a reassuring smile.

"And don't think I didn't see that canon you're carrying," Nina added. "I just think you're better off with it than without it. That should tell you how serious I think the situation is."

"We're both planning on walking back out of here in just a few hours," Cash said.

Nina picked up the intolerant, belittling tone.

"Well, with you wearing that expensive perfume, clean gear, and that perfectly shampooed and caressed hair, the likelihood of you finding anything downwind of you is pretty slim," Nina said, glowering.

Cash smiled, seemingly glad to have gotten a rise from Nina.

"Well, now I know who to come to for tips on how to wipe my butt with poison oak to blend in with the natives, don't I," Cash quipped, turning around quickly before Nina could reply.

A slurry of thoughts raced through Nina's mind, including pulling her gun on Cash before dragging her back to the car and calling the girl scout outing off. She almost was impressed how Cash had blended a personal insult about her looks and hygiene with a broader, racial one. The she felt Benoit's hand on her arm.

"Let's go," she said. "She's a bona fide bitch, and nothing gets her worked up more than getting her way. Ignore her – we all do, including the producers."

Nina rolled her eyes.

"I just want one good punch, just one," Nina laughed.

She let out the breath she'd been holding as a deep, releasing sigh.

"Sorry, I'm not a people person," Nina explained.

"Katie Cash is a lot of things," Benoit laughed, "but people, she ain't."

She smiled at Nina as she glanced over, before steering the truck back onto the track and allowing it to pick up speed again as they continued.

"Do you know where you're going?" Nina asked.

"I've put it in the nav," Benoit replied, pointing at the screen, but it doesn't seem to recognise this as an official road. I'm hoping it joins up with that line of blue at the top of the screen that indicates actual tarmac."

"It does," Nina said, smiling, "but don't go right like it says. Hang left, and we'll cut back up another logging road. Saves us about a mile and a half."

Benoit followed Nina's directions and they were soon driving up the now familiar private road that led to the house of Lucas Christian. As they drew up to the gates, Nina thought the house looked ominously dark. Doctor Benoit slid the window down and pressed the intercom button. As they waited, she exchanged concerned glances with Nina as no answer came. She reached out to press the buzzer a second time, when it suddenly crackled into life.

"She's dead... I think she's dead," came a distraught voice in reply.

Nina was shocked. It didn't sound anything like the confident, self-assured man she'd met just a few days ago.

"Mister Christian, it's Nina Lee with the Ranger Service," she said, leaning past Benoit and hoping she could be heard. "Do you remember me? We need to come in and see if you're alright."

"I... I'm locked in... I need to... the security... oh God, is it still out there?" Lucas Christian stammered.

Nina caught Benoit's look of alarm as her eyes widened in surprise.

"Mister Christian, we know you're in your panic room. Can you access the security from there? If you let us in, we will check everything is safe before you have to come out."

She paused. When there was no reply, she tried a different tack.

"You said somebody was dead. Who's dead Mister Christian?"

"My wife... my ex-wife. I think it killed her."

Suddenly the gates groaned and began to swing open. Benoit put the truck into drive and powered forward, quickly ascending the short, curved road up to the house. She drove right up to the imposing front door and killed the engine but left the light rig running.

"What killed her?" Benoit whispered as they got out of the truck.

"I don't know... but I guess they thought you should come along for the ride for a reason," Nina replied.

They both heard a loud, metallic bang that made Benoit jump. Nina could see genuine fear in her eyes. It made her concerned. If this was a murder scene, she needed to know Benoit could handle it.

"You okay, Doc?" Nina asked.

"Shitty memories," Benoit replied. "I'm fine, honest."

There were two more metallic pings and then what sounded like a deadbolt sliding out of place. Nina caught movement out of her peripheral vision, and instantly drew her weapon. She pointed the barrel of the .357 Magnum revolver at the window, then relaxed. Dark, metal shutters were raising up on the interior. She put the gun back in its holster but took out a flashlight – a Streamlight Protac that she always had clipped to her belt. Nina pushed open one side of the double front door. The main lights were not on, but there was the soft glow of emergency lighting coming from somewhere. She used the flashlight to find the switches on the wall and brought the house back to life with a few flicks of her fingers.

"Just be on your guard," Nina warned, "he has dogs – big dogs. I think they were Tibetan mastiffs."

"Do you think that's what he meant, when he said something had killed his wife?" Benoit asked.

"I only just remembered, but I think it's worth considering."

Nina and Benoit headed along the corridor. Nina was in no rush to get to the panic room before she knew the location was safe and clear. Nothing seemed too out of the ordinary on the ground floor, and Benoit made to head up the stairs. Nina shook her head and directed her past, towards the kitchen and the rear of the house. They entered the room together. Again, nothing seemed out of place, and they followed it through to the adjoining large room that looked out over the back portion of the estate. Nina remembered the state-of-the-art ballistic glass that made up the floor to ceiling windows. She walked over to them and looked out. The same Washington state wilderness looked back, but then something caught her eye. She raised her flashlight and tried to shine it through the glass, but found it was no good. She looked over the frame of each window but couldn't find an obvious way to open them. Giving up, she backtracked to the kitchen and made for the side door.

"Do you think it's safe to go out there?" Benoit asked, the uncertainty showing in her voice.

Nina shrugged and swung the door open. She took out the revolver again and did a quick scan with the torch before stepping out. She moved quickly, resting her gun hand on the one holding the flashlight, giving her a stable shooting platform if she needed it. Nina kept her head as still as possible, letting her peripheral vision do all the work. The air was crisp and still, but within a few steps, she could smell the blood in the air. Working her way across the small rear courtyard, including its expensive outdoor furniture and kitchen, she soon found herself at the path that led away from the house. She paused, now much closer to the object that had caught her attention. She was sure the ominous blob had not been there when she and Travers had visited just a few days ago. Lifting her hands slightly, the beam of the flashlight sought it out. The gasp that escaped her lips was involuntary, and she regretted it immediately as she felt the presence of Benoit behind her. Illuminated for them both to see, was the dead and broken body of one of the dogs. It lay at the bottom of a large conifer, its paws jutting out just far enough to stretch across part of the path. It was hard to believe that such a large and powerful animal had been so violently overcome.

"What in the Sam Hill..." Nina heard Benoit mutter.

"Maybe a mountain lion, or a bear," Nina started to reply.

"Not the dog, look at those prints over yonder," Benoit exclaimed.

Nina turned, and there, just within reach of the flashlight, she saw them. She froze. Etched against the pristine porcelain slabs that made up the path were a series of blood-stained tracks. She took a few steps closer, but she already knew what they were. Their form was obvious – footprints at least eighteen inches long and maybe eight or more inches across. Benoit walked past her and took a pack off her shoulder. Unzipping the front and reaching in, she took out a compact and expensive-looking SLR camera. Benoit poised over the footprints and began taking pictures.

"Don't touch or disturb anything, we're presuming this is a crime scene," Nina reminded her.

"Want to see something cool?" Benoit asked.

Nina nodded, although hesitant and wanting to reach Lucas Christian. But quietly, she wanted to examine the footprints close up too. She took a knee beside the doctor, who was looking over the closest with a steely gaze. It was as if she was going over it with a fine-toothed comb in her mind.

"So, as you can probably imagine, the average sasquatch is a little bigger than us humans," Benoit began.

"Imagine is the right word," Nina smiled.

Benoit took the jibe acceptingly and smiled back.

"Well, imagine how the foot might have to evolve to accommodate excessive bodyweight," Benoit continued. "If you look at this print, we see some of the biological adaptations that go with that."

Benoit started at the heel end of the track.

"Look how wide this is. Then, as we continue up, we see it has flattened arches," Benoit explained. "You and I, we have what's known as an instep – or a longitudinal arch to give it its name from the medical books. It's a natural feature seen in human footprints. We have an arch because our ligaments and tendons maintain it through the way we walk and the way we're built. But if we were bigger, our feet wouldn't have the strength to support our weight, and the arch would naturally flatten. Let me ask you a question; if you were to double in height and keep all your proportions the same, how much would you weigh?"

"I guess twice as much," Nina shrugged.

Benoit shook her head. "You'd think so, but biological physics is more fun than that. Density is the key here. Your structure, the cross-sectional aspects of your anatomy, would increase times squared. That alone means your muscles and supporting tissues would be four times stronger, even though you've only doubled in size. At the same time, weight increases times cubed – so you'd be eight times heavier."

"I've had lunches like that," Nina smiled, raising an eyebrow.

"So, sasquatch anatomy has to be different from ours, otherwise his strength would be cut in half," Benoit explained. "We can see that just in the foot. The toes show an almost uniform size, and there is a double-ball feature at the base of the big toe. We only have one. What I'm saying is, in short, these are strange, uniquely corresponding anatomical features that match what we know about these creatures. And it would be very unlikely somebody just happened to include them all in a fake footprint."

"What you're saying is, we can discount somebody with boards strapped to their feet," Nina concluded, her eyes widening a little.

Benoit nodded.

"Let's head inside," Nina suggested. "We need to find Christian and find out what happened here."

"Let me finish up here and I'll be right behind you," the doc replied.

As Nina walked away, she heard Benoit's phone ring. She left her to her conversation and backtracked to the house, re-entering via the kitchen. Her gun and flashlight were back out and she now pointed them both up the first part of the stairway. It was wide and wooden, and it creaked under her weight. The staircase led to a flat intersection, where another set of stairs joined it at a 90-degree angle, then a further intersection joined with a third and final staircase leading to the upper floor. Nina worked her way up steadily, her back to the wall and her gun and flashlight always pointing up. She felt her chest tighten and her mouth was dry, as if she needed a drink. She took the final step up.

To her right, there was a short length of corridor that led to a window facing the rear of the property. She glanced towards it, clocking the door to its left as she faced it. It was open, and an eerie, soft glowing light crept towards her from it across the carpet. As she squinted, she could see the light was being reinforced by a faint, pulsing orange light that flashed slowly and steadily from within. She wanted to head towards it and investigate, but her instincts were tugging her left. She had learned a long time ago to trust her gut.

Left, the corridor continued to a similar window at the other end of the property, this time facing the front. She followed the wall that met the staircase, until she came to a corner, where the corridor widened. Although she had scanned the walls, she had been yet to find the switches for the lights on the upper levels. Instead, she used the flashlight to scan ahead. Up on the left, almost at a perfect 45-degree angle to her, was another door. It too was open, and light spewed from the room beyond, although she still couldn't see in. And just like outside, she could smell the blood. She took a breath to steady herself and crept forward.

She could see the room was well lit, but her view was obscured by a narrow corridor that led further in. All she could see was another wall beyond the door. With her gun still raised, she carefully and slowly switched off the flashlight in her other hand and clipped it back onto her belt. Nina pushed the door open with her free hand and stepped inside. She noticed the thick, greasy, blood splattered stains on the carpet first. They led from inside the room, out past her into the corridor. Annoyed she hadn't spotted them before, she backtracked. She soon realised why she hadn't seen them. Each print was over six foot apart. Her mind began to race, desperately trying not to confront the reality it was headed towards. Whatever had made the tracks had stepped from the room to the other side of the corridor in one easy stride. It had then made it to the next door – the one with the pulsing light, in two steps. It can't be human she told herself.

Her methodical nature drew her back to the door on the left. She wanted to see where it had been before she saw where it had gone. With each step, she checked to ensure she wasn't disturbing any evidence. Once inside the corridor, she could smell more than just blood. The air was humid, and she guessed that she was entering a bathroom. Adding to that, the scent of a fragranced candle – peppermint and eucalyptus, hung heavily. Together they veiled, but not altogether hid, the odour she'd picked up back at Dalton's cabin; strong and musky, but only a fraction of its strength when she had first encountered it. The overlapping scents did not go well together, and she had to fight the gag reflex it was creating. She fought it back then turned the corner.

Nina had seen death before, but not like this. Her posture stiffened and she felt her muscles become rigid. Her skin tingled and her heart raced, and there was a heaviness in her stomach that protested, wanting to vacate her body. She was rooted to the spot, and she felt her hands turn clammy as a cold sweat sent a shiver down her spine. Unconsciously, she took a step back, seeking the wall to press her back against. It was only when she felt dizzy that she realised she was holding her breath. As she inhaled a gasp of air, she shut her eyes and controlled her breathing, her bladder, and her bowels, to regain control over her body. Her breathing became shallower, and she wiped the dampness from the back of her neck. She tilted her head as she heard footsteps coming up the stairs and then along the corridor towards her. Her eyes snapped open.

"Don't come in here," she commanded.

The woman's body, what was left of it, had its legs splayed across the floor. The torso lay prostrate, the other side of the still full bathtub. Nina couldn't yet tell if the red water was from bath salts, or blood. Guessing by how much of the latter was congealing on the floor tiles, she had to presume the worst. The head propped against the wall at an unnatural angle. The woman's left side, from the collar bone to her naval, was ripped open. Her breast and pectoral muscles were missing and there was a gaping hole in her abdomen. Nina knew it shouldn't be that clean and empty. To create the cavity, some of the insides had been removed and presumably devoured. On the same side, the shoulder and arm were ripped open too. The deltoid and bicep muscles had been stripped down to the bone. Only tatters of flesh and skin remained, which made the rest of the mostly in-tact arm below the elbow joint look out of place.

Her own mother had been victim to an animal attack, and Nina had been with her when she died. Those memories came flooding back now, attacking her integrity as she tried to hold things together. But there was something else too, tugging at her from her subconscious. Nina heard the crunch of glass under her foot, and it brought her back to the present. She looked down to see the floor was covered in tiny, broken shards and fragments. They too were bloodstained, and as she neared, she saw bloody handprints on the rim of the tub. This has been a prolonged attack; one the woman had fought against. There were no windows that Nina could see, and there was more glass than would have come from a vase or ornament. She felt a blast of icy fresh air from above, and she felt relieved as it helped quell her nauseousness and cool her hot skin. She closed her eyes and let it waft over her, raising her head as she did so. When she opened her eyes, she could see the remnants of the skylight above, and there was no more mystery as to where the glass had come from.

"Can I come in now?" Benoit asked from the hallway.

"Have you seen a dead body before, or been around animal attacks?" Nina asked. "I've not seen one this bad. I wouldn't recommend it."

"I was talking to Special Agent Smith," Benoit explained. "Bureau bums and a coroner are on their way. They don't want us to touch anything. But they've asked me to see if I can discern what kind of animal it was."

"If I didn't know better, I'd say a great white shark attacked her in the bathtub, after dropping through the skylight," Nina exclaimed. "I obviously can't stop you coming in, but I..."

Nina turned around, realising Benoit had already entered the room behind her. She recognised the same processing of emotions, nausea, and shock that she had been fighting. She was impressed that Benoit managed to keep her dinner down. This clearly wasn't her first rodeo. Benoit gathered herself and took a few steps forward. Nina pointed out the glass on the floor. But Benoit didn't seem to notice. She took a knee, close to the body – much closer than Nina had gone. Her law enforcement training had kicked in and she hadn't wanted to disturb the scene. She wanted to say something, to justify why she hadn't, or why Benoit shouldn't. But she dismissed the thoughts. Benoit wasn't an idiot.

"Holy shit, I think we've hit the jackpot," Benoit

exclaimed.

Nina moved a little closer, curious as to what she meant.

"We've already got the footprints from outside, but this is the motherload," Benoit said. "I'm going to have to be present when they process the scene, I can't have them missing this evidence."

Benoit leant in a little closer.

"Oh my," she said quietly. "Our boy wasn't being subtle."

"What do you mean?" Nina asked.

"These creatures are masters of stealth and concealment," Benoit replied in awe. "We jokingly call them the ninjas of the woods. I don't know if it's his injuries, or because he felt singled out, but our boy just threw caution to the wind."

"Out of interest, how do you know it's a guy," Nina asked.

"What I'm looking at, running down this poor woman's face and intact shoulder, is semen."

"What?!" Nina said, horrified. "You don't think it..."

"No," Benoit said, shaking her head. "Believe it or not, it's not about sex. It's a biproduct of the testosterone and adrenaline build up when they go into flight or fight mode. It's also thought possibly to be a sign of strength. Great apes – especially chimpanzees, tend to attack the face and genitals. By putting your junk on display, you're saying what a big, aggressive animal you are and you're confident you can deal with an attack."

"Model society," Nina replied, not impressed.

Benoit shifted to her side and glanced between the legs of the dead woman.

"Definitely showing signs of bite marks, so we might have saliva too," Benoit added. "And" she said, pointing, "we have hair too. That's not hers."

Nina saw the strands, much darker than those of the

woman's, smeared against a bathroom tile in two conjoined drops of congealed blood.

"Let's do what we came here to do, if you're confident our friend isn't still here," Nina suggested.

"He'd never let us get this close to a food source," Benoit replied, shaking her head. "He's long gone."

~

Shartale was being led by instinct. He had fed after killing the human female but had not been satiated. Rather, he had indulged his need to punish and terrorise the male human that had moved so blatantly against him. Robbed of that opportunity, he knew better than to stay in one place. His wounds were sapping him of his strength, and it would be dangerous to attract the attention of others, as had been the case in the forest. He was making an obvious, heavy trail, and he intended to do so until he could find what he knew his body needed. Travelling south and following his nose, he soon discovered it. The bank of yarrow plants was not yet in flower, but it was only their leaves he needed. He stripped them from several stems and stuffed them into his mouth, chewing them into a thick paste. Placing it carefully on his fingers, he began to smear it across his open wounds, paying attention to his feet in particular. The natural clotting properties of the plant soon kicked in, and he rested a while, enabling the wounds to cool and scab over.

As he had discovered back in the forest, just after killing Adotey, his body had not escaped the sting of the human's weapons either. He traced his fingers over his leg, arm, and chest, finding a round, metal stone in each, flattened and wrapped in a wad of his own hair and fused into his skin. The one on his chest had barely scratched him, but the ones on his leg and arm had dug a little deeper. For those, he used his claws to extract them, and again chewed yarrow leaves to clot the wounds. With his nose close to the ground and on all fours, he also sought out greenbriar and red clover. These plants he chewed into a pulp and swallowed down whole. Now, he needed water and he moved with more caution and up into the trees. His ears picked up the sound of a slow-moving creek before he smelt it, and he dropped to its bank and lowered his lips to its surface, washing down the medicinal plants. Although he only knew they were making him feel better, their anti-inflammatory and blood purifying properties were already resetting his incredible biological systems.

His thirst quenched, he crossed the water in an effort to both hide his scent and clean his wounds further, and then lifted himself back into the trees. This time, he headed north, in the opposite direction to the heavily laid trail he'd left in the wake of his attack. He needed to rest and began to look for a safe place to bed down. But even now, his instinct was telling him that a threat remained in the forest. Shartale climbed high and then froze, pressing his chest against the trunk of the black cottonwood tree he was in. At first, it was difficult for him to pick up on anything out of the ordinary. He knew humans could be found in the forest. He'd followed them along trails, hidden in the trees as he was now. So, it wasn't out of the ordinary for their scent to lace the air. Their raw, earthy must was often wrapped in acrid chemical taints that were hard to ignore. Most of his kind had learned to treat these unnatural scents with disgust and distaste. They signalled humans were near and to move on. But for him, it was an easy way to trace a potential meal.

He did not know how long he had stayed watching from the tree when he decided to risk moving his nose into the wind. It came to him almost immediately. There were two of them, a male and a female. Shartale was not ignorant to the knowledge that killing humans came with a price. They would search for him. They would make up for their lack of strength and size in mere numbers. It was something he had accepted after the death of his clan, and his decision to punish those that carried out their murders. He had accepted it when he had chosen not to retreat into the forest when the human had tried to trap him. And now, he made his decision to hunt humans once more knowing the risks. But he needed to eat as well as rest, and he could not do the latter until he knew this part of the forest was free of humans and their weapons. He climbed back down the trunk silently and carefully, then reached out for a branch in a neighbouring red cedar. Following his nose, he headed in their direction.

~

Nina stepped into what she guessed had once been a very plush office. What it was now, it was hard to say. The furniture had been torn to pieces. The remains of a desk lay splintered across the floor, barely recognisable. What she guessed was excrement was smeared across the walls, and three smashed computer monitors sat fizzing and sparking in what could only be pools of urine. She couldn't help but think how thrilled Benoit would be. She was co-ordinating the arrival of the feds but would be back soon enough. It was almost impossible to not disturb evidence here. The destruction had been absolute. The frame of a once expensive executive chair sat upturned and twisted, the leather seat torn and shredded in its bent frame. She knew that both her and Benoit's prints, boot patterns, and even probably a hair and DNA sample might be taken, to exclude them when the evidence was processed. And most likely, the same would be required of the man in the panic room, on the other side of the door she was approaching. Nina pushed the intercom panel next to it, hoping it still worked. It flashed green, giving her hope. There was a hissing of slight static.

"I... I can't move," came the distressed, high-pitched voice from the intercom.

Nina found it hard to believe this was the same man she had met and spoken to just a few days before. So confident and assured in his power and capability. An animal, and mother nature, had stepped in to teach him some humility. But Nina recognised shock when she heard it, and the lesser mentioned side-effect and third child of adrenaline fatigue. After fight or flight, came freeze. Mind and body would have to be convinced it was safe to move again. Stay still too long in that condition and the body might just shut down altogether. Nina knew she had to get him to come out of shock and what were now recognised as the initial symptoms of post-traumatic stress.

"Mr. Christian, it's okay," Nina assured him. "Federal agents are here, and whatever animal did this has gone. It's safe to come out, I wouldn't let you if it wasn't."

"I feel like I'm having a heart attack, I don't know what to do," Christian stammered.

"Just concentrate on the sound of my voice," Nina said softly. "We're going to take some deep breaths together, okay?"

"Okay," he sobbed.

Nina could hear the slight hope and release in his voice.

"So first, we're gonna take a deep breath in," Nina instructed. "As we breathe in, we're going to count to four, okay?"

Nina didn't hear anything.

"Mr. Christian, I can't hear you if you nod, so you'll have to keep saying yes I'm afraid," she hinted.

The man laughed, as if she'd hit a valve to release pressure, and she could hear him wiping away tears.

"Okay, let's do it together, deep breath... one, two, three, four. Now hold it for a sec. Now, as we exhale, count to eight."

They did it, and she heard Lucas Christian take a big gulp of air after. It had been a push for him, but it had done the job of getting him to focus. There was a hissing noise and the door suddenly released, pushing open slightly. Nina moved back slowly as he stepped out of the room.

"Mr. Christian, I'm going to take you downstairs and one of my colleagues is going to look after you," Nina explained. "They'll have some questions for you, but if you don't feel up to it right now, you get them to come get me, and I'll get them off your back."

Lucas Christian nodded, and he followed Nina out of the room and down the stairs, head down, and not looking at the carnage around him. By the time they got to the lower level, Nina could see that several black SUVs were parked outside – visible through the open door. They were dwarfed by the dark-coloured big rig that sat behind them. None of the vehicles had any markings that she could make out, other than that of the Medical Examiner. Her green and white Chevy Silverado was out front, and Nina could see she was deep in conversation with Benoit.

Nina was relieved to see someone in authority that she knew. She didn't trust the bureau bums one bit and was half expecting evidence to be covered up. But Doctor Charlotte Taylor was a professional – and she, Nina trusted. Nina had attended her lectures during her time at the University of Washington, Tacoma. The course on cadaver examination and wilderness death investigation was not a mandatory one, but something she had wanted to do. The knowledge she had gained had served her several times in the field, and in turn, Doctor Taylor had come to know and trust Nina too.

"Two doctors for the price of one," Nina said, approaching them.

"Your friend was just telling me about your great white

shark theory," Doctor Taylor smiled.

"Have you been in there?" Nina asked.

Doctor Taylor nodded. "I've had a looksee, but we're currently arguing over paperwork before I go back in."

"What's the issue?" Nina asked.

"They need me here, but at the same time, I'm a fifth wheel," Taylor explained. "This is the sort of thing they'd rather make go away, but they're way too interested in the gory details, so they need me," she grinned. "I'll have to sign some clause or such, but I'll be in soon."

"You can go in now, Doctor Taylor," Nina heard someone say from behind.

She turned to find Special Agent Gregory Smith climbing down the steps of the big rig – clearly a mobile command post of some kind.

"Sorry to have kept you," Smith said politely but dismissively.

Doctor Taylor bowed her head and picked up her bag, following Benoit into the house.

Smith turned towards Nina.

"You've had an interesting couple of days," he offered.

Nina nodded. "Is what she said true... is all this going to be covered up?"

"Right now, all that matters is the truth," Smith replied. "After that, it's not my decision. I know you don't trust us, and I know we didn't help with that, but we're cogs in the same machine, not a spanner in the works."

Nina got the feeling he was telling the truth.

"Is he going to be alright?" she asked, nodding back towards the house.

"We're not disappearing anyone, if that's what you mean," Smith smiled. "Sorry, maybe a poor attempt at humour. It wouldn't hurt if he confirmed our suspicions that it was a mountain lion attack."

Nina stared at him. She had considered the possibility. Black bears were brilliant climbers, but the walls of the house would be way beyond their capabilities. A grizzly would definitely poke around a house if it got the chance, but would enter through the ground floor, and there was no sign of that kind of damage. A cat was a decent candidate. It could have climbed a tree, gotten access to the terrace and scaled the roof from there. A big tom would have no trouble jumping up to fifteen feet. That put it within easy reach. The only thing was the victim. Lions simply didn't kill or eat like that. They had the decency to put you out of your misery first, usually through a suffocating bite to the throat. There had been no wounds to the neck she had seen. Despite dismissing them as suspects, the injuries were like those dealt out by a bear. They offered their victims no such respite. You were alive when they began to feed. It made her shudder as she thought of her mother again.

Nina was shaken from her thoughts as Benoit walked out to join her.

"How is he?" Nina asked.

"Physically, he's unharmed," Mary Beth replied. "But mentally, he's in a world of hurt. I know you don't want to hear it, but he says it was the monster in the woods that did it."

Nina raised an eyebrow. "Convenient, given the subject matter of his next novel," she replied.

"Maybe there's something that'll convince you out back," Benoit suggested.

Reluctantly but obediently, Nina followed Benoit back through the house to the rear courtyard and the path that led towards the forest. They had to work their way around the sections that hard been cordoned off with crime scene tape and moved past the tree where they'd discovered the body of the dog. Benoit moved to the far side of the path and approached a different tree – a Sitka spruce. She stepped on to the dirt to examine it closely and beckoned Nina over to look. What had caught her attention was easy to see. Four slashing claw marks had been etched into the trunk, ripping the bark open and puncturing deeply into the wood beneath. Sap seeped from it. Their length alone eliminated the mountain lion from the suspect list – although she had once encountered a cat perhaps capable of doing such damage. But that had been no mountain lion, and neither was this. Each claw mark was over forty inches long and spaced nearly two inches apart from the others. Her memories began to tug at her again as she thought of grizzlies, and out of place predators she'd encountered before. But her subconscious was telling her she knew better. She knew what this was. She froze and gasped involuntarily as the memory fought its way to the surface.

The meadow was wide and filled with golden coloured grass, scorched by a hot summer. Woven among their blades were numerous wildflowers soaking up the sun before the rains and cool of fall hit. She was six – no, seven, she thought. With her head down, she had not noticed how close to the treeline she was. Excitedly she had scampered from tree to tree, now adding mushrooms to her foraging. Happy and content, she sang to herself as she often did back then. It made her wonder when she had stopped singing like that. Was this the day? It was as she passed a particularly large fir that the creature had dropped to the ground. Nina had turned, expecting to see a black bear – she'd seen one of those fall from a tree before. But this was no bear. The creature had a distorted, ugly face. Its body was covered in thick, dark brown and blackish hair. The thing was at least three times her size. Even though it was on all fours, it blocked out the sun – its shadow enough to engulf hers. As it looked at her, it bore a strange grin that revealed its fang-like teeth. In her mind, it now seemed malevolent, perhaps even evil. It was purposely trying to scare her. As if to confirm this, the beast struck the earth with its fists, sending a tremor through the ground which she felt under her feet. It wanted her to run. She didn't.

Nina had felt her anger burn as she moved with the severity and speed only a life-or-death situation could conjure. In her basket was a thin, pointed stone she had picked up earlier. She whipped it into her hand and flung it with force and precision. It hit the creature in its eye socket, and it stumbled back, more in surprise than anything else. But it bought her the time she needed. She had burst into a lightning quick sprint back towards home – the line of small cabins on the other side of the meadow. The anger was gone now, and as she ran for her life, the tears flowed without inhibition. Her heart thundered in her chest, then she realised the rhythmic thumping she could hear did not come from her, but from the creature in pursuit. Each of its steps were equal to ten of hers, and it roared savagely as it drew near. In moments, it was within a few yards of her and all she could imagine was it reaching for her from behind.

Then, with a cry, she had seen her father. He stood tall and had his bow drawn. She screamed as she ducked under a tree branch and threw up her arms as she sprinted towards him with all her remaining strength. She had watched her father tense and then release the arrow, which took flight as if in slow motion. She didn't look back as it sailed over her head and kept running. But her father wasn't looking at her. He was still looking behind her. He reached behind him and pulled out the deadly tomahawk axe he carried everywhere and forbade her to touch, due to how sharp he kept it. Then, Nina had seen her father relax, lowering the weapon and finally fixing his eyes on those of his daughter. He had knelt and swept her up into his arms, wiping away her tears as she nestled into his shoulder. But instead of walking towards the homestead, he headed towards the trees. Nina knew better than to question her father, but she noticed the fear in his eyes.

"Nothing to fear little one, the Bukwus has gone," he had told her. "But I need my arrow back, and I will show you his mark, so you recognise it from now on."

Her father had put her down on the ground as he retrieved the arrow, then walked over to a tree a little further into the woodline. He again crouched down and put his arm around her as he showed her the sign of the creature he had called Bukwus. Four deep claw marks slashed into the bark of the tree, large enough for him to need both of his hands to show their length and breadth.

~

As often as she could, Katie Cash preferred to delegate the field operations to other members of the team. Her job, as far as she saw it, was to look good on camera whilst giving soundbite summaries of their findings and adventures. However, this seemed as close as they had ever come to getting the golden ticket footage she had always hoped for. And if they did capture a sasquatch on film, then it was also her ticket out of here. Nobody was going to take either of those opportunities away from her. Also, the events of the last few days had made her stressed and uncomfortable, so time alone with Bodhi wasn't the worst thing. She needed a release and if they got the opportunity, she knew he would oblige. He was a natural adventurer and would live in the woods if they let him. Benoit was purely in it for the science, and unlike her, seemed genuinely uninterested in the potential fame that was beckoning with any discovery. Even Joe was more at home in the field than she was, and he was a bona fide geek and conspiracy theorist.

She wasn't sure how far they'd hiked but she was close to

declaring it was far enough, when Bodhi came to an abrupt halt and turned around. He dropped his pack from his shoulder and leant it up against a tree. He was smiling at her with knowing intent.

"I think we're far enough from prying eyes," he declared.

He reached up and turned off the camera on his harness. Katie did the same.

"I think we're far enough from anything," she smirked, sidling up to him and wrapping her arms around his neck.

She kissed him, strongly and passionately, the rigours of the hike releasing into it. Her muscles were hardened and her skin sweaty from keeping pace with Bodhi. Somehow, even now, he smelt good – like sandalwood.

"And I thought we were here to look for sasquatch," she murmured, unbuckling her belt, and letting her pants fall to the ground.

"Didn't you know," Bodhi laughed, "they're attracted to sexual activity. Our pheromones will draw it in like nothing else."

"Then let's get releasing them," Katie implied, turning away from him, and placing her hands up against the tree where he'd left his pack.

Bodhi unbuckled his own pants and placed his hands on Katie's wiggling hips. He explored with his fingers, kneading, and pressing tightly, then massaging her, slowly at first, then harder and faster. As her murmuring increased, so did his own excitement and he thrust against her. He pushed against her obliging body, which squeezed and gripped him from within. First, their love making was violent and fast, then they began to slow as it became more sensual. He leaned over her, cupping her breasts in his hands and pushing his chest against her back. His hot breath stung her neck, sending shivers of excitement down her spine. Then Bodhi suddenly stopped.

"Fuck me," he declared, breathless.

"It's a little hard from this position," Katie smiled, looking over her shoulder.

But Bodhi wasn't looking at her. He was looking straight ahead. His withdrawal from her was sudden and made her cry out, more in surprise than pain. She was about to whirl on him and educate him on the dos and don'ts of illicit intimacy, when she caught movement in her peripheral vision. She froze and turned her head back towards the trees.

What she saw made no sense. She had read thousands of reports on sasquatch and interviewed hundreds of alleged eyewitnesses, but nothing had prepared her for what she was looking at. Katie knew she stood five foot seven, three inches taller than the average female in the US. She doubted she would even be eye level with the creature's naval – if it had one. With thick hair that covered its body, it was impossible to tell. Its head was the size of a county fair pumpkin and seemed to sink into its shoulders, giving the appearance of having no neck at all. Its musculature was daunting yet functional. Nothing looked out of proportion. The creature had significant bulk and was broadly wide at the shoulders with a relatively narrow waste. It was running straight at them, upright and on two feet, yet it made almost no sound. In fact, she realised it was the crunch of the underbrush and the snapping of tree branches in its way she could hear as it approached. It was like nothing she had ever seen. And it was fast – so fast. Before her body and brain reacted to the predator staring her down, it had reached them.

It seemed to pay no attention to Katie, knocking her aside with its momentum as it passed. It connected with Bodhi at full speed. It was like being hit by a pick-up truck. Bodhi flew backwards awkwardly, his pants around his ankles still tying his legs together, and his arms flailing uncontrollably. He smashed into the ground nearly twenty feet away, rolling backwards. His camera harness and equipment twisted and bent around him, biting into his flesh. The light rig couldn't take the beating and snaped off, breaking up as it splintered over the dirt. Katie had been spun onto her back, and she now faced Bodhi – the creature turned away from her as it approached him. Slowly and carefully, Katie slid her own pants back up and fastened the polymer belt. Then, with a smooth, controlled, and equally slow movement, she reached up to her own harness and turned the camera back on.

The creature was in no rush. It almost seemed to leer at Bodhi as he struggled to his feet, distracted by his torn pants around his ankles. He was confused by the sense of shame he felt at being vulnerable and exposed like this. The pack with the shotgun wasn't far – still lying at the base of the tree no more than six feet away now. At least the thing had thrown him in a convenient direction. The creature dropped its head slightly, as if it could read his thoughts. Bodhi dove for the pack, but the creature's arm – nearly matching the length of Bodhi's body, shot out and plucked him from the air, its fingers wrapping around his neck with ease. It lifted him straight into the air, letting him dangle as he fought with both of his hands for release. He couldn't even get the monster's fingers to move. Bodhi felt the blood pounding in his head; his skin became scorched with heat as the flow of air was slowly and methodically cut off. Then horrified, he watched as the creature's gaze fell to his exposed penis and testicles.

Seemingly fascinated, the sasquatch probed the organs gently with a finger. It reached behind Bodhi, then lifted him up higher and rotated its wrist so it could see behind him. Then its maroon-orange eyes met his and Bodhi gasped in renewed terror. Its thumb and two fingers wrapped around his sex organs and simply began to pull. There was no haste or violence about it, it simply increased pressure as it encountered resistance – as if it was conducting a scientific experiment as to what would happen. The burning sensation in his testicles made Bodhi want to scream, but the fingers latched around his throat denied him even that. It was as if a dozen white-hot knives had been inserted into his groin. There was a tearing sound, and then a pop, and the pain transitioned into a less violent, throbbing sensation. Bodhi thought he could hear rain, but as he glanced down, he was shocked to see his own blood, as it poured from between his legs. The creature examined the bloody morsels in its hand and scooped them up into its mouth. It chewed a few times, then thought better of it and swallowed its mouthful. It dropped Bodhi as if discarding a spoiled piece of meat and turned back towards Katie. But she was no longer there. It grunted with surprise as it snapped a glance to its left, where it saw the human female crouched at the base of a tree. Its eyes widened as it saw the weapon she cradled in her hands, angling it up towards its chest.

The explosion was deafening, but then came another, and another. Katie continued to pull at the trigger with ragged determination. She had no idea that Bodhi had loaded the 10-round magazine with alternating solid brass 303-grain slugs, triple aught buck shells, and fragmenting steel slugs. By the time she had pulled the trigger four times, the creature had disappeared. Her entire body shook as she fell to the floor and looked into Bodhi's eyes. He was alive, but she knew he wouldn't be for long. As adrenaline coursed through her body, she dropped the shotgun from her shaking hands and fell to her knees. She emptied the rest of Bodhi's pack out onto the floor, unable to search through it with any control. The red cloth of the first aid kit showed up in the light from her harness and she grabbed it, tearing it open. Then she realised she had no idea what to do.

The bleeding was prolific. Panic stricken, she began to plug the wound with gauze, ripping the plastic-wrapped packs apart with her teeth. Bodhi grunted with pain and then his eyes rolled into the back of his head as he passed out. Katie froze, knowing that was something she shouldn't have let happen. Her hands trembled as her mind raced. She undid a crepe bandage and used a combination of wound closure strips and duct tape to create some kind of compression on the wound and keep the gauze in place. She realised she was out of ideas. Her hands were still shaking when she heard the squeaking from her earpiece, which dangled from her camera harness. It took two attempts for her to position it again successfully.

"RUN, Katie, RUN" she heard both Joe and Tilly screaming over the static.

She looked up as the shadow fell across her. Then she was up and sprinting as fast as she could between the trees, tears streaming down her face.

~

Doctor Mary Beth Benoit looked at Nina with concern and gripped her shoulders. Nina seemed to be in a state of shock.

"Bukwus," Nina murmured.

Mary Beth was familiar with the term. The Bukwus, also known as the Bookwus, Bukwis, or Pugwis, was a creature of legend known to the Kwakiutl people of what was now British Columbia. The Bukwus was a wild, hairy man of the woods. The being was often roped in with similar legends, especially with that of the sasquatch, known first to the Salish nations across the Pacific northwest. But the Bukwus was different – to the Kwakiutl, it was a spiritual being that sought out lost travellers. It would offer them food, in the form of cockle shells. But this ghost food, if eaten by a human, would transform them into a creature like the Bukwus. It was these beings that were thought to be more corporeal, and therefore considered to be what was often called bigfoot. Yet, over the centuries, the origin of the name had become diluted, and now, many tribes in the northwest collectively referred to wild men legends as Bukwus.

Mary Beth had not taken Nina to be superstitious, in fact, she had seemed no nonsense and dismissive of such legends. All the time she had spent with her, she had been shrewd and disinclined to engage with that side of her heritage. Mary Beth knew enough to recognise the reaction of someone experiencing an intensified traumatic memory. Whatever Nina was recalling, it was real – and she was reliving it in minute and acute detail. She also knew that it was likely to be a repressed memory, one that Nina had buried deep within her subconscious. Mary Beth took a step to her right, blocking Nina's direct line of sight to the marks that had been clawed deep into the wood.

"Nina," she said loudly and firmly.

Nina slowly blinked and then jolted backwards. For a moment, Mary Beth saw the confusion in her eyes as she returned from her past into the present. It took her a few moments to realise where she was, and as she did, her legs gave way from under her. Mary Beth and an agent standing behind her were quick enough to catch her. Slowly, they helped her over to the garden furniture in the courtyard. By the time they reached the outdoor dining table and chairs, Nina was showing signs of being back to herself.

"I'm fine," she said, waving the agent off. "I just got dizzy, that was a really weird experience. I've seen marks like that before."

Nina sat with her head in her hands as she took deep breaths. Mary Beth sat next to her with a hand stretched across Nina's back in comfort.

"Urgh," Nina groaned. "I owe a lot of people an apology," she sighed.

"What happened?" Mary Beth asked.

"It was a memory from my childhood," Nina explained. "These things are real, and I saw one as a kid. It came after me. My father called it a..."

"Bukwus," Mary Beth nodded. "I knew something bad had gone down as soon as you said it. Nobody uses that name for the friendly ones."

They both looked up as they heard footsteps approaching them at a rushed pace. Special Agent Gregory Smith looked pale and was making a direct line for them. His expression changed to perplexed when he saw how unsettled Nina seemed, and with Mary Beth apparently comforting her.

"Everything okay?" he asked.

Nina nodded, "I was about to ask you the same thing, you look how I feel."

"Doctor Benoit, I've just been informed that Katie Cash and Bodhi Prince have been attacked in the forest," Smith explained. "I have a team already enroute to them, and your colleague Joe Beazley is also accompanying them. But we're closer. You might be able to get to Katie before..."

He didn't have to finish. Mary Beth was already up and running. Nina was startled by her urgency but nodded at Smith to indicate she was going with her. By the time she caught up, Benoit was in the driving seat of the Wendigo and had the engine running. Nina climbed into the passenger side and was almost thrown out again before she could close the door, as Benoit hit the gas and the truck shot forward like a missile. Nina remembered her partner, Scott Travers, drooling over the vehicle when he'd seen it and how he had regaled her all the way back to the station about its modifications. Right now, the 707hp supercharged V8, straight out of a Dodge Hellcat, was what had her attention.

She glanced over at Benoit, who had been overcome by a determination she hadn't seen in the usually placid doctor before.

"I'm guessing by the way you're driving, I'm not the only one who's had a bad encounter with one of these things," Nina said.

Benoit glanced at her, alarmed, but then her demeanour softened.

"Remember when we met, I told you that being bluff charged by one of these things was what turned me into a believer?" the doc asked.

Nina nodded.

"It wasn't a bluff charge," Benoit continued. "It was an ambush."

Nina glanced at Mary Beth, now feeling a kinship that only strengthened how much she liked the woman. Her newly reformed memories were only minutes old, yet she had already discovered that she wasn't alone in the trauma she had experienced. She knew that was a big deal in coming to terms with what had happened to her. Now knowing exactly what she was facing, she had wondered how she would feel continuing with the investigation. Knowing Benoit had been through a similar situation and had managed to continue with her work, was reassuring.

"Some of what I told you was the truth," Mary Beth stated. "It's easier to conceal a lie within a few strands of reality, I guess. It makes telling the story less complicated and scripted."

Nina nodded in understanding.

"Pennsylvania in fall is just beautiful," Benoit said wistfully, her eyes on the road but also somewhere else, as they continued at considerable pace. "The trees are painted cardinal red and honey gold, with bursts of emerald green woven in from the pines and spruce. The campground we'd commandeered as our base was a little basic – it had cabins, but the bathrooms were separate buildings outside. Don't get me wrong, I have no problem with that. Pretty much the same when I was a kid. And we know the audiences love when we go to rustic, scenic places like that, so it was a big win on all fronts. We'd had a good day filming, with some great eyewitness interviews. Bodhi had done some whoops and roars – some of his best, as I recall. It had been a good day."

Benoit paused for a moment, and Nina didn't want to push her, so stayed silent. But she couldn't take her gaze from the woman next to her, like an expectant child being read a story. One that hid the scare with the anticipation of a thrill. Where you were willing to take the risk of being frightened for the payoff of finding out what happened next.

This is why I don't like horror movies, Nina told herself.

"We were wrapping things up," Mary Beth continued. "No more filming, the night shoots had been done. We'd had our chow, and it was just campfire tales and an early night, maybe a beer or two. I was so happy when I stepped outside that door. I felt so lucky to have the life I do."

Nina was distracted as Benoit tugged at the steering wheel, pulling the truck round a sweeping curve, and pausing as she did so.

"The bathroom block was no more than thirty yards," she said, picking the story up again as they hit a straight piece of trail familiar to Nina.

"There were floodlights on the cabins and on the block, and everything faced each other. It was kind of like a farm in layout. But there was this one, teeny patch next to the bathrooms that was dark. The forest came right up to the perimeter there. Course, my gaze went straight to it," Benoit rolled her eyes and smiled at Nina. "First, I thought they were fireflies," she said, more quietly. "Two little golden lights blinking in the darkness. But fireflies don't come out in fall. It never roared, or growled, or even grunted. It was just coming. Later, Joe wondered if we'd made it mad by doing the calls."

Benoit went quiet again.

"It wasn't overly big," she continued, as if realising this for the first time. "A little over six feet. It was lanky and awkward looking, and it was a female, as far as I could tell. I just froze. I couldn't process what I was seeing, then before I knew it, it hit me. I remember it being as hard as granite. I flew backwards, and it leapt with me. She opened her mouth and I just saw these four fangs – very much like a chimp – gleaming and rushing for my throat. But my hands got in the way, and she slammed against my chest."

Benoit held up right hand, and Nina saw the thin white scar lines that ran across her pinkie and ring finger. Then, with the same hand, she pulled down her jacket a little way. There, a neater scar line showed the tell-tale signs of a surgically sealed wound.

"Next thing, she was towering over me, her arms raised in the air and her hands formed into fists. She beat my head like it was a drum. When I came round, I was being dragged by my leg towards the woods, towards that black space."

"I'm beginning to think I got away lightly," Nina said. "You're kind of a badass, doc," Nina declared.

"I'm not, but Bodhi was that night," Benoit said. "Guess that beating made a fair racket. He stormed out of that cabin, roaring and shooting. You should have seen that thing's eyes. He scared it good. One moment it was there, the next it was gone."

"You, Bodhi... nobody killed it?" Nina asked, shocked.

Whether bear, wolf, or mountain lion, if wildlife was deemed a threat, it was hunted down and given no quarter. She began to wonder if these creatures, with the intelligence to recognise humans as a threat, maybe even hold a grudge, perhaps had cause or reason to hate the people they came into conflict with.

"That was somebody else's job... and out of my hands," Benoit explained.

Suddenly, something bolted from the treeline into the middle of the road ahead of them.

Benoit slammed on the brakes and Nina was thrown forward so violently that she had to brace her hand and arm against the dashboard. The chunky off-road tyres bit into the wet, slippery dirt as the truck's advanced systems fought to bring them to a controlled stop, without breaking into a skid. Nina stared out through the windshield. Staggering towards them, almost unrecognisable, was Katie Cash. Her hands and clothing were bloodstained. She cradled a shotgun between her arms, holding it close to her chest. Her cheeks were streaked with tears and dirt. Both Benoit and Nina flung open their doors and rushed towards her. She collapsed as Nina reached her. Catching her, Nina slowed her descent and dropped down into a kneeling position, gently. She pushed back Katie's sweat-soaked hair with her hand. Katie's expression was blank and distant. Involuntary trembles cascaded along her arms and holding her close, Nina could feel the other woman's heartbeat thundering along like a racehorse. In contrast, her breathing was ragged, haphazard, and strained.

"She's in shock," Benoit said.

Nina nodded in agreement. "Her organs aren't getting enough oxygen," Nina added. "We need to get her warm and stable."

Benoit bolted to the rear of the truck and opened the elongated trunk. She dragged a large, red box over to her, marked as a medical kit. She carried it back over to Nina and Katie, then opened it and began to rapidly sort through the contents. She found an emergency blanket and ripped it open.

"I can't see any serious wounds – mainly scratches and bruises," Nina confirmed. "Help me lie her flat on the ground, and then you can wrap her in the blanket, and I'll elevate her legs against the truck."

Benoit nodded and helped lower Katie to the ground. She took off her jacket and placed it behind Katie's head as a pillow. As Nina picked up Katie's feet and rested them at a 90-degree angle against the Wendigo's passenger door, Benoit wrapped the shiny metallic sheet around their patient. As Nina looked up, she saw Benoit kept glancing into the trees and the forest beyond, illuminated a little way in by the Wendigo's high beams and light rig.

"I'm not desperate to stay here," Benoit hinted. "We should think about moving her and getting her to a hospital or medical centre."

Nina looked out into the forest and caught her drift. "Yep," she agreed.

Nina opened the rear passenger door and then, together, she and Benoit lifted Katie from the ground. Once up, Benoit scrambled into the back of the truck, as Nina pushed and lifted Katie's legs into the cabin. Benoit used the seatbelts on both sides to secure Katie to the bench seat, tucking in the blanket and checking her breathing as she did. Instead of getting out, she climbed through the gap between the two front seats back into the driving position. Nina closed the rear door then jumped back into the front.

Benoit hadn't been kidding about not wanting to hang around it seemed. As soon as the door slammed, the tyres were spinning in the dirt, and they were catapulted forwards as they shot down the trail. Benoit tapped the huge screen in the centre of the truck's console, bringing it to life. She drove furiously for a few minutes, before an electronic ping sounded in the cabin.

"Finally," Benoit exclaimed, relieved.

She pressed a button on the screen and a sound of static burst through the speakers.

"This is Wendigo to base, anyone recieiving?" Benoit asked, loudly and slowly.

"Wendigo, this is base," came the immediate reply.

The voice was female, and although they had only spoken a few times, Nina recognised it as Tilly Miller, one of the producers of Seeking Sasquatch she'd met at the campground.

"We've picked up Katie and are heading your way," Benoit explained. "Has there been any sign of Bodhi?"

"Negative," came the reply. "Katie's camera harness came off when she started running. It was still filming. Bodhi... he's gone."

Nina looked at Benoit and saw she was visibly shocked by what she'd just heard. She was fighting back tears and shaking her head.

"There's an army search and rescue unit in the area," Tilly explained. "They know we've been looking for you and are on standby. I'll ask it to land here so we can medevac Katie. How's she doing?"

"She's in shock, but otherwise doesn't seem hurt. But it was touch and go for a minute there. She must have been running for her life, and who knows for how long."

There was a long pause.

"Understood," Tilly finally acknowledged. "What's your ETA?"

"Thirty minutes," Benoit confirmed, touching the screen to end the call.

CHAPTER TWENTY

DESPERATE MEASURES

It was as if she was sleep walking, as Nina made her way up the steps of her father's cabin. She was aware of Benoit, talking to her from the window of the truck behind her, but did not answer. It sounded like she was underwater. She couldn't have made out the words, even if she'd been concentrating on the conversation. But she wasn't. Her thoughts and memories fogged her senses, and she acted purely on muscle memory. The big, modified Jeep pulled away, removing the outside world from even her peripheral vision. She felt the brush of fur against her side, and for a moment, flinched at its touch. Then she realised it was Achak. She pushed her fingers deep into his ruff and held on tight. He led her to the house and then inside, the door easily opened with a nudge of his muzzle. It was just gone 5am, and the past few hours were a blur. She walked over to the couch and sank onto it, curling her knees up. She stared into the few remaining embers of the fire as Achak placed his huge head on the cushion beside her.

Katie Cash had been airlifted to the general hospital in Tacoma, which had a helipad. The team of soldiers that had intervened at the cannabis farm had been her escort, including the 2nd Lieutenant that she'd spoken with. There had been talk of other deaths, an accident perhaps. When she had pushed to find out more, she had been threatened with arrest by one of the attending bureau agents. Marty, her boss, had ordered her home, on enforced 48-hour leave. The lieutenant, and surprisingly, Agent Jones, the one she had called Chuck Norris's meaner brother, had been the ones that got between her and the unknown bureau bum. Nina blinked slowly. She was beyond exhausted and was still processing everything she had learned – or perhaps relearned, that night. She slipped into a fitful state of unconsciousness.

She woke with a start and a shiver of cold raced down her spine. The warmth of both the blanket over her and Achak's body next to her, calmed her and she relaxed again. Her eyes lifted to the chair opposite, where she saw her father sitting. Her gaze met his.

"Time to talk," he stated, simply.

Nina made the slightest nod of her head, her eyes wide.

"You remember?" he asked.

She nodded again, slowly, and more deliberately. He sighed and looked at his feet.

"You were the lucky one that day," he said. "I often wonder if that was the day, I lost you to the wider world. It was the first time I had to take you to the hospital," he said.

"Hospital?" Nina queried.

"You don't remember everything it would seem," her father smiled, warmly. "You went into severe shock. You didn't come out of it for two days. And when you did, you couldn't remember a thing. We decided that was the way it was to be."

"We?" Nina asked, sitting up now. Achak half growled, half yawned his annoyance at having to move.

"The tribal council."

"Why were they involved?"

Robert Lee chewed his cheek and looked away from his daughter, out of one of the windows.

"Because the Bukwus was angry at what had happened," he continued. "He had been robbed of his prize. So, he took another one. A young girl, two valleys over. They said it was a cougar, but we knew otherwise. We also knew the Bukwus would move on, and it did. We said nothing and let the forest keep its secrets."

"Well, I think Bucky's back," Nina said, yawning.

"Don't be flippant about these creatures," her father warned. "They can be angered easily."

"Dad, I'm accepting there is a monster in the woods," Nina declared, throwing her arms up, "but actually, I don't," she added, quietly. "It's an animal, not a monster. It doesn't have superpowers. I accept it's smart, and strong, and incredible... but it's just an animal."

Robert Lee stayed silent but watched as Nina shuffled over to the kitchen. Just then, there was a knock at the door. Nina turned around. The blanket was still draped across her shoulders. She had a deep need for both coffee and breakfast, probably in that order. What she had no need of, was company. Seeming to sense this, her father rose from his chair and headed across to the door, opening it. They were both surprised to see Doctor Mary Beth Benoit standing there. She was holding something large and white in her hand.

"I wanted to check on you and also pass on a souvenir," the doc explained in her gentle, southern lilt.

Nina nodded and slumped back down onto the couch, indicated with a nod of her head that Benoit should join her.

"How's Katie doing?" Nina asked.

"Okay," Benoit replied. "We're effectively shut down, so all she's interested in now, is getting as far away from here as possible. So, I thought I'd pass what we had to you."

"I'm out too," Nina explained. "A minimum two days of forced leave."

"Well, I thought you might still want to take a look anyway," Benoit offered, passing over the white slab she had been holding.

Nina realised it was a plaster cast and there was no need to guess of what. The shape of the print was immediately recognisable, partly due to its quality. Each toe showed definition, and the plaster had picked up impressive levels of detail. Nina marvelled at it, then offered it to her father. He stepped forward and took it in his hands. He lifted it closer to his face, studying it carefully. He moved across the room and placed it on his desk, before making his way back to his chair.

"Charlotte said the victim at Lucas Christian's place died from exsanguination from laceration of the brachial artery. Bodhi died of exsanguination from laceration of the cremasteric and testicular arteries. Once it made the killing blow, they died fast, from massive and irreversible blood loss. This thing knows how to kill, and it knows how to do it very well."

Nina nodded in understanding, picking up the warning in Benoit's tone.

"I guess I'll see myself out," Benoit said, politely. "You need to get some rest and I didn't mean to bother you. But I'll see you before we go anywhere – nobody's made any official decision yet."

"Thanks Doc," Nina smiled. "I appreciate you keeping me in the loop."

"I got your back," Benoit winked, as she headed for the

door.

Robert Lee stood up to see her out. As he closed it, he turned to find Nina headed for her room.

"On second thoughts, I'm going to do what the doc said and get some rest," she said, over her shoulder.

He simply nodded in understanding. After he heard her bedroom door fasten shut, he walked back over to look at the plaster footprint again. He bent down and opened the lowest drawer of the pedestal desk, moving aside some old newspaper clippings and lifting out a large, rectangular metal box. Taking off the lid, he lifted the item out. It was wrapped in tissue paper, and he began to peel the layers back, revealing a much older, more weathered plaster cast of a similar footprint. It was one he had taken from the treeline all those years ago. He ran his fingers over a deep crease that ran from the centre of the foot to the big toe, meeting a large skin whorl and a ridge of hair striations that seemed to separate the toes from the upper pad of the foot. Then, slowly, he ran his fingers over the identical marks on the fresh cast the doctor had gifted Nina. Robert Lee considering himself a practical man, so there was a tape measure on his desk for no good reason other than he might need it. He reached for it. His cast measured just over seventeen inches. The new one was an inch longer. But the marks were identical. There was no doubt the two prints came from the same creature.

"You've got bigger," he said to himself.

He took out his pipe and some tobacco and headed for his chair on the porch. The pipe was a hand carved egg style, briar type. It had an accent of buffalo ivory, with a black and green ebonite stem. It was both handsome and one of his prized possessions. He settled into the chair and filled it with his own personal blend from his pouch, a mix of Dark Fired Kentucky and American Black Cherry. As he lit it, he thought of one of his favourite books, The Hound of the Baskervilles. He didn't read much, but in school, as part of his forced, western education, he had been made to read several so-called classics, including the Sherlock Holmes novel. It was the only one he had enjoyed. As an adult, he had recalled the fictional sleuth's problem-solving technique with great satisfaction and a connection with his own outlook. It was, to simply sit in a chair and smoke a pipe, most thoroughly, contemplating every aspect of the situation until there was a remedy. In the film starring Peter Cushing and Christopher Lee, the Baskerville curse had been declared a two-pipe problem. The most challenging of cases – such as that of the Red-Headed League, required three. As Robert Lee sucked the first few wisps of smoke from the pipe, he was confident this was a two-pipe problem, almost fittingly, given this conundrum also revolved around a creature with wilful murder on its mind. He sat back and looked towards the mountains, sucking on the pipe in slow, satisfied draws.

It was two hours later when Robert Lee stood from his chair, his pipe empty, and his mind clear. He returned inside and collected a hat – a black wool Yutan with a hawk feather, and a weathered leather messenger bag from the back of his desk chair. He took a black, twisted walking stick that he knew to be sturdy and then quietly and quickly made his way to Nina's door. She was fast asleep, lying face down in the bed. He was relieved to see that she had at least managed to discard her uniform this time. Achak, who lay at the foot of the bed, lifted his head, and acknowledged him before returning to his own, protective doze. Robert closed the door quietly and headed outside. He skirted around the cabin and began to head up the gentle slope towards the treeline. He was soon surrounded by oak, pine, spruce, and madrone.

A little deeper into the trees, he found one of the things he was looking for. The clump of sweet grass had grown tall in a small break in the trees, uninhibited by their shadows. He took a small buck knife from his belt and used it to harvest some of the grass. The other things he needed weren't so easy to find. He searched for nearly an hour before he discovered the tendrils of white sage. He took roots from a lavender plant not in flower and added bearberry leaves to his bag. He ignored the drooping, weathered seedpods of the purple coneflower, and instead, dug into the soil to find its roots – known as black root. He only needed one more ingredient, and he found it further up on a hillside overlooking the Packwood Reservation and where he called home. As he dug the snake root out of the ground and cut it into fibrous strips, he realised he had walked and foraged in a large, wide circle. As he looked out over the rooftops, and beyond to the mountains, he noticed that evening darkness was creeping in from the east. He turned back towards the forest, now hurrying.

Robert Lee found a dry, flat piece of ground within the trees. One of the few western red cedars in this part of the forest was to his back, as he sat with his legs crossed. Black cottonwood, oak, and hemlock surrounded him, with sprinklings of Sitka spruce and Douglas fir adding to the forest's silhouette against a darkening sky further in. From his bag, he took a polished, greenish-white abalone shell – streaked on the inside with blue and silver. He placed his offering of herbs inside it. Next, he took a small dropper bottle of patchouli oil from the bag and a wand of bundled sage, cedar, and sweetgrass. He laced the herbs and roots with the oil, then lit the wand and held it to the bundle. It caught immediately, with a flash of fire and a crackle of dry stems. As it burned, he added one more ingredient from his bag – a handful of black, wild rice. Inside the shell, the offering burned strong and bright. Robert began to sing and chant, guided by his instincts.

Lost to his task, he did not know how long it was before he could no longer feel the heat from the flame, nor the touch of its light on his closed eyelids. All he knew, when he opened his eyes, was that darkness had fallen. His gaze fell to the abalone shell on the ground in front of him. It was filled with a fine, black, powder. Carefully, he picked it up and began to sparsely distribute the ash in a wide, encompassing circle, that he took great care to not cross into. He packed away the shell and the oil dropper, as well as the lighter he'd used. All the while, he knelt with his back to the circle. As he stood up and shouldered the pack, he caught a scent on the breeze – not unlike wet dog. He couldn't help the shudder that raced along his spine as he set off, not once tempted to look over his shoulder. When he reached the cabin again, he hastily set about saging the perimeter. As he completed the circuit of the house, he went to climb the steps of the porch, his intention to smudge the house interior too. Instead, he found Nina staring at him from her own seat on the veranda.

"I woke up and you were gone," she explained. "Where

did you go?"

"For a walk," he said.

Nina eyed him suspiciously. She looked dishevelled, and a blanket was wrapped around her shoulders. He guessed she hadn't been up for long.

"How are you feeling?" he asked.

Nina shrugged. "I'm just beat... physically, not so much. But the world got a lot bigger, real quick. Fighting my boss and some shithole agent pushing me around is one thing. But the machine... the 'man', that's another. I'm not sure I want to go down this rabbit hole anymore. I wanted to know what they were hiding. Turns out I knew all along. Now I don't want to."

Robert nodded in understanding.

"Whenever you think you're too small to make a difference, try sleeping with a single mosquito in your room," he offered with a smile.

"Old Indian proverb?" she asked, wryly.

"Dalai lama actually," he grinned.

He walked up the steps and Nina suddenly sat upright in her chair. She grabbed his coat and held it close to her nose.

"What have you been burning?" she asked.

There was curiosity in her tone, but also accusation.

"Just some roots and herbs. I was going to do inside next," he replied. "I know you don't believe in such things. But like you said, your world got a little bit bigger today. Maybe try trusting your old man for once, hey?"

Nina sunk back into her chair, a little ashamed. She nodded.

"Course dad," she said.

Robert reached for the door handle when a savage growl

from close by made him jump and then freeze. The hair stood up on the back of his neck and for a moment, he dared not turn around.

"Achak," Nina scolded. "What's got into you?"

Robert spun on his heels and saw the big black wolf standing rigid at the bottom of the steps. His ears were pricked up and his salt and pepper dashed muzzle was pointed in the direction of the treeline to the east. His unblinking gaze was fixed on something that only his sharp eyes could see in the darkness, for now. Robert pushed the door open quickly, holding it ajar.

"Let's go inside, Nina," he suggested. "You'll get cold out here."

Nina hesitated, a little surprised by her father's sudden hurrying. But then she nodded and got up from the chair. She entered the cabin and headed for the couch.

"You too Achak," Robert commanded.

Both the wolf and Nina were taken aback by the firm, sure voice that he used. Achak took one more glance at the treeline then trotted up the steps and into the cabin. He passed through the main room and into the corridor that led to Nina's room. Nina followed him, puzzled. The wolf went into her bedroom and headed straight for the window on the far wall. Achak used his muzzle to push the curtains aside. He again fixed his gaze in the direction of the treeline.

Nina walked back to the main room, her instinct telling her that both Achak and her father seemed to know something she didn't. She stopped mid-stride when she found her father with a wand of burning white sage, as he chanted, eyes closed. He meticulously smudged the doors and windows. She went to say something, but his eyes snaped open and he fixed her with a glare of warning that rendered her silent. He continued his chanting and smudging around the entire cabin, leaving his room upstairs until last. As he descended the stairs back to the main room, Nina was standing at their bottom.

"Dad, what have you done?" she accused.

"Thought you didn't believe in this kind of thing... they're just animals," he said.

He stepped passed her and carefully put away the things from his bag. He looked up and met her stare with eyes that pleaded for understanding and forgiveness.

"I've sent for help," he said.

CHAPTER TWENTY-ONE

ENEMY OF MY ENEMY

Nina stared at her father. She felt like her head was spinning and she sought out the safety of the couch again. She slumped down and let the blanket fall from her shoulders. Robert Lee closed the front door and secured it. Although he didn't always do this, she knew it wasn't unusual. However, he seemed shaken and concerned. He walked over to the kitchen sink and ran the smoking sage wand under the cold tap. Crossing the room back to his desk, he placed it in a small porcelain bowl to dry. Nina didn't know what to say and watched as he rummaged through a drawer. When he turned around to face her again, he held out a smooth, light-grey coloured stone. It was very thin, with rounded edges, and was approximately two inches long. It sat easily inside the palm of his hand. Etched into it, leaving a white outline of scared rock, was the image of a wolf's head – its nose pointed towards the sky and its mouth open, depicting a howl. The picture of the wolf was framed on either side by a single, wavy line. He placed it in her hand gently, then quick and silently, took her wrist in one hand and ran his buck knife over her still open palm. Nina flinched and withdrew her hand.

"What the actual fuck, Dad?" Nina barked, accusingly.

Disturbed by her tone, Achak ran back from her bedroom and stood between them, his head moving from one to the other. Robert reached down and took his daughter's hand more gently, turning it over to reveal the small cut and where it had briefly stained the stone she still held.

"It needs to be sealed by blood, and I didn't think you'd let me explain it to you," he said.

"It didn't hurt, but this is weird, even for you," she

grumbled.

Robert went over to a kitchen drawer and pulled it open. He fished out the small pack of band-aids, and took them over to Nina, dropping down onto the couch next to her.

"The creature that killed the logger, that killed this woman, attacked these soldiers," he said, sounding calmer now. "It's dangerous and it's not going to stop. Once adult, they're very hard to kill. And you know what they say, you need to fight fire..."

"With fire," Nina realised. "You're not telling me you've tried to attract another one of these things, have you?"

"No," he said, shaking his head. "Something they don't like. Something more savage, something that hates unbalance in nature and moves against anything that upsets that harmony."

"Dad, what are you talking about?" Nina queried.

"We call them the Limmekin," he said, noticeably dropping his voice.

Nina watched, confused, as he looked over his shoulder, as if to check nobody else was listening.

"There are two kinds," he continued. "The first, we call watchers. If you've ever been in the forest and felt unease, or as if something was looking into your soul, it could be a watcher. They can also be tricksters. They might try to scare you or follow you, or things may go missing from your camp."

Robert paused for a moment and sat up straight, looking down at the floorboards.

"The other kind," he continued, not meeting her gaze, "we don't have a name for. If you do something that goes against the natural order of things, you can attract their attention. That is not something you want to do. If you are angry, or have ill-intentions, it's like ringing the dinner bell for them. If one of them gets on your trail, you're never seen again."

"What are they?" Nina asked, her voice hushed.

"Wild spirits of vengeance, in purest form," her father replied.

He leaned back into the couch and lifted his head to look into her eyes. Nina could see he was deeply troubled.

"So, they're like a ghost, or some kind of phantom poltergeist?" Nina spluttered.

"No," Robert exclaimed, a warning tone in his voice.

"So, what are they then, what do they look like?" Nina shot back, aggravated.

"Like Achak," Robert declared. "But they walk on two feet, like the Bukwus. Not as tall, but faster, more predatory. They have hands like the Bukwus too, but with claws like knives. And their teeth are not like those of a wolf. Each one is sharp and pointed. Some have said it looks like they have too many teeth to fit in their mouths. They have large, broad heads with long, pointed, tufted ears. They can run on all fours, but when they walk on two feet, they hunch and lean forward. Believe me when I say they are very physical."

Nina drew the creature in her mind.

"Wait... Dad, are you talking about a fucking werewolf?! Please, this is nonsense."

"They are not shapeshifters," Robert scolded, standing up from the couch and looking down at her. "They are not, and never were people. In fact, they don't like us very much."

"Us?"

"Humans. At least for the most part. Can't blame them, given what we've done to the natural world," he explained. "My bloodline should protect you, but the stone will guarantee it. I know you find this hard to believe, but please, if you do nothing else for me, carry it with you until this is over."

"Dad, I can't sit around and just accept that you've arranged a ten-round title fight between two monsters... I'm going to need a little more than that."

Robert huffed and shook his head. Just then, Achak ran back into the main room. He stood alert, facing the front door. The fur on his back began to bristle as he became tense and rigid. Although he didn't make a single sound, Nina could tell that he was being led by instinct not to unleash the growl that wanted to rumble in his throat. Then she heard it. The creak of the boards outside on the veranda. There was a muffled thump, followed by another, as something moved from right to left. Each thump ended with a clack of something hard striking down against the wood. It reminded Nina of the predatory, pack-hunting dinosaurs from the movies, tapping their claws on the ground. Another thump and then another. Whatever it was, it was moving on two feet – and towards the window to the front of the house. Nina held her breath as she glanced up, realising the curtains had not been pulled over.

For a moment, there was nothing there. Then a shadow blotted out the remaining light of the sky beyond. The thing that stood there was darker than night itself. A void that eclipsed the entire window. But as Nina stared, there was something she could make out. Two amber coloured spheres that seemed to glow like embers. Her mind raced, trying to convince her that they were anything but eyes. As if reading her mind, and taking some delight in proving her wrong, the spheres disappeared and reappeared again slowly, as the creature blinked. And she knew it was a creature now, as she could see its outline. It was just as her father had described. The head was broad, taking up most of the window. Its ears sat on top of its head and even though she could not see their tips, she could tell they were pointed. They looked like they could have been taken straight from a statue of Anubis, the jackal-headed Egyptian god of the dead. But the rest of the head seemed straight out of a Hollywood werewolf movie. But this thing was real, right down to its untamed wisps of fur.

Nina took a step towards the window, and she could now see the creature was hunched over and stooped forward. By moving closer, she could no longer see the glare in the glass from the cabin's interior lights. The Limmekin, as her father had called the creature, opened its mouth. Nina shuddered but didn't recoil back. Somewhere in the last 24 hours, she had resolved herself to stop running from monsters. This was partly fuelled by what she had said to her father, about them being animals. If that was the case – and she saw no reason for it not to be, then she needed to know more about them. Yes, they were animals, she told herself as she glimpsed the teeth. Unknown, misunderstood, and apex predators without a doubt. But animals all the same. The Limmekin closed its mouth and seemed to pull away from the window. Although Nina had first felt apprehension and a little fear, she now felt calm and less unnerved by the creature's presence.

"Nina," her father murmured.

She turned to look at him and caught the movement in her peripheral vision. Snapping her head back towards the window, she saw it was now empty. The only golden swirls of colour there now, were those of the clouds, soaking up the last of the sunset, nestled against the pink and orange-streaked sky. She rushed forwards, ignoring her father's protestations. Pressing her hands up against the glass, she looked out, desperate for a better look at the thing that had stood there just moments before. Perhaps, it was to try and confirm it was something she had misidentified. But she knew she wanted to see it in more detail. Get a sense of its true size, colouring, how it moved. But there was no trace of it now. Its clumsy, noisy approach along the veranda had been seemingly deliberate. It wanted them to know it was there. As she looked out to the treeline – seventy, maybe eighty yards from the cabin, she realised it was clearly capable of far greater speed and stealth than it had shown around the cabin.

"Nina, you need to respect it, not challenge it," her father warned.

"I'm not challenging anything," she replied. "I just wanted to see it, for real."

"Be careful what you wish for," he grumbled. "Just because you carry protection, I wouldn't want to test how fool proof it is."

"So, given it seemed to taunt us and was looking in the window... was that one a watcher?" Nina asked.

"I didn't invite anything here to watch," Robert said quietly.

"Dad, I have friends out there, who don't have one of these," she said angrily, holding up the stone.

"That doctor said they were shut down," Robert protested.

"She's not my only friend," Nina complained, headed for her room.

She went to put on her uniform shirt, then paused. There didn't seem much point. Instead, she pulled on a thick, ivory and jade coloured flannel shirt on top of her jeans and T-shirt. She picked up the King Cobra revolver and its holster, as well as her badge, putting it on under the shirt. She hesitated, then pulled open the bedside drawer, taking out another leather holster. This one was lighter in colour, like buckskin. On duty, Nina carried a multitool, as full knives were frowned upon. But as she had remembered all too quickly, she wasn't on duty. The five-inch, notched blade was inscribed with delicate scrollwork, and was housed in a handle of turquoise, lapis, spiny oyster, jet, and jasper that measured four and a half inches. She fixed it to her belt, positioning it against the back of her hips. She passed back through the main room, grabbing a jacket from the peg.

"Don't try to stop me," she warned her dad, not looking at him directly.

"I know better than that," he acknowledged. "But more so, I know this is something you must do. I just beg you to be careful."

"I will," she said softly, meeting his gaze now. "I'm just going to warn them that things are more complicated than they think. They don't know what's out there."

"Consider that it might not do them any good if they did," Robert implied, throwing up his hands in surrender. "And be ready for a fight, even if you're not seeking one. You and the Bukwus have a destiny – I feel that."

"I've had worse relationships," she shrugged.

She walked over to her father, who rose from his chair. She threw her arms around him and hugged him tight.

"I have something else for you," her father said solemnly.

He walked over to the desk and opened a drawer. He leant over slightly and lifted something out. Nina knew what it was immediately. His prized tomahawk. He passed it to her, holding it flat across the palms of his hands. The stem was made from a single piece of ash. It curved slightly from the butt of the handle to a notch about three quarters of the way up, where it curved more sharply upwards to the eye, where the carbon steel head was fixed. The main blade was viciously sharp and broad, and a spike balanced the weight on its back. Small, intricate etchings had been carved and burnt into the wood, but overall, it was quite plain. It was a weapon and had no need for decorative elements.

"You have your knife?" he asked.

Nina nodded.

"If it gets close enough that you need them, use the hawk in one hand and the blade in the other," he instructed. "Fight like a demon. Blades and bows seem better than bullets against the Bukwus, but I would strongly recommend using them all."

"Thanks for the protection and the warning," she said. "I'm taking both seriously – at least seriously for me."

Nina released him from the embrace and headed towards the door. She grabbed the keys to her truck as she opened it, then closed it behind her. Achak took a step forward, then glanced up at Robert.

"That's what I'm afraid of," Robert Lee murmured quietly.

~

Agent Jones stood in what, until they had acquisitioned it for their purposes, was the campground's kitchen cabin. On the floor, across from him, were four black bags, laid out in a uniform line. In just one night, his team had been cut down by half. He'd never encountered anything like it before. He knew the families and clans often worked together, especially when hunting. But he rarely had to engage with those. It was the loners – the ones he called rogues that got the attention. This one was different though. It was cunning and ruthless. The night had revealed two strikingly different sides to its character. First, it had stealthily evaded his team with ease, killing two highly trained soldiers without them ever knowing it was there. Then, it had led the soldiers to the family, taking further pieces off the board. Jones was in no doubt that it had killed the big alpha, having separated it from the family group and gotten the weapons of his team to do half the job already. And then, most incredibly, it had manipulated the surviving young male and shown him skills to become a threat of almost equal concern. Granted, the young male was now Clarke's problem. For Jones, his lay in the body bags beside him.

Special Agent Gregory Smith walked in through the double front doors of the cookhouse, stopping when he saw Jones sitting at one of the camp dining tables, overlooking the black plastic sacks. Spread across the table was the paperwork he'd been filling out. It was a task Jones always insisted on doing. The families of the soldiers would be told they all died heroes – Jones always saw to that. But it would be against an unnamed enemy, thousands of miles away, on a different continent. In some cases, the families would be denied access to the bodies. All would be given a military funeral and be provided with full support – from generous pensions to college allowances for the kids. But most of the time, Smith knew that Jones – and Clarke too, chose the single guys with fewer connections. It was easier that way.

"Doc's ready for us," Smith said. He stopped and stood a little way off from Jones.

Jones looked up and nodded.

"These guys are good to go as soon as the chopper is," Jones said, standing up.

He shuffled the paperwork into four neat piles, one for each of the men he'd lost. Then he followed Smith back out through the doors. They crossed the central campground, over the track that led through it, and headed towards one of the cabins, where two military police guards stood either side of the door. They didn't stir as the two agents entered. Doctor Mary Beth Benoit looked up from her makeshift operating table as they entered the interior. She stepped away as they drew close.

The body of the alpha male was immense. With its slightly conical shaped head at one end, its knees dropped over the other, its feet touching the floor and laid out at an angle. Its arms were nearly six feet long, and its fingers too, fell over the bottom edge of the table. The table was easily four feet wide, but still not large enough to contain the creature and all its limbs. So, its intact arm hung over the far side, draped onto the bench seat below. Jones looked down at it. The eyes were closed and the mouth open, exposing the significant, yellow-stained canines and the large, flat molars behind. Chisel-like incisors sat between them, shooting up from odd angles. The tongue was purple and swollen.

"How we doing, Doc?" Jones asked, quietly.

"Still can't quite believe I'm here, to be honest," Benoit replied.

"You're good at what you do, and you were always on the team for a reason," Jones assured her. "We don't get many opportunities like this. What can you tell me?"

"He took quite a beating," Benoit explained, stepping back from the table a little way. "Most notable, is the 50. calibre wound to the arm. Significant muscle and tissue damage, but not enough to kill him outright, although I'm sure a second shot would have done it. His side is peppered with smaller calibre shrapnel. He'd already scratched some out. They didn't have anything like the same penetration. What killed him though, was a heavy blow to the throat – enough to snap his hyoid bone and crush the larynx. Despite all the lead you threw at him, he died of asphyxiation."

Jones nodded in understanding. It was as he had suspected.

"You realise what I'm saying, right?" Benoit urged. "The only thing that could have done that, was another sasquatch."

"I get it, doc," Jones replied. "And it sure as shit wasn't one of the other family members. Thank you. Anything else?"

"Wanna know why their tracks are so flat?" Benoit grinned.

Jones nodded. He had always known that having a

biologist on his own team would prove worthwhile. The military didn't like to share their information, and usually confiscated any bodies before he could get to them. An up-close examination was a very rare opportunity.

"Take a look at the sole of the foot here," Benoit said, moving to the end of the table. "As I'm sure you know, one of the things that distinguishes a typical sasquatch track from a human is the lack of an arch in the foot," she explained. "Our footprints don't show a full outline because our feet have what's called a lateral arch. It's where a good portion of the foot is clear of the ground when we place it down. It helps our feet basically act like a spring."

"But they're too heavy," Jones said. "They have a midtarsal break, like other non-human primates. They can lift their heel independently from the rest of the foot."

"That's right," Benoit said, smiling as if proud of a student. "But there's something else. Press here," she motioned, indicating the left side of the foot, some way above the heel.

"No gloves doc," Jones shook his head. "I'll take your word for now."

"There should be three bones here – the cuboid and two cuneiform bones," Benoit explained. "But there isn't, it's solid. This could be what we call Arcto metatarsus. It's the biological development of a very flat, rigid foot, caused by two of the metatarsal bones converging to pinch off the third."

"Uh-huh," Jones nodded. "Meaning?"

"It would allow the animal to not only support huge weight but also run fast and fluidly, without having to worry about stresses being put on its foot structure. This is built to take it. I can only think of one other animal like it." Benoit said, pausing.

"And what would that be?" Smith asked.

"Tyrannosaurus Rex," she exclaimed. "Huge. Fast. Heavy. It's what we call convergent evolution. Where the same adaptations with similar form and functions appear in species of different epochs of time. It's natures version of if it's not broke, don't fix it."

"Thanks Doc, appreciate it," Jones said, his brow furrowing.

"Thought of a name yet?"

Benoit nodded. "Obviously, I'm not expecting to find it in any textbooks any time soon," she smiled. "But I thought Megalopedus atrox might be suitable. Loosely, it translates as savage bigfoot. It gives them their own taxonomy and separates their family from ours and other apes."

"Works for me," Jones huffed.

Benoit smiled and excused herself. Smith and Jones watched her leave as she headed out of the door. The doc was holed up in one of the cabins, along with the production team and Joe Beazley – Seeking Sasquatch's resident researcher, paranormalist, and conspiracy theorist. Katie Cash was the only one not on site and would be hospitalised for some time.

"When can Cash be safely moved?" Jones asked, looking up at Smith.

"Too early to say," Smith shrugged. "There's an agent with her, one who knows what's going on. She won't say anything – can't really. She's been heavily sedated. The moment she's given the all clear, we bring her home."

Jones nodded.

"Just leaves us with one problem then," he grumbled.

Jones walked over to the wall, where a framed map of the trails and area surrounding the campsite was hanging.

"In a way, we're back to square one," Jones huffed. "Hunting this rogue down without the distractions of the family group, or even the fan club," he added, referring to the Seeking Sasquatch team.

"But we've taken a big hit," Smith conceded. "And there's just as much ground to cover as before. Trying to ambush him or funnel him into a trap doesn't seem to work. We need a new plan."

"Agreed," Jones nodded. "I get the feeling our friend has been hunted before. It led the males from the family group straight to our boys. We need to see him, without him seeing us."

"What about Joe?" Smith asked. "If he can get his toy to actually work..."

"Maybe," Jones replied.

Jones cocked his head and went quiet. Smith looked at him baffled, then he heard it too. A car engine was working hard along the trail, headed into the campsite.

"Are we expecting company?" Smith asked.

Jones shook his head and reached the door in a few strides, throwing it open. He stepped out and headed to the entrance road that led into camp. He saw the lights of a pick-up with a light rig ploughing along towards them. In a few moments, 2nd Lieutenant Wade and Master-Sergeant Dugas were beside him, and two Bureau agents fell in behind, their hands on their sidearms. Jones stared at the oncoming vehicle. The GMC Syclone was an older truck, but this one had clearly been modified to cope with Washington logging roads. It made its way towards them with ease, sliding to a stop about thirty yards from them. Jones relaxed as soon as he saw a familiar face pop out of the driver's side window.

"Don't shoot," Nina yelled.

"Just so you know that's a two-way street," Jones replied.

Nina knew it would be overstating to say the agent smiled, but she felt he meant it warmly. She stepped out of the truck and walked over to them.

"That's close enough miss," one of the agents barked

from behind.

"Shuddup, you idiot," Dugas spat in his direction. "She's more welcome than you are."

"Can we go somewhere and talk?" Nina nodded towards Jones.

He looked her over for a moment, then gave a single nod in reply. He turned around and leaned in towards Smith.

"Go get the doc and Joe," he suggested.

Smith dashed off towards the cabins the Seeking Sasquatch team were housed in.

"Follow us," Jones barked back over his shoulder.

He led Nina and the soldiers to the reception and visitor centre that they had been using as a headquarters. He walked to a large central table where there was a large coffee percolator with a selection of paper cups, as well as milk and sugar. He poured himself a cup, and Wade and Dugas took the opportunity to do the same. Wade turned towards Nina, indicating if she'd like some. She shook her head. In her mind, there just wasn't a situation bad enough for government issued coffee.

"So, how can we help you Ms. Lee?" Jones asked.

"I know we got off to a bad start," Nina stated. "But we all know, including me, you're not hunting a bear. I've come to warn you... my dad, he meant well, but there's something else out there now, and you need to take it seriously."

"What do you mean?" Jones said, stepping forward.

"I don't even know how to explain it," Nina replied. "Please, I am not superstitious at all, and my dad would be the first to tell you that I don't take our myths, legends, or even our aural histories too seriously. But as of right now, I do. I've seen it."

"We all saw it," Jones said quietly. "It's okay, I'm not gonna make you say it was a bear anymore. But we do need to talk about what you're going to say."

Nina stared at him, not following his line of thought, then she caught on.

"No," she said, shaking her head furiously. "I don't mean the bigfoot, or whatever you want to call it. There's something else out there. My dad... summoned it somehow. He expects it to hunt down and kill the sasquatch. But I just see it as something else you're gonna run into."

Jones narrowed his eyes and studied Nina carefully.

"This thing have a name?" he asked, eventually.

"He called it a Limmekin," Nina explained.

"Not heard that one before," Jones shrugged. "Describe it to me."

Nina frowned. "I know how this is going to sound, but it looked like... like a werewolf, straight out of a horror film".

She had expected her audience to burst into laughter, but they didn't. In fact, it felt like the atmosphere in the room had gotten real serious, real quick.

"Sounds like you're describing what has become known in popular culture, as a dogman," came Benoit's familiar voice from behind her.

Nina spun around and gave her a brief, yet confused smile. She was pleased to see her.

"Can't imagine too many Native Americans calling it that," Nina said. "I know Dog Men as Cheyenne elite warriors – I used to live with my mom in Wyoming, where the Cheyenne settled in the 19th century."

Benoit acknowledged the information with a smile and a turn of her head.

"You won't get any argument from me," Joe Beazley added, from behind as he sidled up next to Benoit. "I hate the name, and I think most researchers do too. It doesn't really do justice to what it is."

"So, you know about – have heard about these things?" Nina asked, a little shocked.

"If your Limmekin is what others call dogman, then, yeah, we know about them," Joe shrugged. "Not things you want to mess with."

"That's kind of what my dad said," Nina sighed.

"On the most part, encounters are very scary and intimidating, but nothing actually happens," Joe continued, trying to be reassuring. "However, some now think that earlier reports of aggressive bigfoot encounters were actually these things. And not every encounter goes well. Ever heard of the creature of the land between the lakes?"

"Is it related to the one from the black lagoon?" Dugas smirked. Wade shoulder barged him to shut him up.

Nina shook her head. Joe looked around, ignoring Dugas. Jones was fixing him with a deliberate and unblinking gaze that disturbed him but didn't suggest he should stop talking. That was a look he was more than familiar with.

"The incident I'm referring to took place in the early 1980s," Joe continued. "A family consisting of a mother, father, and their son and daughter, were setting up their RV in a campground on the Kentucky side of the Land Between the Lakes National Park. From what I've read, the father was outside putting the motorhome's yawning up, and the son was outside too, collecting firewood. Suddenly, this thing walks out from behind the RV and leaps onto the boy. The dad makes for a shotgun resting up against the vehicle, but never makes it. Both are slaughtered. From what was found at the scene, it's thought that the momma must have seen this happening or heard enough to barricade herself inside. Didn't help though. The thing broke through the door, and it made her pay for putting up a fight. Apparently, she was ripped to pieces. Blood and flesh were dripping from the walls and ceiling. I'm told there were police officers who attended that day that resigned from the service the very next morning. Then, it turned its attention to the daughter.

She was the last to be found, as when the scene was discovered, she was no-where to be seen. It's suspected she was hiding inside the bathroom of the RV, and this creature heard her or smelled her. Either way, it found her and dragged her away. Her half-eaten remains were found in a tree some way from the campground."

Nina and the others stared at Joe in silence.

"So, nobody survived, yet we know what this thing looked like and exactly what happened," Dugas challenged.

"Apparently agents killed one of the things on site," Joe said sheepishly. "There are also eyewitness reports, about what was heard and witnessed from other campgrounds nearby. And, on top of all that, there are historic references and other encounters. A bow hunter was killed not long before that. In the 70s, a group of guys in a VW microbus became so terrified of what they described as a werewolf, which they said stalked them, they left the campsite they were on – but not before the beast left four deep slashes in the metalwork of the car. They said the howling sounded like diabolical laughter."

"I obviously don't know if any of that is true," Nina said. "But it fits with what my dad said. He suggested there were two kinds. Watchers, which like to show themselves. They might frighten or intimidate you, but they'll most likely leave you alone. But the other kind are much more aggressive. They react purely instinctively, and... he said they can tell if you have bad intentions towards nature or have done something they consider evil. They're pure predators."

Nina felt a shudder pass along her spine as she remembered the teeth.

"I wouldn't be wasting your time with this," Nina protested. "But I saw it. You need to believe me."

Agent Jones studied her for a moment before his features

softened and he nodded.

"I believe you Ms. Lee," Jones replied. "And Dugas, go easy on Joe. My daddy was one of those police officers that quit the next day. He went to work somewhere else. How do you think this circus got started in the first place?"

Nina saw Joe's eyes widen in shock, and Dugas' too.

"Ms. Lee, would your father still be at home?" Jones asked. "I was wondering if I could talk to him. This is new territory for us."

"He'll be at home for sure," Nina replied. "But I warn you now, he's not the most friendly towards authority types."

"Guess it runs in the family," Jones said, with a smile that wasn't unkind.

"Say I sent you, that'll go a long way," she replied softly, a little taken aback.

"Joe, is Merlin ready to fly? Agent Smith here can show you around the Prowler, our big rig, see if we can extend our night vision a little ways," Jones asked.

Joe Beazley looked up, surprised.

"I think it could be... I haven't done any test flights, so, no guarantees or anything. But we can try," Joe offered.

"Gents," Jones barked at Wade and Dugas, "I want you, Hicks, and Dixon to secure a 200-yard perimeter around this HQ. Then, I want Hicks downwind, with Joe and everybody else watching his back. The 50.cal can do them real damage, but so can the M4s if you get enough hits. If you know where it is and see it coming, you'll have the edge."

Wade nodded and turned around with the efficiency of a soldier with something to do. Like they all did, he didn't feel comfortable unless 'on mission'. He guessed it was part of the training. Down time was different, but sitting still when there was still a job to do felt like wasted time. That's why menial tasks, from collecting firewood to cooking and cleaning were always welcome. But now, they were back in harm's way. As he made for the door, Nina reached out and grabbed his arm.

"Be careful," she warned. "It might be best to just let them duke it out, you know."

"I'd be happy with that, if it comes to it," Wade replied in a quiet voice. "But we don't want them doing it close to all these people. We're just putting up defences, that's all."

Nina didn't look reassured, so Wade flashed her the most confidence-instilling smile he could muster. A few seconds later, he was headed to the cabin to gear up with the rest of the team. As Nina turned back around, she noticed Joe, Smith, Jones, and Benoit all headed for the door too.

"Guess I've outstayed my welcome," Nina shrugged.

"Not at all, stick around," Benoit suggested kindly.

They left the camp's reception and visitor centre together. Nina watched as Jones headed straight to an adjacent paddock, used for the pack and trail horses, as well as anyone visiting with their own horses when the site was open to tourists. Currently, it appeared to be serving as a vehicle pool, with a multitude of trucks, SUVs, four wheelers and more parked within. She couldn't help thinking about the havoc their tyres and tracks would be playing with the ground. Not my problem she thought, as Jones climbed into a big, dual-axled Ram truck. With its black paintwork and matching steel wheels, as well as a light rig and flared wheel arches, it made for an intimidating work horse well suited to a clandestine agency man. But Nina strongly suspected the truck was Jones' personal transportation rather than government issue. It had a bad attitude look to it that suited him down to the ground. As it tore out of the paddock, she was pretty sure a Cummins turbo diesel was under the hood too, and she doubted any bureau was picking up the cheque for that kind of power. Then she glanced at the big rig Jones had called the Prowler and had second thoughts.

"I should move my truck if I'm going to be here a while," Nina suggested.

"Give your keys to Agent Hannigan here," Smith suggested, beckoning a young-looking agent over to him.

Nina handed the keys over, and the agent gave her a brief smile in acknowledgement. As with a lot of the others, he would have been hard to pick out of a crowd. Well built, with short black hair and no real distinguishing features. It was like they came off an assembly line. She continued walking with Benoit, only glancing over her shoulder once as Smith drew the agent to one side.

"She's not to leave until I give the all clear, understood?" he demanded.

The agent nodded, then jogged over to Nina's truck. As the agent, who Smith had called Harrigan pulled it round to the paddock, Nina felt a pull in her gut that something wasn't right. She looked around for the 2nd Lieutenant but couldn't see him. She realised there wasn't much she could do about it right now and decided to see where things were headed. She followed Benoit up the steps of the Prowler inside. In the open doorway, she paused, as she heard the distinctive engine of the Wendigo. A moment later, the big, white, modified Jeep pulled up to the rear of the big rig. Joe Beazley jumped out of the driver's seat. Nina watched as he began to unwind several cables from a rear console of the Prowler. He then walked them back to the Wendigo and disappeared round the back. A few moments later, he walked briskly back into view, carrying a large, black briefcase and practically skipping up the steps to join them.

"Show time," he declared, beaming.

Benoit looked at Nina and rolled her eyes. A moment later, Agent Smith joined them, and directed them towards the screen wall that took up one entire side of the rig. Smith glanced at a group of fold-down chairs that were screwed to the opposite wall, and Nina and Benoit took the hint. By the time they were seated, the screens had flickered into life, revealing the exterior of the Prowler, in pixel perfect, monochrome night vision. Nina guessed the camera was sitting on the roof of the big rig, and it was directed out towards the treeline past the campsite's border. A white tail doe shone in hot white and light grey, with even its fine fur and hide picked up by the clearly high-end camera. The doe was browsing on the grass shoots that the camp's hive of activity had uncovered over the past few days. Deer in Washington state had learned a long time ago to hang around the campsites, for free and easy handouts from the tourists who didn't know better. But, in one way, it kept them off the geraniums and roses in Tacoma and even Seattle gardens, so the rangers didn't mind so much.

Joe placed the briefcase on the table in front of them and opened it up. Nina realised it was much more than that, as he unfolded two vertically aligned screens and another two that flipped out either side. She could see there was another screen – much smaller, that was flat to the table and joined to a keyboard. There was also a large remote-control module that Joe separated from the bottom of the keyboard with a determined pulling motion. He pressed a button on the remote control, and the screens blinked on. Each read the same thing: Merlin online. On the larger screens attached to the Prowler's walls, Nina watched as the modified trunk of the Wendigo began to lift on hydraulic jacks, then slowly split in two and fold over. Nestled right at the back of the truck's rear was an incredibly large drone, with the letters M E R L I N stamped into its fuselage. Four rotors on mechanical arms pointed skyward and began powering up. As they did, the screens on Joe's control module blinked on. They shared a single image, split across the four panels.

“Pairing to the Prowler’s systems... now,” Joe declared, still smiling.

The screens on the wall blinked once, and now the same single image was displayed across the eight wall panels – split into two rows of four. As the drone gained height, more of the treeline and surrounding area was revealed in the same hot white and greyish tones of the drone’s thermal imaging cameras.

“Okay, this is where it gets tricky,” Joe said, raising an eyebrow. “Time to introduce Merlin’s friends.”

With the drone hovering, he punched a command into the keyboard. Suddenly, the screens went blank. A few moments passed and then they suddenly blinked back on again. This time though, four images now appeared on the screens in distinct columns.

“Perfect transition, well done,” Smith smiled, slapping Joe on the back.

The eight screens were now split into four columns showing a different series of images, still quite close together but from slightly different angles and heights. Then Nina noticed that each different screen column had a name assigned that blinked in their top right-hand corner. It seemed Merlin had been joined by Arthur, Uther, and Nimue.

“Someone likes their myths and legends,” Benoit said, raising an eyebrow.

“Hey, they’re my toys, I get to name them,” Joe shrugged. “Merlin can carry three other satellite drones, and they can work either collaboratively or alone.”

“Impressive,” Nina said. “Did they recruit you straight out of MIT?” she laughed.

“Caltech actually, by the NSA, as it happened,” Joe replied, a little sheepishly.

“I wouldn’t call what happened recruitment though,”

Smith laughed. "More like community service that enabled him to skip serving five-to-ten for hacking a number of defence systems."

"That sounds like blackmail," Nina challenged, glowering a little at Smith.

"Well, whatever it was, when we worked out what he was looking for, he got our attention," Smith replied, leaning back against the wall of the truck, and glancing sideways at Nina.

"Okay, I'll take the bait, what were you looking for?" Nina asked.

Both she and Benoit looked at Joe expectantly. He in turn looked at Smith, who paused, then gave a good-natured nod.

"I'd heard stories about something called the Bureau of Sports Fisheries Bird & Mammal Lab being a front for investigations into... well, things that go bump in the night, basically. But I was particularly interested in a special army unit, rumoured to be based in Fort Belvoir, Virginia. They were meant to have been in a battle with seven sasquatches, who were hunting people."

"And?" Nina inquired, shocked at what she'd just heard.

"Just ghost stories," Smith interjected. "But nevertheless, Joe got our attention, and we put his passion... and interest in conspiracy theories to more practical, healthy uses."

Joe looked at Smith anxiously, then turned back to the screens. He split the drones up to fall in overhead as they picked up the soldiers moving into the treeline ahead.

"Now we have eyes on the ground and in the sky," Joe chirped, back to being excited again.

~

Agent Jones pulled his truck up outside Robert Lee's cabin, having found the address in Nina Lee's personnel file. He got out of the truck and slowly made his way up the steps to the house. As he reached the deck, a low growl of warning rumbled out of the darkness to his right. Jones wasn't easily startled, but it was enough to make him reach for the Korth revolver in its side holster.

"No need for that," came a commanding voice, as the door opened.

Jones turned to see the Native American man walk out onto the porch and veranda. Robert lee studied him with an amused grin as he walked past. In the light that now seeped from the cabin's interior, Jones could see that a large black dog was stood at the end of the decking, watching them. Its amber eyes caught the light and reflected at them, and he realised it wasn't a dog.

"Tell me I didn't come all the way up here because you've got a wolf?" Jones grumbled, in a way that was meant to be under his breath.

"Don't mind Achak," Robert said, pushing the door open with his arm in a gesture that invited Jones inside. "Wolves can sense testosterone in us guys. From the looks of you, I'd say you have plenty of that coursing through your veins. It's why they get on better with women overall. They see us as a threat and prefer to keep their distance unless they've grown up with you."

Jones walked inside and noticed he was closely followed by the wolf before Robert Lee closed the door behind him. Robert gestured at a chair that sat opposite the couch and Jones nodded, lowering into it. As he did so, he realised how tired he felt. The chair welcomed his aching shoulders and he relaxed into it. When he looked up, he noticed Achak was sitting directly across from him at the end of the couch, watching him intently.

"And as for why you've come up here," Robert laughed, "it's not for Nina's pet. I guess you could say it's for mine."

"I just need to know what we're up against," Jones said,

openly.

"Coffee?" Robert offered, glancing at an old-fashioned metal pot that was bubbling on the stove in the kitchen.

"Yes please," Jones said, not realising quite how long it had been since he'd had anything to eat or drink. "Black please."

"I don't make it any other way, except for the addition of some wild chicory for flavour," Robert replied, taking the pot off the stove, and grabbing two mugs from a glass-fronted cupboard above it. "You game?"

"Count me in," Jones replied.

Robert Lee poured the coffee and handed Jones a mug as he sat down on the couch with his.

"I'm not gonna hide that I'm basically here to satisfy my curiosity," Jones huffed. "First off, I wanna make sure we're not talking about something I've dealt with before. What the Mi'kmaq call a Gugwe?

Robert Lee shook his head.

"What about a Benandanti?" Jones offered.

Robert Lee sat up a little and shook his head again, "don't know that one," he said.

"Guess that's not much of a surprise," Jones sighed. "They're Italian – meant to be a malevolent bipedal wolf that protects crops and battles supernatural creatures. Legends of them spread here when the European settlers did. I thought it was worth asking."

Robert Lee nodded in understanding. "Not the same, I'm sure, but not dissimilar," he offered.

"So, what is this thing... your daughter called it a Limmekin."

"It's hard to explain," Robert sighed. "Do you know what a tulpa is?"

"Yeah, I watched the X-Files before I joined it." Jones smiled. "Sort of a thought-form brought to life – a Buddhist thing, I think."

Robert Lee nodded solemnly.

"Instead of being conjured by our minds, they already exist," he explained. "They seek a connection – an invitation into our reality. At least some of them do."

Jones let what Lee had told him sink in.

"So, interdimensional, something like that?"

"A crass label for such an elegant existence," Robert scoffed. "But again, not inaccurate. Or, to put it in cowboy terms," Robert smiled, glancing at the revolver on Jones' hip, "they ain't from around here."

"How does that work?" Jones asked.

"Forgive me, but it isn't something we discuss, and certainly not with outsiders."

Jones frowned but decided not to push that angle. It wasn't necessarily what he wanted to know in any case. Not the most important thing anyway.

"From what has been passed down, they see themselves as elite warriors and spirits of wilderness," Robert continued. "Their existence is about pure predatory vengeance. They consider it an honour to be called upon. But that's not really what you want to know."

"How do we kill them?" Jones admitted.

"It's not easy," Robert sighed. "You must remember that the wolf is a sacred, spiritual creature. He is the hunter most hunted. The killer most killed. Our oldest friend and enemy in one. So, my honest answer is... any way you can. But I warn you. It is here to do a job. My advice would be to let it do it. If you get between it and its target, it won't hesitate. And I wouldn't piss off any natives either. They don't like that."

"I'll bear that in mind," Jones sighed, getting up. "Thank you for the coffee and the straight talking."

"Thank you for respecting an old man's traditions and

beliefs," Robert offered.

Jones walked to his truck, with Robert Lee and the black wolf watching from the door. As he climbed into the cabin, he saw the door close, and he was left sitting on the road. He took out his phone, checked he was tapped into the secure line, then dialled Major Clarke. As usual, it went straight to an equally secure message box. Jones was used to this and knew that anything he said would be vetted before being passed on.

"Sitrep," Jones growled into the handset. "Redskins have called in a quarterback."

He hung up and looked out into the darkness, just as a slither of rain drops began to trickle down the windshield. A storm was coming.

CHAPTER TWENTY-TWO

A GATHERING STORM

Shartale sprang up, startled and disorientated. It had been a long time since he'd allowed himself to sleep and rest for such an extended period. He stayed crouched and still as he listened intently to his surroundings. He had dug into the ground underneath an overhanging ledge that shielded him from the elements and had allowed his wounds to heal a little, aided by the restorative agents he'd found and his attendance to them. His strength had also been restored, having found some sustenance. The yearling mule deer buck had been malnourished and ridden with parasites. It had survived the winter, but only barely. It had been easy prey and much needed. But Shartale had made the mistake of leaving the remains close to where he had sought shelter. And although he couldn't hear anything, his instincts and his nose told him that what was left of his meal had attracted another predator.

Shartale stood up to his full height. The scent was familiar to him. It wasn't a bear or a wolf. It was a cat, on the lookout for easy pickings. Like him, he sensed it didn't want a fight. It would be foolish if it did, but he knew how the desperation of hunger gave in to risk. He felt the breeze on his face and realised that if the wind hadn't changed, the cat would've made it much closer. Shartale took two steps forward in a slow and deliberate fashion. Standing over the kill, he reached down and ripped one of the deer's front legs off. He snapped off the lower part and hoof, taking the shoulder with him as he headed into the forest. He didn't turn around, but he knew the mountain lion and her cub from the previous year, had descended from the bank above his shelter and were now feeding on the carcass. He left them to it, tugging the skin from his own meal with his teeth, before separating flesh from bone.

Shartale knew that, like his own kind, the humans would return to the forest to collect their dead. He had headed North with this in mind, travelling some distance from the canyon where he and the family had battled them. His direction also took him further from the dwelling where he had killed the female human. He had felt safe resting up during the day, knowing the humans would be preoccupied. But he was all too aware that as night fell, the hunters, like him, would come out again. With both the family's females killed by the humans, his instinct told him to seek a new territory, far from here. He would cross the mountains and travel east, and then maybe south as the warmer weather came in.

He was unfamiliar with this part of the forest, having previously followed the tracks and trails of the family group, and later, the humans. Shartale couldn't sense their presence here. His acute senses picked up on his gain of a couple of hundred feet in elevation, and the storm that was moving in from the west. He could tell it had blown in from the coast and that the downpour would be heavy, and that moisture would cling in the air to form a thick fog. In the morning, the ground would be frostbitten and cold. Travelling on all fours, he moved carefully and with caution through the brush, leaving little trail or trace. Then, as the trees became more densely packed, he left the ground altogether, passing from branch to branch. As if choreographed, his movements were veiled by the wind as it creaked the boughs and shook the canopy overhead.

By heading north, he knew there would be fewer humans. Ultimately, it was also more likely he would come across territories held by more of his own kind. His presence would be unwelcomed unless there was need of an alpha.

Sometimes, as dominant males became older, they would accept outsiders into a clan. Trust had to be earned and a role had to be secured in such situations. Nearly always, it took the approval or acceptance of a female to do so. Although hunting humans was seen as unclean, it was easier than constantly sizing up to new alphas and family groups. And by no means did he always hunt just them. What Shartale looked for, in all situations, was opportunity. And he had one now, to escape with his life and leave the area.

He felt more at ease as darkness fell. To make the passage north, he would have to skirt the central part of the forest where the humans had been active, travelling along a valley that eventually took him up and over the ridgeline. To the west of the valley was an area he was more familiar with, and where he had hunted younglings of the dark-skinned men when he himself had been young. He had not been there for many moons, as they were good trackers and hunters, and sought revenge when one of their own was killed.

In the distance, Shartale could hear the machines of man. He recognised the sound of an encampment, having been around many before. He instinctively veered away, knowing it was likely to be the men he had hunted, and who had hunted him. As the trees became loftier, with fewer lower boughs and branches, he was forced to return to the forest floor. He stuck to solid ground but sacrificed some caution to travel faster. Then, in a gulley that signalled the start of his ascent through the valley, an unfamiliar scent was brought to him as he turned into the wind. He stopped and lifted his nose high. The odour was distinct. Although its power had faded, it had a signature that he recognised as predatory. The situation unnerved him. He could tell that the source of the odour wasn't close and was upwind of him. Shartale had learned his own predatory skills through hardship and necessity. Prey was approached downwind, so it would not detect what was stalking it. His highly adapted brain had been honed by evolution towards natural problem-solving functionality. Both his intellect and his instinct told him that the predator had positioned itself upwind deliberately. That made it about territory and intimidation. Whatever it was, it was so sure of itself, it didn't mind who knew it was there.

The boldness of such an act unsettled Shartale. He had never come across a creature that he couldn't best. Even among his own kind, Shartale had grown large and powerful. Other sasquatch would only confront him in groups. But whatever was lying in wait in the valley, acted alone. He had never encountered arrogant rashness like this before. Confrontations between predators often happened suddenly and haphazardly because they moved stealthily and downwind by default. And then instinct would take over. Fighting something else built to kill others was risky. Injury carried consequences. Most avoided it for this very reason. But this predator invited conflict. More than not caring if others knew it was there, it seemed it wanted them to.

Then there was the nature of the scent itself. Undeniably that of an animal, but not one Shartale recognised. It most strongly resembled a coyote, but it had a strong, metallic overlay that reminded him of a skunk or badger. There was a further warm dampness to it that wasn't unlike the large brown bears. Yet still, Shartale knew it was none of these animals. It gave him pause. In the distance, a streak of light lit up the sky. It was enough for him to notice the wet-looking outline of a footprint, etched onto a slab of rock that marked the path towards the valley. He stepped closer to examine it. It had a large heel, not unlike a smaller individual of one of his own kind. But then, the foot narrowed dramatically, culminating in a triangular-shaped pad with four distinct oval toes. Each of these was accented by a sharp, angular mark of an attached claw. Shartale recognised it as undoubtedly canine. He also now knew why the scent lingered rather than just being carried on the wind. Canines had scent glands between their toes, which made their feet unsavoury to eat. Shartale noticed the print hadn't dried and was still fresh. It hadn't been long since the creature had passed this way.

The next consideration Shartale pondered, was if the animal had detected him already and changed direction to avoid him. If so, that was a good sign. But it meant he had to make his own decision. If he went forward, it would be a flagrant challenge to the creature that had so carefully marked its trail. Yet changing direction came with the danger of encountering the armed men who already knew he was here. It had only been a few seconds when the thunder rumbled over the mountains and through the valley. Moments later, the rain began to fall. Softly at first, but quickly increasing into a persistent patter. Shartale looked out across the forest. He ignored the steep-rising valley to the North for now, instead gazing East. Here, another ridgeline, made up of a steep-sided rockface, slowly rose to meet the head of the valley somewhere beyond. He knew the rocks here were made up of layers, and that they allowed water to pass through them. That meant the possibility of cave systems. There, he might find shelter from all he looked to hide from, for now. As the storm rolled in, he headed east.

CHAPTER TWENTY-THREE

A WILD SPIRIT OF VENGEANCE

Nina had been watching the screens with the others for over an hour when the storm reached them. She had expected it to impact the drone's ability to fly, but Joe had responded with a smug smile, assuring her that the only thing they had to worry about was a direct hit by lightning, and even then, it had shielding to protect it. The squad of soldiers were patrolling the camp in a rough, wide perimeter. One of them, equipped with a long gun, had broken off from the others and was now positioned on a slope facing the camp and the trails that led in. He was undoubtedly well camouflaged, but the drone's thermal imaging meant he shone in dazzling white heat against the dark background. There was nothing behind except the high ridgeline to the north and the west. Unless the creatures were willing to cross mountain tops in a storm, Nina suspected that it was going to be a long night. She'd heard enough talk to know the sasquatch was probably injured. If there was ever a night to lie up and lick your wounds, this was it.

Then she thought of the Limmekin. If something like that was on her trail, relentlessly stalking her, with the sole intention of taking her down, she knew she'd run too. Storm be damned. Nina had also noticed over the last hour that Agent Harrigan hadn't returned with the keys to her truck.

"I'm gonna need to bring the drones back in soon to recharge," Joe said, breaking the silence that had overcome everyone inside the Prowler's snug interior. "Mind if I test out Nimue's party trick?" he asked, turning towards Agent Smith.

Smith looked up, having become disinterested in the screens some time ago. Caught unawares for a moment, he clearly hadn't been paying attention. As Joe's words sunk in, he quickly nodded his approval and stepped forward, focusing once more on the viewers. Nina was glad it wasn't just her who was feeling tired. She turned her gaze to the column of screens marked as Nimue, wondering what Joe meant. There was a small creek a couple of hundred yards East of the campsite, which became a powerful waterfall a little further beyond, emptying into a wide and deep pool. It was a popular swimming hole in summer. Nina noticed the drone was currently hovering over the pool and beginning to dip down towards it.

"As the good doctor noticed," Joe beamed, "my babies are named after characters from the legend of King Arthur. Merlin, the great wizard and teacher. Uther, Arthur's father, and..."

"Careful," Nina cried, jumping up, as the drone came dangerously close to the surface of the water.

Joe just turned towards her with a wry smile, as the drone dropped a few more feet and touched down into the pool. Nina looked at him, stunned. She couldn't believe that he was deliberately trashing what was undoubtedly a very expensive, and apparently unique piece of equipment.

"And then, there's Nimue," Joe said, turning back towards the screen. "Also known as..."

"The lady of the lake," Benoit cut in.

As Nina watched, she could now see one of the other drones – Arthur, had positioned itself above the pool. Through its cameras, they watched Nimue's rotor arms fold backwards ninety degrees, as the drone began to sink below the surface of the water. Seemingly automatically, two spotlights switched on at the drone's front – their strong beams clearly visible below the surface. And instead of sinking, the drone began to glide through the water, propelled by its now horizontal rotors. The camera feed remained sharp and clear. On screen, a small fish came into view, close to the bottom of the pool. Nina recognised it as a slimy sculpin. They were nocturnal and preferred cold, slow, or even still water due to being inefficient swimmers. They lacked a swim bladder, and often looked like they hopped across pond bottoms when they moved. Illuminated by the glow of the drone's spotlights, it made quick and easy pickings for the grass pickerel – a predatory, pike-like fish, that dashed in from the gloom and plucked it from the mud before disappearing again.

"That's a neat trick," Nina exclaimed, impressed.

Joe beamed at her, clearly proud.

"I developed her in mind of a wild theory I heard about how we don't find bodies of sasquatch, because they bury their dead in lakes," Joe explained.

Agent Smith coughed lightly and shifted on his feet. Joe looked back at him nervously and retuned his gaze to the screen.

"Well, I'd call that a positive first test," Joe smiled, a little more sheepishly this time.

Nina sank back down into her chair, glancing at Benoit with a tired smile.

"You look exhausted," the doctor said kindly.

Nina nodded.

"Why don't you grab one of the cabins?" Smith suggested. "It could be a long night. We're just taking precautions and the show's over for now," he added, looking at Joe.

Nina could see the drones were all headed back towards the truck. Nimue had once again risen to the surface and was taking to the air, quickly falling in behind the others.

"The Wendigo's hooked up to a generator," Joe explained. "The drones will need an hour to recharge even with our advanced military technology," he shrugged, adding speech marks to his words with his fingers.

"We'll come get you if anything happens, of course," Benoit suggested.

Special Agent Smith walked to the exterior door of the Prowler and opened it. Standing outside was a Bureau agent, with his back to the door. He was using the awning and overhang of the big rig's trailer housing to shelter from the rain. As he turned around, Nina saw it was Agent Harrigan, who had moved her truck earlier. A thick stream of water trailed off his Bureau of Land Management baseball cap.

"Ah, Agent Harrigan, just the man," Smith smiled. "Ms. Lee is gonna rest up in one of the cabins. Any not occupied?"

"Straight across the way there, No. 5," Harrigan replied with a reassuring smile. "I'll walk you over."

Nina nodded, if a little hesitantly. But the reassuring smile that Benoit beamed at her went along way to rid her mind of conspiracy theories. She followed Harrigan hurriedly across the track and onto a winding path that led to a block of three cabins. Number five was the first one they reached. Harrigan ducked under the porch and opened the door for her. Nina stepped inside and turned to face the alleged BLM agent.

"Do you still have my keys?" she asked.

"Let me hold onto them unless we need to move it again," he smiled. "Consider me your valet service."

Nina was about to argue, but she caught Smith looking over at them from the steps of the Prowler. For some reason, she didn't feel safe with Agent Jones absent from the command post. She went inside and closed the door. The cabin was basic yet snug. There was a small kitchenette consisting of a retro-looking refrigerator, a microwave, an electric hob, and a broiler, all set within a single wall cabinet. In front of it was a round pine table and four farmhouse-style wooden chairs. There was a large couch that had seen better days set against the opposite wall, and a double bed at the far end of the room. She could see two small further rooms at the back, through doors each side of the double bed that were open. One was a bathroom, and the other a bedroom with two bunks. The big double bed was spread with an inviting chequered quilt. She lay down on it, only to find the mattress as hard as granite. She rolled off with a growl and dragged the quilt over to the couch instead. She lay with her feet and head facing the front door of the cabin, and as she settled in under the quilt, she turned on her side and drew her revolver from its holster, placing it beside her, with the barrel also pointed at the entranceway.

~

Shartale traversed a small escarpment that led to a rockface. It towered above him, presenting a wall that could not be scaled or penetrated. Yet he knew there was an opening here. His feet pressed the loose fragments of stone that it had spewed onto the ground. The storm robbed him of most of his sense of smell, but he could taste the dampness of a cave not far beyond. As he clambered up the slope, his feet slipped against the slick rock and greasy mix of clay and minerals beneath. Rather than fall, he leapt forward, landing at the top on all fours.

His head snapped back to the forest behind him. As the rain beat against the rocks like drums, and loose scree tumbled down the slope from where he'd lost his footing, the sound had almost been lost. But he was sure it had been there. A sharp growl of denial that only a predator could know. It was the venting of frustration that came after, when poised to strike, prey moved, or in this case, recovered from a fall or being knocked off balance. Shartale recognised for that split second, as he slipped, he had been vulnerable. And something had been watching him. It had wanted to rush in and make the most of that moment but had been denied. It was a situation he had been in many times, but never as the quarry. It was a new and unwelcome experience. Shartale faced the forest, rising to his full height. Baring his teeth, he unleashed a low, rumbling growl of warning. The sound was ugly and full of intent. As it built in his throat, he unleashed the sharkaah, the dark voice, adding new layers to the warning. He reached out for a nearby hemlock trunk and ripped the tree from the ground with one arm. Unleashing a roar, he lifted it high above his head and then smashed the leafy top branches into the ground as a crack of lightning flashed across the sky. The tree splintered as he drove it downwards with unrelenting force. The roots pointed directly skyward. Stepping backwards, he slowly entered the cave opening, his eyes searching the trees beyond. The sounds of rain, wind, and running water filled his ears, but nothing else. He backed away from the opening until he was surrounded by darkness.

Once inside, Shartale turned around and faced the cave. He could tell it wasn't a natural opening. The humans had tunnelled into the rock. Not quite high enough for him to stand up, he hunched down and craned his head forwards. Water trickled along neat channels either side of the relatively flat floor, and he could smell the moss-covered dead timber that lined parts of the floor and roof of the cave. Most importantly, he could taste the distant scent of fresh air and forest. He travelled in its direction, quickly and silently.

~

Nina didn't know how long she'd slept, but she snapped back into consciousness with a jolt. A bead of sweat ran from her temple and down her neck as she sat upright, her hand on the grip of the revolver. She looked at the door, relying on her night vision and not willing to turn the light on yet. The cabin was still dark. She listened to the soft, sporadic spatter of raindrops as they rapped against the windows. The storm hadn't quite given up yet, but it seemed calmer than before. If she'd managed to sleep an hour or so, that meant there were still a few hours until it got light. She glanced at her watch. It was 4.07.

She didn't know why, but the feeling she'd had earlier, that something wasn't right, floated up from her gut into her chest. Her heart thumped hard as she strained her hearing, trying to ascertain why she felt so on edge. With no further answers coming, she threw aside the blanket and stood up. She straightened out her shirt before walking over to the front door and pulling on her jacket from the chair it was slung over – thankfully now dry. She holstered the revolver against the back of her hip but didn't take her hand away from the grips. Instead, she angled her body slightly away from the door, so it wasn't obvious she had one hand behind her back. However, she knew any government agent with an ounce of sense would recognise a defensive stance when they saw it. Feet and body angled to both anticipate and deflect a potential impact or assault.

She opened the door to find Agent Harrigan's face a few inches from her own. Despite the inky black sky, he was wearing sunglasses and had obviously heard her get up and walk across the cabin towards the door. Otherwise, the thought of him standing there for hours just facing the door was even more creepy.

"I think I've had my fill of both excitement and games," Nina stated. "I've passed on my information and I'm going home."

Harrigan's mouth formed into a grin that attempted to look embarrassed and apologetic, but it just came off smug. He'd been expecting this and seemed to be enjoying the moment.

"It's not convenient for you to leave right now Ms. Lee,"

Harrigan said quietly. "I don't have the men to move the trucks around out of your way. Perhaps if you wait until it stops raining, then we'll see what we can do."

"I said I wasn't playing the game anymore," Nina replied sternly. "Keys, now," she demanded, holding out her hand.

Agent Harrigan's grin dropped immediately.

"Fine, have it your way," he shrugged.

Harrigan half turned away, which was enough for Nina to drop her guard just for a second. But it was all that the agency man needed. He barged towards her and brought his hands up to grip her shoulders, trying to turn her and knock her off balance. But she had caught his change in stance and spun on her back foot, stepping back into the cabin. Harrigan's momentum took him forward and Nina went for her gun, but so did he. His Glock pistol was holstered on his belt, forward facing, and he was already moving towards her as it was. Nina was fast, but Harrigan had positioning on his side. He brought up the pistol with effortless momentum and closed the space between them in a fraction of a second. Her own gun was only half drawn when she felt the cold metal of the Glock's barrel press against her temple.

"I prefer it this way, actually," Harrigan whispered. "I'll take that, thank you," he added, grabbing the revolver from her hand. "I don't have to play nice anymore. Until the boss says so, this cabin is your home. You're not going anywhere. My suggestion is you get comfy – maybe get a bit more rest. You try to leave again, I'll restrain you."

Nina glowered at him.

"I'll be wanting that gun back," Nina warned.

"That's fine – like you, it's going nowhere. Now back inside," Harrigan ordered.

As he stepped outside, Nina slammed the door of the cabin behind him and made sure to bolt it. She then headed to the windows and made sure all the curtains were drawn, including the ones over the little kitchenette. She didn't know what she was going to do, but she knew she didn't want Harrigan to see. Nina slumped down on one of the chairs by the round table and let her eyes flick over the room and the contents of the cabin. There were no windows on the side walls of the cabin, but she seemed to recall there had been one in the bathroom. She got to her feet and stepped lightly over the floorboards. She peered in through the door, her gaze falling on the small, rectangular frame above the toilet. It looked like she'd be able to get through it. The trick would be doing it without Harrigan hearing.

~

Shartale could sense the presence, somewhere behind him in the darkness. He had been followed into the cave. The scent of rain and pine led him through the maze of tunnels and back out into the night. He leapt from the opening and hit the ground running. Swiftly and silently, he traversed the shallow slope that led to the treeline, then leapt again into the branches of a mature Sitka spruce. He climbed as high as he dared, holding his body close to the trunk, and weaving between the branches as he ascended. The thick green boughs hid him well. Through a small gap in the tree's canopy, he faced the opening that led back into the mountain. He supported his weight by holding onto a branch above him with one hand, and a foot firmly planted on another below. The claws on his other hand bit deep into the trunk's bark, and his other foot lay pressed flat against it. To his back was an opening that would enable him to leap clear to the ground. And as before, the wind came towards him. Hidden and downwind, he now had the advantage. His pursuer would not be able to detect him and would not be able to approach without revealing itself. With almost all his body hidden behind the trunk of the spruce, he tilted his head ever so slightly and looked.

Through the darkness and the still falling rain, he almost missed it. The thing stood in the shadow of the opening, only partially visible. It was the movement of its chest that alerted him. Its torso heaved in and out rhythmically fast. The musculature was not unlike his own. Not quite so broad, but more pronounced. Its waist was narrower and more streamlined. Similar to Shartale and his kind, it stood on its hind legs – but the lower parts were turned backwards, like that of a wolf. Its stance appeared to be hunched, as if permanently leaning forward. He could only see one arm, as the other was still in shadow. The fingers on the hand were not so well defined as his own, more like the splayed digits of a paw. The thumb was much further down the hand than his own, more like the dew claw of a wolf or coyote. And each digit had a curved, elongated, and permanently unsheathed talon at its end, clearly sharper and more purposeful than his own.

The creature took a slow step forward. Its top-heavy mass pulled it out into the open. Staying upright seemed to be something that took effort for it. Shartale could tell that the creature did not stand as tall as he did, but its torso and musculature suggested it was extremely strong and built to run fast. Fully revealed, there was no doubting its canine appearance. Two large erect ears scanned the forest, twitching slightly with each sound they picked up. None seemed to alarm it, nor encouraged it to investigate further. The head was large and broad. Like the dogs he'd fought at the house, the creature had a ruff of thick hair that flowed over its neck and shoulders and seemed to originate in a hump of muscle on its back. The jaw was wide and elongated. With its mouth closed, Shartale could not see its teeth, but everything about the animal suggested it was a formidable predator.

Suddenly, the creature looked up, straight at the trees. Its eyes appeared as two golden orbs that glowed in the darkness. Shartale's body responded automatically, as his breathing and heartrate slowed. He felt no alarm. Controlling his body this way was the ultimate act of concealment and he trusted his instincts. The creature had not seen him, and he knew it could not detect his scent. If this were one of the large brown bears, or even a normal wolf, he would have emptied his powerful glands as a warning. But this was no wolf, and he knew that he had the advantage by staying hidden.

The thing took a few more careful steps forward, slowly moving its head back and forth as it did so, scanning the trees as it passed through. This was not something Shartale could do. His neck was a thick band of protective muscle, and to move his head he had to turn his shoulders or his torso. Shartale recognised this meant the creature's throat was more vulnerable to attack than his own. He stayed completely still as he watched the animal come closer. Still, Shartale's nerve held. He knew that by entering the trees, there was no possible way for it to track him. Then it stopped close to the tree he was in. It was still in full sight, but its proximity intensified his urge to go on the attack. Then the creature snapped its head away from Shartale's tree. It dropped to all fours and leapt into the darkness, loping along a trail that led downhill and away from the rockface. Shartale did not stir for some time, until he was sure the creature had not doubled back. Slowly, he descended the tree and faced the direction the animal had taken. Above the patter of the rain and the trickle of water from the rocks and leafy branches around him, he picked out what had caught the thing's attention. Somewhere out in the forest ahead of them, the sounds of a human encampment sang out into the night and gave them away. He began to follow the same trail the canine-like creature had taken.

~

Nina stepped up on to the toilet seat. She could hear the rain against the window – more of a gentle thrum than a violent beating against the pane. The frame was old and wooden, and kept locked by a folding metal opener with holes in it that aligned with pegs along the base. The rectangular glass was small and high enough for bears not to be an issue – but she figured a lithe, athletic Native American woman might just be able to squeeze through. Gingerly, she lifted the opener and pushed against the frame. It wouldn't budge. Her memory recalled nights spent in similar cabins at summer camps and the like, and she knew all too well that in many cases, windows were nailed or screwed shut to keep errant teenagers in. She couldn't see any screw or nail heads though, and pushed again, this time letting the opener hang loose as she shoved with both her hands.

There was a small bang, as the vacuum of air that had sealed the window shut for so long, broke with a puff of dust. There was no resistance now, and the frame swung upwards freely. Nina was careful to lift it high and not let it fall back to knock against the frame. She decided there was no time like the present and scrambled up further onto the toilet seat and bathroom cabinet. She was able to gain enough of a foothold to push her head through the open window, tilting it to do so. She wiggled her shoulders, wincing as the hooks for the opener scraped against her sternum and the upper frame of the window pinched at her back. She took a deep breath and slowly and more deliberately, she edged forwards.

Her midriff had just cleared the bottom of the frame when she heard footsteps. Her head shot to her right, along the side of the cabin. The front was obscured by a small line of ornamental conifers, and the cabin sat on a bed of gravel. It was the crunch of boots on the latter that she could pick up. They moved from the front of the cabin in her direction. A few moments later, Agent Harrigan appeared. He stopped when he saw her, a smug grin creeping across his face. He drew his weapon and held it down by his side as he began to walk towards her, casually and in no rush. Nina was angry at herself for being caught in such a vulnerable position. He wasn't pointing the pistol at her, but she took it as a suggestion to stay where she was rather than retreat. He stopped when he was a few feet away. She had to twist her head to the right to look at him.

"Guess I wasn't clear when we first spoke," he sighed mockingly. "Now, what are we going to do about that."

"I want to talk to Agent Jones, now," Nina demanded, glaring at Harrigan.

"Well, I want a lot of things," Harrigan smirked, his voice quieter. He took a step forward.

"Oh, I bet you do," Nina growled.

"One of us for sure, is going to be shit out of luck," he replied.

Harrigan lifted his free hand and ran a finger down Nina's cheek.

Nina snapped her head away, glowering with anger. She instantly started wriggling back through the window. Harrigan brought up the pistol and flippantly smacked her across the chin with it. It wasn't hard enough to do anything but wound her pride. Then he grabbed her by the hair and began to pull her towards the ground. Once her buttocks had been dragged through the opening, gravity did the rest and she tumbled onto the gravel. She rolled away from Harrigan, but he dashed towards her. She was surprised by the physical strength he showed as he lifted her chin with one hand and slammed her head against the wooden outer wall of the cabin. But doing so enabled her to sit up slightly, her back straight and legs bent. As Harrigan dragged her upwards, she let her left hand drop to her side and fall behind her. Her fingers unsnapped the button on the hidden knife holster nobody had bothered to check her for.

Nina was used to racism. Inside government agencies like the Ranger Service, it was almost encouraged. Native Americans were still marginalised, denied rights, and treated as inferior and ignorant. She knew the story all too well. Somebody had ordered Harrigan to keep her under house arrest. His interpretation of that was he was free to do with her as he pleased. She didn't know if that meant just violence or if it extended to rape. But she did know the same story was being played out in jail cells, parking lots, back alleys, and countless other places across the country. Being treated as a second-rate citizen came with one advantage though – being underestimated.

"You look like you've still got plenty of fight in you," Harrigan sneered. "Gonna have to knock that out of you I'm afraid. Job like this has got to have some perks. Technically, what we're up here hunting doesn't exist, which means neither do I... nobody to tell tale on. Shucks."

Harrigan lifted the pistol again. It was a standard issue Glock 17. He held it by the barrel, clearly intending to hit her with the weightier grip and magazine. His other hand was still clamped around her throat. Her own hand moved like lightning, unsheathing the blade with the back of her hand, and driving it up to rest flat against Harrigan's throat. She took some pleasure in watching his eyes widen in joint surprise and terror. But her other hand wasn't as quick as his instinct and training. Harrigan lurched backwards, putting distance between himself and the blade. In a cowboy-esque move, he flipped the gun and caught it by the grips, pointing it at Nina. At the same time, Nina had dashed forwards and brought her knee up into his groin whilst swiping at his gun hand with the knife. Harrigan was again quick enough to bat it away as he stumbled backwards. She found herself staring down the barrel of the pistol, which was pointed directly at her head.

"Enough foreplay, you're not worth it," Harrigan gasped, wiping spittle from his mouth. He took another step back, straightening his gun arm for a steadier shot.

Nina didn't know why she had an urge to look at her feet, but she did. That's when she noticed the stone her father had given her. It must have slipped from her back pocket when she had fallen from the window. She no longer cared what Harrigan would do to her and reached for it. At the exact same moment, a black mass dropped from the roof above her and landed behind Harrigan. Nina froze as it rose behind him. She could hear the creature breathing in ragged, laboured wheezes. As its legs straightened, its torso lifted and there was a loud and obvious popping sound that seemed to emanate from its hips. At the same time, it took a sharp intake of breath. The heavy wheezing stopped, and it now stood at its full height, towering nearly three feet above Harrigan. Nina could smell the creature. She imagined it wouldn't be dissimilar to what you'd get if you found a dead coyote and a skunk together, in putrid swamp water. Harrigan had spun on his heels as it had passed over him, but now stood motionless. His mouth was open, and he stared unblinkingly into the two piercing yellow eyes that gave the illusion of glowing softly in the darkness. Nina realised that even now, she couldn't quite make out the creature beyond its silhouette. Yet she was in no doubt what it was. The Limmekin.

As if snapping out of a trance, Harrigan gave a little gasp of realisation and raised the gun ever so slightly before he began to put pressure on the trigger. The creature's claws ripped open his forearm and wrist, slashing so fast and deep that neither Harrigan nor Nina had blinked. The gun fell to the floor and Nina dove for the stone her father had given her. She cradled it in both hands as she curled into a ball against the wall. Picking up the stone seemed to get the wolf-like animal's attention, and it bent its broad head down towards her. It wasn't looking into her eyes, instead it appeared to focus on her neck. It pushed its snout towards her, stopping a few inches from her exposed jugular notch. Nina trembled as she felt its hot breath wet her skin as it expelled a snort from its nostrils. Momentarily, it had lost interest in Harrigan, who was writhing on the floor, clutching at his wounded arm with his good one. He had already lost a lot of blood. Involuntary tremors ran up and down his body. The Limmekin tilted its head, clearly focused on Nina's neck. Then it turned away and looked down at Harrigan.

The creature reached down and grabbed Harrigan by the leg. It lifted him with ease and swung him against the cabin wall, where he landed in a crumpled heap, several feet from Nina. She remained curled against the wooden frame of the building, hugging her knees, and clutching the stone so tightly, her knuckles turned white. Letting go of Harrigan's leg, the Limmekin wrapped its clawed hand around the agent's throat and dragged him upwards. In a few moments, his feet dangled helplessly below him. He kicked and writhed, his face slowly turning red as the creature continued to squeeze. A guttural, gurgling snarl that almost sounded like a laugh rose into the monster's throat and stayed there, resonating as it grew in strength. Nina's eyes widened as she saw its lips curl back. It's grinning she thought. Its enjoying this.

The light from the window above her illuminated Harrigan's face just enough for her to see the trickle of blood as it oozed from his ear. That's when she saw its claw, imbedded in Harrigan's neck, just below the jaw. The creature was not just suffocating him. It had cut off the carotid artery with precision. The blood that had surged into his head as it had begun to throttle him now had nowhere to go. So, it sought outlets through his facial orifices. Nina knew blood would be evacuating his nostrils, his other ear, and filling his eye sockets and throat. The creature knew what it was doing. It seemed to watch, waiting as the life literally drained from Harrigan's body through his eyes. Then, just as it was about to extinguish, there was a sudden, violent snapping sound as it broke his neck with just the slightest of pressure from its fingers. Harrigan's corpse dropped to the ground, and the Limmekin sunk back down onto all fours. It showed no interest in the dead agent, other than lifting its rear leg as it liberally and casually urinated onto the body. Finished, it slowly loped past her, indifferent and without a second glance. When she glanced in the direction it had gone, there was nothing there but darkness again. Then, over the sound of the rain, a gunshot. And a cry of terror.

Her arms and hands trembled as she crawled over to Harrigan's lifeless body. Another gunshot and a scream ran out from the front of the camp. Her head snapped upwards in the direction it came from. When she looked back down, Nina tried not to look at Harrigan's grotesquely coloured face and bulging eyes. She couldn't shake the idea the Limmekin had somehow homed in on her, perhaps even come to her aid. Yet she felt no pity or remorse for Harrigan. History and experience told her that she would not have been his first victim. And if she'd had a gun in her hand, she would have pulled the trigger, no question. But there was a difference between self-defence and the Limmekin's deliberate cruelty. She remembered her father's words. A wild spirit of pure vengeance that hated unbalance in nature. It now seemed like an understatement.

Gingerly, Nina began to frisk Harrigan's body. She found what she was looking for in the inside pocket of his dark blue, federally issued, BLM-emblazoned jacket. She removed the Colt King Cobra and checked it was still loaded, before returning it to the holster on her hip. As before, she covered it up with her outer layers. On her second pat down of Harrigan's corpse, she discovered the keys to her truck in the back pocket of his pants. She stood up and turned around. Ahead of her, she could pass through the line of conifers and come out onto the main path, opposite where the Prowler was set up and presumably, where the rest of the team still were. She glanced to her left. If she headed through the trees, on a roughly north-eastern path, she'd come to the paddock to the east of the campsite, currently being used as a parking lot. She launched into a silent, loping, yet fast-paced run.

It only took a few minutes for her to emerge from the trees, finding a simple two-bar fence separating her from the swathe of black SUVs on the other side. The rain was more sporadic now, falling in a half-hearted drizzle. She could hear the soft pings of the metalwork on the vehicles as each drop fell. She ducked under the high bar of the fence and passed through. She came to a sudden halt as she approached the nearest vehicle – a dark-coloured Dodge Durango. A set of four, deep scratches had invaded the bodywork, and sliced through both tyres, following the same line right along the side of the car. She moved along to the next vehicle, finding similar damage. Curious, she passed to the second row of trucks. These were untouched. Quietly and constantly alert, she made her way down the line until she came to her own truck. She opened the driver's door and took out her father's tomahawk from behind the seat, securing it to her belt behind her back.

Suddenly, a series of gunshots rang out from the central

area of the camp. These were quicker in succession than the previous, isolated ones she'd heard earlier. She could also tell that more than one weapon was being fired. As with what had done the damage to the cars, she was in no doubt what was disrupting the camp. Nina flinched as another louder explosion echoed into the night – this one clearly from a shotgun. Something urged her to step inside the truck. Escape was within easy reach if she wanted it. But she realised it was fear, not instinct guiding her towards the safety of the front seat. Then she was running, flat out and with the Colt drawn, in the direction of the camp.

CHAPTER TWENTY-FOUR

ESCAPE AND AMBUSH

Wade ensured that every step he took was precise and silent. It made for slow progress, but he had no intention of giving away his, or the team's, position. The rain had been persistent, and it hampered their ability to stay quiet whilst on the move. He touched his ear as Hicks asked them to hold their position, whilst he and Dixon scouted along a side trail for a place to set up a sniping nest. Wade took a knee underneath the shelter of a sprawling, old-growth oak. It always amazed him that you didn't have to wander far off trail in places like this to find pristine, untouched wilderness. Yet, after the events of the last few weeks, he wondered if he'd ever go off trail again, now he knew what was out there.

"You boys might want to join us up here," Hicks' voice echoed quietly in his ear.

"Found something?" Wade asked, turning towards Dugas.

"I'll say," Hicks replied. "Think our boy has been through, and I think we figured out how he gave us the slip."

Wade and Dugas double-timed it along the side trail, a little more relaxed in the knowledge that Hicks and Dixon were ahead of them, monitoring their progress through the powerful night vision scope of the latter's MK15 rifle. In just a few minutes they travelled nearly eight hundred yards deeper into the forest. The path was narrow, and soon gave way to nothing more than a game trail. They noticed they were on an incline, and the trees were beginning to space out a little, when they saw Hicks's silhouette ahead of them. He turned, and they caught the flash of the whites of his eyes, as he indicated they should look past him.

It wasn't obvious at first, but as the quarter moon above them burned through a sliver of thinner cloud, the wall of rock that represented the head of the valley and the end of the canyon, revealed itself. A tiny flicker of a red headlamp gave Dixon away, further up. That's when they saw the opening. He was exploring the partially collapsed entrance to an old mine.

"Pretty sure it goes all the way through to the other side," Dixon surmised over their open channel.

Wade, Dugas, and Dixon moved up to join him.

"Washington State has a significant number of gold, silver, lead, and zinc mines," Joe explained, clearly listening in. "There are even small numbers of uranium seams, not to mention a rich history of coal mining in the state. It's long been purported bigfoot uses them for shelter and to stay hidden, just like they would a natural cave system."

"Not much to do, other than make sure we block off its escape," Dixon explained.

If there had been any doubt about Hicks and Dixon being former special forces, it was eclipsed as Hicks swung his pack down from his shoulder and unpacked a block of C4 from its top like it was groceries. Taking out his knife, he used the four-inch Tanto blade to cut the plastic explosive into three equal pieces, discarding the shredded wrapping from each back into his pack. From the same top pocket, Dixon removed a small tin box, opening it up to reveal a selection of SPD detonators. He took one out with three cord relays and made his way back to the entrance of the mine. Wade had to admit he looked very slick as he reached out with both hands simultaneously, slapping an explosive patty on the opposing walls of the mineshaft, just a few yards in. Then he reached up and fastened the remaining charge to the ceiling.

As he jogged down from the entrance, Wade noticed the soft green glow of a black rectangular device he held in one hand. It was no larger than a matchbox, and had one small, black switch.

"Might want to find some cover boys," Dixon quipped, passing them, and not stopping.

They quickly fell in behind, falling back to where they had first seen Hicks waiting for them. Each slipped behind a tree or hunkered down behind the deadfall and rocks that lay scattered across the sloping path that led to the mine.

"Fire in the hole," Dixon whispered.

The explosion was immediate and deafening. The collective experience of the soldiers meant that none of them flinched, be it due to Hicks and Dixon's hands-on experience, or Wade and Dugas's close calls with IEDS back in the sand pit of Afghanistan. Wade stepped out from the weathered Black cottonwood tree he'd sheltered behind, one of the few species in Washington he recognised from his native state of Louisiana.

"Look over here lads," Hicks gestured, his proximity giving them a little feedback in their earpieces.

With their eyes naturally adjusted to the dark, they stooped down to look at what Hicks was pointing at with the barrel of his rifle. The footprint was clear, pressed deeply into the mud. Still, this was the first one Wade had seen for himself, and its size unnerved him. He guessed it to be nineteen inches long and roughly half as wide. The imprint had filled with rainwater, making it stand out much more than if the conditions had been dry. It pointed in the direction they had just come, which sent a shudder down Wade's spine. Had it been watching them? Had they passed it by?

"A little more bad news for you boys," Joe announced. "The eyes in the sky need a recharge. We won't have visuals back for forty-five minutes to an hour. Stay frosty."

Dugas flashed a grin at Wade as he rolled his eyes. Wade shrugged a knowing smile in reply. They waited as Dixon clambered down from the mine entrance to re-join them. Together, they trudged back along the path in silence, unsure of their next move, with Wade on point. Suddenly, every fibre of his being screamed at him to freeze. Having learnt to trust his instincts by now, he came to an immediate stop, holding his hand up in a fist to alert the others. Dugas dropped to one knee and covered their immediate right. Hicks hunched over his rifle and did the same for their left. Dixon, bringing up the rear, didn't have time to sling down the rifle from his shoulder. Instead, he steadied the MP7 submachine gun, slung under his left arm for easy reach. He planted his feet in a side stance, ready to defend in any direction, including behind them. But as he looked at Wade, he could see the soldier was staring directly ahead.

The thing that crossed their path was like a wraith, moving silently and so incredibly fast, it was gone before he had blinked. It had been a passing shadow, only its rippling form giving its presence away. Wade's rifle was at his shoulder in a flash, but nothing revealed itself in the gloom.

There had been no sound to give it away. No warning. Just a primeval reaction as his senses registered danger before his consciousness did.

"Did you see it?" Wade whispered.

"Just for a moment, maybe," Dugas replied. "Was that it?"

"I don't know... felt different," Wade replied. "More inclined to say it was something else, like the Ranger was talking about."

"Well, it's at the right party," Wade sighed.

As a shot rang out in the distance, back towards camp, followed by another, the soldiers turned as one, and broke into a run.

~

Shartale caught the scent of the men before he saw them. He couldn't gauge why, but the strange creature that had tracked him through the cave, had diverted away into the woods – heading straight towards the dwellings the humans clearly inhabited. He had no trouble hearing the buzz of activity, from the strange contraptions and machines they used, to their clumsy movement. The creature, with its tall, erect ears, must have also heard them, but showed no caution. It was Shartale's hesitancy that had saved him from being revealed. Hunkered down, by the side of the trail, he'd first smelled them, then heard them. As he realised they were headed away from him, he gave a short, quiet huff. He was not used to feeling the tension that had built up in his chest. It wasn't fear he felt, just unease. Ultimately, he felt challenged, and he could feel the anger and rage building inside him as a result. Part intellect, part biology, he focused his thoughts on how he had been chased and outmanoeuvred since he had first killed in this area. He let a deep, drawn-out, guttural growl linger in his throat as he dropped to all fours and broke into a run.

~

Wade and Dugas sprinted down the trail, the lights of the camp now ahead of them. The outer perimeter of cabins was just over a hundred yards from their position. They slowed their pace and Dugas took point, raising his shotgun. Quickly yet carefully, they made their way forward. As they rounded the closed off, wooden porch of the nearest cabin, Dugas snapped round and brought the barrel of the gun up as he detected movement. Wade was next to him in a second, but Dugas had already checked himself. Huddled in the far corner of the porch was Doctor Benoit. Her eyes were wide in terror as she glanced from them to the rest of the camp.

"Do... do you see it?" she stammered.

"No ma'am," Dugas replied, crossing the porch, and making his way over to her. "But you're safe now," he declared.

Benoit's eyes snapped to his. "Like hell I am," she declared, standing up, with Dugas' help.

"What happened, what is it?" Wade intervened.

"Exactly what Nina said it was... the Limmekin, dogman, werewolf, whatever you want to call it. But it's here. It's hunting, and..."

"And?" Wade demanded.

"It's enjoying it," Benoit replied.

The tremble in her voice was echoed across her shoulders, down her arms, and into her fingertips. Her eyes constantly darted out into the darkness. Even as Dugas still held her hand from helping her up, she backed away towards the outer wall of the cabin behind them. Another gunshot and a scream rang out. A figure appeared out of the rain and gloom, staggering wildly. Wade rushed out from the shelter of the cabin, raising his rifle, and switching on the flashlight attachment underneath the barrel.

The BLM agent swayed unsteadily, then dropped to his knees. Wade ran over to him, freezing as he drew close. Half his face was missing. His one good eye twisted in its socket and his mouth opened, but no sound came out. Part of his scalp was missing, and blood oozed from raw flesh, opened by the four deep slash marks on the left side of his face. That's when Wade realised his ear was missing too. The blue BLM jacket was shredded, and his left arm hung in tatters. But the agent raised it anyway, revealing a bloody, gushing stump where his hand used to be. The man took a violent, single last breath as his whole body relaxed. Instead of slumping to the ground, his shoulders drooped, and his head fell to the right. The body fell backwards, folding in on itself unnaturally into the mud. Wade just stared, then turned back to the others.

"Where's everyone else?" Wade asked Benoit.

"I think Joe and Smith are still in the Prowler," she answered, still scanning the darkness from the perceived safety of the porch. "The Bureau of Land Management agents – they're all over the place, spread out."

Dugas mouthed the word "literally", nodding at the fallen body behind them.

Wade glared a warning.

"What do we do?" Benoit pleaded.

"We get you somewhere safe," Wade replied. "Right

now, that means getting you out of here. We head for the vehicles and all non-military personnel fall back to point Beta."

With a single touch of his right earpiece, Wade relayed the instructions, hoping Joe was still monitoring their communications. Joe, in turn, would order the BLM to rendezvous with the soldiers and retreat, via Smith.

"Dagger formation, straight up main street," Wade suggested, the question clear in his tone. The others appreciated he wasn't giving orders but asking for approval. They all gave it.

Wade took point, with Dugas and Dixon either side of him. Benoit followed them, with Hicks bringing up the rear. Main Street, as Wade had called it, was a generic term, referring to the clearest route from A to B. In this case, it was the slightly curved, unmade bit of track that led from the entrance road into the camp's central area, passing the paddock to the front. It was approximately three hundred yards. On the way, they would pass the Prowler, parked on their right, next to the reception building, which they had used earlier to gear up. The kitchen hut, currently Benoit's makeshift morgue and hospital, was opposite the reception on their left. Next to it was the first row of cabins, the closest of which, Nina Lee had been escorted to. Wade glanced towards it. Partially concealed by foliage intended to separate the accommodations from the utility areas, he could only see one side of it, but it didn't look like there were any lights on inside. He glanced at his watch. It was approaching 4.30am, but the likelihood of a trained Ranger like Lee sleeping through gunshots and screams was close to nil.

Wade lifted his right hand and indicated they were

moving up. Each soldier monitored their immediate station – Wade directly ahead, whilst Dugas and Dixon covered the left and right respectively. They had made it past the kitchen hut when Wade held up his right hand again and closed his fist, bringing them all to an immediate stop. Directly ahead of them, two BLM agents had appeared on the trail, stumbling into the beams of an overhead set of lights along the track. The agents had their backs to them, firing their pistols simultaneously into the darkness. One let out a shriek as a hulking form appeared in front of him, cutting him down with a lightning slash of a grotesque, elongated arm, equipped with talon-like claws at the end of its bent, bony fingers. Then the thing leapt forward, engulfing his partner, who Wade only now realised was a woman, and throwing her to the ground. Wade lifted his rifle and began to put pressure on the trigger when a burst of gunfire erupted from behind him.

"Incoming, on our six," Hicks screamed, in between short bursts of directed shooting.

Wade turned around. A sharp exhale escaped his lips in shock as he watched the creature dart from left to right, as if anticipating the gunfire. Then, it was running directly at them, closing the distance at impossible speed. Hicks and Dixon dived to their left, rolling, and bringing up their weapons as one. Dugas jumped back, grabbing Benoit, and dragging her with him. For a flicker of a moment, Wade locked eyes with the creature, as it barrelled towards him. Time seemed to stand still. He'd seen silverback gorillas move like it on TV, its bent knuckles and powerful feet driving into the ground as it charged, crouched and purposeful. Yet it moved much faster, its pace and gait almost cheetah-like. In that split-second, Wade realised it wasn't looking at him, but beyond him, further up the trail.

The impact took him off his feet, launching him into the air with violent, unbridled force. He landed on his back, dropping his rifle, and twisting his ankle badly. He fought to take a breath, with his lungs on fire, as they were denied the oxygen that had been knocked from his body. His throat opened and he croaked an unhinged, desperate suck of air.

"Anyone get the license plate of that truck?" Wade rasped, as Dixon helped him to his feet.

"That was one pissed-off monkey," Dugas laughed, passing Wade his rifle. "You okay?"

"No," Wade groaned.

He looked around, dazed, confused as to why nobody was shooting. Then, he looked back up the trail after the bigfoot. A second female BLM agent had rushed out from behind the Prowler to try and help their wounded colleague, who lay on her back and was unresponsive. They were too close to risk automatic fire down range. As if reading his mind, Dixon swung the big Mk.15 sniper rifle from his shoulder and dropped to a prone position, using his pack as a gun rest.

"Got him?" Wade asked.

"Got em both," Dixon whispered as he pulled the trigger.

The boom resonated painfully in their ears. As Wade winced, he could see Dixon cursing as he chambered another of the .50 BMG rounds.

"What happened?"

"Fucker moved, darted to his left," Dixon spat. "The werewolf-looking thing reacted to the movement; it was like they saw the damn bullet coming."

"They heard you," came Smith's voice in Wade's earpiece, at barely a whisper. "They have exceptional hearing. They heard every word you said, and odds are the big guy knows the sound of someone pulling back the bolt of a rifle."

"Where are you? Wade asked.

"Joe and I are still in the Prowler."

"How many of your BLM agents are left?

"I have two unaccounted for," Smith replied. "Harrigan and Martinez."

"Odds are I'm looking at Martinez right now – trying to administer... oh God," Wade exclaimed.

Wade watched in horror as the creature they knew as the Limmekin leapt forward with savage speed, closing the distance between itself and the sasquatch. It landed behind the BLM agent and lifted her from the ground, its curved claws slicing through the back of her neck and bursting through her throat. She writhed as the creature positioned the agent in front of it like a shield, making Dixon look up from the scope of his rifle. Still alive, the woman kicked futilely as blood filled her throat and spilled out of her mouth – the creature's claws making for effective plugs to the wounds they had just made. In the moonlight, the dark blue of her jacket slowly turned black.

Nobody tells you blood looks black in the moonlight, Wade thought. You learn that when you see it, recalling something his grandfather had told him once, whilst hunting racoons. As his grandfather had also said, it was something you never forgot. Then his gaze moved to the sasquatch, which had come to a sudden stop, next to the wounded and unconscious agent on the ground. It was no more than six feet from the Limmekin, or as Benoit had called it, the dogman. *Wonder if it's so bad-tempered because it's got a shitty name,* Wade thought.

The sasquatch let out a roar, throwing its arms back and opening its hands. Living up to its popular name in folklore, it lifted its foot from the ground and brought it down with unrelenting force onto the agent's skull. Her head exploded like a watermelon hit with a sledgehammer, the flat-footed sole smashing it into goo against the ground. The dogman threw the agent it had harpooned with its claws at the bigfoot, who caught her with one hand. Doing so made the creature take a step back as it matched the momentum. The Limmekin lunged forward, seizing the opportunity to strike at the sasquatch, slashing it across its chest whilst it was off-balance and exposed. The bigfoot didn't hesitate, letting out a primal roar of pain and rage, as it swung the agent still in its grasp. The human's skull met the wolf-like head. Even at the distance they were, Wade and the others heard the sickening crack as the blow broke her neck.

"Light 'em up!" Wade yelled, lifting his rifle to his shoulder, and squeezing the trigger.

The big rifle in Dixon's meticulous hands boomed, and bursts of automatic fire erupted around him. A haze of smoke rose from the hot barrels, momentarily blocking their vision. As it cleared, Wade felt a swell of anger and disappointment as he realised the trail ahead of them was now empty. The only bodies on the ground were those of the agents, mutilated and murdered by the creatures.

Wade was on his feet and began to move up the trail at a light jog. His rifle was at his shoulder, and he swept from side to side with a fluid roll of his shoulders. The rest of the squad formed up behind him as before, with Benoit protected in their centre. As they passed the Prowler, the door opened, and Joe scurried down the steps to join them. He shot nervous glances in the direction of the camp's entrance as a distant roar rose from the vehicle paddock. Smith followed close behind. A movement in Wade's peripheral caught his attention and he called it out, his finger on the trigger. He immediately raised his hand and formed a fist to signal a stop and cease fire. There, ahead of them on the track, Nina Lee stepped forward. It took less than two minutes for them to reach her.

"You and I have business," Nina glowered in Smith's direction. "You may not want to survive this, if you get the choice."

Smith met her accusation with a look of acceptance, if not admittance.

Wade noticed Nina held her revolver in a standard defensive stance, the barrel lowered towards the ground, but her arms straight and her torso braced for readiness. He nodded in approval and towards Benoit, whom she joined. Wade made a forwards motion with his hand, pointing it twice in the direction of the paddock. They moved together and in silence as they passed under the entrance archway and main gate of the campground. A few moments later, they were headed towards the lines of vehicles. As Wade moved towards those nearest the fence, Nina grabbed his arm and shook her head.

"They're no good to us," she whispered.

Wade paused, then changed direction to the back of the field. Nina could see a large vehicle parked there. Beyond its futuristic-looking, edgy front and headlights, it looked like a stripped-out, doorless pick-up truck. The bulky off-road tyres and reinforced frame and chassis spoke more of its capabilities. With five seats easily visible in the cabin portion, and a further two side seats in the rear cargo bed, there was more than enough room for them all. That's when she noticed the gun turret, tucked into the roofline of the vehicle, and connected to the truck's bed. Wade caught her gaze.

"ISV – Infantry Squad Vehicle, heavy gunner variant. We get all the toys," he chimed.

They climbed in quickly, Dugas eagerly setting himself up in the turret. Benoit and Nina sat either side of him in the cargo bed fold-down chairs. Wade climbed in behind the wheel, with Smith in the passenger seat. Joe looked uncomfortable, squeezed into the middle of the second row of seats, between Hicks and Dixon, who covered their respective sides with their weapons. Wade pressed a button on the dashboard and the vehicle instantly came to life. The headlights glowed an eerie red, as did the instruments on the dash. And there was no noise at all from the engine, other than a slight hum.

"Completely electric," Dugas grinned down at Nina, noticing her puzzled face. "Everyone likes Detroit muscle on the street, but in a fight, it kind of lets everyone know you're coming from miles away," he explained. "This way, we stay a little stealthier. And even fully loaded like this, we can probably go 80, 90 miles maybe. Plenty for combat purposes."

"Far enough to get us out of here, at least," Nina whispered under her breath to Benoit.

As they moved off, his attention went back to the large

machine gun in front of him as he swung the barrel left and right in slow sweeps as they moved off. Wade wasted no time in turning the vehicle west, headed along the track and through the pine forest back towards civilisation. It was a good twelve miles away and Nina knew that no matter how fast they went, it was going to be a long journey. Two monsters of myth were now at large in the same part of the forest they needed to get through.

The electric motor of the ISV meant they were all able to hear the savage growl that echoed through the trees to their left, followed by a sharp snap of a branch. It had sounded like it was right next to the vehicle. It was answered by a wrathful roar to their right, much louder yet clearly further away.

"That was the sasquatch," Benoit said quietly to Nina. "That's a roar you don't ever forget."

"Meaning we have the Limmekin on our left," Nina surmised.

"I've heard reports of them working together – if it's truly what we call dogman," Benoit added. "Do you think that's possible?"

In the glow of the lights coming from the ISV's interior, Nina could see the worried look on the doc's face. She shook her head.

"My Dad said it was here to restore balance... like the sasquatch had broken the rules or crossed the line somehow. I don't think it's here to buddy up."

Benoit nodded but didn't look reassured.

"Why did it attack us then?" she asked.

Nina shrugged. "It's not like I know for sure... but Dad said they could pick up on ill intent. We both know those agents aren't BLM. And even if they are, they're here under false pretences. I don't think it's very tolerant of us. It only takes the slightest provocation."

Nina saw Benoit turn away. In the side seat, her back was to the trees and from where the roar had come. Every few seconds, she cast an involuntary glance over her shoulder into the gloom. Nina took out her revolver and placed it casually on her leg, keeping her hand on the grips. It seemed to do the trick, and Benoit gave her an appreciative smile. They both braced slightly as the military vehicle leaned into a right-hand bend, perhaps a little faster than it should have, taking them slightly off balance.

The impact came without warning. Metal groaned. A roar erupted close by. Nina was thrown backwards violently, and she collided with Dugas before she hit the ground. The air was sucked from her lungs as she was brought to a sudden stop. The back end of the ISV flipped over them, spewing the team, equipment, and debris as it went. She heard Benoit screaming before the sound was cut off, suddenly. She rolled onto her front, grimacing with the pain. Raising her hand to the back of her head, it felt warm and wet. A groan from her right revealed Dugas. Nina made her way over on her hands and knees, brushing away the mud and brush that surrounded him. She froze, an involuntary gasp escaping her lips. Dugas was in a bad way. A deep, crimson gash had split his forehead and blood was trickling from his busted nose. She glanced behind them at the ISV, still on its side. The rear wheel in the air span slowly, robbed of power and traction. Nina looked at the buckled frame of the half-turret that Dugas had been standing in. As she turned back, she saw his leg – twisted back on itself at an unnatural angle. Moving closer, the pale sheen of his splintered fibula was visible in the dim light of the crescent moon, behind its veil of dark cloud.

"I'll be right back," Nina rasped to Dugas, getting to her feet. "I just need to check on the others."

She staggered a few steps to the upturned ISV. As her hand reached over the doorless rear entry point, now facing directly upwards into the sky, a hand shot upwards from the vehicle's interior and grabbed her own. Nina anchored her feet in the mud as Dixon hauled himself upwards, resting his elbows on either side of the opening, pushing what was left of the camouflage netting aside. His face was smeared with blood and grease. His left forearm was torn up; his bloodied uniform shredded. He panted hard with the exertion of getting to his feet but began to clamber out of the wreck. He was banged up but okay.

"Find your weapon, soldier," Nina said grimly. "We're not out of the woods yet."

Dixon chuffed, and she noticed he momentarily clutched at his ribs as he did so.

"On your six," he grimaced.

Nina spun around, her revolver drawn and up at an instant.

"Don't shoot" came a familiar voice from the darkness.

A silhouette took form and Hicks stepped closer to the vehicle. He seemed okay. His rifle was gone, but he had a sidearm out and semi-raised. She wondered what good the 9mm ammo of the pistol would do, against the creature that had rammed and overturned a military pick-up truck laden with a full crew and equipment. She shuddered as she realised that was exactly what had happened.

A groan to her left alerted her to Wade. He lay on his back in a mash of ferns, and she saw him raise his right hand in the air. She rushed over to him, then stopped in her tracks. The left side of his face was covered in blood. The skin on his neck looked raw, and she could see tiny specks of gravel had imbedded themselves into tracts leading down his cheek and throat. Like Dixon, his uniform was torn and bloodied. He had multiple lacerations along his arm, and his left hand was mangled. It was a bloody mess of tattered flesh. Crimson droplets hung from his ragged fingertips like the thick corn syrup they used in horror movies.

"Who taught you to drive," Nina jeered, checking him over.

"I can weave through cones fine," Wade winced. "Bigfoots, not so much. That was what hit us, right?"

Nina paused, then nodded. "I think so,".

Nina didn't think there was anything preventing Wade being moved, so she pulled him up into a sitting position and helped him rest his back against a tree.

"Why hasn't it attacked again? It had us."

Nina met his gaze, letting him know she'd already thought that too, but didn't have an answer for him.

"Still two unaccounted for," Nina explained. "I'll be right back."

"Think I heard the Doc scream back there," Wade suggested, nodding towards the trees.

Nina glanced in their direction. The moon was helping a little, but the cloud and water vapour made things hard. She desperately wanted a flashlight and considered there might be one in the upturned ISV. She hadn't seen any equipment, but it was a military vehicle, and it made sense there would be basic gear stashed away inside. She was about to turn away when a quiet and familiar voice spoke from nearby.

"I'm right here," Mary Beth Benoit said, a distinct elevation in her tone.

Nina froze, recognising somebody trying to stay calm. Like when their life depended on it.

"And I think I can answer your other question too," Benoit added, the tremor in her voice growing. "About why it hasn't attacked again. I'm not alone. To your right."

Nina's head snapped in the direction Benoit's words had come from. There, in the dark, she realised she could see the outline of someone, resting up against a tree like Wade. But this person was hugging their knees, gripping them so tightly that the tremble was visible down her calves. Nina realised it was the movement that she noticed first. Benoit seemed to be ducking her head down as low as she could place it, like she was in a brace position. Then she saw the other silhouette. It was hunched and stood rigidly still. Nina recognised the same, forward-leaning stance she'd noticed before in the Limmekin. As if to confirm it, two round orbs of yellow lit up, nearly seven foot off the ground. The eyeshine was unmistakable, yet she had no idea what it could be reflecting off. She shuddered, realising just how close the creature was to all of them.

From behind, Nina heard the faint metallic click of a gun safety. It was answered with a low rumble growl of warning.

"Nobody move and definitely don't shoot," Nina warned.

She hoped whoever had the itchy trigger finger had heard. With no following burst of fire, she guessed they had. Then a cry came from the other side of the dirt road and much deeper into the treeline. Nina knew instantly that it was Smith and that he was in pain. There was a desperation to the moaning wail that echoed through the trees. It was as if you could sense the hope draining away as the cry faded. Then it came again, sharper, and clearer for a moment. That's when she realised that Smith wasn't just in pain. Something was hurting him, repeatedly. Like it wanted him to make noise.

Smith's cries seemed to also catch the interest of the Limmekin, as Nina noticed the eyeshine blink off, then on again, looking in the same direction. She turned her head slightly as she sensed someone approaching on her right, along the other side of the upturned vehicle. Instinctively, she knew it was Hicks. Of the team, he was the most able and least injured. Unfortunately, she trusted him less than the others to keep his finger off the trigger in the heat of the moment. And as moments went, the temperature had spiked. When Nina turned back towards Benoit, the eyeshine was gone. Nina moved over to the doc.

"I think it's gone," Nina assured her, holding out her hand.

Benoit reached up and took it, allowing Nina to help her to her feet.

"I'm sorry," the doc stammered, looking down at her feet. "When I was thrown from the car, I landed on my back, and I was looking up into blackness. Then suddenly, it was looking down at me, with gleaming yellow eyes and teeth... such awful, awful teeth."

Benoit stared into empty space, her thoughts, and memories elsewhere, as she seemed to relive the moment.

"Yeah, only a mother could love that face, huh," Nina

said softly. "Believe it or not, I think it was protecting you, if that helps," she added.

Benoit shook her head violently.

"I think you're giving it too much credit," Benoit warned. "It was downwind. It was waiting to see if the sasquatch would move in. It was too late to intercept the attack on Smith, but I was the next closest."

Nina paused. She realised there was no way of knowing if either of them was right. But it gave her pause for thought when it came to what her father had told her. There was danger in assuming the creature was more friend than foe. Just as her dad had said, it didn't care for people much. She tried to imagine its sense of mission; focused on vengeance and restoring a natural balance. It didn't take long for her to conclude she and the team didn't fit into that. It was as happy to use them as bait as it had been to kill Harrigan. She thought back to that moment. Had it intervened on her behalf, or had it taken pleasure in an opportunity to kill. Perspective was able to cloud judgement just as well as it provided clarity.

"Doc, why don't you see what you can do for Dixon and Dugas, they're pretty banged up," Nina suggested.

With Benoit close to going into shock, Nina knew it was important to give her purpose and bring her back to reality. Mary Beth stood up and nodded at Nina, who led her back to the other side of the upturned ISV. Wade and Hicks were on their feet, with Dugas and Dixon pulled to one side in the brush. Nina was glad to see Wade had fixed a tourniquet to his wounded arm and padded and plugged his cuts with gauze. His left hand was wrapped in bandage. Discarded packets of clotting powder also littered the ground. Unlike her, they had known exactly where to look for the supplies stashed around the vehicle, and a large, bright red first-aid kit was beside their two wounded comrades. Nina noted they both had flashlight attachments to their sidearms too.

"I think we should go after Smith," Wade suggested.

"We didn't give Campbell the same option," Dugas protested, as Benoit knelt beside him and began examining his wounds.

Nina nodded. "You know it's a trap, right?"

"It's learnt from the other one," Wade sighed. "It must have been watching when we took on the younger male. It knows we won't go in after somebody it's killed. Smith is alive, and its gonna keep him that way."

"Think you're up to it?" Nina asked.

"I'll go with you, straight at it," Wade said. "Hicks will flank. Hopefully, it will smell my blood and that will be enough to keep it distracted. But we need to move now. We don't want it to get bored."

Hicks stepped into the trees behind where Dugas and Dixon were being attended to by Benoit. In a flicker of a moment, he had disappeared. If he was moving through the brush, he was doing so silently. Nina was impressed that even she couldn't hear him. Wade moved up behind her as she turned. Together, they crossed the trail. Wade's flashlight beam appeared from directly over her shoulder, pointing the way and, as she realised, acting as a further distraction to the sasquatch. The forest seemed to close in around them immediately as they left the track. The moon struggled to penetrate through the canopy and thick branches, and she was glad of the flashlight. But as she narrowed her eyelids to combat its glare, she knew it was covering the forest outside of its touch with a veil that made it harder to see through.

They had gone about thirty yards, when, as she pushed aside a low branch, the beam fell across the white collar of Smith's shirt. As Wade angled the light downwards, Smith's right arm rose to block it directly hitting his eyes. He lay on the ground, his shoulders and head resting against the trunk of a tree.

"Dumb move, Ranger," Smith groaned, "but one I appreciate."

Nina noticed the blood stains on his shirt front. His blazer was covered in mud, as were his pants. On one side of his head, his hair was messed up and bloodied. She realised some of it was missing, as if it had been torn out. He also had a nasty welt above his left eye, with bruises quickly turning black and blue on the side of his head to match it. As Nina stepped forward, there was the slightest of movements to Smith's left. The large, hairy foot came down flat and hard on Smith's upturned forearm. There was a sickening crack, and Nina knew that the ulna and radius bones had snapped like twigs under the pressure. Smith winced and grunted with the pain but took it. He had obviously learnt not to move or complain whilst under the sasquatch's charge. When it wanted him to call out, it made him.

Smith's eyes were desperate, but Nina's were drawn to the foot holding him down. The five toes were visible in the torchlight. Like the rest of the foot, they pressed down flat towards the ground. It was why breaking Smith's arm had been so easy. There was no arch, like in her own foot, that would have maybe given some leeway. This foot was as flat and heavy as an anvil dropping on the bones. She could hear

Wade breathing as the flashlight moved upwards. She realised that the soldier hesitated only for a moment when the beam reached what, for them, was eye level. That's when she realised, she was staring just above the creature's navel. Its legs were solid like tree trunks. The torso was broad and barrel-chested. And its arms, that hung down pendulously almost to its knees, were covered with thick, shaggy hair. As the beam hit the head, nearly four feet above their own, the sasquatch growled and raised its hand, just as Smith had. Nina noted the thick slabs of muscle that covered the neck, giving the creature the appearance that it didn't have one. The sagittal crest wasn't as pronounced as on say, a gorilla, but it was there. All features of an animal that needed incredible jaw and bite power.

As if reading her mind, the sasquatch opened its mouth wide and gargled a growl of warning. The pronounced, canine teeth gleamed in the light. With the slightest flex of its foot, Smith called out sharply, writhing on his side in a desperate but futile attempt to get free. Wade lowered the beam.

Is it grinning? Nina asked herself. It sure looked like it.

There was an explosion of sound around them and a rapid succession of flare-like eruptions of light as Hicks appeared. He had expertly flanked the creature and was firing the Sig Sauer pistol from no more than ten yards away, straight into the creature's side. Nina felt the slight pressure on her right shoulder and instinctively dropped to her knee and brought up her own revolver. She fired the 357′ Magnum almost in sync with Wade's own Sig Sauer. The sasquatch reared backwards, using its arms to protect its head. Released from its pinning foot, Smith rolled several times towards Nina and Wade. Nina stopped firing and grabbed his good arm, dragging him closer. The sasquatch leapt towards them, putting the tree Smith had leant against, between itself and Hicks as it did so.

Wade kept his pistol high, using his damaged hand as a rest for his good, extended arm. Sure, and true, he stood his ground and continued firing. He had to trust that, at what was point-blank range, 17 rounds of 9mm luger would still make the monster think twice. Just as he realised he was wrong, he heard a dreadful, rageful snarl in his left ear. He moved through instinct, spinning on his heels to meet the threat. But his movement seemed so slow, he might as well have been under water. The Limmekin found Wade now directly in its path, and knocked him aside with a sharp, backhanded cuff of its arm. Which was all the time it took for the sasquatch to reach them. The Limmekin took the brunt of the charge, letting itself fall backwards as it brought up its powerful hocked legs. Its toe claws scraped at the bigfoot's stomach as they found purchase. In turn, the ape-like bigfoot's hands had connected with the Limmekin's shoulders, and its own, claw-like nails of each thumb tunnelled into the flesh for extra hold.

The Limmekin lashed out with a savage double kick that sent the sasquatch flying backwards. Before it hit the ground, the Limmekin was already up and charging, baying for blood as it stooped forward. The sasquatch lifted its hand to defend itself, and the Limmekin's jaws opened to welcome it, closing either side as it brought down its dagger-like teeth. The creature was clearly capable of inflicting more damage than Wade's bullets were, as the sasquatch roared in pain. But the Limmekin had sacrificed its footing to deliver the bite. The sasquatch struggled upwards, lifting its werewolf-like attacker off its feet, and swinging it round with impressive force. Losing its grip, the Limmekin spun away from the sasquatch, colliding with Hicks as it skidded backwards. Enraged, it turned on the soldier, sending him to the floor with a decisive swipe of its claws.

Nina froze as she heard Wade call out in shock. She turned, but all she could see was his flashlight, directed back at her, as he was dragged away from her through the trees.

CHAPTER TWENTY-FIVE

BATTLE OF THE BEASTS

The Limmekin had disappeared back into the darkness too. Nina trembled as she made her way over to Hicks. She helped him sit up as he took ragged, gasping breaths. He clutched at his left arm, which hung loosely and unnaturally across his chest and lap. She realised it was dislocated. He winced as she helped him to his feet, and she recognised the hunched to one side stance that meant a broken collar bone. To add to that, his nose was gushing with blood, and it too was clearly broken. She directed him to lean back against the tree as she helped Smith gingerly get on his feet too.

"Go... go get him," Hicks stammered, offering her his pistol.

Nina glanced to the forest floor, where Wade's own pistol had fallen. She considered just how swiftly and forcefully the sasquatch would have had to attack Wade to make him drop his weapon. Hicks noticed her gaze.

"He dropped it in the mud. It's probably fine, but you don't want to risk a misfire or a clogged trigger. Mine's clean," he explained.

His hands shook as he performed a tactical reload, taking out the half-used mag and replacing it with a fresh full clip. He handed the gun to her, along with his third magazine, and the half-empty one. Nina nodded and tucked the gun into the back of her belt whilst pocketing the ammo. She then reloaded her revolver.

"Get back to the truck," she suggested. "Find a radio. Call in the cavalry."

"Never heard Jones called that before," Smith said, smiling to stifle the pain, unsuccessfully.

He nodded at her in understanding and acceptance. She smiled too.

"Just don't tell him I called him that," she replied.

Nina darted through the trees quickly and quietly. She didn't need to look back to see if Smith and Hicks were underway. She could hear their laboured progress, as they supported each other and half-hopped, half-lurched their way towards the vehicle and the others. Soon though, there was silence, as she put distance between them. Now, all she could hear was her own pulse, thundering in her ears. She alerted as something large, and unseen, passed through the brush to her right. She followed its progress with the barrel of her revolver. Her eyes couldn't pick anything out in the darkness, so she closed them. Nina slowed her breathing as she listened to the surrounding forest.

At first, there was nothing but the sound of the breeze moving through the branches. They raked against each other with gentle knocking and creaking sounds that masked everything else. Then she heard it, off in the distance. Wade was yelling at the top of his voice. Nina's eyes snapped open, and she sprinted in the direction of his call, carried as it was on the wind. She couldn't believe how far the sasquatch had travelled already. Wade sounded distant. As she made her way, she realised he was also doing his best to leave a trail for her. He had dug in his heels and was leaving a wide and obvious drag mark. She continued, following the trail faster and more confidently now.

From somewhere up ahead, a savage, animalistic roar of pain ripped through the silence of the forest. Nina froze.

Then, Wade too cried out. Nina guessed he had been struggling and wasn't going down without a fight. Somehow, he had found a way to put the hurt on the sasquatch, even as it dragged him. She was sprinting now. As she broke through some low branches, she came skidding to a stop as she saw a glint of metal on the ground, caught in a slither of moonlight. She bent down and picked up the small, but viciously sharp knife. The blade was bloodied. At three and a half inches, Nina imagined it was the perfect boot knife, and Wade had been able to grab it as the sasquatch dragged him along.

"IT'S ME YOU WANT," Nina screamed into the night. "YOU KNOW IT'S ME, DON'T YOU."

The echo of a breaking twig sounded off to her right, and she snapped around to face it. Then, just as the forest returned to its eerie silence, a soft, huffing growl reached her ears. Nina tried to shrug off the feeling it was mocking her. Her mind raced as she tried to think how she could goad the beast. Did it really remember her, like her father had suggested. In the blink of an eye, she went back to that day in the meadow, skirting the treeline as she sought mushrooms and herbs. She was happy... she was singing. She always sang to herself when she foraged as a child. She opened her lips and the words flowed like the memory. The harmony was simple and rhythmic. As it came back to her, she sang louder, as if it were a chanting war cry.

"Look to the sun and stay in its sight. Be warned, if you don't, you'll be in for a fright," Nina laughed, trying to steady her nerves. "Gather your flowers, mushrooms, and grasses. But be sure to run home before daylight passes. For the woods have a watcher, happy to wait. Yes, the hairy man hunts when the hour is late. You'll know when he's near, by the terrible smell. Get away if you can, before he drags you to hell."

Nina concentrated on controlling her voice. She wanted it to stay soft, like a child's, as she repeated the words. She knew she was clutching at straws, but anything that distracted the sasquatch was an advantage that would let her get closer. She froze in her tracks as she heard Wade cry out suddenly and the crack of breaking branches sounded out like the blast from a shotgun. Whatever had just happened had been sudden and violent.

~

Shartale stopped as the human female's voice reached him. He let out a soft grunt of surprise, low enough not to carry. The memory came back instantly. The human infant had passed beneath the big fir tree he had hid in. The sounds she made were similar. No, they were more than that. They were the same as those that drifted through the forest now. He growled in recognition that this female was a foe that he'd faced before. One that had escaped him.

The memory was strong. He had been confident as he dropped to the ground behind her. He had known that hunting so close to the human dwellings was a risk, but the opportunity the youngling represented was too tempting. Shartale had flashed his fangs, hoping to startle her into running away, deeper into the forest, away from the safety of the others of her kind. When she didn't run, he'd struck the ground with his fists. He gently lifted his finger to his left eye, and the tiny fleck of white scar tissue that indicated where the stone the girl had flung hit.

The human male he was still dragging, began to struggle

more persistently. In one fluid movement, Shartale lifted and flung him hard against the nearest tree. The human's body went limp as it slumped to the ground, and Shartale turned in the direction of the female's melodic voice. He neither saw nor heard the shadow that passed in the branches above him.

~

Nina drew the revolver and brought it up. To help control her breathing, she stopped singing. She held the revolver in a tactical stance as she scanned the forest ahead. The forest was silent. A collective sign that a predator was close by. Two predators, she thought, reminding herself that she too was a hunter, not just the hunted. Something primal ignited in her and she suddenly remembered Benoit's story of being charged out of the darkness, so silently and swiftly. That spark of recognition jolted her instinct, and she spun on her heels and dropped to a knee as she fired two clean shots into the creature as it tore through the mist towards her. It let out a primal scream of rage and veered away from her as it rapidly accelerated towards cover. She steadied herself and took her time, remembering the advice of a former Navy Seal she knew. Slow is smooth. Smooth is fast. Despite its speed, she followed its arc, with the barrel of the revolver poised just ahead of it. She squeezed the trigger just as it passed into the trees. The slightest of flinches suggested she'd landed a glancing hit before it disappeared from her line of sight in the gloom.

Nina was up on her feet immediately. She turned her body slowly, imagining the path the creature was taking through the woods. Rather than move forwards, Nina stayed rooted to the spot. She knew it would come to her. She thought she saw a shadow pass close to her left, and she spun, surprised at how close the creature had somehow gotten. A momentary panic ignited in her gut, and she pulled the trigger before she could stop herself. The bullet smashed into the trunk of a Douglas fir some thirty feet away. Then she fell to her knees, her weapons splayed either side in limp hands that dangled at the ends of her powerless arms. She fought the wave of nausea that wrenched her stomach and burned her throat, fighting with everything she had, just to stay upright.

~

Shartale concentrated hard as he fixed his gaze on the female human. He was hurting, but he controlled his rage. He was unleashing a powerful weapon in his arsenal, one that allowed him to stun and weaken his prey without getting close. He rarely used it – as he usually enjoyed the rush felt when he confronted other predators, especially the larger of the brown bears. Shartale not only readily fought them, but he found their meat especially favourable. But the humans had developed weapons that could reach him from afar. He knew these – what his kind called vahk. There were others, like the sharp-edged stones wielded at the end of dead wood or flung fixed in a point. They gave humans the advantage to attack and fight from a distance. His own ability gave him the same advantage.

He used his peripheral vision to check the wound to his bent leg momentarily. The world appeared to him in a mix of light greys and browns as his retinas expanded and the mirror-like structures at the back of his eye drank in the light. The blood on his calf, which was already drying, appeared dark and purplish. It did not concern him. He returned his full focus to the female human as the reverberation built in his throat. It was possible that at this level, she could now hear him – but it wouldn't matter. The chiikaah, the dark voice, would render her powerless. And maybe even kill her.

~

Nina's eyes widened in terror as she felt the erratic thump of her heart in her chest. It felt too big, like it was hammering against her ribs to get out. Sweat poured from her brow and she was helpless as her bladder began to empty; slowly at first, but then uncontrollably, like a torrent from a broken dam. Her stomach gurgled as her bowels spasmed too. The constant ringing of tinnitus sounded in her ears and the sounds of the forest now seemed even further dulled, like she was underwater. Yet she heard something. A low rumble that she knew was close by but sounded far off. She barely recognised her surroundings, and her head began to spin as her eyes rolled back and she felt the pull of unconsciousness beckon.

~

Shartale reached towards the ground with his fingers but with his gaze still fixed on the human female. At first, they found soft ground and the touch of moss. But that pleased him, as he knew that what he sought wouldn't be far. He bent his knuckles, digging his digits underneath the springy carpet of vegetation until they found what he was looking for. The cold, hard touch of stone. He searched, using his fingers as a guide. One crumbled at his touch. Another was too thin and angular. Then, he paused as he pressed his palm around a smooth, rounded surface. He lifted it from the ground, maintaining the penetrating reach of the dark voice in his throat. Continuing it this long was putting strain on him, and he lifted the stone. The human female wasn't dead yet, but he would use a tool to do the job from afar, just as they did. The efforts of the night had made him weary, and he longed to feed and rest. Knowing it would soon be over, Shartale bent his arm back behind him, holding the stone flat at waist level in his open palm. His prey was not moving, and he was confident it would be a killing blow.

He caught the movement in his peripheral vision too late. Jaws opened over his exposed forearm and clamped shut on the flesh. He roared with pain and dropped the stone as he instinctively leapt upwards to his full height. It felt as if his flesh was on fire and his arm shook violently as sinew and nerve were shredded. He tried to lift his arm and shake the creature attached to it loose, but he found his strength compromised. As he arched his back to gain a better position, the searing pain in his arm was joined by a sharp, ice-cold stab of pain in his side. He glanced down to find the creature's claws withdrawing from beneath his fur, stained with his own blood.

Shartale roared and flung himself backwards, dragging the creature with him. He now knew what the beast was but had never seen one. His kind called them Yawartoq – blood wolves. From them stemmed a hatred for all dogs. He knew the Yawartoq were an enemy not to be underestimated. Shartale had heard of those that had faced them and never returned. In a moment of clarity, he remembered the distant cries of a clan as they were chased from their own territory by a pack. His eyes enlarged in a moment of panic, as he considered the potential of there being more than one enemy to face. But even as the Yawartoq bit down harder, Shartale regained a clear passage of thought and realised it would have been near impossible for more than one creature to have approached downwind and flank him.

Shartale growled as he turned to face the Yawartoq more fully. Using the arm between the creature's jaws as a weapon, he forced it backwards towards the nearest tree. There, he pinned it against the trunk and used his free arm and his own considerable weight to push his trapped limb further back into the blood wolf's mouth. It didn't move readily, but slowly, the backward curving teeth of the Yawartoq, helped in part by the slickness provided by Shartale's own blood, began to lose their grip. Shartale's shoulders heaved as he forced the jaws of his attacker apart. He moved his arm further back into the mouth, partially blocking the throat. Then he clamped his free hand around the snout of the beast.

It only took a few moments for the Yawartoq to open its mouth as it attempted to gulp down some air. Shartale ripped his arm free but used his hand to push down the creature's head. With its back still against the tree, the Yawartoq used it for purchase and lifted its feet from the ground, scrabbling at Shartale's belly with violent kicks and slashes from its viciously curved toe claws. But now it was off balance and Shartale pushed the creature away from the tree and him. As one hand drove its head further downwards, the other came down on the top of its skull with all his might. The Yawartoq was knocked to the ground and Shartale moved swiftly to bring his foot down on its neck with crushing force.

His blow met nothing but soft earth. The Yawartoq dashed backwards on all fours, snapping its jaws defensively as it put distance between them. Like him, it was quick to draw up to its full height, which Shartale saw was not equal to his own. However, he had already experienced the creature's speed and strength and would not underestimate it again. The two attackers began to circle each other, with menacing warning growls lodged in their throats.

~

Nina slowly came to her senses. The wet stain on her pants was icy cold, almost painfully so, and it was what had brought her back to reality. Her vision was blurred, and it still sounded like she was underwater. As she forced herself to take a deep breath, one ear popped, and then the other. Her head snapped round as she picked up the terrifying sounds coming from nearby. She tried to gauge the distance, but it was impossible to tell. Yet she knew it was two animals in a horrendous fight. Once, she'd witnessed a small band of desperate wolves take on a large female grizzly and her cub. What she heard now wasn't unlike that, but this was worse. Much worse. As her mind resettled itself, she was in no doubt of the identity of the two creatures battling to the death. She blinked slowly and began to search through the leaf litter of the forest floor. She let out a sigh of relief as her fingers found the wooden grips of the revolver.

She took a knee as she prepared to stand. The sense of nauseousness still washed over her, and she swayed slightly as she found her feet. Unbalanced, she half-tripped, half-stepped forward. She slowed, preventing herself from falling and allowing more of her senses to return. Off to the left, she noticed the bleary swirls of movement and how the sounds grew louder. She raised the gun and trained the barrel on them. Three bullets left. Perhaps time for one shot if one of them charged. Nina decided she would have to trust the wolf creature was not interested in her, as her father claimed. But that put her in a new quandary. To find the right target, she would have to get closer. Much closer.

~

Shartale feinted away from the Yawartoq. As he hoped, it lunged towards him eagerly, but he side-stepped and delivered a powerful kick to its ribs. The blood wolf rolled over the ground. It scrabbled to right itself, but Shartale was already standing over it and on the attack. He brought both fists down in clobbering blows that landed heavily on the creature's back and side. The yelp of pain it emitted brought a feeling of pleasure to Shartale and he sank to his knees to pin it to the ground. Then the shoulder of his already wounded arm erupted into a violent spasm of pain, and his ears rung with the echo that could only come from a weapon of man.

He leapt to his feet and roared. His change of direction was immediate, and he covered the ground with furious speed. He found his target almost immediately and roared again as he realised the human female had dared take up her attack again. Shartale closed the distance within the space of a single breath. So savage was his fury and intent, he didn't hear the second blast of the weapon, and its impact on his lower torso barely registered. He reached her and lifted her from the ground by the throat with his good arm. His other bloodied hand batted away the weapon from hers with such force that it ripped open her flesh as the gun was flung far beyond reach into the forest. Shartale growled with delight, the mucus and spittle from his throat spraying onto the face of what was soon to be his prey. He opened his jaws wide and lifted the human female towards them.

~

Nina knew she had moments to live. She was disappointed that she felt so calm and rational. Her life didn't flash before her eyes. She felt no regret or sorrows. In a way, she felt proud of who she had been. Then, in a microsecond of realisation, she corrected herself. Who she was, she thought. Unable to focus on anything else but the yellow canine teeth that bore down on her, her uninjured arm reached for the knife, found it, and plunged it into the lower torso of the sasquatch. It screamed and dropped her, where she crumpled onto the ground.

She was spent. Her energy was gone. She pushed herself backwards, wincing in pain as something hard dug into her spine. She used her good arm to move and find purchase. Nina looked up into the eyes of her killer and smirked as she noticed the bloody wounds she had inflicted on the immense creature. Perhaps she had not been able to kill it, but she'd done enough damage for Jones to finish the job. Nina let out an uncontrolled, hysteric laugh as she considered she had done the hard work for them. Then, in an instant, her cackle turned into a scream as the Limmekin landed on the back of the sasquatch and buried its teeth into the side of its neck. As it yanked its head back, a spray of arterial blood erupted from the wounded bigfoot, which clawed at its attacker in a desperate attempt to dislodge it.

Nina watched as the sasquatch spun, roaring in pain and for the first time, what sounded like fright. It wrenched the Limmekin from its back, pulling it over its own head with both hands and throwing it to the floor. It lifted a foot and

Nina could see the bigfoot planned to cave in the chest of the wolf-like creature. As if in a trance, something ignited in Nina. She didn't know where she found the strength, but she twisted up onto her knees and reached for the thing that had dug into her back, now knowing what it was. She watched the handle of her father's tomahawk leave her fingertips in what seemed like an out-of-body experience. It flew straight and true, as if in slow motion. Then time stopped altogether, as a microsecond became an eternity, and her eyes locked with the sasquatch. The blade struck the face, at an angle across its nose and between the eyes, just below its heavy brow ridge. It hit deep and stayed fast. As it turned to look at her, she could see it was embedded down to the bone below its left eye. It opened its mouth, but no sound came from it. The sasquatch swayed violently as it staggered towards her, its arms outstretched, zombie like.

~

Shartale felt his life force flow away from him, fast and impossible to stop. He could feel the throb of his heart as his neck pulsed and blood poured from his wounds, like a torrent over a waterfall. He took deep, panting breaths as he motored forward. His only intention now was to kill his tormentor. Shartale did not realise he had fallen to his knees until he slowly blinked, and the human female was eclipsed from his line of sight. He heard nothing now, and he looked up, confused, and fearful. Fearful that he was to be denied this final act after all. Two orbs of golden yellow peered down at him in an unblinking stare. Shartale winced only slightly as the slash of claws opened the wound on his neck further, and he fell forward. The ground raced up to meet him. There was jolt of pain. And then nothing.

~

Nina watched as the Limmekin stepped in between her and the sasquatch. As it slashed at the bigfoot's neck, it stepped away and she watched as the ape-like creature slumped forward. She couldn't control the cry of shock as its head slammed into the ground, forcing the blade of the tomahawk deeper into its skull. If there had been any uncertainty before, it was dead. It was over.

Then the Limmekin turned its head towards her, as if noticing her for the first time. It let out a growl that could have been of delight or malice. Either way, it was enough for Nina to fall backwards in fright as a chill ran down her spine. Already unsteady, she tried to get to her feet, only to trip on the root of a large oak and crash to the floor. She looked straight up, glimpsing the night sky above through its branches. Then she gasped as the stars disappeared and were replaced by the bear-sized head of the Limmekin. It stood over her on all fours. Its lips curled back in what almost looked like a smile. If she had been kidding herself about any sense of kinship with this animal, it dissolved instantly. All she could sense was its rage. Its malevolence. And she decided she didn't care. She slowly drew the stone her father had given her from her pocket and held it up, inches from the mouth full of kitchen knives that lingered over her throat.

"Get out of jail free card, asshole," she whispered.

As her world went black, she felt the hot breath of the creature against her skin, and she heard a distant scream – which her last thoughts concluded had probably been her own.

CHAPTER TWENTY-SIX

ENDINGS AND BEGINNINGS

Nina awoke with a start. The room was bright, and she winced as the light scorched her eyes. For a moment, she squinted. Her mouth was dry, and her throat was parched. As she slowly blinked, adjusting to the strong sunlight streaming through the window opposite her bed, she moved her head slightly. A cardiac monitor beeped away beside her. A rustling noise brought her attention back to the window, and the chair beside it in the shadows. Agent Jones ran his fingers through his hair as he got to his feet. He seemed sheepish and at first, was unable to meet her gaze.

"Ms. Lee, it seems we all owe you a debt of gratitude," he said quietly.

"Does that mean you're picking up the hospital bill," she croaked, a smile spreading across her face.

She glanced down at the different electrodes attached to her chest and above her ribs, and the intravenous drip plugged into her arm.

"And then some," Jones nodded, drawing nearer, and standing by the bed.

"The others?"

"Dugas is a few doors down. He'll be in here longer than you, but he should be okay. Dixon got cleaned up pretty good and checked out this morning. And the only time you'll find Hicks in a hospital is when he makes it to the morgue, which he hasn't yet."

Nina's eyes widened and her elbows pressed into her sides as her whole body became tense. She felt like a rabbit caught in the headlights.

"Don't get all excited," Jones exclaimed, holding up a hand. "Wade's in pretty rough shape, but he's gonna make it".

Nina nodded. She was relieved that Wade was alive, but she couldn't bring herself to feel happy about his condition. Yet she inferred from Jones' tone that he'd not only pull through but also recover and return to the unit.

"It's not often that I have to take up a whole wing of a hospital," Jones smiled. "Katie Cash is just next door. Benoit is in with her now, as is Joe. But it makes the security easier at least."

"About that..." Nina pressed.

Jones let out a deep sigh but smiled.

"Believe it or not, I don't make those kinds of decisions. I don't tell people what they can and can't say. That's beyond my pay grade. But you're not the first Ranger we've involved in all this. Usually, you'd be pressured into joining a unit within the Forest Service. Like you, they have encountered these things and know what to expect. When a park or forest starts seeing activity, we transfer one of you in to monitor and take care of things. What happened here... that's not how it usually goes. In fact, it's never happened before."

Nina stiffened and opened her mouth, her eyes wide and accusing. Jones held up his hand for a second time, this time in surrender.

"I told them that wouldn't work with you," he half-laughed. "You don't do great being told what to do, I have come to accept that. But I have a different offer for you."

Nina stayed quiet, waiting for Jones to come out with it.

"I gather things didn't go great after I left the camp. Smith overstepped. At the same time, I suggested to the powers that be, that the Army nearly got us killed. Twice."

"So, you're gonna quit?" Nina smirked.

"No," Jones shook his head. "We start anew. Do things differently. Maybe not so clandestine. Just solving problems. How would you feel about joining my team. Wade, the guys, Benoit, Joe. Hell, you're already part of it anyway."

"No Cash?" Nina asked.

Jones shook his head.

"Katie was always waiting in the wings for some big network to call, or some such. She's seen enough. It's not for her."

~

Mary Beth Benoit squeezed Katie's hand as Joe lifted a nice bouquet of pastel-coloured roses, alstroemeria, lilies, and sea thistles, onto a table against the back wall. It joined several others and a plethora of cards – the number of which was growing by the day.

"There was a bit of a burst of activity on social media before it got shut down," Joe explained. "Think someone clocked you being admitted."

"You know our fans," Benoit smiled. "They love a conspiracy theory. Like with me, they think you've been attacked by a bigfoot."

Cash's eyes narrowed with a flash of fury, but it was gone just as quickly.

"You were attacked by a bigfoot," she said coldly and quietly. "So was I. Bodhi was killed by one. I think it's time we let slip a little more than the odd rumour and some Sunday night entertainment."

Benoit glanced at Joe with a smile.

"We feel the same way," she said. "I think we owe it to Bodhi."

Katie looked around the room, and through the small glass window in the door.

"It's okay, I've already swept for bugs, and jammed the room," Joe assured her. "It's just us".

"Did you get it?" she asked.

He nodded, grinning.

"The footage from your camera, most of what we've got from this trip – saved to three different servers on the dark web," he explained. "An edited stream of clips should be released from untraceable, anonymous emails. I spent some time playing with the angles and filters to make it look like it hasn't directly come from us. It'll look like off-cuts, or like somebody left the cameras running."

"When?" Katie demanded.

Joe looked at the clock on the wall. It was seven minutes past midday.

"About seven minutes ago," he grinned again.

~

Jones looked up as an agent knocked on the door and entered the room.

"Sir, Special Agent Smith needs you to see something. It's urgent," he informed them.

Jones looked at Nina.

"You're gonna have more than a few days to think it over. I've got your number. We'll talk soon."

"That's nice and everything, but you can have my answer now," Nina replied. "I'm in."

Jones was halfway to the door but paused. He turned to

face her and gave her a single, appreciative nod. He hadn't expected her to agree so soon. But if he'd learnt anything from working with the Forest Ranger, it was that she knew her own mind. He'd seen that on the first day they'd met. He turned and followed the agent out the door. A few minutes later, they were marching out the front entrance. Just opposite, across the strip of tarmac that led to the parking lot, was a picnic area. Smith was sat at one of the benches. As Jones reached him, his partner smiled and handed him a tablet device with his one good arm. The other was in a black sling, that matched his suit. Jones smiled as he turned his attention back to the screen. A YouTube video was paused, and he tapped the triangular 'play' button.

He watched as clear footage of the bigfoot appeared within a few seconds. Jones smiled, impressed how the cameras had caught nobody but the Seeking Sasquatch team. Him, Smith, the team, even Nina... they were all missing from the video. Then Jones noticed there were several more in the queue. Some of the names on the posting accounts he recognised as bigfoot researchers, podcast hosts and the like. But then there were the major news channels. He smiled and shrugged as he passed the tablet back to Smith.

"Shit's gonna hit the fan," Smith declared.

"Always was gonna," Jones said. "Any thoughts on where it came from?"

"The lead theory is that Bodhi stashed footage and in the event of his death, it was to be released," Smith sighed. "He died. It was."

"Kind of does sound like something he'd do," Jones acknowledged. His gaze only momentarily flickered to the third-floor window, where Katie Cash's room was.

"Tilly and Jason, the producers, said the editing was pretty slick," Smith continued. "They think it must have been done by the TV companies. Some of these researcher guys who analyse so-called evidence, they're pretty good with digital stuff too. Point is, we can't stop it. Everyone has it. They're predicting it'll get more than 100 million views in the next 24 hours."

"And shaking down everyone who posts it, to see if they might have been involved, is now officially a waste of time," Jones huffed.

"Shutting the proverbial barn door," Smith said, looking down at the table.

"Heard you're off to Fort Skookum."

Smith nodded slowly. "End of the road for us, I guess. I... I just want you to know it's been an honour. You've done your dad proud."

Jones eyes snapped to those of the man who'd been his partner for the last seven years. As he had been with Nina a few minutes before, he was surprised by the rawness and honesty. He gave a silent nod.

"Know where you're headed?" Smith asked.

Jones didn't answer for a while, his gaze moving towards the distant peeks of the Cascade mountains.

"Montana has crossed my mind, seeing as I'm part-ways there already," Jones admitted.

Smith nodded, the concern in his eyes easily registered.

"Think he's still out there?"

"It," Jones growled. "Three air force pilots paid with their lives to confirm it."

"Taking your new team with you?" Smith asked.

"Some of them only just learnt of the existence of one

monster," Jones replied, shaking his head. "They get some R and R, then a trip down South. They're not ready for what I have in mind. Not sure I am either."

They both looked around as the Prowler pulled into the hospital drop-off zone with a blast of its air brakes. Smith smiled and offered his good hand to Jones as he stood up. They gripped each other's hand firmly and genuinely as they shook. Jones watched as Smith walked away, towards the big rig, the engine of which was still running. Suddenly, he turned back towards Jones, a quizzical look on his face.

"Does... does this mean we're on opposite teams now?" Smith asked, loudly.

Jones grinned.

"I hope not... for your sake."

EPILOGUE

Lucas Christian had watched reports on the death of a star from a popular bigfoot show into the early hours of the morning. Although his actual murder hadn't been shown, the imagery of the attacking sasquatch was hard to deny. That wasn't stopping government officials, academics, and many more from trying. But for the first time, it felt like the balance had shifted. The footage was compelling to say the least. Right now, more people believed than didn't.

He sat in the remnants of his study, the doors to the terrace fully open. The broken furniture had been cleared out. For now, he abided in a leather armchair, with a laptop resting on his knees. The rest of the large room was empty and dark. The only light inside came from the soft glow of the computer screen. Outside, light streamed in from the bright full moon as the night air huffed chilled blasts into the house. Lucas logged into the private server on the dark web and entered the live chat forum. Just as he was, everyone there was anonymous. But his research had revealed this particular group was made up of people with real power. From guerrilla journalists to network CEOs, they all sought stories here. And he was about to give them one.

He had always known the government would scrub his files and footage, confiscate his equipment, and threaten to silence him. For a time, he had considered the very real possibility that they would kill him. But they hadn't. And in their haste to track the beast that had attacked his home and killed Josie-Mae, he realised he had moved very far down their list of priorities. Especially considering today's events. His 'proof' had been duplicated and sent to over thirty different backup platforms automatically. Naturally, the government were good at what they did. They had tracked them down. All but six of them.

He watched the loading bar at the bottom of the screen that told him the files were ready. As Lucas moved his finger to the enter key. He hesitated. In a few moments, the world would learn that this was no hoax. They would watch the same creature from the news reel as it butchered and devoured a pig. As it roamed and destroyed his home. There would be no doubt in anybody's mind. He pressed the button and closed the laptop.

~

Cona had recovered quickly, like all his kind did. For the first few days, he had roamed the unfamiliar ground, only to discover he was trapped. And he wasn't alone. Others of his kind were here. His size and scars had saved him from any territory disputes. His hunting prowess didn't go unnoticed either. He took the deer trapped with them with ease. And all the time, he observed the others. He watched as they separated into small groups that stayed and roamed together. As he moved around, he realised just how many of them were gathered there. That's when he had started sharing his meals. He picked a few of the younger males and showed them how to bring down the deer as swiftly and easily as he did. How did they not realise they numbered so many. They could be a clan of a size never seen. He remembered what the one called Dark Claw had shown him. That by working together, they could take the fight to the humans. That together, they could kill them.

THE END

NINA LEE

WILL RETURN

IN

SOUTHERN ROGUE

A NOTE FROM THE AUTHOR

Thank you very much for reading Rogue. By doing so, you've supported an independent author and the independent publishing industry. If it wasn't for thousands of readers like you, taking a chance on an unknown writer, it would never have been possible. So once again, thank you.

For us little guys, spreading the word is really important. So, I make one request. Whatever your thoughts about the book you've just read, good, bad, or otherwise, please consider leaving a review on Amazon, Goodreads, or both! It really can help make the difference.

If you'd like to get in touch, please do so by following the Black Beast Books Facebook page, or dropping me an email via luke@blackbeastbooks.co.uk

You can also find my other books on Amazon.

ABOUT THE AUTHOR

Luke Phillips has always been a keen student of the natural world. When studying zoology at Liverpool John Moores University, he was surprised to find the Loch Ness Monster referenced in the first lecture he attended, as an anecdote about what could be out there. But even before then, having spent time on the shores of Nessie's home as a young boy, and with a keen imagination fuelled by creature features glimpsed through childhood fingers covering his eyes, his interest in myths and monsters was evident from an early age.

He lives in the county of Kent in the UK, and was always encouraged to write by teachers and readers alike. Rogue is his fourth novel.